Wiping his blade, the Justicar turned and fixed the stunned Polk with a glare.

"Stay here."

The man turned, the wolf pelt shimmered, and he was gone. Sandwiched between two corpses, Polk the teamster slowly scrubbed his hands through the leaf litter and nodded to himself in a daze.

"Yes, sir. Never interfere in another man's work. . . ."

GREYHAWK

AGAINST THE GIANTS
Ru Emerson

WHITE PLUME MOUNTAIN
Paul Kidd

DESCENT INTO THE DEPTHS OF THE EARTH
2000

White Plume Mountain

Paul Kidd

For Jeff and Malcolm, Derek and Brad, Rory and Damien—in celebration of many dice rolled and many monsters slain. . . .

WHITE PLUME MOUNTAIN
©1999 TSR, Inc.
All Rights Reserved.

Cover Art by Ravenwood
Map by Sam Wood

First Printing: October 1999
Library of Congress Catalog Card Number: 98-88154
9 8 7 6 5 4 3 2 1
ISBN: 0-7869-1424-6
T21424-620

U.S., CANADA, ASIA, PACIFIC, & LATIN AMERICA	EUROPEAN HEADQUARTERS
Wizards of the Coast, Inc.	Wizards of the Coast, Belgium
P.O. Box 707	P.B. 2031
Renton, WA 98057-0707	2600 Berchem
+1-800-324-6496	Belgium
	Tel. +32-70-23-32-77

Visit our web-site at www.tsr.com

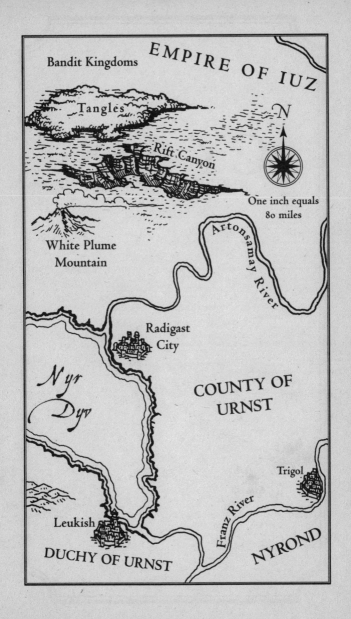

CY 588

Prologue

To a newcomer, the Flanaess had a distinctive, brilliant smell, vibrant and alive, sharp and pure. It sang in a predator's nostrils with promises of blood. All the life, all the wealth, all the thrill of a newfound playground shook and shimmered in the morning breeze.

A predator stood upon a hillside, eyes closed as she felt the currents of her new world ebbing and flowing beneath her. It was a land drained and torn by war—a shadow of the greater battle that raged unchecked across an entire continuum. But it was a *living* land, a world of sun and grass, of cities and animals and birds dancing in the winds, a world that she could one day dominate and command.

New winds ruffled the feathers of her pure white wings. Saala was of the race of baatezu, demons that existed in a dozen different shapes and forms. An erinyes, she was a lean and exquisite huntress who wore the body of a beautiful winged woman, her skin shining pale and exotic as her body gleamed beneath the sun. In her hand, she held a black sword, a deadly weapon now safe in a scabbard decorated with cut obsidian. Despite its temporary prison, the sword chattered like a hungry animal, gibbering madly with the need to feast on souls.

A master of deception and fear, Saala had long used her weapons in the service of her dark masters. Now, abandoned and disgraced by the twists and turns of politics, she had come far afield in search of fertile hunting grounds. The erinyes was a solitary huntress, preferring the use of slaves rather than allies. She roamed the forgotten corners of countless worlds, forever seeking opportunities.

Her search had finally yielded treasure.

Saala turned her golden-eyed gaze upon the lands below her. A city lay there, a place with shantytowns and military camps spilling out of its old stone walls. There were temples and palaces, docks and taverns, all the glorious tangle of streets and plots and plans that made the hunt so rapturously wonderful. Saala gazed down upon the city in all its fabulous complexity and gave the simple smile of a little girl at play. It was a place of opportunities, a place utterly ignored by the erinyes's own race.

Beyond the city lay the wastelands, and beyond the wastelands lay a kingdom ruled by Iuz, a demonic king who had attained the powers of a demigod, spreading terror and destruction across this green world. Yet, unknown to even him, Iuz had brought her a gift beyond price. To further his own power, Iuz had summoned demons of the tanar'ri race, and in so doing, he had become a pawn in an even greater war, for tanar'ri and baatezu had been locked in savage conflict for millennia untold. This conflict had spread to countless different worlds, and minor wars between mortals often became the testing grounds of baatezu and tanar'ri. Each species manipulated their unwitting allies, laying entire nations waste as they grasped for tactical advantage in the greater war.

By summoning tanar'ri as his allies, Iuz had overtipped the balance of power and given Saala the opportunity to enter this world. The erinyes could now conquer a local kingdom as a base and turn it into a tool for her own kind. When her masters raced to this world to stem the tanar'ri threat, Saala would be able to present them with a secure base and thousands of unwitting slaves. A tiny slip of chance might win her entire kingdoms, and the gratitude of her baatezu overlords would be incalculable if she only brought them the gift of victory.

All she need do was conquer a kingdom—and all on her own. The current situation merely needed a little misdirection, a little misrepresentation.

The sword suddenly shivered in its sheath, whimpering and calling for a human hand to wield it. With the weapon as her tool, the erinyes could bring a city to its knees from within. She needed only a little forethought, a little patience, and imagination. Feeling the movement of her thoughts, the sword moaned, and Saala smiled.

All things came to those who knew the value of subtlety. Saala flexed her claws, folded up her wings, and set her mind to the pleasurable task of intrigue. A city to conquer, a land to subdue, and an entire world lying supine at her feet.

There were some days when it was simply good to be a girl. . . .

On a windswept heath in a blighted land, seed heads rattled against the teeth of an old, yellowed skull.

It had been only a year since the war's end, only a year since the corpse king Iuz had sent his legions through these fertile lands like a disease. Finally battered to a standstill, the enemy had gone, leaving the land bleached and empty.

It was a land where the grass had become an ocean. No villages marked the skyline. No taverns spread their wood smoke to the wind. Across the plains, no two stones stood atop one another. Wild grasses grew in untilled fields, and weeds jutted through the blackened ribs of dead, decaying farms.

Yet, life was tenacious even in the face of death. Wild crops grew across the battlefields and covered up the bones. Refugees had crept from the woods to repopulate the borderlands in huddled camps. Once again, the caravans marched as trade and communication struggled to reknit shattered civilization.

It was a world that had begun once again to find its feet.

It was a time when justice reached no farther than the end of a sword. . . .

I

"Razor Wood! Over there! It's called Razor Wood!" The teamster swept out his whip to indicate the approaching terrain, almost taking the ear off one of his own oxen. "You can still see the swords poking up through the brambles! Nigh on a thousand men died there not three years a-gone."

Polk the teamster sat on his driving bench, lord of all that he surveyed. Scrawny, boisterous, and graced with a huge hatchet of a nose, he drove his cart with a singular lack of skill. Heavy wooden wheels screeched like tortured cats as the ox cart lurched its way along the open grass, forcing the teamster to shout to be heard above the noise.

His audience was a man walking alone with a slow and steady tread beside the cart. He was a big man with a shaven head and dark eyes that carefully scanned the heather-covered hills. A scar ran outward to the point of his stubbled jaw. Over plain clothes he wore armor made of rawhide scales laced into strips and backed with heavy felt. The armor was silent, well worn, and as tough as steel. A sturdy helmet hung from the man's belt below a long, heavy sword with a pommel shaped like a wolf's skull.

The walker stayed silent, and Polk approved. A good listener. Now *that* was a rare thing to find! The teamster took a pull from an old clay jug and watched the evening sun setting above the bleak gray woods beside the trail.

"Razor Wood. Yes indeed. I saw me a battle once! Saw me a whole big battle. Even saw me some fellas dueling with swords!" The teamster scratched beneath his hat as though stirring up memories. "You ever seen a sword fight? I mean a real fight, a fight where they mean business?"

Plodding along stolidly, the stranger kept his eyes on the horizon and replied, "Can't say I have."

"Well I saw me one. Big fellas they were, big men. Long blades, too—big as trees!" Leading a procession of wagons and feeling like a general on parade, Polk puffed his chest. "Bein' a fighting man myself, I left them to it. Never interfere in another man's work—that's what I always say. Never interfere."

His audience's attention seemed to be wandering. As the wagon continued rolling by, the shaven-headed man stopped to kneel beside the trail and part the grass. His eyes narrowed as he examined a day-old horse dropping nestled in the weeds.

The County of Urnst stood at the northern edge of civilization. Beyond its northern march, there stretched only the lands of the demon king Iuz. Recovering slowly from the years of war, the County of Urnst had begun to plant colonies in lands laid waste by years of battle. With the fields new-dug and crops still not yet ready for harvest, the new settlements relied heavily upon supply caravans as their lifeblood, their only reliable source for food and clothing to survive the coming winter. Until their crops matured and real farming could begin, each little enclave lived a precarious existence, but the resettlement program was vital. The Countess of Urnst needed to take refugees from her overcrowded cities and sow them back onto the lands before plague and famine struck at the slums.

The latest caravan had traveled cautiously along hidden valleys and unmarked plains, carefully watching for bandits and other predators. There were twelve wagons in the procession, heavy slab-sided vehicles each drawn by half a dozen oxen and piled high with boxes, sacks, and bales. A dozen more traders marched beside the column towing packhorses and mules. Six crossbowmen sat atop the wagons or trudged waist deep in the heather blooms, keeping the procession safe from casual acts of war.

The teamsters trusted the soldiers. The soldiers trusted their gods. No one seemed inclined to watch the watchers. Letting the carts roll ponderously past, the shaven-headed man looked out along the column and carefully let the grass cover up his prize.

Up ahead, Polk leaned over the side of his wagon and called back past the wheels. "I said I never interfere! Wrong gettin' in the way of a man's work. We all have our calling. Ain't for me to distract a man when he's doing good work."

The woods were close, forming a tangled mass of brambles and stark, dead trees. The shaven-headed man hefted his heavy backpack and stalked beside the wagons without giving the eerie woodlands a second glance.

A long black wolf tail dangled from the man's backpack. Eyeing the fur, Polk pulled at his nose and made a conspiratorial jerk of his head toward the man's cargo.

"You a hunter?" The teamster never waited for an answer. "Reckoned you were when I saw you packing all those furs. Winter comes hard up north, and there's folks going to need those furs. That the business you're in? You a trapping man?"

The stranger nodded. "I trap things."

"Right glad to hear it." The teamster prodded his lead oxen away from a juicy thistle. "Gotta admire a good fur."

Before the teamster could think of anything else to say, a rider spurred his horse from around the edge of the woods ahead. With his long greasy hair streaming in his wake, the rider raised his bow in greeting and thundered his black horse through the clinging heather toward the caravan. As the man reigned in his mount next to Polk's wagon, the teamster passed his stone jug of home-brewed ale.

"Hey, scout, how's the trail?"

The scout casually holstered his bow and said, "Clear. Head into the woods and camp for the night. Plenty of firewood, plenty of water." Circling his horse, the scout stood in his stirrups and circled his arm like a banner about his head. "Make camp! Make camp in the woods! The woods are clear!"

The rider took a long drink from the jug, then threw it to the teamster and cantered back along the wagon line. The teamster watched him ride, corking his jug and giving an admiring smile.

"Now here's another man knows his business! Some other scouts, they might keep you out on the plains. But a campfire? Well now, you can see that from a powerful ways away! So into the forest we go. That's the thing to hide a fire!"

The shaven-headed man took a long, quiet look at the woods. "I suppose so."

Drawing closer to the dark, silent sprawl of Razor Wood, the caravan cast long shadows across the grass. With the sunset spreading a dark wine-red light across the lands, the first wagon crunched through the underbrush and made its way beneath the eaves of the forest. The cumbersome wagons moved between dead, silent trees. All about the caravan, dry branches raked stark fingers against the sky. Brambles made tangled thickets between the trunks, blocking off the slanting light of the sun. Dead blackberry bushes cracked and crunched beneath the wheels, dragging sharp tendrils across the oxen's hides. Here and there, small black shapes sped off into the shadows, turning about to stare at the intruders with hostile little eyes.

As the last of the day's light failed, the wagons were wearily parked in a circle. Men slid to the ground to stretch their legs. A harsh wind filtered through the brambles to promise a bitter night, and several of the wagoners began to gather dead branches for a fire.

Polk's wagon was entirely laden with barrels of fish oil. It stank like a fisherman's nightmare, making most of the other wagondrivers park upwind. Ignoring such little niceties, the talkative teamster drove up amidst the stench and chose to halt there for the night. He stood, suddenly discovered that his entire backside had gone numb, and lurched down to the ground on legs made wooden by a long day's haul.

"Cold night's coming! Better feed the livestock a peck of ale with their bran." The man cricked his back with a noise like a breaking branch. "What's your name, son? Never did remember hearing you speak your name." The teamster hung his hat from a nearby branch. "M' name's Polk, by the way! Polk the teamster, or Polk the adventurer. Transport to adventure!" The gangly Polk gave his wagon a slap. "Never drink with a man you can't pin a handle on, son! So what's your name? What do you do?"

The shaven-headed man shot a dark sidewise glance at the teamster and said, "Justicar."

"Justicar? Is that religious?"

"The only religion that counts." The shaven-headed man dropped his backpack on the ground. His huge sword stayed hanging at his side. He dug into his backpack and drew out a blue glass flask, uncorked it, took a sip, then passed it over to the teamster.

"Drink."

The teamster drank, sucking back the raw alcohol as though it were lemonade. He sighed in appreciation, caring not a fig for the cold, the wolves, the empty forest, or even the fires beginning to sparkle to life around the camp.

"Now that's a fine drop! You can cure a thirst, son! Much obliged!"

"Keep it. Stay here, be quiet, and drink." Moving his big hands with practiced speed, the Justicar fussed with his pack, watching the caravan guards from the corner of his eye.

The evening routine had begun, just as it had for the last dozen nights on the trail. Weary men moved slowly, still working out the kinks caused by a long day's travel. Dry branches were thrown on smoking fires and blanket rolls were tossed onto the ground. Men began unhitching the oxen. Eventually someone would have to see about watering the creatures at the nearby stream.

Filled with an uncharacteristic energy, the caravan's mounted scout whooped and leaped off his jet-black horse, picketing the beast to a tree and wandering off toward the stream. He neither unsaddled his horse nor led it to water. The horseman even walked straight past a bucket that hung from a wagon's tail.

The Justicar raised his head and watched the scout with a careful gaze. "You have a clever scout. I've watched him work. Where did you find him?"

The scout disappeared off into the dead gray trees.

"Assigned to us! We're an official expedition. The Countess must have paid for him, 'cause he never cost us a penny! Joined us back at Bulette Creek." The teamster had taken permanent possession of the plum brandy and already seemed rosy-cheeked and hale. "Never turn aside free help, son! Long as they bring their own ale, I'm glad to have him. There's two caravans ventured out this way that no one's ever seen again."

"Three." Rising carefully from the ground, the Justicar examined a strand of horsehair hanging from a bramble leaf. The hairs shone golden bright in the failing sun. "You're missing three caravans."

"Three is it? Then it's good to have some extra help along!" The teamster pummeled his numb backside with his fists. "Not that we'll need it! Simple job. Spearheads, winter food, and blankets to the settlements, then back home. Done it a dozen times."

The Justicar turned to brood upon the dark, still woods. "Then we'll make sure you do it a dozen more."

A cold wind blew through the desolate trees, making the wagoners huddle about their fire for warmth. With the woods becoming dark, men turned more and more to staring at the fire. The Justicar watched, picked a moment when the men were looking elsewhere, then lifted his backpack and faded behind the wagons. As sparks crackled madly from a brushwood fire, he opened his backpack and unrolled a lustrous black wolf pelt across the ground.

The skin was resplendent with claws, tail, a black nose, and teeth that would have done credit to a crocodile. Its grin shone bright as firelight caught across the huge, bared fangs.

Polk had followed the Justicar around the wagon and stared at the wolf skin in unstinting admiration.

"Now that's a fine pelt, son!" The teamster planted his fists on his hips as he examined the fur. The thick black guard hairs were tipped with fiery red. "What kinda fur is that?"

The Justicar slapped his helmet on and fastened the straps. The man swept the wolf pelt across his shoulders and settled the diabolical canine head over his helm. As he donned the skin, a dark red glow seemed to spark inside the animal's eyes.

"He's called Cinders."

The heavy black sword jutted horizontally through the big man's belt. He settled it in place, scanned the campsite, and rose soundlessly to face the trees.

"I have to work now."

"Exactly! We all do, son—that's life! Fact of the matter is, we all have to toil!" Polk followed in the Justicar's footsteps, dogging him all the way into the woods. "That sword now, that's real pretty, a nice wall hanger. No good for a sword fight, though. You need a *real* two-hander—six foot long and thick as your leg! That's the thing for a sword fight!"

"Sword fights are for fools." The Justicar looked briefly at a holy symbol slung about his neck then slipped it underneath his rawhide cuirass. "If the enemy gets a chance to hit back, then you're doing something wrong."

With one hand on the wolf-skull pommel of his sword, the Justicar turned to stare at Polk. "Stay here. Sit still. I have to work."

Polk thought about it, but the Justicar's words had offended his heroic soul. He let the man stalk in sinister silence off into the brambles and then jumped up and followed him.

"Not hit back? *Not hit back?*" The teamster gulped, trying to encompass the enormity of his outrage. "No fights? Steel to steel, man against man? Well, that's not *hero* talk!" The teamster walked pace by pace with the fuming Justicar and energetically waved his hands. "The thing you have to understand is *heroes.* Knowing how to be a hero is ... well, it's the difference between being an average man and a *great* man. Once you understand how to be a hero, then the world's at your feet! You can't be a hero if you don't square off and face 'em man to man!"

Polk lifted his chin, setting himself square against unseen enemies. He speared a lofty glance toward the Justicar.

The black pelt seemed to fade and shimmer against the brambles. Big canine fangs grinned with malevolence as the Justicar turned slowly around.

"Shut up. Go back to the wagons."

"And leave you in the woods all alone?" The teamster gave a firm, competent shake of his head. "You're addled, son. It's clear to me that you need advice. I'm just going to have to look after you and stick to you like glue."

"Fine."

The Justicar planted a brotherly hand upon the teamster's shoulder, smiled, then felled him with a massive left cross. Polk crashed through the brambles and lay amidst a maze of stars. Astonished, the man stared about himself at woods that suddenly seemed devoid of life.

A steady rustling and crackling in the blackberries sounded like footfalls. The teamster lurched to his feet, cradled his jaw, then staggered toward the nearby stream.

Though the clinging brambles and trees masked most of the light from the caravan's fires, he could see a tall figure walking steadily toward him. The teamster made to call out and then balked as he saw the glitter of chain mail and the gleam of a huge two-handed sword.

Towering above the brambles, much too tall for a man, the creature stepped into the uncertain firelight, spreading a vast, dark shadow against the woods. The monstrous figure turned, saw Polk, and pelted straight toward him with his sword raised high. The teamster froze in terror, half raised his hands, and then blinked as nearby leaf litter erupted from the ground.

A feral figure exploded from the underbrush.

A black sword whipped upward as the Justicar rose, cutting his target across the jaw. A second swipe followed, hacking through the enemy's midriff and driving out the creature's breath in a savage mist of blood. The figure folded in two, its head thudding from its shoulders as the black sword scythed down in a single fluid blur.

The monster's huge body thumped to the earth. Fully nine feet tall, the ogre's corpse still twitched as it sprawled at Polk's feet. It had all happened in a split second of near silence. The Justicar crouched over his victim, his wolf skin snarling with bright, silent fangs. His black-bladed sword dripped blood—and then quite suddenly the man was gone.

"Holy Fharlanghn!"

The teamster sat down, staring at the severed head that lay an arm's length from his side. The bestial head had jutting fangs and was smothered in warts and horns. As he stared at the thing in fright, Polk suddenly heard the whole forest rustling with the stamp of armored feet. He shrank back against a tree and stared in panic at a night that suddenly boiled with enemies.

A second ogre parted the bushes with its spear, saw Polk, and gave a predatory snarl. It yelled in triumph and lunged toward the teamster.

An instant later, the creature was struck from behind. The Justicar's black sword hammered down in a two-handed blow, making a sound like an axe thumbing into waterlogged wood as it split the creature's shoulder and sheared through its spine. As his target fell, the Justicar planted a foot on the corpse's neck and wrenched his blade free.

From the woods nearby came a shout. Someone had finally heard the sounds of combat. Wiping his blade, the Justicar turned and fixed the stunned Polk with a glare.

"Stay here."

The man turned, the wolf pelt shimmered, and he was gone. Sandwiched between two corpses, Polk the teamster slowly scrubbed his hands through the leaf litter and nodded to himself in a daze.

"Yes, sir. Never interfere in another man's work. . . ."

✻   ✻   ✻   ✻   ✻

Trigol City's law officers moved with exaggerated distaste as they tiptoed through the alleyway. A foul strew of blood had painted the walls like a bizarre piece of art. Scattered parts of bodies lay all over the street, and flies buzzed thick and fast across the offal. Most of the victims seemed to have been slaughtered from behind.

Three officers advanced slowly forward, keeping their faces covered from the stench with their cloaks. The nearest corpse stared back at them with an expression of sheer terror etched onto its face.

The victims lay as they had fallen. Some had been slashed. Others had been hurled forcibly into the alley walls. Each and every one of them had taken a deathblow from a heavy sword. The corpses lay twisted in a frenzy of terror, as though more than their lives had been ripped from them.

"Sweet Pelor!" One officer stood and carefully examined an outstretched hand that held a dagger. The hand lay at least three feet away from its original body. "What in the name of the Abyss did this?"

Hovering at the alley entrance, a small boy stared in horrified fright. The boy's father pushed the lad quickly back out of view and kept himself well away from the blood-spattered cobblestones.

"We heards them fighting, the lad and me, heards them fighting a while after sunset." The man bobbed his head as he spoke, looking left and right like a terror-stricken bird. "Screaming like fear itself, they were. Kept screaming for nigh ten minutes till it was done."

At least a dozen men lay slaughtered in the alleyway. Dark clothing, hoods, cloaks and sheathed weapons had been scattered like chaff. One law officer rolled over the torso of a corpse, dislodging a storm of flies. The dead man had a pocket in his cloak lining that contained several thin strips of birchwood.

"Sir? Birch."

Flat birchwood strips could be wormed through cracks in doors and window shutters to lift latches free. A cursory search of the bodies turned up climbing hooks and ropes, lockpicks, and chisels.

The senior officer pondered. This had been a very large party of burglars. Trigol was blessed with three different thieves' guilds—organizations that robbed rich and poor alike while running protection rackets across the city. There was no way of telling one guild from another.

Waving the stink away with his cloak, the senior officer backed fastidiously away from the corpses. "Why were they here?"

The peasant at the end of the street edged nervously forward, watching the shadows and the skies. "They drink there sometimes, sir, in the cellar tavern down at the end of the street. We sees them, but we doesn't go in. But you didn't hear it from me, sir! Common knowledge, sir. Common as muck!"

It was all news to the three law officers. Law enforcement in Trigol consisted of armed patrols to keep the streets safe. The doings of the thieves' guilds remained an absolute mystery. With refugees from fallen kingdoms flooding into the city and bringing their cults and feuds, there was already more trouble than the law could handle. The new temples with their private armies and their mutual hate were a far more present source of danger.

There was nothing to be gained from standing in an alleyway filled with carrion. The law officers retreated, waving the town guard forward to do their job. A heavy cart was backed into the alleyway, and long firepoles prodded a gelatinous cube into the lane. The giant jelly moved slowly over the corpses, absorbing them into its ever-hungry mass one by one. As the creature slurped and slobbered, one officer, more conscientious than most, stalked over to the nervous peasant and tried talking to the man.

"Did you see what happened, Citizen?"

"No, sir!" The peasant kept his eyes searching the roof lines overhead. "We heards them, though, heards them start and heards them finish! Stayed indoors with the doors bolted until the other gentlemen arrived an hour later."

"Other gentlemen?"

"Big fellows, sir—swords and cloaks." The man kept up his vigil, looking the rooftops up and down. "Not from your side of the law, if you catch my drift, sir. But we didn't want no trouble. We told them what we heard just like we done with you."

The man pushed his son out of sight behind him and backed hastily away, leaving the three lawmen standing in the street alone. The men faced each other, unwilling to confess that they had pieced together no real clues.

One officer tapped slowly and thoughtfully at his chin. "Two thieves' guilds? Two groups attacking one another?"

"Then why aren't any of the dead locked in combat?" His comrade motioned to the corpses. "These men look like they were slaughtered as they tried to flee."

Two of the officers shrugged and went their separate ways. Their comrade stood gazing in anxiety down the alley-way, his brow furrowed as he tried to picture just what horror might have come to roost in Trigol.

A flicker of motion amongst the trash suddenly caught his eye. The man walked a little way into the alley and stooped to examine a huge white feather that had been trapped underneath a corpse. The feather was long and stiff. It looked like a feather from an eagle or perhaps a swan. The officer made to touch the thing but hesitated as a sudden sensation of revulsion set his flesh creeping. The man jerked his hand away and suddenly looked up to scan the rooftops.

With a nervous stir of motion, a thin face peeked about the alley corner. The peasant's son saw the law officer and crept a little closer with awe shining in his eyes. He spared another glance at the rooftops, then nervously came forward.

"Is the lady going to punish all the thieves, sir?"

The law officer stared from the boy to the feather and slowly rose. "What lady, son?"

"The white lady. The one who said she was going to eat up all their souls." The boy watched the shadows, his big eyes gleaming with terror. "She came here with a man, and the man had the star-sword. Are they coming back?"

The officer backed out of the alleyway, shepherding the boy back out into the light.

"I don't know, son." The officer slowly wiped clean his hands. "Get inside. And tell your family not to go out when it gets dark."

2

Crouching as he ran, the Justicar sped through the shadows, making enough noise to wake the dead. Dried blackberry brambles cracked as he crashed through the dark underbrush. For the moment, speed came first and foremost.

His enemies would be unable to hear anything above their own clumsy progress through the brush. By the time they thought to stand still and listen, the Justicar had found a hollow covered over with bracken fronds and had gone to ground. Utterly invisible, he lay with his sword gripped in his left gauntlet, his sharp senses feeling every stir and movement in the night.

A second set of senses worked alongside his own. The Justicar lifted his head and slowly scanned the darkness. "Cinders? Talk to me."

Sentience rippled through the black pelt hanging across the Justicar's shoulders. Tall canine ears twitched, and the black fur seemed to tingle as the creature scented approaching prey.

A whisper sounded in the Justicar's mind. *Left.*

"Human?"

Ogre and one man.

That would be the caravan's "scout" with more of his ogre ambush party. The Justicar's hard gaze glared at the brambles, distaste wrinkling his face as he planned punishment for the unworthy souls.

There would be another human, a man riding a horse with a golden tail—most probably the leader of the bandits. The Justicar tried to picture just where the man might be even as he heard the ogres crash toward him through the dry ferns on their way to the caravan.

Close!

The Justicar lay flat, his own senses tingling as the pelt's canine ears swiveled to track the enemy that came blundering through the brush. They passed by the Justicar's hiding place. He let them move past him, rose to the ragged rhythm of their movements, then drove his sword through an ogre's spine.

The dying creature screeched in agony, its death screams causing other ogres to stop and search wildly through the brush. The Justicar twisted his blade and ripped it free, whipping about to face a maddened charge.

Three ogres roared in blood-curdling fury as they lumbered through the ferns. One leaped high to clear a stand of blackberries, and the black sword met it in mid-flight with a heavy, deadly sound. The force of the blow doubled the massive creature in two. The Justicar ripped his blade free before the creature even hit the ground, leaving the huge corpse to crash beside him in a thunder of blood and broken steel.

The other two ogres lunged toward him with heavy clubs, attacking in a berserk, snarling rage. The Justicar sliced beneath a maddened swing and whipped his blade about, cracking his target's shoulder blade beneath the coat of scales. Roaring, he hammered his sword pommel hard against the fractured bone, but the ogre staggered free and let its cousin smash its club down at the Justicar's skull.

This ogre moved far faster than the last. The Justicar parried and made a two-handed cut only to have the blow blocked. The ogre's club cracked against his armored ribs with a sharp, biting pain. He trapped the club with his elbow and punched the ogre in the face, only to curse as the creature ducked to take the blow atop its steel helm. The Justicar almost broke his knuckles, and the ogre roared in triumph as it dragged its weapon free.

His scarred jaw snarling, the Justicar turned and let the club whip past him, his sword blade shearing a bright curl of wood shavings from the haft. He hacked hard at the ogre's forearm, throwing his weight into every blow.

The black sword suddenly bit into a wrist thick as a young tree, and sparks showered from an immense steel bracelet on the ogre's wrist. The monster wrenched its hand back, blood pouring down its arm. With one arm ablaze in agony, the brute attacked one-handed with a vicious sideways swing. It bellowed, obviously intending to smash its enemy's head.

An instant later, its target disappeared. The Justicar dropped to one knee, let the club whip past his head, then hacked into the hamstrings of the ogre's knee. The monster fell with its right leg severed just as the other ogre launched itself at the Justicar.

The man threw himself forward to crash into the huge creature's waist. He lifted with a huge explosion of strength. Flesh crashed into flesh with a noise like thunder. Screaming, the ogre spun head over heels and smashed into the ground. The Justicar turned and kicked the monster in its broken shoulder, making it tumble howling through the ferns. He reversed his blade and stabbed two-handed down into the creature's open mouth. Black blood flew up to spatter all across the blackberry grove.

An arrow flashed from the underbrush a dozen feet away, piercing the Justicar's armor and ripping a vicious line of pain across his flank. He whipped his head about to glare at the archer.

Above the Justicar's face, the wolf's red eyes gleamed. *Hello.*

The woods sheeted with light as a huge tongue of flame thundered from the pelt's jaws. Fire engulfed the screaming archer, blinding him as his clothing ignited. The archer dropped his bow and clapped hands across his eyes as he staggered, shrieking through the brush.

The Justicar rose to his feet, hissing in pain as he touched the arrowhead jutting out from his cuirass. "Thanks, Cinders."

No problem.

Cinders's red eyes gleamed, and the hell hound pelt seemed to glow with canine satisfaction. The Justicar felt the line of the arrow that had cut across his ribs and ripped the shaft painfully free. He planted an open hand against the bleeding wound, let the magic flash, and healed the injury.

In the bushes nearby, the archer still screamed as he burned. Chain mail and riding boots identified him as the caravan's scout. The Justicar wiped his sword clean of blood while above him, Cinders sniffed the scent of scorching meat upon the wind.

Burns nice! The hell hound sniffed hungrily for blood. *Kill with sword?*

"No. Let the bastard burn."

The scout had been an inside man for this merry little bandit gang. He must have led caravan after caravan into pre-planned ambush sites, setting the victims up for the kill and then guiding the ogres into the attack.

Let the traitor die hard.

Red hell hound eyes gleamed above the Justicar's helm as the man gazed across the corpses. The man's face rippled with the reflected light of the fire as he turned his heavy frame and stalked back toward the camp.

The wagoners and merchants had heard the sounds of violence in the brush. Six crossbowmen stood with the fire at their backs, making fine targets as they stared into the deepening dark. The Justicar halted in the brambles, sinking to his knees as he probed the shadows with his gaze.

Evening had dimmed the sky beneath oceans of purple-rose. Little light now filtered through the dark trees, and the woods were growing black. The Justicar tried to see into the brush up ahead, but the light of the wagoners' campfire had turned the place into a maze of dancing shadows.

Hidden in the underbrush, the Justicar and Cinders carefully tested the breeze.

"He's in there."

One creature. Evil. Not human. The hell hound's ears lay flat as he scented prey. *Smell magic.*

Some of the teamsters had dogs. The attackers had deliberately approached the camp from downwind to keep the animals from scenting them. This placed the last attacker upwind of Cinders and the Justicar. The big ranger rose and hefted his sword, feeling a light breeze winding through the brambles and into his face.

"Polk!"

"Is that you, son? Is that you?" The talkative teamster held a cudgel in his hand and sheltered behind the six cross-bowmen. "I told them it would be you! 'Now that's the sound of a man at work,' I said!"

"Quiet!" The Justicar felt like a target standing on a carnival shooting range. "There's one of them in front of you. Throw firebrands into the brambles and burn him out!"

A sudden blast of light speared from the nearby brush. The Justicar hurled himself aside and turned to take a fierce blast of heat across his back. The hell hound pelt jerked as flame licked across it, the fireproof fur shielding the Justicar from the blast. Flame licked along his left arm, and the Justicar fell sprawling in the smoking ferns.

Feet pelted toward him as the last bandit made good his retreat. As he came near, the Justicar erupted from the ground with a lightning-fast swing of his sword.

His opponent was swift. The sword blow that should have sheared him off at the knees instead whipped through empty air. The Justicar cursed and sprinted in pursuit, his right arm suddenly crawling with pain.

Something dodged into the dead trees. A flame blast thundered out from Cinders's nostrils, instantly setting the brush afire. The flames lit up the figure of the running bandit, and he turned just in time to block the Justicar's black sword with his own glittering silver blade. The raw force of the blow threw the bandit back toward the camp, and he fell sprawling in the dirt.

Placing himself and his deadly sword between his enemy and escape, the Justicar's heavy, savage figure stood backlit by the flames. His enemy made a feral hiss in the firelight. As the trees behind him burned, the creature's demonic face shone mottled and skull-like in the gloom. The creature was scaly, inhumanly slim, and dripping with lordly disdain. Long needlelike fangs disfigured an already ugly face. It gazed in distaste upon the savage sight of the Justicar, and firelight flickered inside the creature's eyes.

Shifting his blood-smeared blade, the Justicar gazed at his enemy as though slowly measuring it for its grave.

Cambion.

A half-demon, part man and part monster, cambions were an abomination. As the Justicar poised his blade, breathing slow and hard, the cambion gave a sudden scream and charged forward.

They traded blows—the silver sword moving fast as lightning to block the Justicar's black blade. The two swords met again and again, the force of the Justicar's barrage driving his enemy down, and then the man viciously kicked his enemy in the knee. The creature cursed and grunted as the Justicar hacked his sword into its armored hide.

The thing's flesh jarred like teak, almost denting the Justicar's blade. Scarcely scratched, the creature twisted and stabbed its sword at the man's head. Steel screamed as one cheek guard almost tore free from the Justicar's helm. The big man roared and butted his head into the hellspawn face. As the creature staggered back, the black blade chopped a thin wound across its cheek. Scenting the kill, the Justicar brought his sword back around in a blow designed to shear the creature in two.

Screaming an arcane incantation, the cambion shot a force bolt from its palms that staggered the Justicar back an instant before his blade could strike.

With shocking speed the Justicar bulled into the attack. His sword blow came blindingly fast, flicking aside the cambion's blade and sweeping in a blur to cleave toward its neck.

The cambion streaked aside, launching itself away from the terrifying black sword. It sped toward the wagon camp, racing past the teamsters and crossbowmen and heading away from the blazing woods.

Lumbering hard in pursuit, the Justicar bellowed in anger at the caravan guards. *"Shoot, you damned fools!"*

Whipping up its hand, the cambion cast a spell as the crossbowmen sighted and fired. Crossbow bolts ricocheted away from a half-seen disc of force. The barrage failed to touch the cambion—yet it stalled the creature long enough for the Justicar to bring it back into the range of his blade. Whirling about, the cambion saved itself an instant before it could be sheared in two. The colossal force of the Justicar's blow still drove the creature back and chopped a gash deep into its side.

The two combatants hammered at each other while the caravan crews gathered to stare in shock. Sparks spattered across the dirt, steel screaming as the Justicar drove his enemy back. With a roar, the cambion parried, shrieked another incantation, and slapped its open palm against the Justicar's blade. A savage crackle of lightning wreathed the sword, and the Justicar spilled backward, swearing in pain. His enemy tried to stab down with its own blade. The Justicar roared and kicked the creature in what should have been its crotch, but it merely made the thing stagger one pace back and skin its blade past the Justicar's armored hide.

The creature rebounded off the fish oil wagon, hissed through its needle fangs, and took a firm grip upon its sword. With his own blade lying three paces away, the Justicar tensed in order to dive away from the inevitable blow.

Die!

The hell hound seemed to scream with laughter as it blasted out its third and final flame for the day. The cambion ducked underneath the firebolt, which smacked into the wagon, instantly catching the oil-stained barrels afire.

"Cinders!"

Fire! Burn! The hound seemed to dance with utter glee. *Burn! Burn!*

Flames climbed the wagon, wreathing the oil barrels in light. Framed against the fire, the cambion raised its hand and let the air crackle with the power of a magic spell. With a scream of triumph, the creature prepared to blast the Justicar into nonexistence.

Oil barrels suddenly burst open in the heat, and blazing fish oil gushed out to drown the cambion with flame. Blinded, the creature instinctively whipped about, giving the Justicar the instant he needed to snatch his blade and attack. The cambion tried to heave itself out of the black sword's path. It lifted a hand to shield itself as the Justicar whipped his blade downward in a terrifying blur of speed.

The sword rang as it hacked into demonic flesh. A severed hand flew into the fire, the cambion screeching in pain as it clutched at the stump of its wrist. The mutilated monster staggered wildly aside, then quite suddenly sprinted off into the dark.

"Damn it!"

Shielding his face, the Justicar tried to pursue through the flames, only to fall back as more and more oil barrels exploded in the heat. Oxen reared and screamed as blazing oil burst amidst the trees, the whole forest suddenly catching flame.

His teeth set in a wide, unmoving grin, Cinders gave a gleeful wag of his tail. *Good fire! Good fire! Burn! Burn! Burn!*

"That's *great*, Cinders. That's about a thousand gold nobles worth of oil!"

Burn!

The Justicar irritably sheathed his sword and cursed. The bandit chieftain had escaped, and burning fish oil had set the entire forest ablaze. Swearing bitterly, the Justicar shoved his shoulder against one wagon and helped the teamsters roll it slowly away from the flames.

Oxen stampeded off into the night, and the scout's horse broke its tether to bolt off to gods-knew-where. Scorched and sweating teams of men managed to roll wagons out onto the soggy plain, losing their bedding and their tents to the rushing fires.

In the end, three wagons were a total loss. The Razor Wood wreathed the entire sky with flames, trees crisping and huge sheets of fire soaring up into the sky. Sitting on the grass a few hundred yards from the blaze, the Justicar could only curse and grumble as he used a fistful of weeds to scrub clean his blade.

Having managed to collect a brace of oxen, Polk the teamster came over to sit at his side. The teamster watched the forest burn, unable to hear the tittering glee of Cinders in his own mind. Taking a bite of barbecued oxen, he passed a lump of meat over to the Justicar and then uncorked a brandy jug.

"Sentient hell hound pelt, hey? That's a mighty strange partner, son." Apparently unconcerned by the sulphur hissing from Cinders's jaws, Polk took a drink. "It's a nice touch. Unusual. A real fighter needs a touch of the unusual about him."

Polk parked himself beside the Justicar, forgetting to offer a pull from his brandy jug.

"Your technique's good, son! Don't get me wrong!" The man worked a piece of meat out from between two teeth, then pitched the morsel at the fires. "See, I knew they had to have someone watchin' over us! A special agent, a guardian angel. You work for the County Guard?"

"Special commission." The Justicar shook his head. "Countess of Urnst. She asked. I listened." The Justicar examined his blade. The enchanted steel was unmarked by the evening's work. "She knew I'd be . . . *inclined.*"

Polk thoughtfully screwed the cork back into his jug, settling it in place with a decisive *thud.*

"How did you know that scout feller was a spy?"

"He was heading off to lead the ambush." The Justicar carefully examined his tools. "When a rider goes to the stream after making camp, he takes a bucket or he leads his horse."

"Good reasoning, son! Fine reasoning." The teamster watched as an oil barrel deep inside the burning forest somehow shot itself up into the sky. "Unless he watered his horse when he first went into the forest—before he came back to the caravan."

The Justicar glared at the man and stripped the grinning hell hound pelt away from his back. "The ogres made a convincing argument."

"I suppose so, suppose so. . . ." The teamster watched as his companion began to brush the hell hound pelt into a lustrous shine. The creature leaked sulphurous smoke from its nostrils, squeezing its eyes shut in pleasure as it basked beneath the brush.

Most other men would be loath to intrude upon a man and his dog—particularly a fire-breathing sentient hell hound pelt—but Polk had obviously decided he was made of sterner stuff.

"Well, at least you picked up a few pointers from me. Not many folks are smart enough to know when they have a failin'." The teamster patted the big man with a paternalistic hand. "See, I told you that you needed a good sword fight! I admire a beginner who's not ashamed to learn, son. I admire it, I really do."

More explosions sounded from deep inside the forest fire as more oil barrels fed the hungry blaze. With half the landscape aflame, Polk strode off to see if any ale had been rescued from the camp. Sitting cross-legged in damp grass with a skinned hell hound purring in his lap, the Justicar could only gnaw upon his half-cooked meat and pray that tomorrow would be a better day.

Someone was trying to make sure Urnst's northern border settlements failed, and whoever they were, they were good. The Justicar could chalk at least three caravans up to his enemy's credit, and the gods only knew how many other raids had gone unreported. Whoever orchestrated these bandits had power enough to secure inhuman help and an intelligence network that let them slip their own men into each expedition. That meant the leaders had wealth, had power—and had a larger plan. Yet, they were subtle enough merely to try to make the settlers lose hope and leave. This seemed to rule out the obvious culprit, the half-demon king Iuz. Iuz would have simply eradicated the settlements through violence, and he had far more power to call upon than a handful of ogres and a cut-rate cambion.

The Justicar's current employer, the Countess of Urnst, was a wise woman. She knew that her counselors were security risks and that her border patrols had been infiltrated. Obliterating this problem would require a certain silent, savage touch. Hence came the Justicar. He had a simple commission: Get the wagon trains safely moving. To accomplish this, he would have to eliminate the cause of the raids.

Because the caravans left from secret locations and took secret trails, someone was obviously seeding agents among the caravans to lead them into ambush. This meant that the enemy must have a spy that somehow discovered the caravan routes.

To find that spy, the ranger had accompanied the teamsters on their journey back to their usual home base. Somewhere here, there was a spy, the next step up a ladder that would lead the Justicar to the head of the conspiracy. He had followed the trail back to where the caravans began, and now once again he hunted for unworthy souls.

Along the Franz River, on the border of the County of Urnst and its eastern neighbor Nyrond, there lay an area of careful neutrality. Both kingdoms watched each other in mutual hostility and therefore had opened a niche for exploitation.

The river had become a haven for showboats and pleasure barges. As long as gambling, prostitution, and alcohol were peddled on the river, the boats were technically under no one's tax and no one's law. The barges were careful never to touch upon the shore, plying rowboats back and forth to pick up passengers and supplies. Huge, lordly, and teeming with revelers, each barge existed as a tiny kingdom with its own power struggles, its own politics, and its own maze of petty crime. They were floating worlds the size of villas, crewed by dozens of sailors, waiters, cooks, prostitutes, card sharks, and armed guards.

A typical barge of its kind, the *Saucy Gannet* measured two hundred feet in length, soared three stories tall, and had been decked out in painted wooden feathers from gilded stem to crested stern. Onboard gambling halls, bars, and brothels catered to a bizarre array of tastes. Cheap tavern housing could be found below decks while the upper levels were as opulent as a palace. The whole contraption plodded through the water, propelled by a huge stern wheel. Guests who had tried to skip their gambling debts now walked along a treadmill that turned the wheel.

Festooned with banners and with its idiotic figurehead grinning at the world, the *Saucy Gannet* was a universe all of her own.

The Justicar did not approve.

In a world where so many suffered and where so much work still needed to be done, he objected to seeing such effort being wasted upon sheer banality. Watching a pair of leggy women wiggle past, the Justicar leaned on a rail and distastefully wondered if merely touching the ship would somehow taint his soul.

Two tourists seemed to be enjoying their little dip into debauchery. They were dressed largely in ostrich feathers, most of which were placed to the rear. They looked the shaven-headed man slyly up and down, leaning back upon the rails in invitation. All of a sudden, one girl saw the hell hound skin grinning wickedly at them from the Justicar's backpack, bugged her eyes out, and dragged her companion into a hasty retreat to the farthest possible corner of the ship.

From his nest inside his friend's backpack, Cinders gave a happy sniff of the air.

Girlie girl smells nice!

The Justicar pulled an apple from a passing tray. He bit into it, chewed for a while, and carefully examined the barge with its waving bunting and its dens of sin. Every person aboard was being fleeced by the captain, robbed by crooked games and thieving waitresses, yet more and more visitors came aboard at every stop. With the end of the war, people seemed in a frenzy to spend their time upon frivolity.

It was a monument to wastefulness, illusion, and greed. Cursing in disgust, the Justicar pitched his apple core down into the river. "I hate this place."

Burn! Cinders seemed to jiggle with glee. *Burn! Burn!*

"Look, just have a snack, will you? And no burning!" After shoving a piece of coal into the hell hound's mouth, the Justicar angrily snatched another apple from a passing dish. "You *do* realize they're trying to make us pay for all that damned fish oil?"

Just to make the day perfect, a bystander decided to invade the Justicar's private retreat beside the rail. The intruder had the physique of a piece of knotted string, a huge axe-beak nose, and had decked himself out in an archer's cap adorned with pheasant plumes.

"So there you are! Thought I saw you there. Said to myself, 'Polk', I said, 'now there's a fellow in need of company!' "

"Oh, *lovely.*" The Justicar seethed with raw hatred for the entire universe. Polk the teamster was *exactly* the right thing to worsen an already irritating day. "You've woken up."

"Had to, son. I'm your host! Brought you here, should look after you. No telling what trouble a young 'un like you might blunder into in a place like this. You need an old hand to watch out for you, someone who knows the ropes, has an investigative mind." Polk helped himself to a bite from the Justicar's apple. He decided to keep it and finished the entire fruit as he talked.

"This is the life. This is the payoff. Here's where we come at the end of every trip." The man managed to shower droplets of apple juice all over the front of the Justicar. "Wagoning! That's the life. You take my word for it, son. Give up this ne'er-do-well trapping you do and take up a proper job!"

"Yeah, right." The Justicar had worked long and hard to make himself into a fearsome figure. He had eliminated bandits and preyers-upon-the-weak from Celadon forest to the borders of Iuz. In stark, unyielding efficiency he had no equals. Wrenching his eyes away from the sight of the river-banks, the Justicar turned himself to the job at hand.

As annoying as it seemed, Polk was his first, best, and only source of information. The big ranger turned to glower down at his companion.

"Talk to me, Polk. So, this is where you were just before you went out on your job? All of you?" The man tried to leave Polk no openings for fuzzy logic. "This exact barge at this exact town?"

"Right here! The *Gannet*'s the best punt on the river, and every teamster knows it. Best spread of crowds, too."

"So I'd heard." The Justicar rested one hand on the pommel of his sword. "Who do you talk to when you get here? Is there one barmaid who always listens, one gambler you always see, one woman you always request?"

"You mean do we blab about where we're going? *Pffft!*" The teamster mimed his own mouth being stitched tight. "Our lips are sealed! That's for us to know and the world to find out! You know me, son—professionalism first! Never interfere with the job!"

Apparently, someone *was* interfering with the job. Someone knew the days and dates that the northbound supply caravans were leaving. Since the teamsters and wagon crews had all been slaughtered to a man, it seemed unlikely that the spy was one of their own.

Clearly, a spy had made a business out of eavesdropping on the wagoners. All in all, it would be easiest to let the spy seek out the wagoners. Much as it pained him, the Justicar decided to attach himself to Polk and his friends.

A gaggle of teamsters had gathered to spend their wages on booze and women before heading out on yet another supply train. Walking slowly after the wagoners, the Justicar followed them down through the gambling dens and into the barge's painted halls.

A big tavern overlooked the broad, curved stern. It was a noisy place filled with the sounds of dice, clanging beer steins, and revelry.

Teamsters and wagoners were readily recognized. They wore leather jerkins, heavy boots, and had money to burn. Every bar girl in the tavern instantly looked the teamsters up and down then began to circle their prey like sharks homing in upon the scent of blood.

At one of the tables, a waitress carefully snipped a gambler's purse free from his belt. The Justicar felt a flash of raw hostility but judged that the thieves were only stealing from other thieves. Justice was being served—none of this was his affair. Seeing his glowering, all-knowing stare, the waitress backed hastily away and whispered in the ear of a man behind the bar.

The barkeep tugged at his nose and waved one hand at the Justicar. "Hey, soldier! Care to set down your pack and sword?"

"No."

The Justicar scanned the tables. Some teamsters were being sped upstairs by some of the girls, but most were clustering about a table where men played a game of cards. As he tried to read the pattern of the crowd, the Justicar felt the bartender stalking over to his side.

"Soldier? Most folk find it better to leave their weapons at the bar."

"Go away."

"Is that a magic sword?" The bartender seemed to sniff like a weasel as he ran his eyes along the skull-pommeled blade. "If it is, we can take real good care of it for you."

The weapon was *intensely* sharp, enchanted, and cared for by a man who knew the value of his tools. Turning, the Justicar slowly pushed the bartender away only to have the tavern bouncer suddenly appear on the scene.

The bouncer growled, then saw a kindred hostility in the Justicar. They met each other's eyes in cold silence, each measuring the other carefully. The two men nodded at one another, then both turned aside to go back to their own affairs. Escaping with his life from between the two heavy-set, grim men, the barkeep scuttled quickly back to the shelter of his bottles, jugs, and jars.

A pert blonde waitress made it her business to perch on a table at the Justicar's side. She cocked her head and nudged at the man's black scabbard with her toe.

"Hey stranger! So what do you do? Ranger? Soldier?"

The Justicar settled his pack on the deck. "It isn't important."

"Do you dance, soldier?"

"I don't." The Justicar found himself a place at the card table and wiped clean a chair. "Never learned."

"I can teach you. It's cozy!" The girl gave a winsome smile. "Why don't I just keep you company?"

Growling like a surly wolf, the Justicar settled in his chair. "I *hate* company."

"Don't you want to be friendly?"

"No."

The woman finally took the hint. She sniffed and stalked haughtily away, leaving the Justicar alone. From inside his backpack, a happy Cinders tickled his thoughts into the Justicar's mind.

Girlie smells nice!

"Well a sniff is all we get. Now keep your nostrils open."

Sitting beside him and shuffling cards, Polk clucked his tongue and fixed the Justicar with a disappointed eye.

"Son, you have to learn to lighten up. That's the mark of a real hero. Devil-may-care, full of life! They take adventure in their stride."

"Shut up. Deal the cards."

The Justicar had only a small purse of gold left—a purse he kept in a badger-skin sporran at the front of his belt. Its proximity to his wedding tackle made it far too sensitive a place for any cutpurse, but until he finished his commission, the Justicar's sum total of wealth stood at seven nobles, a poor sum to last a game of cards. He watched one round of the card game, then concocted a set of self-made rules that minimized financial risk. He wanted to nurse his funds and watch the tables so that he could listen to the talk. Cinders's ears would have been helpful, but the hell hound skin was an extremely recognizable mark. Instead, the Justicar kept his backpack underneath his feet with the hound's nose just peeking out into the air.

Ringed about the table were a dozen assorted teamsters, wagoners, and riverfolk. A fur trapper with a whole fox skin serving as a collar for his coat gave the Justicar a sharp nudge in the armored ribs.

"Hey, baldie! Are you betting?"

"I'm betting." The Justicar advanced the minimum bet. "Deal me two."

There were no women at hand. They would wait to see who was winning before making their moves. Hunched about the table, the gamblers made a fast and friendly game.

There was enough money at hand to make the ale flow freely, and Polk had a cavernous thirst. The man found time between beer steins to play a wickedly lucky game. Wearing a moustache of foam, he whooped as he laid down a winning hand and hammered at the table with glee.

The Justicar watched his own money disappearing and slowly supped his beer.

"Polk, you play well. You play this in a lot of places?"

"A hundred towns and a hundred trails with a hundred girls in every one of 'em, son!" The teamster raked in the pot, then gleefully tossed coins to the waitress and ordered a round of ale for the whole table. "I'm a teamster, son! A merchant adventurer, explorer, hunter, scout! We're heroes one and all!"

The blonde waitress returned with drinks—pointedly thudding a mug beside the Justicar in an attempt to spill his beer. She retreated and kept her distance from the entire table as though convinced the Justicar was the carrier of some unsightly disease.

Much as it annoyed him, the Justicar's mission required him to make conversation. Clandestinely changing his mug with the man next to him, the Justicar watched Polk drain his stein.

"So it's a good life? You can't go that far that often."

"Well I do the borderlands, son. That's where the money is!" The teamster dealt cards with a speedy skill. "Heroes! When we head out day after tomorrow, there's folk going to be cheering our arrival with tears in their eyes."

Excellent. His mouth was spreading the news. Arranging his cards, the Justicar silently assessed the crowds. A new man had come over and silently joined the game while a shifty-eyed foreigner had leaned back in his chair at a table nearby.

"Cinders?"

Feet smell bad! Magic girlie-girl smells good. Spicy! The hell hound seemed relatively happy in confinement. *Prey found?*

"No."

Burn now?

"No." Although Cinders echoed only in the Justicar's mind, the Justicar had to whisper in reply, and he had attracted attention. He hastily tripled his usual bet, then remembered too late that he was almost at the bottom of his funds. "Damn!"

"Never blame the cards, son! A good workman never curses his tools." Polk dealt extra cards all around—unwittingly giving the Justicar a winning hand. With an ironic snort at himself, the Justicar scratched his shaven head and laid down the cards. He gathered in a good ten nobles, gaining a hard glare of irritation from the trapper with his mangy-collared coat. Summoning the grumbling waitress, the Justicar arranged for a platter of hot sausages and mustard for the table.

Happily ensconced with sausages to his left and beer to his right, Polk somehow managed to both fill his mouth, drink beer, *and* keep a firm grip on his cards.

"That's the way, son. Spend it while you have it. No point counting your coins when you're freezing your butt off on the Rift Wastes."

Wonderful. The Rift Wastes were a very specific stretch of countryside. Polk was well on the way to blowing his secret destination. Casting his eyes surreptitiously across the table, the Justicar carefully assessed the other players, looking for a single change in breathing or a twitch of the eyes that might provide him with a clue. He rubbed his nose and used the move to cover another whisper to his backpack down below.

"Cinders?"

Magic girlie-girl smells nice!

Looking up at the all-male table, the Justicar blinked. He sniffed loudly, caught a whiff of a spicy feminine scent, then whipped his head quickly to the right. The fox-skin draped about the trapper's neck met his gaze in shock, the dead fox jerking with a quiver of fright.

"*Ha!*"

One fist lashed out in a blur as the Justicar caught the fox-collar by the throat. The fur screamed and instantly turned into a huge cobra. The snake gaped its fangs, and the Justicar instinctively yelped and threw the thing away. As it hit the ground, the cobra shimmered and changed into a skinny, naked little woman a mere two feet high. She immediately flipped out a sturdy pair of translucent wings and flew madly off across the crowd.

"*Get down!*" the Justicar screamed as he pulled Cinders from his pack.

The Justicar surged huge and angry up out of his seat, spilling the astonished fur trapper to the floor. With one hand he grasped the holy symbol around his neck while the other hand crackled magic all about his fingertips. He hurled a spell that streaked across the room and smacked into a potted fern beside the doors. Laughing at his aim, the pixie spread her wings and whirred gleefully from the room.

The fern lashed out like an insane octopus and grappled the girl with its fronds. The pixie screamed in fright, her torso trapped and her legs kicking as she desperately tried to fight free. The little creature looked up at her pursuer with a thin, exquisite little face. Her pointed ears quivered in alarm as she tried to break open the ferns. As the Justicar thundered across the deck planking toward her, spilling every chair and table in his path, the pixie jerked, struggled, and then suddenly wormed one hand out of the fronds. She pointed at the plant, screamed a frantic syllable, and a stream of magic darts blasted the fern apart. With bits of pot and clods of dirt showering the floor, the little creature righted herself, ripped away the fern fronds, and then raced in panic through the door. Fern fronds trapped her wings, but her legs drove her forward with an astonishing turn of speed.

The whole tavern erupted into chaos. One man tried to block the Justicar's way and was straight-armed to the floor for his pains. Arriving at the doorway a second after his prey had gone, the warrior kicked the door open and lunged out onto the open deck.

Magic!

A spell blast ripped past his head. With Cinders giving an instant's warning, the Justicar jerked back and felt the doorjamb beside him explode into flames. He leaped instantly through the heat, sensing flames hungrily tearing at the wooden walls above.

The pixie saw him land. Snarling, she backed a step away and suddenly disappeared from sight.

"Cinders, shoot high!"

The hell hound blasted a huge sheet of flames across the escape route and into the open river. Invisible and cursing, the pixie dodged back the other way, fleeing to the upper decks of the barge.

With the tavern in flames behind him, the Justicar swore as he tied Cinders into place about his helm. He ran fast as he leaped past deckchairs wreathed in fire.

"Talk to me!"

Girlie-prey runs left! Invisible or not, the hell hound's nose and ears could pinpoint her to within a fraction of an inch. *Runs fast!*

That put her sprinting along the deck between a row of chairs. The Justicar ran hard and heavy in pursuit, matching his prey twist for turn as she fled in a panic up the super-structure and onto the highest promenade.

Magic!

The Justicar dived and rolled, his heavy body hitting the deck in a practiced move that brought him back up to his feet. A lightning bolt ripped past his ribs, missing him by the thickness of a hair. The bolt struck the ship's stern castle, severed a flagpole and sent a banner arcing down into the panicked crowds below. Crew members were already running for water buckets and bellowing "Fire!" at the tops of their lungs. Flames blossomed as a brandy cask caught fire inside the tavern door, blocking the stairs to the upper levels as blazing liquid sluiced across the decks.

Roaring with anger, the Justicar hurled a deck chair through the empty air, heard a thud, and suddenly saw a naked, skinny pixie skidding hard across the planks.

Fern-covered and disheveled, the blonde girl speared him with a glare of such pure, smarting malice that it almost hit him like a blow. The pixie spun onto her feet, one hand trailing a stream of glittering sparks as a new spell formed around her fingertips.

Magic.

"I see it. Thanks!"

The Justicar summoned magic of his own and punched it out along the deck. It caught the pixie in the rear. The girl froze like a statue, caught in mid-stride by a spell designed to hold her paralyzed in place.

A naked study in panic, she stood balanced with her eyes bugging wide. Pleased with a job well done, the Justicar dusted off his hands and stalked menacingly along the deck toward his prey.

Chaos still reigned on the barge below. Gamblers and drunkards fought to escape the smoke-filled tavern as the fire bells screamed. Waitresses and working girls stampeded off toward the bow. The guards decided that the law had finally arrived upon the *Saucy Gannet* and immediately jumped ship to swim for shore. Pleased by the commotion, the Justicar stood with the hell hound pelt gleaming on his back and gave a triumphant, predatory smile.

Cinders seemed to dance and wriggle as he sensed the panic all over the barge.

Flames! Burn!

"Sniff it in good health." The Justicar stalked around to face his prey and squatted down on his heels to contemptuously meet the pixie face to face. "So, what have we here? A pixie that casts spells?"

Suddenly breaking from her sham, the pixie moved with lightning speed. With a squeal of glee, she slapped her hand across the Justicar's face. Glittering pixie dust spattered him like a rainbow, and the huge man froze in place instantly. The pixie danced across the deck, around and around her victim, who merely squatted on his heels and watched with dull, blank eyes.

Naked as a brat and seething with joy, the pixie finally leaned her elbow on her victim's cheek and twiddled magic dust into the air.

"Faerie dust! Pure as dew, straight off the faerie's butt!" The little creature had a husky voice with a twangy foreign accent. "Always know thine enemy! Faerie dust! Once a day! Befuddles enemy. *Bam!*" The girl made a triumphant punch at empty air. "So suck on that, wolf boy! One in, one down—the faerie takes the prize!" Prancing, the pixie rubbed her knuckles into the Justicar's skull. "Who's the big man now, huh? Who's my slave? Who's my drooling boy-toy! Come on! Come on, say it!"

Looking dazed and bemused, the Justicar stared dully at the girl. "Yes, Mistress. I am your boy-toy slave."

"*Ha!*" Lean and skinny as a snake, the pixie made a dancing little turn and slapped her rump. "Make that 'Perfect and Exquisite Mistress'!"

"Perfect and Exquisite Mistress!"

"Too hoopy!" The pixie pranced and sat upon her victim's knee. "And who's the smartest damned girl that ever flapped her wings?"

"You are, O Perfect and Exquisite Mistress."

"And who"—ripping away the last wriggling strands of fern, the pixie flicked out a brilliant cascade of blonde hair—"who is the most beautiful, most exotic, most sensual sight a mortal ever beheld?"

"You are." The Justicar repeated the words with absolute conviction. "You, O Perfect and Exquisite Mistress."

"Of course." The pixie turned a pirouette. "Praise me! Do you like my hair? My nails? Don't you just adore the smell of my skin?"

"Yes, O Perfect and Exquisite Mistress. Your hair is perfect, your wits are keen, you are graceful as a swallow's flight."

"Exactly." The pixie sighed then folded her fingertips beneath her chin, perched in front of the Justicar, and prettily fluttered her lashes. "Is there anything else, O slave?"

"Yes, O Perfect and Exquisite Mistress." The Justicar's eyes suddenly flicked to spear the girl. "*Gotcha!*"

He snatched her like a bug and held the girl kicking and squealing in his hands. The Justicar rose to his feet and shook a last glimmer of faerie dust from his prize.

"A pixie with an ego problem. *Lovely.*"

Gaping, the pixie writhed with fury, unable to hide the astonishment in her eyes.

"I hit you with faerie dust, you bastard!"

"I went to school in Celadon forest." The Justicar shrugged. "We ate that damned stuff like sugar."

"Bastard!" The pixie began a frenzied *kick-kick-kick* of her little feet. "Let me go!"

"Oh yeah—well that's an option. I can see that!" The Justicar took a loop of cord from a pocket and dropped it over the girl, roughly trapping her wings and arms in place. "Come on! It's high time we had a little talk about some wagon trains."

The pixie instantly sank tiny teeth into his hand, breaking the skin and making the man curse her and let go. She landed on her scrawny bottom on the deck, looked up, and hissed with triumph as a shadow loomed over the Justicar from behind.

A thin man in black tried to stab the Justicar in the spine. Cinders whipped his own head about, fixed the assassin in his mad red eyes, and gave a scream of glee.

Prey!

The Justicar whirled, caught the stabbing blade with the same motion, and broke the assassin's arm. He stabbed the man with his own knife, leaving the envenomed blade in the assassin's gut as he continued to turn completely around.

A second man had risen up over the rails. This man fired a bow—aiming not for the Justicar, but for the little pixie. The naked girl froze in terror, helpless to do anything but watch the arrow come straight for her throat.

The Justicar moved with a speed almost too fast to see. His sword cleared the scabbard quicker than thought and cut the arrow out of the air. Both halves of the dart passed to either side of the pixie's face, and she sank numbly down onto her knees.

The second assassin leaped the rails and whipped out a short sword well coated in a greenish, sticky venom. He ran at the Justicar, who dropped to one knee and flicked his sword to strike the assassin's blade away. The assassin's short sword fell, ringing on the ground, and the Justicar instantly punched with his fist, the blow lifting the man up and slamming him down five paces away.

The assassin flashed to his feet, whipped back a hand that suddenly held a throwing knife—

And then screamed as a thundering blast of fire wrapped him in agony from head to toe.

Burn! Burn-burn-burn!

"Cinders! Damn it!"

The assassin would have been the spy's contact—the next step in the chain that led to the mastermind. Now the man was bubbling like a well-done roast, and the whole upper deck was aflame. Cinders had managed to set the entire promenade on fire, and strings of burning bunting fell to spread the blaze all across the lower levels of the barge. The management was definitely going to be annoyed.

The Justicar sheathed his sword, snatched the dazed pixie in his arms, and held the creature tight against his chest.

"Do you like water?"

"No!"

"Good."

With a heavy bound, the man launched himself across the rails and plunged thirty feet down into the icy river. The pixie wailed, then disappeared amid the splash as the Justicar, his hell hound skin, his black sword, and his armor all speared deep into the water. Swimming with slow, powerful strokes, the Justicar traveled underwater for a dozen yards then broke the surface, letting the struggling pixie take a breath. The man looked back once at the blazing pleasure barge and then grimly struck out toward the northern shore.

4

"Now I'm not saying that I have always been exactly *good*, but I have tried, in my way, to lead a life devoted to certain *positive principles*." Remaining perfectly calm, the pixie tried to let reason speak for itself. "So although on the surface some of my actions might appear *questionable*, I can assure you that I have always been pure at heart." The little creature shot a dark sideways glance at her companions. "Look, are you listening to me or what?"

Soaked, dark, and glowering, the Justicar collected twigs and branches and stacked them in a pile. Cinders helpfully shot a small flame jet into the kindling, and a sturdy campfire was instantly ablaze. Bound hand and foot and dangling helplessly above the ground, the pixie anxiously watched as yet more wood was stacked upon the fire.

"Um, all right, I am aware that I have not been . . . as good as I should. However, I believe I can try to be better."

The flames crackled as more and more wood was tossed into the suspiciously large blaze.

"Look! Would you stop doing that while I'm talking to you?"

The lands north of the River Franz were largely covered in fern and marsh. Autumn had broken the riverbanks and flooded the low-lying fields beyond. What in summer were tangled thickets and little hillocks had now become a maze of islands stranded amongst knee-deep, freezing ferns. The Justicar had waded doggedly onward for at least two hours, leaving the river, burning pleasure barge, and vengeful pursuers far behind. With an hour to go before evening, he had finally climbed onto an islet, cut down some bushes, and dangled his captive from a tree.

Helpless in the clutches of a huge, violent man and a pyromaniacal sentient dog skin, the pixie could only kick her heels and jitter in despair. With her hands tied, she could cast no spells, and if she shifted shape, the dog skin would smother her in flame. This left only her considerable powers of persuasion, which would have been more comforting if her captor would perhaps deign to even look her way.

The flames rose higher, spreading heat across the little island. The Justicar planted two forked sticks, one at each end of the fire, then glared at the pixie and began to shave a long, thin sapling into a spit.

Beginning to sweat a little in fright, the pixie gave a squirm. "Look, I'm sure we can make some kind of deal. I mean, you're with the forces of good, right? And . . . and I'm a faerie, and faeries are cute, lovable little icons of forest fun, right? So . . . so there's a joining of interests right there, huh?"

The Justicar rose, holding his sturdy spit as he marched toward the pixie. He slapped the rod in his hand as he walked, and the pixie's twin antennae stood madly on end.

"Um, look, you're a reasonable man. I can see that. So perhaps it's time we just came to a logical arrangement?"

The Justicar drew a knife from his belt, cut the pixie from her perch and shoved the skewer up through the back of her bonds. The girl dangled beneath the stick like a rabbit trussed for roasting and instantly began to kick and squeal.

"*Oh no! Oh no-no-no-no-no!* Faeries have a curse on them, you know! You eat a faerie and—ooooh—and you'll go sterile! No sex drive at all, I swear!" The pixie wriggled frantically as she was carried toward the fire. "And you'll get fat!" The girl tried to shrink down to the bottom of the stake. "You'll get eczema, plus your eyesight will go! A-all food will taste exactly like week-old ham!"

"Shut up." The Justicar seated himself by the fire, holding the trussed, naked pixie up in the air. "You're annoying. All pixies are annoying."

"Oh my goodness, it's a vision of Saint Cuthbert!" The pixie stared in amazement off into the empty scrub. "It's a sign from the gods! I'm converted to the good life from now on, Good be praised!"

The Justicar jammed the bottom of the pixie-stick into the sod, propping the little creature comfortably close to the fire.

"Shut up. Get warm. Keep quiet."

The pixie relaxed, her breast heaving a little as she was slowly drained of her fright. The Justicar had taken a knife and sawed the bottom off his own coarse tunic. He began cutting the cloth into a rough, pixie-sized dress, and looked damned annoyed to be doing so. The man's armor had been hung out so that its felt lining could dry.

Casting a quick eye left and right, the pixie quite suddenly felt safe. "Sure, I'll keep quiet. My name is Escalla, by the way. That's Princess Escalla or Lady Escalla. Sometimes *Your Highness* or *Brightflower Maid*. Or—or a pet name? I mean, you could even give me a pet name."

The Justicar glared at his captive through cold, dark eyes. "Pixie."

"Uh, yeah . . ." The girl tried to coax a little more cooperation out of her host. "Or maybe a more *bonding* kinda term?"

"How's about *fishbait?*"

The pixie hastened to agree. "Endearing! I mean, a sense of humor is good. We can laugh together now, I can see that. We have a rapport!" Escalla blew a strand of stray hair away from her face. "But about the 'pixie' thing. Funny thing is, most people look at me and say, 'Ooh! Pixie!' when I'm actually a *faerie.* I mean, a proper name for everything, and everything done properly. Am I right?"

Having finished a rough strip of cloth to serve as a pixie dress, the Justicar glowered at the girl and hissed, "I said *quiet!*"

He untied the girl from the stick, roughly wrapped her torso in coarse cloth, and tied the dress in place with woollen thread. Escalla began to say thank you, only to find herself immediately bound hand and foot again and threaded right back onto her stake beside the fire. She decided to glare in annoyance at the Justicar, watching him as he drew a fishing line from his pouch and sent a line trailing off into the water.

She considered changing shape into a snake and slithering from her bonds. Unfortunately, the hell hound skin lay propped on the ground a foot from her rear, and she could feel the creature grinning at her. The pixie tried surreptitiously picking at her ties until the Justicar came to sit directly in front of her and glare into her face.

"Speak. Who were you spying for?"

Escalla made a little wiggle-waggle of her head, and the Justicar frowned at her warningly.

"Well how can I tell you if I have to keep quiet?"

The huge warrior gleamed like a demon in the red light of the campfire.

"You will tell me who paid you to spy. Where were you sending your information?" The Justicar glared at the pixie and folded his arms. "Start *now.*"

"Or you'll *what?"* With a sudden, brilliant surge of inspiration, Escalla gave a derisive toss of her hair. "You're not going to stick me in that fire! I can tell. Oh yeah, you *look* tough, but there's no way you are going to take a sleek, pretty, helpless young woman and simply burn her alive."

The pixie stuck out her tongue. "So I guess I'll just keep my little secrets after all!"

The Justicar gave the faerie a level look, then picked her up, levered open Cinders's jaws, and fed her feet first into the hell hound's maw. He closed the hound's jaws about her rump, then simply went back to tending his fire.

Sweating rather large, genteel beads of perspiration, the faerie tried to remain perfectly calm.

"Um, he still has a tongue in here, doesn't he?"

Cinders gave a snigger, wig-waggling his ears.

Girlie taste good! The hell hound's nostrils leaked sulphur into the air. *Burn now?*

"Oh, gods . . ." Wide-eyed, Escalla bit her upper lip and gave a dazed, measured little nod. "All right, I'm going to scream like a peeled weasel now. I just wanted to warn you that you've only brought this on yourselves."

Escalla took a deep breath and suddenly began to shriek and thrash in abject terror. Her screams sent echoes shooting all across the swamp.

"Get me out! For the gods' sake, get me out! Don't-kill-me-don't-kill-me-don't-kill-me! God-oh-god-oh-god please-please-please-please-please! I'll spill my guts! I'll tell you everything I know!"

As a demonstration of pure spineless, backsliding terror, it was rather impressive. The Justicar fished the girl back out of the hell hound's maw, and Cinders mentally smacked his chops.

Aftertaste. Yummy!

"You're welcome." The Justicar planted the faerie's stake into the ground and regarded the weeping, wailing girl. "Spill your guts. I'm listening."

Now several shades paler, the girl hastened to be as helpful as possible.

"All right all right! N-now you have to understand that I'm not malicious! I have been outcast from my rightful position as a leader in the forest community by—"

Escalla went into a panic as the Justicar opened Cinders's jaws. *"They paid me fifty gold a time! I needed the money! I repent! I repent! I repent!"*

"Who paid you?" The Justicar pulled out a tuber he had found in the woods and began carefully peeling it with his knife. "Names. Descriptions. Whereabouts."

"Ah, it was just a guy on the boat. He found me stowing away behind the figurehead and cut me a deal." The faerie gave a shrug. "He was just an extortionist! He worked a ton of different deals—took a cut from pickpockets, gamblers, had his own enforcers. His men were the guys who tried to stab you in the back!"

"And one of them tried to shoot you dead." The Justicar threw tuber peelings in the fire. "You're at the top of their hit list. What did you see that makes them so keen to have you dead?"

Escalla bit her lip in anxiety.

"Well . . . there was one other guy they reported to. A priest guy or maybe a sorcerer! He-he's the one who wanted to know all about the caravans. Tall, skinny, long hair but only at the rear. They met at Trigol City docks once. That's all I know, I swear!"

Wiping clean his knife, the Justicar gave a satisfied growl. The information was enough to lead him back up the chain. If he found the paymaster of the spy scheme, then he might be able to bring the conspiracy to justice.

"Excellent. When we get to Trigol, you can help me search for the man."

"No! No, I can't go! Cities are really bad for my complexion!" Escalla jerked at her ropes in alarm. "Really! I can give you a description, paint you a picture, write you a poem!"

The Justicar glared at Escalla in ill humor. "I need to find him, so you're coming along."

"No! No way! They'll kill me!"

"They are *already* trying to kill you." The Justicar saw his fishing line give a tug and roused himself to pull in a large black bass. "Right about now, they'll be hiring an assassin—maybe even throwing a scrying spell. They should be on your trail by around dawn."

The girl dismissed the thought with a superior little sneer. "Hey, if they could do all of that, why hire a spy!"

"A scrying spell costs two hundred nobles, but *you* work for fifty." The Justicar threaded dinner onto a stick above the fire. "You're not only a snitch, you're a cut-price snitch. Gives you a real glow of pride, eh, Your *Highness?*"

Behind the faerie, the hell hound skin gave another snigger. Seething with hate, Escalla went into a magnificent huff. She kept her hurt silence for almost ten minutes, finally unbending when a sniff of her nostrils told her that dinner was almost done.

Over the next few minutes Escalla let her regal sulk slowly waver; the mere effort of keeping quiet was almost killing her. As she saw dinner cooling by the fire, she finally relented and allowed her captors to hear her speak.

"*Hmph!* So are you going to starve me or feed me like a good servant should?"

"Ooooh—one look at you, and I can just *see* that you're a lady, real princess material." The Justicar had been happily at work, constructing a cage out of sticks and woollen twine. "Have you got to go?"

"Go?"

"Relieve yourself." The Justicar finished his cage. "Or don't faerie princesses obey the call of nature?"

"What?" Escalla bridled. "No, I don't have to 'go,' and it's no business of yours anyway!"

"Fine."

The Justicar scooped up the faerie, pulled off her bindings, and unceremoniously tossed her into her new cage. He tied the door shut, leaving the furious little woman to rattle her bars. Moments later, a chunk of fish, a slab of tuber, and a capful of apricot brandy were thrust through the bars. The Justicar sat Cinders nose-to-nose with the bars, then settled down to thoroughly enjoy his meal.

Escalla ate her fish, burned her fingers on the tuber, and consoled herself with brandy. She looked up to see herself under the unwinking scrutiny of the hell hound's baleful eyes.

Hi.

A few final tasks remained before the evening was done. Clothing was dried and then put back on. The Justicar apparently intended to sleep fully armored with his boots on and his black sword at his side. The ranger brushed Cinders's fur into a nice clean shine, then banked over the coals, bedded himself down upon the hell hound pelt, and went to sleep.

Left alone inside her cage, the pixie muttered to herself, seething with plots of revenge. She planned a hundred ways to escape. Unfortunately, they all required that the hell hound drop dead or fall asleep. Showing no inclination to do either, the canine merely fixed her in his gaze, watching as the prisoner paced her cage.

Eat. Scratch tummy. Sleep.

"Yeah right, red-eyes." Escalla sneezed and waved a sulphurous wisp of smoke away with her wings. "And a good night to you too, you flea-ridden throw rug!"

With nothing else to do, the faerie burrowed into a bed made of dead, dry grass and drifted off into a muttering, dismal sleep.

*   *   *   *   *

Up! Kill! Kill!

Jerking up out of sleep instantly, the Justicar rolled over and wrapped Cinders about his shoulders. He immediately slithered into the cold water and lay almost submerged.

Nerves tingling, he searched the empty night, feeling Cinders bristling instinctively in hate.

"Cinders, where?"

High!

Awakened by all the untoward activity, Escalla poked her head out of her nest of grass, saw that it was scarcely midnight, and made a huge, irritated yawn.

"What is it now? Don't you bastards ever sleep?"

A chilling scream suddenly echoed over the fens. The howl sobbed and yammered in unearthly hunger as a palpable aura of evil flooded through the night. Summoned by the echo of Escalla's voice, a hunting screech came from above. With a rush of wings, something huge and terrible came plummeting wildly down out of the sky.

The faerie wailed in fright, instinctively turned invisible, and fluttered madly about inside her cage.

"Open the cage! Open this gods damned cage!"

High above the island, a dark shape banked and flung itself straight toward the sound of the faerie's voice. With ragged wings spread wide, the monster lofted low across the water and screamed for Escalla's blood.

Sickly moonlight sparkled from the water, illuminating the monster's face. A head shaped like a huge human skull gaped over a muzzle full of fangs. Huge bat wings held aloft a body that ran with mucus like an enormous rotting corpse. The beast hissed, chemicals slobbering from its mouth to drip a phosphorescent trail into the water. Escalla stared at the apparition in fright, trying to wrench apart the bars of her cage as the monster blasted a putrid column of acid straight toward the isle.

As the fiend neared the campsite, the water beneath its wings erupted. In a sudden flash, the Justicar's black sword smacked a long gouge into the creature's wing. With an outraged howl, the monster sawed aside, spinning toward the source of the blow.

A blast of stinking fluid thundered from the creature's mouth, eating away the plants and soil as it hosed across the campsite. Deflected by a handspan as the creature wrenched in pain, the acid hissed past the faerie's cage. Escalla made a dazed little sound as she saw one side of her cage simply slump and disappear. An instant later she flapped out into the open sky.

Surging up out of the water below her, the Justicar saw huge bat wings swerve to pursue the girl and gave a shout of warning. "It's an abyssal bat! Get down in the water or it'll see your body heat!"

Cursing, the Justicar hefted his sword and sped to the remnants of the campfire. He dug out the warm ashes with his helmet, tossing them across the tiny island until the place became a maze of coals and fine white dust.

* * * * *

High above the swampland's spindly trees, Escalla blurred her wings and flew as fast as her skinny little body could go. A savage, bubbling shriek revealed that the monster was coming up fast from behind. Escalla frowned, looked back across her shoulder, and let her brilliant mind deal with the problem. The monster couldn't *possibly* be pursuing her. She was invisible and also far too clever to have left a traceable trail. The monster merely happened to be flying in this direction.

Escalla decided to haul off and simply let the creature pass her by. She made one of the graceful loops for which she was so justly admired, looked derisively over at the monster, and saw a seething jet of acid coming right toward her eyes. The faerie screamed and made a mad tumble through the skies, the acid clipping her across the back as she tumbled free. She felt one wing collapse, and agony spasmed through her as she tumbled through the air. She hit the treetops, ripped through twigs and branches, then felt herself caught by a waiting pair of hands.

"Hold still!"

A blast of healing magic crashed into the faerie's wounds. She gasped and jerked as her body reacted to the sudden, shocking absence of pain. The Justicar held her cradled against his chest, wiped her hair back from her astonished little face, and then stuffed her beneath a warm layer of ashes that lay across the ground.

"Lie still!"

Ashes lay everywhere—hot, gray, and choking. Escalla blinked, but the Justicar had disappeared into the dark. A screaming shape came whipping through the trees, and the faerie could only watch in fright as a huge beast hovered above the isle. With a vile sound, the creature spat acid once again, landing the deadly stream square upon a little human-like shape sculpted out of embers that lay beneath a tree. The acid sent up clouds of toxic steam as it burned the sculpture into sludge. Shrieking in triumph, the monster landed on the acid-spattered ash to tear into its target with its claws.

An instant later, the entire island lit up beneath a pure, brilliant light. The Justicar launched a light spell, blinding the abyssal bat. The monster screamed and lurched into a tree, flapping its wings in an attempt to shield its eyes. Smoke hissed from its skin as the light burned into it like fire. Riveted with horror, Escalla lifted up her head and stared at the thing that flapped and gibbered in hunger for her blood.

The monster stood like a giant dessicated cadaver, its black skin stretched over an inhuman frame of jointed bones. It spread huge batlike wings, fixed its gaze upon the faerie, and gave a roar of pure demonic rage.

Lying stunned beneath the ashes, Escalla stared at the thing and felt her courage slowly deflate.

"Oooh, *poop!*"

Half-blinded, the monster reared aside as a human figure erupted from the ash below. The eight-foot abyssal bat dwarfed even the Justicar. Trailing dust, the Justicar's black sword smacked into the monster's gut. The blade rang as it chopped into stony flesh, black steel flashing as the blade beat aside the fiend's claws and smashed down into its shoulder joint. Screaming in pain, the monster staggered backward, simply shook off a blast of flames from Cinders's snout, and lunged to wrap its huge bat wings about the Justicar. Escalla gave a scream of fright and lifted up her hand, a spell half-formed, but froze in indecision as she saw the human warrior trapped inside the monster's arms.

The Justicar's face stood out in the stark shadows cast by his own illumination spell. Trapped in the monster's arms, the man roared and smacked his shaven head straight into the creature's face. He hit it a second time and then a third, blood streaming down his face from cuts made by the creature's breaking teeth. As the creature's grip loosened, the Justicar raked his boot down the beast's long shin.

It relaxed its hold, and the Justicar wrenched one arm free to rip his fingernails down into the monster's shoulder wound. The man ripped and tore at the exposed end of a bone, and the fiend threw the man aside in agonized rage.

The monster staggered one half-pace back. Gripping his sword halfway down the blade like a quarterstaff, the Justicar rammed the weapon's point into the beasts's throat and twisted at the blade as it came free.

The monster still lived. The creature fought free and lumbered bleeding and howling straight toward Escalla's hiding place. The faerie scrabbled backward and felt her back jam against a tree as she blasted her very best web spell at the creature. The monster ripped its way out of the web and lunged straight for Escalla, its needlelike teeth gaping wide enough to fill her entire world.

The Justicar's shout echoed through the night. Stepping between the faerie and her demonic attacker, he decapitated the monster with one savage swing. Its fangs snapped shut an inch from the faerie's throat. Escalla blinked as the severed head thudded down onto the ash, gaping at her with its wide-open jaws.

Acid leaked from the corpse to burn a hole into the ground. With a shudder, the monster finally stopped beating its wings. The faerie stood up very, very carefully. With mincing, delicate little steps she withdrew from the monster's maw. She wobbled her way over toward the Justicar as the man winced and sank down onto the ash.

The girl blew out a dazed breath. She saw the Justicar holding onto his own ribs and came to stand at his side.

"You, ah, you do little spells, but you do good ones." She touched a hand against her side where the acid had burned away a sheet of skin. Her flesh was now pure, seamless, and as perfect as ever. "Thank you. And the, uh, the warm ashes idea . . . pretty good."

The man cursed and thumped a spell into his own flesh, hissing the invocation in annoyance.

The Justicar's light spell lit up the island in a pure white brilliance. Covered in warm ashes from head to foot, Cinders, the Justicar, and Escalla looked like ghosts. The girl began to dust herself off, casting a frightened glance upward as something dark passed across the image of Luna, the larger of the two moons now riding the sky.

As light rippled reflections from the water, a distant hunting cry echoed through night. It was answered by an even fainter call from somewhere across the marsh.

Appalled, Escalla froze and stared up at the sky. "What *are* those things?"

"Varrangoins, abyssal bats, a type of demon—very dangerous. They're hunting *you.*"

"Me?" The faerie blinked in horror. "Just me?"

"Just you . . ." Stark and dangerous, the Justicar simply looked at the faerie. "Stick close to me if you want to live."

The faerie nodded blank agreement. Ruefully inspecting the ashes clinging to Cinders's wet fur, the man gave a growl. "Hey, Cinders, are you all right?"

All right.

"Good. We're going *now*."

The Justicar tightened his cuirass and snatched his helmet. He whirled, swept up Escalla, and lumbered straight toward the water at a dead run. Escalla saw what was coming and frantically tried to fight free.

"Oh, oh, now look! Guys, it's really cold, and the water and I really don't agree with each other ver*eeeeeee*—"

The Justicar plunged beneath the water just as a black shape cut across the sky. Escalla snatched half a breath, almost drowning as the big man plunged her down into the dark, chill waters. Claws struck at the water, then an acid blast stormed down into the mire, but the Justicar had already darted aside, swimming slowly and powerfully like a leviathan from an ancient world.

Long suffocating seconds passed. Still underwater, the Justicar and Escalla sheltered beneath a submerged branch, shadows showing through the water as more bat-winged shapes passed mere inches overhead.

Terrified of drowning, Escalla thrashed in a mad dance of fear. Her lungs screamed for air, and she desperately lunged toward the surface. She was caught from below and hauled back down. The faerie thrashed, desperate for breath, then suddenly bulged her eyes as she felt the human covering her mouth with his own. She tried to spit the man away—only to have herself crushed tightly in place. She took a breath straight from the man's mouth as a sinister black shape skimmed over the waters just above.

An instant later, the light spell stuttered and went out, plunging the whole marshland into darkness. Escalla and the Justicar hung beneath the water for a long moment more, then rose up through submerged branches and took swift stock of the upper world.

Hunting cries echoed in the night as the creatures searched the far side of the island. The bats found the slaughtered body lying on the island and lifted up a scream of rage. As the remaining monsters flew madly off into the swamp, thirsting for revenge, the Justicar slipped underwater once again and swam quietly away.

Surfacing, he cruised through the thigh-deep water, planting the faerie atop his neck where she could cling to Cinders's fur. Escalla spat and blustered, scrubbing her tongue as she fearfully hissed into the human's ear.

"You kissed me!"

"You're alive." The Justicar's growl implied that this could easily be changed. "Shut up."

"You frotting-well kissed me!" Escalla tried to abrade the taste buds off her own tongue. "I've kissed a damned human! That's the most disgusting thing I've ever done!"

"Unlikely."

The faerie bridled, was about to launch into a stream of curses, and then shrank against the human's broad back as something dark flapped past a line of distant trees. The girl looked about in dawning fear.

"You've seen these things before?"

"I've seen them. I've watched them over Iuz." The Justicar crawled through the water without even raising a ripple. "They're hunters. They like to kill."

"A-are those things really hunting j-just for me?"

"Just for you, and they take quite a bit of summoning."

The Justicar rose dripping from the water to check the skies for sign of pursuit, then swam through a few mere handspans' depth of water, never once leaving a trail. "Looks like I'm not the only one who wants you to shut up."

The abyssal monsters quartered and searched the water-logged isles, spreading a chill of evil across the entire marsh, but the Justicar's skills apparently had thrown them off the trail. Climbing up between Cinders's tall damp ears, Escalla clung to her two companions in fright. She swallowed, following the sounds of the demons hissing through the dark.

"Powerful wizard, huh?"

The Justicar gave a grim, measured nod. "Yup."

"A-and kinda p-persistent too, would you say?"

"Yup."

Wet and bedraggled, the faerie cleared her throat and struck a thoughtful little pose. "All right, I can see that . . . that in the cause of justice, you need my help. And, ah, as a really, *really* reformed and deeply *good* kind of person, I will be really pleased to offer you my aid." The girl shrank flat as a bloodthirsty scream echoed out over the woods. "Um, they can even see me when I go invisible, can't they?"

"Yup."

"That's . . . that's good. That *is* a challenge. We can handle that. You and me and dog breath here, all *together*." The faerie took a stronger grip upon her two new body-guards. "All of us together."

"Oh, really?"

"Look, it's . . . it's my pleasure!" Another hunting scream echoed in the dark. Escalla felt quite sick. Whoever wanted her dead was clearly pretty dedicated to the job, and the Justicar was the only protection she had. "You need a guide, and . . . and a *mentor!* Someone to help you on your quest! So I guess we'll just stick really close together from now on. Really, *really* close." The girl scrubbed at her mouth with the back of her hand. "So I'll help you find this guy you're looking for, but we have to have just a little understanding first, all right? We need a protocol of professional courtesy."

The Justicar cocked an eye upward in annoyance as he swam. "Such as?"

"*No one* touches the faerie! Right?" Vaguely aware that her bare bottom was exposed to the night, Escalla tugged her acid-burned tunic into place. "Do we have an agreement on that?"

"Whatever." The Justicar rose onto all fours to crawl over a hidden mound of drowned grass, then slithered back into the water. "Let me know next time you just want to drown."

Escalla kept watch on the sky and patted the Justicar upon his head.

"Oh, and later on, you and I are going to work on polishing some of those social skills."

"Shut up and let me swim."

* * * * *

In a vast, dark chamber, a thin figure worked late by the light of magic spells drifting down from above. In a place utterly filled with books, maps, charts, and scrolls, he labored with a curt, unforgiving energy. Equation followed equation running simultaneously down slates and parchment scrolls. A tiny, crumpled booklet written on sheets of flexible metal sat before the figure as he worked. Translating the code of the tiny journal through memory, the figure worked in dedicated silence.

Trigol's library had yielded great treasure. It was a place that obsessively stored relics—even those it could not begin to understand. Here amidst the shelves, pieces of the great dream had been found. Patient years of study had slowly brought reward.

His work had built itself slowly. Here, beneath the soaring scroll shelves, a vision of greatness slowly rose. . . .

It was a magic from before the time of the great sorcerers such as Tensor, Bigby, and Otiluke, a lore millennia old and intermingled with dark skills gleaned from a dozen other worlds and other planes—the brainchild of a single man.

This great work finally had a student to bring it to fruition, a successor worthy of the great secret buried for untold centuries here amongst the shabby scrolls.

The moment of ultimate greatness was still an elusive dream, but at last the plans and requirements were laid. The chambers of the ancient master had been discovered once again. Only a few simple tools were needed, and the last phase finally could begin.

The scholar finished the last line of the final equation upon the chart. In cold satisfaction, he laid his hands flat upon the table, staring into empty space as he held his majestic vision in his mind.

His two assistants stood waiting in the shadows. One man inclined his head toward his master and came softly forward into the light. His master turned a thin, bald head, the long strands of red hair at his shoulders catching the light of candle flames.

"The pixie?"

"Has evaded us, my lord." The assistant inclined his head, his voice habitually held in the whisper of his trade. "Our ally will require great payment for the services of his beasts. Shall I request their aid for another day?"

Arising from his desk, the master slowly folded his hands into his sleeves. One side of his face shone bright beneath the lights while the other side gleamed darker than a slice of night.

"Dismiss the demons. We need no more debts to our *ally*."

"And the pixie, my lord?"

"If she is fleeing in fright, she is hardly a danger." The master carefully stored his reference books away, indexing them with an unconscious, habitual skill. "The northern settlements are already as good as gone. We are secure to begin our work at last."

A second assistant waited with his fingertips steepled. The man drifted forward, his voice scarcely louder than the slow drifting of the dust across the library shelves.

"The third weapon has been found, my lord. Blackrazor is now in the city."

The master closed his eyes and drew in a slow, deep breath of ecstasy.

His first assistant raised an eyebrow and turned toward his comrade in mild surprise. "All three weapons are here?"

"All three."

Still standing with his eyes closed, the master let the glory of it run like fire through his mind.

"All three weapons, and the great maze prepared at last." The long, slow spell of an ancient sorcerer was coming to its triumph. "We shall begin the final phase."

Turning, the master swept open his hands and uttered the syllables of a spell. A glowing portal flashed open in the air behind him, filling the entire library with an eerie golden light.

"It has begun at last. All will be as it was. We shall recreate the triumph of the Great One, but this time, we shall exceed even the Great One's dreams."

The figure closed its copy of the wizard Keraptis's journals. Its equations had been so tantalizingly close to completion yet so tragically flawed. It had taken a successor to realize the dream, to find the courage to reach out and grasp true greatness.

The master turned, and in the light of the magic portal, his face shimmered with painted shadows, one half black and one half white. He sent his acolytes through the portal, took one last glimpse at his workplace, then simply stepped through into the light.

The portal flashed and closed, leaving the library in utter darkness. Trigol dreamed onward in its restless sleep while from the north, a cold wind began to blow. . . .

5

The lowlands of the County of Urnst yielded a rather mixed scenery. Ruined homes and castles bleached their timbers like the bones of beached whales. Here and there, tiny villages ploughed fields of winter cabbages amidst ruined forts and walls. Sheep flecked the hills with little white shapes while militia drilled clumsily between the village lanes.

The walls of Trigol City—big walls, freshly heightened with a layer of newer, cleaner stone—could now be seen from the road. The fortifications spread squat and broad as a defense against the inevitable earthquakes.

Trudging steadily amidst it all, the Justicar gave a growl of irritation. The source of his annoyance rode upon his shoulders, leaning her elbows atop his stubbled skull.

The road had been lonely, and Escalla needed entertainment. One way or another, she would squeeze a reaction out of the accursed man. As a chosen travel companion, the Justicar had a lot to learn about the art of conversation, and Escalla considered herself to be the world's best teacher.

Sticking happily with her newfound bodyguard, Escalla wagged her dainty wings, her fingers interlaced beneath her chin as she turned a puzzle slyly over in her mind.

"Borran?"

No answer came, and so the girl tried again.

"Britt? Breggan?"

Silence reigned. The Justicar refused to answer.

"Kevin? Kenneth? Filbert?" The girl touched the corner of her lips slyly with her tongue. "Or Hubert? You look a little like a Hubert. . . ."

The Justicar growled. Reclining across his shoulders, Escalla played with her hair.

"Humphrey!"

"No!" The Justicar kept his head down and marched. "Shut up!"

"Isabod? Hey, is it Isabod?"

Trying to ignore her, the Justicar ate up the miles with his long stride. The faerie could feel him seething in ill temper. Riding happily on the man's back, Cinders grinned his unchanging feral smile and listened to the fun.

Tilting her head, the pixie wrinkled her nose prettily in thought.

"How about *Wilbert?*" The girl felt a little twinkle of success. "Yeah, I'm willing to bet you were a Wilbert."

Below her, the big man clenched his teeth. "I told you, I am *the Justicar.*"

"Yeah, *right.*" The faerie sat up and made a nice, poised motion with her hands. "*The Justicar* is not a name. Your mother did not lay her firstborn in her arms and say, 'Oh look! It's little the Justicar.' " The girl speared one green eye in a sly look at the man.. "The Justicar is what a fighter calls himself when he thinks that all the other fighters have bigger weapons."

The faerie felt her ride stiffen his neck muscles. She coiled a little lower, her wings fanning at his ears. "Tell me!"

"No!"

"Go on! What could it hurt?" Tickling his skull with a wisp of her own hair, Escalla wheedled mercilessly on and on. "Be your best friend! Give you a sterling! Walk your dog!"

Very clearly, her powers of persuasion were going to need a lot of rethinking. Annoyed by her failures, Escalla irritably flicked her wings. "Hey, pooch! Is he always this deeply in character?"

From below her bottom, Cinders's thoughts drifted upward with a grin. *Yup.*

Sighing in frustration, Escalla slumped across the man's head and irritably watched the world roll by.

"I'm bored!" The girl lounged back to stare at the sky. "Bored, bored, bored!"

"Shut up!" The Justicar tramped tirelessly on. "Try going to sleep."

"Then I'll be *asleep* and bored!" Escalla gave a groan. "Talk to me you shaven-headed git! Just tell me your damned name!"

As they drew nearer to the city, more and more people began to appear. It suddenly seemed that this portion of the Flanaess was not so depopulated after all. There were now farmers standing in the fields and merchants marching along the roads. Ignoring the stares from a passing cartload of peasants, Escalla rummaged in the top of the Justicar's backpack and pulled out her brand new set of clothes.

At a wayside stop the night before, Escalla had made a windfall. She had swiped a length of buttersoft chlamys leather from a jewel merchant. After being forced to return the jewels, she had still contrived to make the piece of hide her own. Sitting happily behind the Justicar's neck, she had stitched and cut and sewed all morning, hoping that he would notice the activity. The man remained silent for three solid hours—hours enlivened by the chatter of the faerie at his back. Escalla put a last few finishing touches upon her handiwork, cast aside her stained old woollen clothes, and happily dressed herself in real finery.

The chlamys felt softer than a lover's tongue. Escalla drew long leggings up her thighs, paused for a moment to admire herself in a mirror image spell, then bent over to check the fit of her new new costume and smack her own behind.

"Oooh, there are hearts breaking in the enchanted forest tonight!"

Even more pleased with herself than usual, Escalla whirred up into the air and hovered ahead of the marching Justicar. She struck a lithe, stretching pose in midair.

"Ta-daah! Real clothes! So how do I look?"

The girl wore long fingerless gloves that reached to her upper arms. Long leggings and a tiny corselet that would have gotten her arrested if she were three feet taller completed her attire. The faerie made a pirouette in midair, quite pleased with the fact that the velvety leathers fit her body like a second skin.

"So? Do you like it?"

The Justicar had stopped walking. He examined Escalla, wrinkled his nose, and then went back to his march.

"You look like an elven trollop."

"These are *adventure* clothes." Somewhat miffed, Escalla flew beside the man and threw him a haughty sideways glance. "Adventurers are supposed to be all toned and wear tight leather."

"So do trollops." The Justicar took a closer look at the expanses of exposed pixie-skin. "Did the fact that winter is coming sink into your mind?"

"Hey, I can accessorize!" Escalla flipped up Cinders's long tail and wound it about her like a stole. "Sexiest thing you ever saw. Am I right?"

Her only answer from the man came as sigh of annoyance. He tried to ignore her and kept tramping along the road.

"We're getting near the city now. Turn invisible and stop making a spectacle of yourself."

The faerie let Cinders's tail drop out of her hands. Unamused, she hovered in midair and folded up her arms.

"So I'm guessing you're a really specialized ranger, right? Did they not go much for merriment and social interaction at ranger school?"

"We are about to enter the city." The Justicar deliberately ignored the faerie flying at his side. "The last thing we want our enemy to do is to discover the whereabouts of their favorite pixie."

Escalla gave the man a frosty toss of her hair.

"Hey, I'm a *faerie*, remember? Not a *pixie*, thank you very much."

"What's the difference?"

"A faerie is a pixie who's learned discipline and ambition." Escalla lifted up her chin, her eyes slitted in pride. "Pixies are like sparrows, but faeries . . . ?" The girl looked at one of her slim, perfectly milk-white arms and gave a satisfied sigh. "Faeries are like falcons."

The Justicar grabbed the girl and tucked her out of sight. "Well why don't you falcon-well shut up!"

"Hey! No one touches the faerie!" Escalla jerked out of the human's grasp and sat herself back down atop his backpack. "You are such an annoying twerp!"

"I'm cut deep by that one." The Justicar had always valued a life of introspection and blessed quiet. Between teamsters and faeries, he seemed condemned to have his ears battered by brainless natterings. "For the last time: Get out of sight, keep your ears open, and shut up."

Escalla slyly touched the corner of her mouth with her tongue, then silkily slid closer.

"All right, here's the deal. Half an hour of golden silence—at a time of your choosing—*if* you tell me what your real name is."

"What?"

"Cross my heart!" The faerie sat up and crisscrossed her breasts with a fingertip. "You can store it up in credit to use bits of it at need. Just tell Escalla your name. Come on, you can do it!"

The ranger stood in the road and *seethed*. He flexed his fists and imagined a hundred thousand dire fates for the scrawny little faerie on his back.

"I *hate* pixies!"

"Come on! Tell the faerie your name!"

The ranger mumbled something inaudible under his breath and began to move on. Sparking instantly in interest, Escalla put a hand to one of her long pointed ears and leaned in closer.

"What was that? Hmm?"

"Evelyn!" Embarrassed, the Justicar stamped one foot in childish annoyance. *"There,* all right. Are you happy? I was raised by villagers who happened to like the name."

Sensing a nerve laid bare, Escalla opened her hands in hasty protest. "Hey, I never said a word! Evelyn is . . ." The faerie tried to search for something sufficient to say while desperately trying to keep a straight face. "It's a *wonderful* name! Evelyn . . . Good, fast, powerful. I mean, I just hear that and I say, 'Tough-guy ranger'!"

"Shut up!"

"Hey, you're the boss . . . *Evelyn."*

Basking happily in the sun, Cinders gave a wheezing sound of glee. *Evelyn! Funny!*

Growling, the Justicar marched his way down the road toward the city.

His original name had been a gift from villagers who were now withered dust and bones. In the aftermath of war, the Justicar had created a new identity, a purpose that defined him, a role to be followed with unforgiving intensity. He had labored for years to purify the world of the unworthy, the parasites who slaughtered innocents for their own monetary gain. "The Justicar" embodied everything he had achieved, everything he wanted to be.

"Don't call me Evelyn!"

"Hey!" The pixie touched her heart. "Never slip my lips again. Our secret, you and me." The girl relaxed across the top of his skull. "So, Ev, what's our plans in the city?"

"And don't call me *Ev!*"

"How about Jus?" The girl flew on her back in front of the human with her hands pillowing her head. "Come on! We're partners, right? I can't go around calling you the Justicar!"

The Justicar was too tired with the whole subject to fight it any longer.

The faerie whirred around and settled cross-legged upon his shaven head. "So, Jus, what do we do in the city? How do we find this guy?"

The man weighed the badger skin hanging from his belt. The results were not comforting.

"It had better only take a few nights. I now have precisely twelve nobles left."

Escalla made an airy wave. "No problem. We can get more."

"No thieving!"

The girl pantomimed total innocence as though the thought had never crossed her mind. Glaring, the ranger halted at a hummock by the road. He rummaged in his backpack, inadvertently tickling Cinders.

Preening herself, Escalla hovered just above a thistle bloom. "So, bristle-boy! How do we track this sorcerer down? Even if I can recognize him, we still have to *find* him."

"We can deduce a lot about him from what we already know. Someone is arranging to ambush vital supplies heading to the border colonies. Whoever it is, he's not highly placed enough to simply find out the caravan routes at the court or from the military, so we won't have to go penetrating high society."

"Oh good. I was wanting to broach a few thoughts on changing your personal dress habits." Escalla caught a stinging glare from the Justicar and held up her hands. "Fine! Right, hell hound skin, shaven head, skull sword. The look's definitely you."

The Justicar continued his lecture. "He's trying to keep the north border empty of settlements. North is desolate land. North is also the direction of Iuz, so we're probably looking for a spy from Iuz, someone who can summon those abyssal bats. He therefore either *is* a sorcerer or has one readily at hand. Sorcerers have a need to purchase some pretty strange supplies. We'll start asking at shops that cater to magic-users."

Escalla made a face. "And if he brought his own stuff along with him?"

"We'll cruise the taverns for a while and ask questions." The Justicar felt a glow of inner fire as he anticipated the hunt. This was what he did best, and at the end of it the world would be just a little better. "We see if anyone new has set up in town—anyone with money. Do you know what this person looked like?"

"Um, yeah." Escalla blinked. "Tallish, kinda short; fattish, kinda thin; bald with long red hair; a big hatchet nose; robes with lots of charms hanging from it . . ." The girl creased her brows in thought. "Oh! And he had his face painted black on one side, white on the other!"

Her partner stared at her with a heavy-lidded gaze. "For future reference, the face makeup is probably the most important point of reference."

"You think so? Oh, sure!" The girl gave a shrug. "Whatever."

Annoyed, the ranger shook his head and let the subject drop. "Face painting. It's either a cult, a loony, or a damned good disguise." Working with practiced efficiency, the man hung an old horse blanket about himself—one of the few treasures he had bought along the road—and hid the hilt of his sword. "Nothing for it. We go dig for information. You keep invisible, and we'll see what we both hear."

"Sure. Sounds like a plan!" There was a brief *pop*, and Escalla winked out of view. "I can only keep it up for half an hour, though. It gets tiring, and too much of it gives me dandruff!"

"So make a nest in the backpack for when you need to rest."

"Hoopy!" Invisible wings whirred. "Hey, Cinders! You and me get to be cozy!"

Cozy . . .

The trio traveled down a muddy road. They were soon joined by farmers, traders, and weary militia men. Walking along beside a reeking wagon load of pickled cabbage, the Justicar felt pixie wings tickle at his ears.

"Hey, Jus!"

"Yes?"

"Can we get an inn room with a hot bath?"

The ranger rattled his purse. "Using just exactly what to pay for it?"

"I'm working on it!" The girl seemed immensely cheerful for someone on a deathlist. "No thieving! We just have to apply our talents to the problem at hand."

The concerns of money were a distraction from the work. Frowning, the Justicar thought about it and wearily shook his head. "We can live rough. The job is all that matters." He gripped his black sword. "Justice must be done."

Escalla's voice became silkily sly. She gave sweet reason a honeyed tongue.

"Hey, you're a law enforcer. You need to be able to collect your thoughts, yeah?" Invisible little wings purred. "How can you investigate if there's nowhere to take a load off your feet after a hard day's grind?"

"We'll see."

The road up ahead had become blocked with traffic outside the city gates. Trigol's city guards flanked the gatehouse, and the Justicar looked grim as he heard the distant jingling of coin.

The gate guards were bored-looking men in mail armor carrying halberds or bows. Sure enough, the traffic jam was caused by these individuals extracting a fee from every person seeking to enter the city. The Justicar sighed, impatiently waited his turn, and then marched forward to hear the bad news.

A guard proffered his open palm in the time-honored sign. "Pass chip?"

The Justicar glowered. "What?"

"No pass chip? That's one gold noble entry fee." The bored guard snapped his fingers. "Keep it moving."

One whole noble! The Justicar seemed to grow three inches in height as he crackled with outrage.

"You want *how* much?"

"Militia tax." The guard wore a silk shirt beneath his armor—apparently levied as a tax from a traveller. "Unless you join the militia or ship in supplies, you pay to pass the gates."

About to argue, the Justicar suddenly found something prodding into his hand. He open his palm and found a gold piece gleaming in the sun.

The guard took it and threw the coin into a collection barrel beside the gate. "Have a nice stay."

Looming over the guard, the Justicar seethed for a moment and then went on his way.

As he stalked away, Escalla's voice lilted behind him through the air. "Bye guys!"

Bye.

Guards jerked about in suspicion, but saw nothing except the gleam of fangs and eyes inside the Justicar's backpack. Frowning, the men turned away and went back to the daily business of extortion.

Walking down a wide, cobbled street hung with a hundred different wooden shop signs, the Justicar simmered with indignation.

"I was going to bring them to heel. They're charging ten times the rate they've been told to and are keeping the excess for themselves."

"It's no problem!" Escalla's invisible bottom settled upon the ranger's head. "Why worry?"

"Exploitation of the weak must be *punished.*" The Justicar's voice boomed like the pronouncement of doom. "And we needed the money."

"Money? You still have twelve nobles. You're no worse off than before."

Halting, the man touched his purse. He flicked his eyes to stare at the blank air behind him. "You stole!"

"I took it from the guard, so it wasn't thieving. It was a redistribution of misdirected assets."

The Justicar gave a bristling growl. "It's still stealing."

"No, no! It's anti-stealing!" Escalla could twist logic with the best of them. "Think of it as un-money."

"What?"

The faerie hovered invisibly in midair. "Well, is there a difference between normal goods and stolen goods?"

"Of course there is!"

"And you yourself would *never* use stolen goods—so that means there's a taint, right?" The girl drove home her logic point by point. "So, if stolen goods are different from unstolen goods, then stolen-ness is a quality added to normal items to mark them as stolen. Am I right? In this case, the coin was already stolen, so I myself didn't transfer any quality of stolen-ness onto it."

Breathing slow and hard, the Justicar sensed the distinct presence of a fallacy. "It's still stolen property."

"How about this one? A mathematical proof." Escalla drummed a little tattoo onto the Justicar's skull. "Look, theft is a negative thing. Now a minus and a minus is a positive, right? Therefore, two wrongs must make a right. I just did a good thing, and you should therefore congratulate me."

The Justicar drew a long, slow breath. "I'm letting it pass just this once because you only took one coin. Don't do it again."

"Sure. Fine. Whatever!"

Clamped inside Cinders's gleaming teeth were three more coins. Escalla's invisible fingers carefully closed the dog's mouth to hide her ill-gotten gain from view.

"You all right, pooch?"

All right.

6

The trio stood in a street thronged with crowds intent on getting indoors before the autumn evening brought the cold. Here in the outer regions, refugees had made rough shelters leaning against the city wall. Their rags were a stark contrast to the bright clothes of the merchants who flowed from the gateway to the city marketplace. With the fall of the Duchy of Tenh to Iuz during the wars, thousands of refugees had come flooding into Trigol. The poor now sheltered in makeshift shantytowns while the wealthy purchased property, patronized their imported temples, and started riots in the streets.

Even on a quiet evening, the city was a strange and marvelous thing. Crowds hurried with heads down, dispersing into the light and warmth of countless houses. Standing with his head craned back to see the rooftops and the painted wooden shop signs, the Justicar took a moment to simply enjoy the view. Excited at reaching a big city at last, Escalla made a brisk flitter-flutter of her wings. Cinders gave a happy wag of his tail.

Many houses! Very flammable!

"Don't." The Justicar growled then tugged the straps of his backpack. "We're in no position to pay for repairs."

The hell hound grinned his pointy grin and kept wig-wagging his tail.

Hundreds of things seemed to be happening at once. Mothers, babies, and brats surrounded a puppet booth on a corner. Pack horses, carriages, and wagons trundled down the roads. Taverns spread open doors onto the street, filling the air with sounds of music, drinking, and merriment. The Justicar scanned the street to see if he had been tailed then turned to talk to the hell hound at his back.

"Cinders? Sniff."

The dog's nose swung to all points of the compass, snuffling happily at the richly scented air.

Smell fire! Smell food! Good meat! Hot coals!

"And?"

Smelly socks, pine cones, beer, old leather, new leather, girls, dry bones, warm rugs! The hell hound pricked his ears. *Beer! Meat! Coals!*

Raising one brow, the Justicar cocked an eye back toward the hell hound. "We are supposed to be locating a magician's supply shop."

Escalla stirred, eagerly sniffing the scent of roasting meat from a tavern door nearby. "It's almost evening. Let's eat."

"We have work to do. We have to find your black and white spy."

"So where better to ask than a tavern?" The faerie's wings whirred. "Come on! We've been living on your damned camp cooking for days. Eat! Eat!"

The Justicar stood his ground. "What's wrong with my cooking?"

Escalla cleared her throat and leaned conspiratorially closer. "All right—*real* meals? *Real* meals don't look up at you from the plate and offer to negotiate. . . ." The invisible girl slapped him on one shoulder. "I'm kidding! Now, come on! There might be cake or something."

Trigol's taverns were mostly two-storied, wide, and overcrowded. Stomping in through the doors, the Justicar ducked beneath the low ceiling made by a surrounding gallery and walked down into a gigantic sunken taproom. He wondered briefly how the place could be kept clean, then noticed a sink hole and a sewer grate large enough for a man to wriggle through at the center of the stone-flagged floor.

All in all, the place looked as though it had once had another function—such as a public bath, an opera house, or a cattle barn. The roof arched in a dome high overhead, while sleeping rooms ringed a balcony that rimmed the circular central hall. Tall enough to look over the heads of most of the patrons, the Justicar found himself a sheltered table, planted his backpack beneath his feet, and raised a hand to summon a short, sweating little man who obsessively wiped his hands upon a spotty apron.

The innkeeper was almost completely bald, sporting only a few juts of orange hair, which made him look as though he had been colonized by shelf fungi. He seemed rather over endowed with enthusiasm.

"Sir, sir, sir! Welcome to you, sir. Welcome to you. Welcome to you, sir!"

Leaning forward into the blast of verbiage, the Justicar thumped his elbows onto the table. "I need a place to stay. Is there room here for the night?"

"Of course there is! Of course there is, course there is, course there is!" The innkeeper finished wiping his hands and began all over again. "Plenty of room! Big floors, lots of space! Lots of space on the floor! One common copper, plus one for breakfast! Barley porridge! Very nutritious! Nutritious!"

Drumming his fingers on the table, the ranger gave a sigh. "Are there any rooms?"

"Rooms? Rooms? Of course there are!"

"Can I have one?"

"No, of course not! They're all taken!" The innkeeper began to briskly polish the table, chair backs, and oil lamp. "Refugees in town. Winter merchants coming in. We're full, we're full, we're full, we're full!" The man flicked out his polishing rag with a crack like a whip. A little squeak of outrage showed that he had just managed to hit Escalla's invisible rear. Keen on his own voice, the innkeeper seemed not to hear. "There's only the royal suites, that's all. Just that, just that, just that!"

Drumming his fingers in impatience, the Justicar growled. "How much are those?"

"Ten nobles each, but that's because they're royal!"

A little voice whispered in the Justicar's ear. "Ask him if it has a bath!"

"Shhh!" The Justicar rummaged for small change inside his badger-skin sporran. "Floor space, then. And bring me a large mulled ale, some mulled ale in an egg cup, and some of that roast beef."

And coal!

"Yes." The ranger patted Cinders's fur. "And a piece of coal."

"Fine sir! Fine, fine, fine!" The innkeeper proffered his hand. "Two coppers for bed and breakfast, and one noble for the meal."

The Justicar's mind boggled.

"One gold piece!"

"One sir! Just one, just one, just one!" The innkeeper waved his hands in an attempt to fan out the flames of his customer's outrage. "Supplies are at a premium, sir! The city's overcrowded, and the fields are all choked with weeds! Food, sir! It's almost priceless!"

Angrily paying for his meal, the ranger passed over the coins and watched the innkeeper thread his way off between a heavy crowd of minstrels, townsfolk, and gamblers.

"There had better be bread with this." The man sniffed the torturous smell of fine roast beef and felt his stomach growl. "Escalla, do you need me to make you a seat?"

There was no answer. From his comfortable den inside the backpack, Cinders waved his tail.

Girlie go bye-bye!

"Great. Maybe she's doing her job." The Justicar settled himself more comfortably in his chair. "She'll be back for her meal."

*　*　*　*　*

At a far part of the tavern, a suave gambler dressed in black held sway over a large game of cards. With almost a dozen players, the pot grew to huge proportions—and weirdly enough, the profits rarely seemed to fall into the gambler's hands. The fact that the major winners were all assistants to the gambler seemed quite beyond the mental capacity of the other players to grasp. The constant chink and hiss of money cascading into happy hands served as a magnet to draw victim after victim over to the game.

Watching unhappily from one corner, a scraggly youth stared at the fall of money with a wistful, hungry eye. He seemed ill fed and unhappy and thus could scarcely believe it when three gold pieces fell into his lap from the empty sky. The boy looked about as though expecting someone to demand the money back—then blinked as a little voice whispered in his ear.

"Hey, kid! *Psssst!* Hey! Over here!"

A rather sleek and perky ginger cat sat in the shadows of his chair. The boy blinked then leaned a little closer as the cat jerked her head and beckoned him near.

"Hey, kid! I'm your magic wishing cat! Make a wish and we'll see it come true!"

"Ummm . . ." The boy blinked. "I wish for true love!"

The cat's ears flattened. "Fine, you're now destined to meet Miss Right. Now is there anything maybe on a *smaller* scale we might try?"

"Um, I could use some money."

"An excellent choice! You're a gem, kid, no matter what the neighbors say. Now pay attention, kid, and we'll get some cash into your hands."

The cat had sleek curves and strangely feminine eyes. A little concerned about his sudden turn of good luck, the skinny boy looked the cat carefully up and down.

"Where did you come from, O Magic Wishing Cat?"

"Um, from the beast lands. What's-her-name, the Queen of the Cats, sent me."

"Why?"

The cat gave him an irritated glare. "Because you're such a legendary good pal to cats."

"Really?"

The cat cocked an eye. "Did you ever just pat a cat for no reason other than the fact that it rubbed around your legs?"

"Um, yeah."

The cat gave a shrug. "So it's payback time. Now pay attention, kid."

The boy immediately tried to pat the cat and had his hand swatted for his pains.

"No one touches the magic wishing cat. All right?"

"All right."

"Right!" The cat curled its tail about its paws. "Now I, the magic wishing cat, will help you win a great fortune at cards tonight, but to show your gratitude, you must be willing to give half of your gains to my nominated agent so that he may redistribute the money to the needy."

The youth gave a shrug. "All right."

"Good. So go play cards and listen for my voice whispering in your ear!" The cat suddenly turned invisible, and the air seemed to hum with the beat of little wings. "Play what I tell you to play, use the three gold pieces for your stake, and we'll have you rolling in dough in no time!" Wings passed low over the boy's head with a little whirr. "Kid, the cards are gonna burn hot tonight!"

*   *   *   *   *

The Justicar's dinner took half an hour to arrive, and it arrived without bread. A giant bowl of pickled cabbage with chopped onions accompanied the hot roast beef, as well as a bowl of beans. If everyone else was eating the same fare, then the common room would be no place for open flame once everyone went to bed. With no sign of Escalla, the Justicar shrugged and simply dug into his meal, making sure he kept aside one of the good, crackly end-pieces of the roast for the missing girl.

He listened carefully to conversations. He questioned a pair of long-bearded burghers for the location of sorcerers' supply shops and made carefully innocent inquiries of the waitresses. The Justicar bought drinks for three city guards and scanned their talk for anything that might have been a clue. With the evening wearing on and no leads gained, the man bought himself another drink, borrowed a stable brush from the landlord, and flopped Cinders out over his knee to brush the hell hound's fur. The sentient pelt growled happily inside his friend's mind, basking in the warmth of the open fire and seeming utterly content.

Into this strange domestic scene, a thin youth appeared. Flushed with excitement, the boy staggered under the weight of two large bags of coin. He thumped one bag onto the table, seemingly exhausted by the weight.

"Hey, mister! The magic wishing cat told me to give you this money to distribute to the poor and needy."

Slowly putting down his ale, the Justicar suspiciously drummed his fingers on the tabletop.

"Magic wishing cat?"

"She was sent by Queen What's-her-name, the cat lady!" The youth breathed out a sigh. "So there you are! Now I'm off home!"

"*Wait.*" The warrior eyed the heavy bag of coins. "How did the wishing cat get all this coin?"

"She helped me win it at cards. She magically let me know what cards to play."

"Oh, really?"

The fleeced gamblers were having an angry meeting in one corner of the room. Since they were thieves themselves, the Justicar felt a sour stab of satisfaction at seeing them so suddenly impoverished. "Son, you really ought to celebrate. Go order yourself one of the royal suites."

"Um, all right." The boy blinked. "If you think it's best."

"It's best. And when you take that money home tomorrow, make sure you travel with good friends."

The boy walked away, leaving the Justicar alone. He reclined with Cinders in his lap and put his hands behind his head.

"You really like this 'stealing from thieves' thing, eh?"

A piece of lukewarm roast beef hovered in midair, disappearing bit by bit as Escalla stuffed her invisible self with meat.

The faerie spoke with her mouth full, licking invisible fingertips. "Hey, it's natural justice!"

"Hmm." The Justicar leaned his head on his hand. "And doing good actually feels good, doesn't it?"

"You betcha!"

"Thought so. Let's see just how much good we can spread around." The Justicar summoned the innkeeper over to his side.

"Landlord, how many refugees do you think there are sheltering in the nearest streets?"

The little man with the shelf fungus hair rapidly blinked his eyes in thought.

"Oh a few! A few, a few, a few! No money on them, you see. Never come in here!" The landlord wiped his hands as though contaminated by the whole idea. "Must be a couple dozen of them."

"Is there room for them in the common room?"

"Of course there is! Of course there is!" The landlord spread his hands. "But it costs two copper pieces. Bed and breakfast, barley porridge, and a warm fire!"

"Good." The Justicar began to count out large gleaming piles of gold. "Floor space accommodation for twenty of them. Roast beef for all of them. Pre-paid for . . . oh, let's see . . ." Ignoring agonized flutters about his head, the ranger counted up the piles of coin. "Three days. That gives them time to buy that old barn out the back with the rest of the cash and turn it into a proper waterproof home."

A wail of pain came from the empty air. Counting over a second pile of money, the Justicar shot an impatient glance toward the noise.

"And I'll have one of the royal suites please, with a hot bath." The man sniffed himself. "Make it three baths, with soap and towels."

The innkeeper left. Escalla grumbled. Taking his ale back up, the Justicar looked straight at the invisible girl. He was learning the knack of finding her. She had a particular smell reminiscent of marked cards and forest flowers.

"One night only, then we switch to a normal room."

"All right, all right!" Escalla sat on the immensely shrunken bag of coins and went into a huff. "I'm good already! See, generous deeds aplenty, and they're all done simply for that warm, special glow it gives me inside." Escalla swiped a dozen coins to hide them in reserve.

Warm room! With coals! Cinders wagged his sooty tail. *Eat eat!*

Escalla made a confused little noise. "Coals?"

"He likes the taste." The Justicar grabbed his equipment

and rose. "And I also think it's time you-know-who had a B-A-T-H." The man rolled his eyes. "You haven't lived until you've tried giving one to a hell hound."

Settling his huge sword, the man stalked over to the door. "I'll be back with twenty refugees. You can have first bath while I'm away."

"Hoopy!" The faerie whirred her wings and climbed up into the air. "See you!"

✻　✻　✻　✻　✻

Out in the streets, the nighttime chill had raised a clinging, gloomy fog. The Franz River echoed with the sound of voices as showboats came nosing slowly to the docks. With street performers finishing up their acts for the night, the alleys were swiftly emptying.

Working quietly and methodically, the Justicar found refugee families and sent them running to the inn. He cleared the alleyways one by one, until finally there was but a single hovel left. He put his head into the dismal little shelter, only to have a disheveled figure erupt and shake him by the hand.

"Son! It's you, son! They thought you'd drowned, but I said they can never keep a good man down!"

Polk the teamster slapped the Justicar on the shoulder in pontificating glee.

"So you survived the wreck of the *Saucy Gannet*? That's grand, son, just grand. We floated on the wreckage here to town. It's hard luck, but you can't stop a teamster who has faith in adventure!"

The Justicar turned the man about, pointed him at the inn, and gave him a shove. "Just get inside, eat a meal, and go to sleep. It's paid for three days."

"I will! I will! And much obliged. You don't have to tell me how much you owe me, son!"

Polk went on his way, leaving the Justicar muttering behind him. With a last look down the street, the ranger turned to head back into the warmth—then noticed a man wheeling a puppet booth past him down the street.

The puppets hung by their strings from the stage, and amongst them was a little gold-robed wizard with a face painted black and white.

The Justicar immediately walked over, stopped the puppeteer, and pointed to the puppet. "What's this?"

"What is it?" The puppeteer blinked, only to find new enthusiasm when a coin was placed in his hand. "Why it's the puppet show of mysteries! The greatest heroes and the darkest villains! The wildest monsters ever to stalk the Flanaess!"

"The black and white puppet. What is it called?"

"Keraptis!" The puppeteer rattled his manikin, and the grotesque little figure waved a magic wand. "The sorcerer at the edge of night! The Overman, inhuman, superhuman, evil incarnate!"

The Justicar squatted down and touched the wooden puppet with a fingertip. "Is he based on a real figure?"

"Just so, my friend! The sages will tell you so. Keraptis believed that he was a new stage in the evolution of man and therefore was above puerile concepts like good, evil, mercy, and justice. He even changed the structure of his body so that he wouldn't feel related to his fellow men." The puppeteer nimbly made the puppet bow. "Why do you ask?"

The Justicar stood, laying one hand upon the hilt of his sword. "Where would I find this Keraptis?"

"Where?" The puppeteer seemed astounded. "At the bottommost layer of the Abyss, my friend—and good riddance!"

The warrior tilted his head, not quite understanding.

The puppeteer frowned and began putting his puppet away. "Keraptis is dead, my friend! You're too late. He's been dead for thirteen hundred years."

7

"*Up!*"

A stiff finger nudged Escalla in the ribs. Bathed, warm, and with a whole double bed all to herself, the faerie rolled over beneath the blankets and made a plaintive little whine of sheer pleasure.

The Justicar jerked Escalla's blankets free, exposing her to the cold night air. With a moan of irritation, the girl forced herself awake. She sat blearily up, clutching sheets against herself to preserve a fragile dignity.

It was still pitch black. Unimpressed and decidedly *not* an early riser, the faerie growled.

"All right, Steely Thews! There had better be a damned good reason for getting your face in the way of my beauty sleep!"

Already strapped into his armor, the Justicar was silently unsheathing his sword. His voice whispered in the gloom cast by the coals glowing in the firegrate. "Cinders can hear something. It's time for tonight's little visit."

The faerie let her sheets slip in amazement. "Visit?"

"No professional gamblers are going to let a rube get away with fleecing them. Gamblers usually have contacts with someone in the local thieves' guild." The Justicar had stuffed his bedding with pillows until it looked like a sleeping man. "Right about now, some midnight visitors are going to come calling on your gambling friend."

Escalla pulled on her leathers as quickly as she could.

"You mean the thieves are coming to this room? Why? Isn't our boy staying in the suite next door?"

"I hung a sign from our door saying, 'Tinkby's Tavern Congratulates Our Big Winner.' "

"Humorous, yet pointed. That ought to do it." The faerie cracked her knuckles and rose up out of a perfectly good, warm bed. "So what do we do?"

"I've seen you do lightning bolts, and I've seen you throw fireballs. Do you do any immobilizing spells?"

The girl rubbed at her eyes as she collected her thoughts.

"Well I can charm, I can freeze 'em in place—oldie but a goodie. Oh, and I've got a web-spell-thingie! Will that work?"

"It's fine." The Justicar clipped Cinders into place about his neck, the hell hound's eyes shining a faint, sinister red. "Just sit above the doorjamb, slip behind them, and stop them from making an escape."

The room descended into silence. After a moment, Escalla's whisper drifted down from above the door.

"Hey, Jus!"

"What?"

"Why are we doing this?"

From his place behind the door, her partner gave a growl. "Because thieves know a lot about illegal doings. I want to catch some thieves and ask some questions."

"Right. Now that's a plan."

They sat in silence, their own breathing echoing strangely loud until suddenly the tiniest of scrapes sounded in the door's iron lock. Well oiled and cared for, it gave only the barest click as the lock was picked open from the outside. A thin strip of birchwood appeared, wiggling softly through the crack of the door. The birch strip lifted up the door latch with the barest little metallic *click*. The ring-shaped handle carefully turned, and the door slowly swung wide.

Two dark shapes crept into the room. A sense of presence made it feel that there was perhaps another visitor standing silently on the balcony beyond.

The two shapes stalked silently into the bedroom, moving to flank the bed. A knife gleamed in the dark as the intruders approached. Moving with careful precision, the Justicar swept down his sword and prodded the blade against an intruder's lower spine.

"Freeze!"

A brilliant flash instantly lit the room as the thief triggered a spell. Blinded, the Justicar staggered and felt a blast of heat crack out from the hell hound's maw.

"Cinders! Damn it!"

Someone screamed in pain, and another figure raced past the Justicar toward the door. The whole rear end of the room was in flames with a thief dead and burning in the middle of the floor. The hell hound's manic grin glowed in the firelight as his red eyes shone with glee.

Burn! Burn! Die-die-die!

"For the gods' sake!" The Justicar's vision was a mad blur of dancing lights. He rescued his backpack and ran out onto the gallery above the tavern's common room. "Escalla!"

"I've got 'em!" Dazed, the girl had fallen against a railing and was blindly blinking her eyes. "I got 'em! I got 'em!"

The pixie called out a sharp syllable, and a mass of rope-thick spiderwebs shot from her hands. Still dazed by the flash, she managed to target the wrong figures. Half the sleepers in the common room were suddenly tangled in the sticky nets, while two black-clad shapes safely dived for the drain at the center of the room.

The Justicar snatched Escalla up by the scruff of her bodice as he pounded heavily past. A one-handed cut of his sword cleared a path through the magical webs, and he leaned over the big square drain. The metal grating had been levered aside, and the resulting hole was more than large enough for a man to clamber through.

"Cinders, do it!"

The hell hound blasted flames down the open drain, and a screech of pain revealed that the thieves had been waiting in ambush for their pursuers. The Justicar immediately jumped down through the hole, his sword and backpack trailing behind him. He landed in a wet tunnel still lit by sizzling fires.

"Cinders?"

Two men running—this way!

The hell hound could hear them, smell them, even see their heat. The Justicar threw a spell, surrounding himself with clean, white, magic light and then jogged down the sewer tunnels in pursuit.

A thoroughly annoyed Escalla passed overhead. Snarling, the faerie sped down the tunnel and threw a charm at a retreating shape, only to see the magic ricochet from her target and spatter uselessly across the walls. She braked madly to take a sudden ninety-degree turn and caught sight of her quarry silhouetted in the tunnel a dozen yards ahead.

One dark figure whirled, lifted a hand surrounded by a crackle of light, and shot a blast of lightning straight at the pixie's eyes. Already lunging back around the corner, Escalla gave a squawk of fright as the lightning bolt missed her by a wing's breadth, struck the tunnel wall, and bounded back the exact way it had come. The whole sewer lit up with a brilliant blue flash, stones crashing from the walls and ceiling as wet mortar blew apart in a flash of superheated steam.

Still moving at a lumbering run, the Justicar passed Escalla and charged around the corner before the tunnel could cave in. The faerie followed dizzily in his wake, ploughing through a haze of dust to see the human looming like a demon above two blackened, fallen men. He whipped his sword back for a killing thrust, the black blade gleaming and sulphur steam hissing from the hell hound's head cresting his helm.

One of the two men was already quite dead, but the other screamed in terror and tried to cram himself away from the quivering blade.

"No! No! No!" The injured thief tried to hide himself behind his arms. "Don't take my soul!"

Backlit by his light spell, the vast, sinister shape of the Justicar loomed above his victims like a shadow of doom.

"Thieves . . ." He let the word drip like bile from his mouth. "Unworthy souls."

"Not the blade! *Not the blade!*" Scorched and blasted by the ricocheting spell, the thief shrank backward over the smoking body of his companion, shrieking with mindless fright. "We can betray the last of the guild to you! We'll turn! We'll follow the White Lady!" The thief reversed into a pile of stones, gibbering in terror as the black blade hovered an inch from his throat. "All the guilds will be yours!"

Letting his voice growl in threat, the Justicar took his best possible chance to wrench information from the thief. "I want the black-and-white-faced man."

The thief quailed and tried to press his shoulder back through the fallen stones.

"I . . . There is no such man!"

"The black-and-white-faced man." The Justicar moved his sword fractionally backward, his muscles bunching as though about to drive his sword into his prey. "Where is he?"

Suddenly the thief ripped a short sword from his belt. With a screech of fear, he turned, rammed the blade over his own heart, and leaped upon it. Recoiling away from the expected attack, the Justicar could only stare at the dead thief in a daze.

There was a long, pained silence as faerie and human both gazed blankly down at the corpse. Finally, the Justicar's sword tip clinked as it sank and struck the floor. The noise echoing down the tunnel made the two companions stir.

The Justicar kept his eyes riveted on the body and slowly shook his head. "What the hell was that about?"

Appalled, Escalla kept herself well away from the cadaver.

"That guy was terrified. He killed himself to save his soul." The faerie blinked, then looked at the Justicar's black sword. "Is there anything about that sword we both should know?"

"It's enchanted enough to be damned useful, and I keep it very, *very* sharp." The Justicar lifted one hand and his illumination spell shone more brightly. "It sounds like a soul-eating sword is being used in Trigol. I am not pleased."

"And by the competing thieves' guild from the sound of it." Escalla wiped her hands, and showed not the slightest inclination to search the corpses for loose change. "That makes for a guild war with a difference."

A soul-eater. In all the catalog of foul deeds, there were few things the Justicar could measure as more cowardly. It sucked out the very essence of a victim's soul—a vampire that existed only by sending other creatures to oblivion. It was lethal, and it was loose inside Trigol's underworld.

Shaking his head, the Justicar bent over the corpses. He helped Cinders lower his nose and sniff for magic, then pulled a golden ring free from a dead man's hand.

"Here you go. Magic ring." The Justicar tossed it to the faerie. "Resistance against charm spells, I imagine. That's why your spell misfired."

Escalla blinked, a little taken aback by the man's generosity. She slipped the ring over her finger and saw it flash and mold itself to her size.

"Resist charm!" It was a rather useful tool. "Don't you want one?"

"Already got one." The Justicar pulled off one of his gloves to show a plain bone ring upon one finger. "Had it all along."

Escalla stared at the ring, looked at the man, and felt herself fluffing up in indignation.

"On the barge! You lying twonk! You never saw faerie dust in your damned life!"

"Nope." The human prodded his companion on the rump. "Damned stupid story. Don't know why you fell for it."

The sewer tunnel leading back to the tavern had largely collapsed—and no bad thing considering the repair bill they probably owed for the scorched room. The Justicar levered a few stones out of his way and squinted down the tunnel that lead off to who-knew-where.

"That thief was terrified. He wouldn't have lied in the face of that sword."

Escalla raised one brow. "Meaning?"

"Meaning that whoever your two-toned man is, the thieves had never heard of him " The ranger slowly sheathed his blade. "So it's not him that owns the soul-eating sword. But if he wants power, then he's going to want to control it."

The faerie could hardly conceal her delight at being expected to chase a soul-eating sword.

"Ooh, I can just feel those gears turning inside your big, misshapen skull. You want to locate a soul-eating sword then hang around in hiding until *our* guy comes to steal it." Escalla gazed drolly over at the Justicar. "Let us just come to terms with the fact that this is not a workable plan."

"It's a lead."

"Get out of the sewer, Jus, or I'll bite you."

Her wings whirring, the faerie led the way off down the sewer toward a manhole far beyond. Growling in annoyance, the Justicar took a last glance at the dead thieves and then followed his companion up into the dawn.

*   *   *   *   *

She awaited the dawn upon the dockside roofs, her white wings folded to cloak her in their warmth. Tall and magnificent, Saala the erinyes let the wind stir through her long auburn hair and let her mind drift upon the pleasures of the day.

Slowly and steadily, like a wasp larva gnawing on its host, the erinyes had made herself a home. The Black Claw Thieves' Guild was now utterly beneath her domination, and with the sword Blackrazor, they had liquidated all resistance in Trigol's underworld. With the underworld held in her grasp, Saala could begin to make the city entirely her own. She looked out across the rooftops as they were lit by a golden dawn and gave a quiet, predatory smile.

Trigol held two treasures, two keys that could be used to unlock a civil war. Here in the early morning by the river, the erinyes planned to seize those keys and let the violence flow.

Beside her, a dozen of the Black Claw thieves lay watching in the shadows. The guild leader had been placed utterly under Saala's magical domination. It took concentration, but the thief now acted as Saala's puppet, behaving only as his mistress saw fit.

He made an admirable tool. Fast and skilled, he was capable of wielding Blackrazor, which the erinyes was not. Made by an enemy race, the sword would burn her if she held it, but the guildmaster was the perfect species and temperament to use the weapon. Without glancing at the man, the erinyes stood and opened her pure white wings.

"You will remain here for one hour, until I have created a diversion. Let the riot draw the guards away. When their magic weapons are taken from their vaults, slip inside. No one will guard an empty vault." Saala was pleased with the elegant simplicity of her plan. "We shall steal their treasures from the inside out. When the weapons are returned to the vaults, take them and run."

Senior thieves gathered at her side. Saala laid down a map for the leaders of her two groups and pointed to the maze of sewer openings and tunnels that laced their way beneath Trigol's streets.

"First group, enter the temple of the river god Geshtai. Your escape gate is beneath the water, ten feet from the docks. It is marked by the red and yellow buoy. Swim upward into sewer branch nine." The woman's hands were perfect—long, slim, and flawless as she pointed to her maps.

"Second group, slip into the temple of the craft god Bleredd. Your escape is behind the chimney of the bakeries, a secret entrance leading to sewer line twenty-one."

She rolled away the map and handed it to her attendant, the guildmaster. At the man's side, Blackrazor gibbered in its scabbard as it hungered for fresh souls.

"This vantage point overlooks both escape routes. Blackrazor remains here to cover your escapes. We will meet back at the guild hall." The erinyes flicked a look of cold, professional evaluation across the faces of the two dozen assembled thieves.

The men had all dressed as priests of the two temples down below. Those who were to raid the Geshtai temple were dressed as the rival priests of Bleredd. Those who raided Bleredd were likewise dressed as priests of Geshtai.

"You will not loot bodies. You will not touch any other treasures. Each temple has a single item on which they place great value: their gods' weapons. Geshtai's priesthood has a magic trident named Wave. Bleredd has a magic hammer called Whelm. Do not touch the metal. Do not attempt to wield the weapons. Steal them, leave behind a holy symbol of the opposing temple, and get out. Leave none of your own party behind, dead or alive."

The trick was a sure way to start a most promising little war.

Over the past few years, the two temples had grown at a fantastic rate under the patronage of wealthy refugees. Their private armies, their unruly worshipers, and their arrogance had kept Trigol shaking with street brawls and occasional murders for the best part of a year.

With their precious relics stolen, the two temples would begin an outright civil war. The thieves guilds could stir the pot, and Saala would reap the rewards of a city in chaos. Blackrazor would let them tip the balance and become makers of kings. Saala would pull the strings of a new puppet, and the city would be hers.

All in all, it promised to be a beautiful day.

8

For Escalla, Cinders, and the Justicar, the morning had mellowed into the beginnings of a lovely golden day. The sorcerers' supply shops had yielded no information, so the investigation hovered at a dead end. Making the best of their circumstances, they made their way down to the riverside markets and organized some breakfast. Sprawled out in a warm beam of sun, Cinders sucked upon a coal and made satisfied little noises. With fried fish wrapped in warm bread, Jus and Escalla sat in a quiet niche beside a jetty. Fully visible, Escalla lounged against the Justicar and enjoyed the morning sun.

"Did you find any clues at that supply shop?"

"No. They say they have a professional code. They won't pass on information about their customers." The ranger watched a river skiff drifting slowly down the stream. "If worse comes to worst, we can hide you inside a shop to watch for the guy."

"Wizards have a habit of seeing through my invisibility."

"Yes, I suppose so." Jus scratched his stubbled head and laid his worries aside. Breakfast was good, and the sun was warm. To Escalla's eyes, he actually looked relaxed.

Cinders—now recovered from the trauma of his bath the night before—soaked up the sun. He happily flopped his tail from side to side as Jus brushed his pelt to a shine. Escalla watched the Justicar as he petted Cinders's grinning skull. The sight seemed so ludicrously homey that she smiled.

Escalla stretched and looked up at the Justicar. "So, Jus, where did Cinders come from, anyway?"

"Found him during the war." Big and mellow, Jus proffered a tub of garlic sauce to the faerie girl. "Got him off a paladin."

"A *paladin?*" Escalla stood and leaned upon the Justicar's shoulder. "Aren't they usually good guys?"

"This one thought that tanning a hell hound and keeping him as a tormentable trophy was a good joke." Jus warmly scratched Cinders underneath the jaw. "He thought wrong."

Escalla blinked. "So what happened?"

"I killed him."

The faerie raised her brows in surprise. "You killed a paladin?"

The Justicar quietly stroked his hell hound's ear. "I don't care if they claim to be good or evil. You pick on something helpless, and one day you might just have to explain yourself to *me.*"

With a little laugh, the faerie looked fondly at her companion. "Oh, man, you are *so* harsh!"

"Thank you."

"You're welcome."

The morning sun was warm, and the river proved to be a remarkably relaxing view. Escalla lay flat on her back upon Cinders's fur, spread her wings, and watched the clouds drift past in a bright blue sky.

"Oooh, I'm comatose. Gimme a jug of wine and just bury me here!"

"Too much work to do." Jus drew a few inches of his sword from its sheath, contemplated honing the already razor-sharp blade, then decided to leave it until evening. "You seem too clever to be a thief. Tell me, what made you take up crime?"

Escalla gave a sigh. She watched the clouds and quite suddenly looked a little sad. "I was living in the bilges of a big, leaky barge. I sold three really dumb bits of information to some guy I scarcely knew and blew my amassed fortune on wine, faerie cakes, and tangerines."

"Why were you living on the barge?"

"The barge?" Escalla suddenly looked a little blank. With her face falling, she gazed up at the sky with a saddened stare. "Let's just say that for some of us, being a lovable icon of forest fun is . . . unfulfilling. It's only when you try to be different that you realize just how vicious *nice* people can really be."

Beneath Escalla's bottom, Cinders wagged his tail. *Cinders likes faerie.*

"Thank you, Cinders." Escalla patted the hell hound's fur. "You're a weird guy, and I like you too."

The Justicar deliberately kept from meeting Escalla's eye. He patted Cinders's skull, then reached into his backpack and unwrapped a little gift for the faerie.

"Faerie cake. I found it at a stall." The big man drew in a sigh. "And I bought you a silk scarf and some rabbit skins to turn into clothes."

"Thanks, man," Escalla said. She seemed very pleased but a bit embarassed at the ranger's sudden kindness.

Down in the water a small brown frog floated with its toes splayed and a look of lazy pleasure in its golden eyes. Around the jetty pilings, water weeds bloomed and damselflies flew. It was obviously a fine place just to be a frog. The Justicar joined Escalla in sprawling at the water's edge and watching the frog, the plants, and even the flies. When Escalla sat very, very still, a damselfly landed quietly on her hair. She sat straight and tried to see it from the corner of her eye, careful not to scare the pretty little thing away.

"Hey, Jus?"

"Hmmm?"

"You know a lot about the north." Escalla carefully bit into her faerie cake. "I mean Iuz, abyssal bats, and everything."

"Yes." The Justicar watched the frog floating dreamily in the shallows. "Yes, I suppose I do."

"So are you going to tell me why?"

The Justicar remained silent. He sat and stared at the frog floating in peace and quiet down below. Ripples spread as the frog made a lazy turn. All around him, a city flowed past, distant and forgotten.

"You don't remember it much." The Justicar had eyes only for the river shallows. "It was a green country up there before the war. The far north of the river was all bandit kingdoms, but Urnst was fairly calm, a pretty place—cattle country up by the river, manor holdings all through the hills." His stubbled face quirked up in a rare smile. "I went south to study in Celadon—learned the sword from the elves, then learned to fight from the dwarves. I came back north, though. It was the kind of place that seemed worth coming back to. Lost all of it in the war, of course. Lost pretty much all of everything. Just ashes . . . one end of it to the other. Even the corpses were gone."

The Justicar's hand rested upon Cinders's fur

"I killed a lot of Iuz's minions then, hunted them like pigs. You lived alone, you trained alone . . . and then you hunted them alone. That was just what you did. Then one day, they stopped coming."

Escalla looked at Jus quietly, her face propped up by her hand and the brilliant red damselfly still preening in her hair.

"So after the war, you joined up with the law?"

"No. Too much has happened to worry about law."

The man rested his sheathed sword across his folded legs, his long fingers tracing the stark shape of the wolf-skull pommel.

"You *think* more when you're alone. You take a look around, and you see that the law is there only to protect power, to make things run. The common people just get ground down. When the wars were done, no one helped the little folk. They just looked at them and demanded taxes or told them they were serving the state and rounded them up like slaves. They keep rebuilding shattered kingdoms. You'll see plenty of law, but what you won't see is any justice."

Escalla looked at him and seemed to finally begin to understand.

"So for Justice, you need a Justicar?"

"Yes. You need a Justicar."

Jus had invented himself and created a name for his new role. Monastically simple, incorruptible, and grim, he was the perfect instrument. Escalla felt the damselfly whirr away into the air then gave the man a kiss upon the ear.

"We'll get 'em, big guy. We'll get 'em."

On the road up above, the sounds of morning traffic had increased. Escalla rose and dusted the faerie cake crumbs from her lap, ready to face the rest of her day.

"Well, Justicar, let's go catch this two-toned sorcerer."

"Call me Jus." The big man rose to his feet and threw Cinders about his shoulders. "Let's go."

They climbed the wood-boarded walkways that overhung the riverbanks. The Justicar tromped his way past boat owners and troupes of dancing girls alighting upon a pleasure barge and walked out into Trigol City's main marketplace.

The wide square was lined upon three sides by buildings and lay open to the river at the south. Overshadowing each end of the marketplace stood huge, frowning temple gates, and behind the wrought iron were two temples, one decorated with symbols of water and fish and the other with images of hammers, flame, and steel. It was architecture imported from the Duchy of Tenh: gaudy, bright, and indolent. Escalla made vomiting sounds as she took a long, hard look at the decor.

The stalls in this busy place were rather strange. Half were tricked out in blue-green ribbons and the other in red and iron gray. Coded ribbons, hats, or feathers similarly marked people on the streets, and both opposing mobs eyed each other with hostility.

Now invisible and sitting upon the Justicar's left shoulder, Escalla drew up her feet to avoid touching the crowds. Spying the Justicar's lack of ribbons, followers of both temple factions tried to block his way as he approached, but the big man simply shoved them out of his path. His silent stare froze a dozen others in place. Several glances at the ranger's massive sword decided it for them, and suddenly it became much easier to walk through the crowds.

Escalla frowned. "These are *seriously* rude people!" The faerie spat and sneezed as a passing lady swung her feathered hat into her face. "What are all these damned ribbons for?"

Jus thrust through the crowds by sheer force of ill temper.

"Worshipers from two competing temples: Geshtai and Blah-something." The ranger strode forward through the street, pushing the hostile crowds apart. "Refugees from the Duchy of Tenh brought their cults with them when they moved in about five years ago. Now the wars are over, and they're both flexing muscle and trying to get their claws into the city. It really puts the polish on the place."

"Yeah, *real* homey." Perched upon Jus's shoulders, Escalla cracked her knuckles and wriggled her posterior in glee. "Hey, I can do an illusion spell. Do you think they'd clear the streets if it suddenly rained pus?"

"*Don't.*"

"Hey, just a suggestion. I'm trying to offer positive work solutions here!" The faerie planted her hands on either side of the Justicar's face and steered his view to a midpoint between the two temples. "Hey, look. A library! That's pretty smooth."

The library spread its squat shape along the northern edge of the markets, frowning like a toad at all the noise and bustle outside its doors. Immediately intrigued, the Justicar marched inside, paid a stiff entry fee, and walked into an echoing hall that smelled of beeswax, candleflame, and dust. Shelves thirty feet tall reached up to the ceiling, each one filled with leather- or wood-bound books or with pigeon-holes for countless scrolls. Scholars in dust-streaked robes rode long ladders that rolled on tracks, travelling sound-lessly about the rim.

Perched happily atop his friend's head, Cinders began to wag his tail in glee.

Paper!

"Keep a lid on it, flame boy." Escalla swatted the hell hound's ears. "We are rapidly running out of places to stay."

A rampart of desks, each of them covered with maps and scrolls, surrounded a central dais. In deep conference behind the barriers were three librarians, each wearing immaculate gray robes. The two junior men were paying devoted attention to the orders of their senior, and all three men ignored their visitor. Thus freed from exchanging pleasantries, the Justicar walked heavily over to a reference desk, fished a vast ledger up from its hiding place, and made space for the huge book by simply shoving scrolls and pamphlets off the desk onto the floor.

The ledger held confused notes upon the scrolls owned by the library. The Justicar searched for "Keraptis," "Sorcery," and "History" and found that the appropriate entries had been cut from the pages. Annoyed, he slammed the book shut, making enough noise to attract the attention of one the librarians upon the dais.

The senior librarian turned. He was a tall man with an expression dominated by a superior gaze. His long hair streamed down behind a balding pate, rippling like the mane of a manticore.

He raked a cold, disgusted glance across the Justicar, then simply turned away and announced for all to hear. "This is not a public library. It is the library of the Black Newt Sorcerers' guild. Remove yourself from the building at once."

With no time for scholars and their airs, the Justicar simply approached the man upon his dais and said, "I'm looking for a book."

His audience could not have cared less. The three librarians carefully watched the marketplace through a window. Greatly angered, the Justicar sealed their attention by banging his sheathed sword down upon the desk. The echo boomed like drums of doom all through the library hall.

The senior librarian flicked a sign at his assistants, who glanced coldly at the Justicar and faded swiftly off into the maze of shelves. Left facing the Justicar and Cinders, the senior librarian glowered at his guests.

"Be swift. The library is closing in five minutes."

The Justicar had no intention of leaving. Ignoring a sudden raise in volume of the market crowds, he leaned forward onto the cluttered desk.

"I want to find a book describing the life of the wizard Keraptis."

"Keraptis!" The librarian's huge beak of a nose lifted loftily into the air. "What would a warrior need with tales of Keraptis? Go ask a storyteller or a puppeteer!"

The Justicar glowered. "You teach your children about evil?"

"It is a sad fact that time reduces even the greatest of men to mere abstractions." The librarian drew in a long, cold breath of pride. "Keraptis was a visionary. He realized that the only true nobility is the nobility of the intellect. A true sorcerer is therefore liberated from the moral codes invented to restrict lesser men."

The librarian clicked his fingers, and the lights within the library doused themselves one by one. Marching from between the shelves came three very large, very heavily armored men who glared at the Justicar.

The librarian indicated the door. "I have other work to do. The library is closed. You will leave now."

❀   ❀   ❀   ❀   ❀

High above the floor, Escalla was in her own little world. Minding her own business and fluttering about the shelves, she had been poking through the scrolls and finding interesting tidbits here and there. Sitting atop a bookshelf, she found an old lamp shield made of blown glass rolling about in the dust. The faerie blew it roughly clean and looked through the smoke-stained glass to peer at her two companions down below.

Jus had given up the argument and was preparing to leave. Cinders grinned like a mad thing above the man's head, red eyes twinkling. Escalla lifted up the glass tube and looked through its sides at the room, childishly pleased at the way it dimmed her view of the window light.

She turned her toy upon the librarian and gazed at him, shading half of his face black with the lantern sleeve. She stared at the two-colored face, with its long, limp hair and hatchet nose, then let the glass tube sink quietly to her side.

"Oh, no."

Escalla backed frenziedly away, trying to hide herself behind a shelf. A scroll rolled free behind her and fell onto the floor below. The librarian turned to scowl. Escalla blurred low over the floor. Jus was leaving through the door, and he almost fell as Escalla shot between his legs and out the door. The faerie swooped up to flatten herself against the library wall and saw the librarian suddenly running to the window to scowl across the square.

The librarian stared for a long, hard moment, then sniffed and turned away. He had the air of a man interrupted in the middle of business. Escalla felt her little heart racing as she tugged at Jus's belt and dragged him out of sight of the library door.

"Jus! Jus, it's *him!*" The faerie flapped like a mad moth in fright. "It's him, two-tone, the black and white guy!"

"What?" The Justicar whirled. He stood on the library steps, staring at the door in cold calculation. "You're sure?"

"I'm sure! Hey have I ever steered you wrong?"

Jus and Cinders both swivelled their eyes sideways toward the invisible faerie, their gazes speaking volumes. Escalla waved invisible hands in annoyance. "Oh, fine! Well, you two guys just kick the door down and march straight in there. You can ask him yourself!"

"All right, we believe you." The Justicar tapped his fingers thoughtfully against the pommel of his sword. "So our man is here?"

Burn! Cinders flapped his tail madly up and down. *Burn! Burn!*

"No . . . not yet, anyway." Jus stood in grim thought, Escalla settling onto his shoulders. The big man scratched at his stubbled chin. "The two-toned man is either the top of the chain, or he's a link to the top. I don't want to kill him until I know which." He drew a long, hard breath. "We'll come back when it's dark and take a careful look for clues."

"Hoopy!" Escalla leaned to look closer at the library. "Hey, do magic scrolls have significant resale value?"

"They're not ours to take."

Escalla sat prim and erect on Jus's shoulders and announced, "If he's an enemy of the public, then the public deserves a little compensation for troubles caused." The faerie fanned invisible wings. "Since I am a member of the public, I consider myself qualified as a representative."

The argument wasn't working this time. As Jus stalked his way down the library steps, Escalla tried again.

"Hey, look. If this guy steals, then he's taken money out of public circulation, right? By reselling his stolen goods,

I'm actually injecting all that cash back into the economy. It's like *giving* it back, only better because it generates trade at the same time! Granted as an unfortunate side benefit, I may be forced to outfit myself with a pure spidersilk dress and a few new hats, but think of the benefits to the lingerie trade alone!"

Escalla kept speaking as they reached the halfway point down the stairs. She stopped just in time to see a priest of Bleredd run through the markets, make a massive swing of his warhammer at a priestess of Geshtai, and smash the helpless woman to the ground.

9

The murder took place right in the middle of the square. The Geshtai priestess fell without a sound, her blood spraying out across the market stalls as her murderer laughed and disappeared, running toward Bleredd's temple at the far end of the square.

For a few seconds, a crowd of a thousand simply stood and stared, dumbstruck. Then Geshtai worshipers suddenly looked at Bleredd supporters and gave a wild scream. The Bleredd worshipers put a hand to their weapons, and an instant later the whole marketplace shook beneath a tidal wave of hate and rage.

Street merchants threw themselves at their neighbors while shoppers grappled one another, hammering daggers into one another's guts. From each temple, gate guards and soldiers began to run into the battle. Maces and halberds smashed into unarmored civilians, clawing bloody swathes through the crowds until both private armies met each other face to face. Priests joined the soldiers, and the blast of spells began to gouge into the rioting mob.

Behind it all, Escalla and Jus stood on the steps of the library, overlooking the churning chaos of the melee.

The Justicar shoved through a pair of brawling fishwives, cracking their heads together and letting them fall. Shoving battling merchants aside, he tried to catch sight of the murderer of the Geshtai priestess.

"Damn! Cinders, where did the killer go?"

The hell hound sniffed, using senses born on a far-distant plane. *No killer. Killer is illusion!*

"Just the killer, or the victim too?"

Victim real, but not dead. Blood is illusion.

Escalla dodged a jam jar thrown by someone in the melee.

"An illusory murder? Great! Someone's inciting a riot!"

It was more than a riot. It was a war. A thousand citizens battled in the marketplace, with temple priests and temple guards thickening the fray. Striding from both temples came their high priests with chosen warriors who had been issued weapons from the temples' vaults. From the Geshtai temple came a long silver trident and from Bleredd's halls, a magic hammer. The wielders of the weapons launched themselves into the crowds. Backed by high priests and warriors, they began to wreak pure carnage as they hacked their way into the unarmored mobs.

Magic. Strong!

"I see it!" The Justicar kicked a charging ironmonger off the library steps. "Escalla, the murdered priestess must still be alive! We have to find her!"

"Gotcha! I'll cover you." The faerie whirred up into the air.

The Justicar surged down the library steps, heading for the center of the melee. With his sword sheathed, he strode into the brawl, wrenching men aside. Just overhead, Escalla tried to peer into the chaos to catch a glimpse of their prey.

A swarm of men decided to attack the Justicar. His response certainly wasn't art, but it was beautiful to behold. A huge blacksmith threw a punch straight at Jus's face, and the ranger parried with a forward-stepping move. He stepped aside, dodging the blow, caught the blacksmith under the chin, spun him about, and slammed the man to the ground with one of his arms held in a lock.

The man's apprentices came racing up to save their master. The Justicar took a look at the new onrush of attackers, briskly dislocated the blacksmith's shoulder, and then strode forward to meet the charge.

All three apprentices screamed for blood. The Justicar ducked a wild swing, flicked a hand to his sheath, and rammed the hilt of his sword into one man's solar plexus. The apprentice folded, stumbling back into his companions.

The Justicar still had not drawn his blade.

Another man swung clumsily with his fist and was punched in the jaw for his trouble—a single massive blow that lifted him off his feet and sent him senseless to the ground.

The last man came at the Justicar with a hammer held high. The ranger caught the man as he charged, turned with the passing blow, and hurled the man to the street. He knelt, hammered the apprentice three times with his left hand, and left the unconscious youth sprawled across his friends.

Six feet overhead, Escalla dodged random pots, pans, and missiles flying from the melee.

"You do good work!" The faerie had to shout to make herself heard above the mob.

"Where's that dead priestess?"

"No sign!"

Cinders suddenly jerked his ears, and the Justicar whipped his head about to follow the hound's lead. Escalla followed their gaze and saw a blood-spattered female figure borne by a pair of young Geshtai priests.

The supposedly dead priestess suddenly sprouted claws and tore into the priests' spines. The men fell dead, and the woman laughed as she strode away from her self-made civil war.

"*There!*" Escalla's little voice cut through the battle.

Beside the temple, the "dead" Geshtai priestess whipped about to give the faerie a stare of pure malice. The priestess shimmered, cast away her previous form, and became a tall, slim female with long tresses of red hair. Her old clothing dropped away to leave her a gleaming nude. Several of the nearby rioters stopped fighting to stare at the voluptuous figure in open-mouthed shock.

Escalla cast a spell, and a thick, putrescent cloud quickly spread through a sizeable chunk of the market, sending men and women retching and staggering aside. The red-headed woman strode uncaring through the cloud, building up to a run as she changed shape into a powerful black dog.

"Damn!" Escalla blew a strand of hair out of her face. *"An erinyes!* Just what this town needs." She knew of erinyes, but she had never seen one before and had certainly never dreamed of having to actually fight one. "Oh well, first time for everything."

The dog sped beneath tables and stalls, heading for the edges of the markets. It dodged and doubled back, sprinting through melees. Clinging to her quarry like glue, Escalla finally outsmarted the thing. Picking the dog out as it ran toward an alleyway, the faerie whipped beneath a line of stalls and suddenly had a clear shot straight at the black dog's back.

"Hey! Suck on this!"

A fireball ripped from Escalla's hands and blasted straight into her victim's back. To the faerie's surprise, the dog barely staggered. It whipped its head about and stared at her, its eyes suddenly turning a poisonous green. Escalla felt fear slam into her like a physical blow and wrenched to a complete stop. The black dog snarled and slowly approached the faerie, who could scarcely move as the fear spell twisted through her mind.

The Justicar came striding through the stinking cloud, his hell hound skin cloaking him in sheer, savage anger. The black sword came free from its scabbard, swinging light as a toy in the big man's hands. The black dog looked at him with its evil green eyes, then blinked as its fear spell failed. Hackles raised, it began to back away.

The dog suddenly shifted form. In a flow of melting shapes, it became a magnificently naked woman with pointed ears and pure white angel's wings. She hissed in a raw explosion of hate, savage hellfire gleaming in her eyes.

"Jus!" Escalla shouted. "Jus, it's an erinyes! Watch out!"

The devil-woman whipped out a long rope and lashed it straight at the Justicar. The rope whipped around him in a blur, trapping his arms and binding him in loop after loop of cord. The erinyes gave a scream of triumph. The Justicar stood his ground, stared at her, then nodded his head toward the rope. Cinders gave a manic grin and blasted out a jet of flames to burn the rope in two.

Appalled, the devil-woman backed away, holding the end of her rope and screaming in anger. The Justicar freed himself from the limp coils, flicking free his sword. With a thundering growl, he charged toward his enemy.

A flash of motion streaked from the rooftops above. Four figures, each armored in black leather, landed on the ground between the Justicar and the erinyes. One of them was dead almost before he struck the ground, his guts ripped open by a flash of the Justicar's sword. A second man tried to parry the ranger's sudden attack. He caught the first blow then spun as a huge swipe of the black sword cut him almost in two.

The last two split up. One, wielding twin swords, veered left while his companion with a double-ended spear ran to the right. Jus tracked one, had Cinders burn him, then whirled and caught a spear blow with his sword. The double-ended spear flashed fast and bright, ringing sparks from Jus's blade as he caught attack after attack. A sudden upward flick of the ranger's sword hooked the man's left foot out from beneath him. The ranger followed with a savage stab into the torso as the man smashed to the ground.

Twin blades flashed as the last attacker, burned and furious, came rampaging into the fight. Sparks rained down as his two swords cut and flickered in a blur. The Justicar backpedalled then flashed sideways, his sword whipping downward with an almost inhuman speed. His attacker managed to catch the blow with crossed blades but was hurled a pace backward by the Justicar's sheer strength.

With a wild cry, the man charged. Jus whirled sideways, ending up behind his enemy. As the man passed, the Justicar sliced the full length of his sword across his enemy's abdomen. The man lurched forward, horror in his eyes as he fell dying to the ground.

With a snarl, the erinyes looked to the rooftops to summon her last reserve. Rising dazedly from hiding, a black figure silently sprang down from the rooftop above and landed behind the Justicar. Cinders hissed in alarm, and Escalla blasted a sudden mass of web down upon the newcomer, plastering him against a wall.

Escalla breathed hard, still shivering with the aftereffects of the demon's fear spell. She lowered her hand, wisps of spider web still floating down from her fingertips.

"Jus, look at his sword!"

The newcomer roared. A myriad of faintly pulsing and flickering stars seemed to dance slowly along the blade, and a weird energy pulsed up from the blade into his flesh. The man began to move with unholy speed, each sweep of his black sword severing a dozen sticky web strands. The sword eked a sinister black radiance and moaned in ghastly hunger as it smelled the scent of blood. With a final slash of his sword, the man ripped out of the web and threw himself toward the Justicar

"Jus, look out!"

Escalla saw the devil-woman charging toward her friend's back and fired a spell. Swarms of biting, stinging insects formed high above the street then slammed into the woman, wreathing her in a cloud of agony.

The erinyes began to fight off the insect swarm. Escalla cursed like a stevedore and backpedalled madly in midair as the woman sprang aloft to lunge up at her. Escalla led the screaming monster away from her friend, firing a stream of little magic missiles at the creature in an attempt to hold it at bay.

❖ ❖ ❖ ❖ ❖

Far below, the Justicar readied himself to fight the sinister, moaning sword. The sword's wielder—a tall, scarred man—raised the screeching blade and raced forward. He made one huge, twisting cut, and Jus's parry rang against the weapon like a bell, both black swords meeting in a flash of light.

The Justicar moved as fast as he could to block another strike, but the man was pushing him to his limit. His attacker was filled with a magical energy that seemed to skitter him forward through time. Moving insanely fast, the man made cut after cut with the evil sword, laughing and overconfident in his magical speed. He sliced at the Justicar's feet and when the blow was parried, he whipped the hellish blade around in an overhand cut intended to shear his enemy in two.

The Justicar parried, pivoted aside, and struck, aiming for his enemy's forearms rather than the sword. His blade struck, severing the thief's arms clean through. Screaming, the thief spun away, and the black blade fell skittering across the cobblestones. Still accelerated by magical speed, the thief bled to death in a single horrific gush of blood.

From high above, the woman gave a terrified scream.

"Blackrazor! No!"

The creature forgot her attack upon Escalla and whirled to save the sword. She had only just begun to move when a figure stepped suddenly forward from the nearby crowds.

A gigantic opaque fist shimmered into existence, picked up the sword, and whipped it though the air. Floating above the street, the fist settled above a thin, balding sorcerer who awaited the sword with open hands.

The Justicar started as he recognized the face of the librarian laughing in triumph. As the erinyes lunged for him, the librarian simply stepped through a glowing portal in the air. With a silent flash, librarian and magic sword instantly disappeared from view.

The devil-woman screamed in loss and panic, passing through the empty space where the librarian had stood. She searched wildly for the portal, found nothing—then saw the faerie and the Justicar racing toward her.

"Jus, be careful!" Escalla screamed.

Escalla hammered at the erinyes with a spell that sent swarm of darts shaped like little golden bees arrowing straight for their foe. Staggering under the assault, the erinyes broke into a retreat. She raised her hand, and sinister energies twisted at the air. All about the Justicar and Escalla, butchered corpses streaming blood rose to their feet and made a barrier between the devil-woman and her enemies. She spread her white wings and shot up into the sky, moving at a pace that left Escalla tumbling in her wake like a butterfly.

Six shambling corpses charged the Justicar. He smashed the arms from one and clove another's shoulder off its torso. A third corpse ripped a wound across the ranger's shoulder. Cinders raked flame across two of the undead abominations and set them afire, sending them blundering off into the crowds.

Two of the undead still locked swords with Jus. Escalla poised in midair, licked her index finger, and pointed at a zombie. A stream of little explosive golden bees blasted into the creature's spine, raking the monster as it tried to turn. The last zombie turned to make a clumsy swipe for the faerie but was smacked apart by one savage blow from the Justicar's black sword.

The city's military had finally come on the scene. Soldiers came running into the marketplace, and priests and temple guards instantly withdrew from the fighting. The trident and magic hammer were hurried back into their respective homes. This left the common people fighting, leaderless and insane with fury as soldiers armed with staves tried to bring the fighting to a close.

A law officer stood bellowing helplessly at the crowd, waving his warrant over his head as though it were a magic scroll. A dozen rioters instantly surged toward the man, and he backed against a wall and drew his sword. The Justicar wrenched himself back from staring after the fleeing erinyes and began to shove his way toward the struggling man.

"Escalla, help the lawman!"

The faerie backed away from the open skies. She turned, spread her fingers in a sleep spell, and sent six members of the crowd slumping to the ground. The Justicar leaped over the bodies and brought his blade down on a rioter from behind. He killed a second man with a stab through the back, then joined the lawman side by side.

Rioters surged forward to attack only to be flung back by huge blows from the Justicar's sword.

With the onrush of armored soldiers, the rioters soon began to scatter. Some dove into the river while others fled into alleyways. A great many of the refugees from the Duchy of Tenh managed to pour into their respective temples, barring the doors against other citizens following behind.

The Justicar hacked the legs out from under a last enemy and them stabbed the man through the heart. He wrenched his sword free with a look of absolute distaste and knelt to wipe the blade upon a dead man's clothes.

Escalla had managed another sleep spell to clear a path for an inrush of city militiamen. Winded, panting, and scored by a rioter's blade, the rescued lawman watched the soldiers come. He fought for breath, looking up at the grim shape of the Justicar as the huge man sheathed his blade.

"Whoever you are, I thank you."

Escalla came twinkling down from the sky.

"All part of a day's work, hon!" The faerie perched herself prettily across the Justicar's huge shoulders, reclining across the grinning hell hound skin.

With an expressive glance toward the faerie, the Justicar strode forward to help the law officer to his feet. The city streets were littered with corpses, and the main marketplace was awash with blood. Jus kicked a weakly flopping zombie out of his path as the stench of burning slowly began to fill the air.

Escalla peered down from between the ears of the grinning hellhound skin. "Hey, could any of you boys go for a drink right now?"

Beer! Cinders wagged his tail.

Helping the law officer keep his feet, the Justicar led the man away from the carnage. A tangled maze of corpses now marred the city streets, while from the temples there rose a fresh new chorus of screams.

10

"Who? *Who* did it?" Naked and screaming in rage, Saala shoved one of her thieves, the sheer force of the blow sending the man slamming a dozen feet back against a wall. "Who stole Blackrazor?"

"Lady, we weren't there!" A senior thief half hid himself behind a chair in the Thieves Guildhall. "Our operatives swear they have never been followed or observed at any time."

"Liars! *Incompetent* liars! I'll rake out their hearts and eat them whole!" The she-devil whipped her wings in a lather of rage, sending a sulphurous breeze twisting through the hall. "Of course they were followed! Someone knew exactly who to watch and where to strike! I demand to know who!"

The senior thieves of three different guilds quivered. The erinyes had welded them together by bloody force and terror, and it had been Blackrazor as much as sheer fear of her powers that had made the thieves her slaves. She sensed the thought and whipped her head about, her eyes suddenly flashing green. Her spell instantly brought a senior thief kneeling at her feet.

"I want Blackrazor back, and I want it *now*." Saala drew a dagger from her belt, and it dripped an acid that burned sour patches in the floor. "All guild magicians are to use every scrying spell at their command. I want to know who has foreseen our plans."

Her spell held the kneeling thief helpless as a lamb. Saala cradled her chosen victim against her lean, silken belly, feeling the man's mind fight helplessly against her control. The erinyes slowly cut his throat, sawing her dagger back and forth to let the man's blood spurt up over her naked flesh. She breathed in the terrified horror of her audience, then slowly sawed her victim's head free from its neck.

The head thudded to the ground. Picking her nails with the blood-drenched dagger, the erinyes turned toward her underlings with a smile.

"I'm a reasonable woman. Now does anyone here have anything to contribute to this discussion? No?"

Men stood and stared at the bleeding body of their comrade as blood flowed across the floor. The erinyes sat herself in a chair and used her victim's corpse as a footstool. Her long, blood-spattered legs gleamed in the candlelight as she sensuously wriggled her long toes.

With her dripping dagger, she pointed lazily at the door.

"Now then. Let us discuss our successes. We now have the trident and the hammer. At least something has gone well." The erinyes crossed her feet, heedless of her nakedness—shape shifting could change a body, but it did nothing about providing proper clothes. "Open the door and bring the weapons in. Let us see just what we have."

No one moved. The thieves seemed to shrink in upon themselves, afraid to meet their mistress's eye.

Saala interlaced her bloody fingers and used them to rest her chin. "Yes?"

"L-lady . . ." One of the guild's senior sorcerers swallowed in fright. "Th-the strike t-teams have—"

"What have the strike teams done?" Saala leaned forward, her skin gleaming slick with patterns of fresh blood. "You will never get anywhere in life unless you learn to articulate."

"Lady, th-the strike teams b-both report that they w-were attacked just after making their escape from the temples." Quite terrified, the sorcerer turned a pale shade of gray. "Each group was attacked by a single sorcerer dressed in gray robes. Th-the magic w-weapons were taken from them. The hammer Whelm and the trident Wave . . . are g-gone."

Keeping her face perfectly controlled and expressionless, the erinyes leaned back in her chair. Her eyes seemed to chill the room with an infinite dark.

"Find them."

"Y-yes, Mistress!" The sorcerer began to back away. "It shall be done, Mistress."

Slit-pupilled eyes danced with flames as Saala flexed her dagger blade.

"I was attacked by a huge warrior armed with a fire-breathing hell hound skin. He was accompanied by a faerie, a pixie that has elected to become an accomplished sorcer-ess." The erinyes lifted her pure white wings. "They are involved in all of this somehow. I suggest that you also spy on *them.*"

"Of course, Mistress." Thieves began to move, realizing that they had survived their mistress's rage. "At once, Mis-tress."

"And cancel my appointments for the rest of the after-noon." Saala slowly caressed her dagger blade. "The strike team leaders and I shall be in . . . *discussion* . . . for a great many hours to come."

✢   ✢   ✢   ✢   ✢

Heavy oak doors shuddered, the latch splintering as a boot slammed against the lock. A second blow sent the doors crashing inward, followed by a huge dark shape that dived and rolled across the ground. The Justicar slammed up against a wall, then sped into the shadows, his black sword hunting for prey.

The interior of the library remained still, the lights extinguished and the windows shuttered. Jus rose, took a glance around the corner, then dived amongst the tall library shelves.

Whirring in a panic behind him, Escalla hid herself behind her friend.

"Jus! Jus, this is not a good idea! I'm out of spells, and doggie's fires are low!" Escalla flapped and fluttered, weaving from side to side to make herself a hard target. "Jus, are you listening to me?"

The big man swiftly hunted through the line of library shelves, slamming a hand against the last shelf as he failed to find anyone. The building was deserted apart from the scratching of a rat somewhere deep inside the reference section.

Annoyed, the Justicar signaled to the faerie and said, "Start searching. Look for places where books are missing from the shelves. Look for books on Keraptis. Look for secret exits. Anything!"

Emerging timidly through the library's front door came the shaken figure of the young law officer Jus and Escalla had rescued in the market. Still dazed from the fight, the man blinked in nervous horror as he saw Jus begin tearing at the library shelves.

"Um, I don't think we should do this. This is private property."

The Justicar dug into his purse and pulled out an amber token—the personal symbol of the countess of Urnst.

"This private property has been used as a base for banditry, murder, and attempted assassination." The Justicar shoved the countess's token away. "I am under commission from the countess of Urnst. There's a soul-eating sword in town, and your librarian has just stolen it!"

"Soul eating . . . ?"

The Justicar began looking behind rows of books on the shelves that adjoined the walls, hunting for secret triggers and hollows. He had less time than usual to waste on polite conversation. "Eats life energy, accelerates the user's speed . . . It's called Blackrazor. It apparently belonged to an erinyes. She seems to be controlling your local thieves."

"An erinyes?"

Jus finished with the shelves. Above his helmet, Cinders sniffed, hunting for the slightest hint of magic.

"Erinyes," the ranger continued, "a type of diabolical agent from the plane Baator. Seductive like a succubus, only smarter."

The young law officer froze. "How . . . how do you know that?"

"If you want to dispense justice, first *study*. It makes for a universe filled with fewer surprises." The Justicar dragged a book from a shelf in passing and threw it open on a desk. "Read. They'll be in there under 'Baatezu'—very nasty."

The Justicar began using the pommel of his sword to check flagstones of the floor for hollow spaces, moving fast in the hope the job would be over before the sorcerer's guild could arrive on scene.

High above, Escalla was making an inspection of the library's books. She had found a big, valuable-looking tome bound in gold, but it proved far too heavy for her to lift. There was scroll after scroll piled in confusion all over the shelves, most written in who-knew-what sort of languages. Escalla began to pry at a big, brightly colored stone that graced the cover of a gaudy volume entitled *Manual of Puissant Skill At Arms*—then suddenly noticed a tasty pile of documents on the library's main desk right in the middle of the hall.

Gold glittered amongst the documents. Intrigued, Escalla opened her little wings and drifted happily down to inspect her find.

"Hey, Jus! Look!"

A pile of parchments teetered on the desk—big heavy sheets covered in maps and diagrams. The whole pile was held down by a golden jewelry box that seemed to cover over some sort of symbol written on the uppermost parchment sheet. Escalla hovered above the pile, looked this way and that at the jewelry box, then reached out happily toward the jewelry box with her hand.

Standing at a nearby bookshelf, the Justicar turned, saw the delicately balanced pile of documents begin to teeter, and caught a glimpse of the magic symbol written in fresh blood beneath the jewelry box. Moving at a shocking turn of speed, he hurled himself across the floor at a dead run, shoving the young law officer into a bookshelf as he passed. As the law officer fell, Jus was already launching into a flying tackle that smacked Escalla hard against his chest. The faerie croaked, the breath smashed out of her chest. A noise of surprised indignation was half out of her mouth when the entire room suddenly lit up with a titanic blast of flame.

The symbol covered by the teetering jewelry box flashed as light touched at the wet ink, then magical force exploded outward. The desk disintegrated, bookshelves blew apart, and wooden wall panels instantly caught fire. Turning on his side in midair and hunching into a ball to shield the faerie with his own bulk, the Justicar caught the force of the heat against Cinders's fur. The shock wave of the explosion tossed the ranger through the air, and he crashed through a succession of flimsy library shelves. Even as he hit the floor, he was rolling to shield Escalla from the blow. He hit the wall with jarring force and snarled in anger as books and rubble crashed around him.

Escalla emerged from beneath a flap of Cinders's pelt to stare at the library. The scrolls, books, and shelves were thoroughly ablaze. Emerging stunned from beneath a fallen cupboard was the law officer. Jus gave a vicious curse, shoved a healing spell into himself, then lifted himself up from the floor.

Escalla woefully watched the book collection going up in flames. "Whoops . . ."

The Justicar rose, ash and burning parchment scraps sliding from Cinders's fur.

"Fire symbol."

"Yeah, I gathered." Escalla rubbed beneath her ribs, still trying to recover from being tackled by two hundred and twenty pounds of flying Justicar. "Bastard knew we were coming!"

"He knew *someone* was." Jus strode through blazing wreckage and kicked at the few blackened fragments that marked where the library desk had once stood. "Cinders, are you all right?"

Cinders didn't do it! No burn! Not Cinders!

"Yeah, we know. Don't worry about it—just enjoy the blaze." Jus found a burning chunk of book to stuff between Cinders's champing jaws. "There you go. Good boy."

Where the librarian's desk had once stood, a trapdoor hung open beneath the rubble, blown in by the shock of the explosion. Jus kicked away a few chunks of burning chair and stared down the gaping hole.

"Here's where he went. There's a ladder and some light."

Burning chunks of scroll illuminated a room below the library floor. Jus dropped down into the hidden room, landing upon a hard stone floor. He looked about, glancing at the lanterns burning in each corner of the room. A corridor easily ten feet wide led in a straight line away from the room, the empty spaces echoing to the sounds of fire and mayhem coming from the library above.

Escalla and the law officer peeked over the edges of the entry hole. Escalla irritably blew a spark away from her pristine golden hair.

"Any sorcerers down there?"

"None." Jus felt Cinders sniffing for magic. "Cinders?"

Magic! Magic down passage. Bad—very bad!

For the benefit of the others, the Justicar passed the message on.

"Cinders doesn't like it. He says there's bad magic."

"Just what we need," said Escalla.

Escalla leaped down from above.

Giving the faerie a warning glance, the Justicar hefted his sword into killing position and began to walk down the corridor. Escalla followed at his heels.

Jus stalked cautiously along the broad, level passageway. Behind them, the law officer nervously descended into the corridor.

"The name's Allain, by the way." Receiving no answer, the young man followed unhappily behind the Justicar, hell hound, and faerie. "I'm law warden of the Temple Quarter."

Jus held up a hand to silence the young man. He flattened himself against a wall, checked the corner with a mirror taken from a string about his neck, then looked into a huge and gloomy hall.

A vast underground space, damp and cold, stretched out across hundreds of square yards. The hall seemed to be a titanic cellar, the vast expanse of roof supported by long parallel walls. Row after row of brickwork divided the room into passages. A few lights gleamed from somewhere at the far side of the corridors, while water dripped from the stone ceiling up above.

The water drops were brown and smelled of mud. Jus caught one on his fingertips and gave a casual sniff.

"River mud. We're under the river."

Escalla padded swiftly over to the nearest passages and peered within. Each one had a broad, flat floor that seemed to have been made from hard-rolled gravel.

"It's clear," Escalla said. "The floors are kinda funny—really hard, compacted gravel. I can't see anything moving."

Jus made a silent motion to Allain, ordering him to stay in place. Moving silently despite his size, the ranger stole forward up one of the parallel passageways. Escalla blinked out of sight, whirring ahead of him on invisible wings.

The passage opened into a broad open space that linked a dozen of the strange passageways. At the center of the hall there stood a wide table laid over with maps and plans. A lantern burned, spreading a reek of fish oil up into the air. A heavy, upholstered chair stood at the table's side. Escalla hovered carefully above. Her lesson learned, she touched none of the parchments until the Justicar arrived.

"Hey, Ev," she whispered, "lookie! We got maps!"

"Don't call me Ev!" The Justicar tested the floor for traps, then leaned over the table to look at the parchments, careful not to touch anything. The drawings showed sketches of corridors and rooms, and a drawing of a mountain pierced by tunnels. Various rooms were marked in red ink, the writing in no language that the Justicar could recognize.

At his side, Escalla peered at a list peeking out from beneath a paperweight.

"What's this, a recipe?" The girl read. " 'One crab. Six lobsters. Six scorpions. Green slime . . .' "

The air reverberated to a sudden rumble. As the whole hallway began to tremble, Jus looked upward, expecting to see the ceiling in mid-collapse.

Escalla hastily withdrew away from the tabletop. "It wasn't me! I touched nothing!"

"Shh!" Jus listened, turning his head back and forth. The ceiling seemed solid. "It's not the river. Something's moving in here!"

Bad! Big magic thing! Fast!

Cinders swiveled his ears. The faerie and the Justicar both turned. Erupting from one of the passages came a vast, top-heavy monstrosity that moved at such speed that the entire hall shuddered beneath its wheels.

Two stone rollers ten feet wide supported a crude stone statue shaped like a hobby horse. Stone pistons pumped out ahead and behind of the horse, jabbing back and forth with each turn of the stone wheels. The juggernaut swiveled to face the Justicar then surged forward.

Escalla flew one way and Jus ran in the other. The ranger dived into one of the multiple passageways just as the juggernaut ran over the table, lantern, and chair. Wood flew to pieces as the huge mobile statue reached the Justicar's hiding place and began to turn into the corridor.

Flattened against the wall and waiting, Jus gave a huge warcry and hacked down in a massive blow of his sword. The enchanted steel of his black sword struck at the piston pumping the juggernaut's front. In a huge spray of sparks, the sword sheared through the stone, crashing the severed piston to the ground.

The juggernaut turned inexorably into Jus's chosen corridor. Jus turned and ran, fleeing hard and fast down the passage. Behind him, the juggernaut rumbled forward, slowly gaining speed until it rushed along the corridor, sparks spitting into the darkness where its sides scraped against the walls. Fast as a charging horse, the juggernaut swept down on the Justicar, intent on crushing him underneath its rollers. Jus thundered down the corridor with death following hard on his heels.

Escalla flew up from behind the monster, poised beside its front roller, and jammed a broken chair leg between the roller and the axle fork. With a sudden flash and bang, the monstrosity pitched onto its face. The stone horse gave a screech of tortured stone as it slid along the floor, crashing and banging against the walls. It finally came to a halt in a heap of rubble right at the Justicar's feet.

Jus stood, breathing hard and staring at the wreckage. The juggernaut spun its wheels and rollers, unable to turn right way up.

Curious, Escalla flew down to inspect the damage. "Hey, I do good work! That thing really had you running!"

Jus growled, settling Cinders back into place atop his head.

"Say, did that bust up your sword?"

"No." The Justicar inspected the fallen juggernaut and decided to leave it as it lay. "I told you it's enchanted."

A voice drifted from behind them, somewhere in the dark. *"Interesting . . ."*

The Justicar whirled with a snarl, his black blade poised to ram through any enemy. Floating in the gloom there hung a huge apparition: the face of the librarian now painted half black and half white. The image of the sorcerer bobbed slowly up and down in the air.

"Interesting." The sorcerer's voice echoed down the passageways. "Yes, *you* are worth encouraging onward. Strong. Disciplined. You might well make a good contribution to the physical form of the new Overman! Come and take the test of Keraptis! As it once was, so again it shall be! Come to my halls and retrieve the three!"

Hovering in midair, Escalla looked sourly at the librarian's ghostly face.

"Hey two-tone, you call that poetry?" The girl made a rude noise. "You know, if *I* was powerful enough to project images of my swelled head all over the universe, I think I'd spend a bit more time in polishing my prose!"

The image turned hungry, knowing eyes upon the faerie and seemed . . . pleased.

"You too, little one. Take the test of the mountain. Retrieve the three prizes. Who knows? Even *you* might provide worthy substance to the new lord of space and time."

The face faded away, leaving nothing but darkness, a thrashing juggernaut, and a growing drip and hiss of water. Escalla blinked into the gloom.

" 'Contribute to the Overman'? 'Provide worthy substance'?" The faerie bit her lip. "I really wish he'd phrased those invitations differently."

A section of wall beside the juggernaut suddenly collapsed. Above the monster, a stone block fell from the ceiling, and river water streamed onto the tunnel floor. Jus grabbed for Escalla's hand and towed her rapidly down the passage, accelerating to a run as more and more stones could be heard collapsing far behind.

Escalla tried to look back "What about those maps?"

"We're leaving!" Jus broke into the main corridor that led back to the library. Allain the lawman still stood waiting in the door. He saw Jus running toward him, and an instant later he saw the river water spilling out of the passageways. As a distant ceiling collapsed inward with a watery crash, all three explorers fled back into the room beneath the blazing library. Jus held Cinders's pelt up as a shield for his companions as they struggled out of the secret room and up into the flames.

The library shelves were burning in earnest now. Fire had spread to the ceiling and the tapestries, the window shutters, and the walls. Jus led his companions through the heat and sagging doors out into the sun.

Soot stained, blood-spattered, and near exhaustion, Jus stumbled to the bottom of the steps and leaned upon his sword. The library burned behind him while big bubbles rose from a new whirlpool out in the river shallows. Cinders wagged his tail, happily basking in the heat of the burning building.

Drawing the stares of a shocked crowd, Escalla fluttered down to land upon the Justicar's shoulders.

"Hey, troops! We've had breakfast, we've fought a demon, and we've burned your library down." The faerie gave a tired sigh. "What now?"

Allain cleared his throat. "We should see the baron. Tell him about your mission." The young man looked back at the burning library. "He'll know what to do."

Jus sheathed his sword and shrugged. For the moment, there might be advantages to cooperating with the law. The Justicar settled Escalla on his shoulder, dusted ashes out of Cinders's fur, and led the way down into a marketplace still streaked and smeared with blood.

II

Over the past twenty years, the county of Urnst had survived invasion by Iuz, raids from the Bandit Kingdoms,
strifes internal and external, and a hundred other problems
big and small. The countess—an old, sharp-tongued
woman with little patience for fools—kept her capital in
the west where she could keep a sharp watch upon her taxes.

The great headache of her realm was Trigol, a city gov-
erned in the countess's name by a baron. The post had little
to recommend it. Bandit raids, refugees, and civic riots were
rife. The baron's daily life was anything but restful.

The central keep of Trigol served as the administrative
center for the entire southeastern marches. There was a constant traffic of couriers and patrols. Military scouts and
sorcerers came in to file their reports while squads of crossbowmen patrolled the walls. As darkness fell over the city,
the keep sheathed itself in light. With new wars gathering
on the borders, nighttime brought no rest to the hard-
worked garrison.

The keep's main hall had been cleared of its usual clut-
ter of mess tables. A heavy bench stood in the middle of the
hall, and here sat the throne of the baron. The baron himself—a surly, thickset man with a neatly pointed beard—sat
sternly in place, leaning his elbows on the table and glowering at a dozen arguing, shouting men. To give himself
patience, the man drank wine—and had apparently been
drinking ever since the riots a dozen hours before.

Soldiers sat along the table beside priests, scholars, and sorcerers. Cinders lay like a rug in front of the hearth. Two large hunting dogs sat nose to nose with him, staring at him in puzzled amazement and anxiously wagging their tails. As silent as the baron, the Justicar crouched beside the great hall's hearth and fed hot embers to his hell hound skin.

Having set up shop on a side table all her own, Escalla had gathered a choice selection of wines, glazed fruits, and other sticky treats. She ignored the arguments behind her and stuffed her face, occasionally casting an eye at the baron's silver cutlery.

A civil war of apocalyptic proportions was about to grip Trigol. The temples of Geshtai and Bleredd, with their thousands of worshipers, were preaching holy war against each other. The baron had heard their first screams of outrage as each had decried the other's crimes, and now he made a last attempt to enforce a parley.

At the conference table, a high priest of Geshtai faced a high priest of Bleredd, each man staring at the other with a look of unremitting hate. Both men were wealthy refugees from the lost Duchy of Tenh. Fat and gorgeously decked out in robes, rings, jewels, and vestments, they left to their underlings the tasks of screaming threats, hurling invectives, and demanding justice from the baron. Instead, the two priests stared at one another in silence, the air between them shimmering with half-formed spells.

So far, the meeting had been utterly futile. The heralds of the two temples roared at each other almost continuously.

Slamming at the tabletop, the Bleredd representative turned scarlet with outrage and shouted, "War! This time we will wipe Geshtai's sacrilege from the face of the city!" Gold rings encrusting the herald's fists left scars upon the table. "The hammer Whelm has been stolen by agents of Geshtai's temple! We have eyewitnesses who saw Geshtai priests fleeing with the sacred hammer!"

"Lies." The Geshtai herald made up in pure disdain what he lacked in fury. "Piddling lackeys of a third-rate god, they have stolen the trident from our treasury and now invent tales to distract attention from their crime."

This brought about the inevitable fresh burst of anger. Clerks and witnesses from both the temples shouted out their evidence, and the baron could only breathe hard, drink deep, and try to sift evidence from invective. Finally, he hammered on the tabletop with a heavy iron mace, tearing a fresh set of scars on the walnut table. The noise brought no results until the man roared in a voice more used to parade grounds than palaces.

"Shut up!"

An offended silence fell.

"Quiet!" The baron slammed his mace flat upon the conference table. "If neither of you are lying, then you have each raided one another's temples! If both weapons have been stolen, then you are both even."

"Search our treasury!" The Geshtai herald rose, his whole being seething with hate. "Cast scrying spells. You will not find Bleredd's hammer in our halls!"

"They have shielded it from spells!" Bleredd's herald threw open his arms in rage. "Where is justice? If the army will not help us, then the temple will take the law into its own hands!"

The baron leaned forward across the table and said, "Transgressions against the civic peace will not be tolerated. If either of you move against the other's temple, if you riot once again, the city guard will fight you! Both of you will be declared enemies of the state!"

There was a confident sneer from the priests.

"It will take more troops than you have here to take down Bleredd's temple . . . or Geshtai's." The Geshtai herald spewed forth his words like poison. "Will you run whining to the countess, my lord? What will she think of a man who cannot even keep the peace in his own city?"

The baron wrenched his mace up from the table, only to be held in place by a interruption from the far end of the conference room. A young man stood, deliberately blocking the way between the baron and the herald.

"M-my lord? Neither temple may have wronged the other after all."

Seated amongst Trigol's three law officers, young Allain had risen to his feet. He intruded into the midst of the hatred, trying to let reason calm the storm.

"My lords and holinesses, there may be another explanation." The lawman waved a hand at the shaven-headed, scar-faced man who kept well to the far side of the hall. "This man is on a commission from the countess herself. He has an . . . *alternate* solution."

All eyes turned toward the Justicar. The priests slitted their eyes and made a calculating appraisal. The law officers beside Allain shifted uncomfortably in their seats. The priests leaned back in their chairs and did not deign to speak. The Justicar had a grim, monastic simplicity that contrasted starkly with the law officers and priests in their golden robes.

The senior law officer shot a distasteful look toward the Justicar and said, "Who is this . . . *person?*"

The baron poured more wine, took a sip, and said, "He is on direct commission as an agent of the countess of Urnst." He seemed far from happy about this, since it meant that the Justicar was beyond his own jurisdiction. "His credentials are correct."

"Credentials," the lawman sneered. "Why should we place faith in a damned *adventurer?*"

"I doubt if he gives a damn if you do or not." The baron drank. "He doesn't answer to me. He doesn't answer to you. For once, just shut up and listen."

The baron jerked his goblet at the Justicar, signaling him forward. Contemptuous of the priests, lords, and clerks, the ranger arose with a creak of leather armor, striding dark and huge toward the watching men.

"Yesterday we saw a set of illusion spells used to trigger off the riots in the marketplace. An erinyes is in the city. She had control of a soul-eating sword with a black blade."

Priests stiffened, and law officers stirred uncomfortably. The heralds leaned in to conduct whispered, intense conversations with their masters.

Bleredd's herald finally straightened, wiped the palms of his hands against his tunic hem, and spoke. "How . . . how do you know it is an erinyes?"

"I fought it." The Justicar turned toward the herald, his black armor gleaming in the firelight. Behind him, Cinders leaked sulphurous steam. "It was a baatezu, a shapeshifter, a seducer—and it controls a force of human thieves within the city."

The herald hastily waved away the scent of sulphur and said, "So this devil-creature now has our sacred weapons?"

"Unlikely."

The Justicar's own blade caught sparks of firelight, its wolf-skull pommel glittering in the gloom. "The erinyes had her own weapon stolen during the market riot. The thief is a sorcerer of considerable power." The man slowly raised up his hell hound skin and draped it across his helmet and his shoulder blades. "If the temples' sacred weapons are missing, the same culprit is responsible. He boasts that he now holds three weapons for us to retrieve."

The Geshtai herald gave a sour laugh and leaned contemptuously back in his chair. "How you know?"

"I *know.*" The Justicar turned, his face cold and savage beneath the grinning hell hound mask. "He has a date with justice."

The baron held out his goblet as a servant poured more wine. The Justicar drank but did not join the politicians at their table.

"Who else saw this . . . *erinyes?*" the baron asked.

"I did, my lord. Briefly." Allain licked his lips. "And for the past month, there have been . . . occurrences. Bodies of murder victims. Each and every one of them had . . . had lost its soul."

"The erinyes's sword is called Blackrazor." The ranger put in. "It is a soul-eater. The man who stole it from the erinyes was chief of the Sorcerers' Guild library." The big man tossed back his wine. "Your city is breeding maggots."

Far down the table, a clerk cast a disdainful glance at the Justicar.

"An erinyes? Soul stealers? Mysterious wizards?" The clerk set his goblet down with a thump. "A convenient little fantasy concocted by you alone. My lords, you can't seriously be suggesting that we take the word of this *vagabond.*"

The Justicar gave a low, feral growl. His red eyes gleaming, Cinders echoed the noise with a thump-thump-thump of his tail. At this point, Escalla popped into view above the center of the table and briskly clapped her hands like a carnival announcer.

"*Bzzt!* All right, important safety note at this point! Do *not* piss off the Justicar!" The girl rowed backward through the air with her busy wings. "This is a nice room, a flammable room. So, lest we all want a demonstration of the mystic fighting arts, let's at least show *minimal* belief in each others' integrity."

The Bleredd high priest finally deigned to speak. He resettled his golden mitre, spared a scathing glance for Escalla, then turned to face the baron.

"And what is this . . . this winged *thing?*" The man prodded at Escalla with one huge fingertip. "Why is a pixie at this council?"

"Hey, for your information, I *happen* to be a faerie!" Escalla swatted the fat man's hand. "And no one touches the faerie!"

"What's the difference?"

"We have cuter butts!" With a sudden flash, Escalla provided herself with illusory scholar's robes. "Now, just to recap: We have a new theory on these thefts, and it has the added bonus of avoiding internecine war."

A temple clerk glared at the faerie, leaned back in his chair, and folded up his arms. "So to corroborate this . . . Justicar's story, we are relying upon a pixie?" The man gave a sour laugh. "What do you take us for?"

Escalla popped out of her illusions and bent over in her leathers, slapping at her athletic little rear. "Faerie, bright boy! See that lift and clench? That's faerie derriere! Read it and weep!"

The baron seemed tired of the whole business. Taking another drink, he gave a sharp, annoyed hiss and flung himself back into the depths of his throne.

"It's absurd that Blackrazor could ever have been here." The baron shook his head briskly, dismissing the whole idea. "To have Whelm, Wave, and Blackrazor all together in one city again is an unlikely circumstance."

The Justicar lifted up his head. He seemed to be in a poor humor. "This has happened before?"

"These three weapons were all stolen once before. At that time, they were stored in the City of Greyhawk." The baron waved a hand as though brushing the thought away. "A wizard stole them. Some adventurers got them back. It was all a few years before the wars."

Escalla lounged in the middle of the table, ostentatiously made herself comfortable and gave a weary sigh.

"Oooh, I can see this one coming from a mile off. Please, do tell the details."

The baron merely drank more wine.

One of his scholars cleared his throat, decided that this was the perfect time to assert himself, and assumed a pedantic tone. "The hammer Whelm, the trident Wave, and the sword Blackrazor resided in the City of Greyhawk once. The weapons were stolen by the wizard Keraptis, who sought to demonstrate his superiority over local heroes by placing the weapons at the center of a maze and daring one and all to come and take them." The scholar shrugged. "A powerful sorcerer, but a man of somewhat childish proclivities."

Focused upon his mission, the Justicar finally found himself a chair, turned it the wrong way about, and sat down. In the hours since the riots, he had spoken long with the local law officers. Trigol's librarian had held his position for only three years, having come here from Greyhawk some time before. The man had settled in Trigol, had finished what he came for, and now had fled. The librarian had to be found. Thus far, the only lead was the librarian's fixation on the legend of Keraptis.

The Justicar leaned his chin upon his folded hands. "Tell me about Keraptis."

"Ah." The scholar pulled at his nose with a superior air. "Thirteen hundred years ago, Keraptis was one of the region's major sorcerers, a genius, though quite power mad. He ruled a considerable empire, slowly draining the lands with greed. He had some rather absurd theories about absorbing the essence of others to enhance his own abilities. When he began to butcher his subjects for the purpose of massed human sacrifice, the people revolted. He escaped— and there we lose him." The scholar shrugged. "He disappeared for an entire millennium. Then for reasons unknown, he returned ten years ago to Greyhawk to conduct the theft of three magic weapons: Whelm, Wave, and Blackrazor."

Jus poured himself more wine and said, "Legend said he died years ago."

"Rumors of his death seem to have been somewhat precipitous." The scholar steepled his fingertips. "However, he was quite definitely slain during the Greyhawk wars in a battle seven years ago. He was decapitated by a vorpal blade while fighting as an ally of Iuz."

The Justicar fixed the other man with his dire gaze and asked, "Where is the body?"

"It was destroyed." The scholar raised one eyebrow in a superior little air. "This is no mere story. It is history! There are definite relics of the event. A lock of Keraptis's hair is encased in a crystal cylinder and kept in our own library's vaults."

Escalla clapped her hands and leaped importantly up onto her feet. "All right, let us take it as fact that the big K is deader than a dwarven fashion plate, but we *do* still have a crime! Your librarian has already told J-man and myself that he wants us to retrieve three weapons in some kind of weird little test he's set for us. So let us assume that your librarian has already raced off with your toys and put them in hiding somewhere."

The senior law officer opened out his hands and said, "Why?"

"Because your librarian has a real thing about Keraptis!" The faerie circled her fingertips madly beside her skull. "This guy likes to *read* about Keraptis, *write* about Keraptis—now he even dresses up as Keraptis! Call it a wild guess, but maybe he even wants to *be* Keraptis!"

The high priest of Bleredd sank down into the collar of his robes and thought.

Beside him, the temple's herald mused then said, "Why would anyone seek to copy a dead sorcerer?"

"Because he's a loon!" Escalla flung open her hands. "This guy has a *serious* Keraptis fixation! Maybe he wants to recreate the big K's greatest joke? Maybe he wants to go one better and out do the guy?" The faerie gave a shrug. "Maybe the guy really is Keraptis? Who knows?"

"Keraptis *cannot* return." The baron's scholar rapped his knuckles on the tabletop. "His remains were destroyed and cannot be reanimated. To clone the wizard, someone would need a sample from his actual body."

Escalla gave a nasty little snort. "You mean like a lock of Keraptis's hair? Like the one in your library's vaults? The library where our sorcerer worked for the past few years? *Think*, people!"

Several of the priests turned pale and began an embarrassed study of the tabletop before them. The senior priests simply seethed.

With Cinders's hide rippling sheer black upon his back, the Justicar turned to face one of the hall's painted walls. A mural of the entire continent gleamed and glittered in the lamplight. Allain joined him and stared at the painted plains and hills.

The Justicar glared at the wall as though sheer force of will could project him at his prey. "Where were the weapons taken the last time they disappeared?"

"Here." The lawman pointed to a position almost three hundred miles to the north. "White Plume Mountain, a volcano on an ash plain. It's a wasteland now. The bandit kingdoms there were annihilated during the war with Iuz. We're trying to repopulate the zone with colonies."

The mountain marked on the map was well past the northern borders of the County of Urnst. It adjoined the region of new settlements, the regions that relied upon wagon trains for food and winter clothes. The Justicar stared at the map, then settled his black sword, already planning his route.

"This was a stronghold of Keraptis?"

"Extensive. The first exploring party hardly scratched the surface."

The Justicar grunted as he ran a hand across the map. White Plume Mountain was dangerously close to the settlements that were reseeding the wilderness. If the librarian was setting up the mountain as his kingdom, then the colonies would be a danger to him—too many eyes to see, too many troops out on patrol. . . . The raids on the supply convoys were finally explained.

"He's at White Plume Mountain. He's been trying to depopulate the nearby border to keep newcomers away. Keraptis may have left considerable relics there that he intends to exploit." The ranger's deep voice drove through the facts one by one. "Yet he has now almost deliberately revealed himself. Why?"

A priest hissed petulantly from the conference table. "This is all merely supposition! There is no proof that this librarian-wizard ever took Wave and Whelm!"

"The first step is to search White Plume Mountain." The Justicar turned away from the gigantic map. "If the weapons are found and returned, then your proof is there. You will have no further cause to threaten war against each other's temples."

Bleredd's high priest looked up sharply and said, "You propose to find the weapons?"

"I propose to bring this librarian to justice for crimes against the innocent." Huge and sinister, the Justicar seemed to breathe in the scent of prey. "In White Plume Mountain, I can find him."

Escalla flicked a look between the map and the Justicar, then tried to drag the man away. "It's been a long day, and my friend here is a little tired. C'mon, Jus. Time for bed!"

Jus glared at the girl and said, "We're going. The librarian must be brought to justice, and Whelm and Wave must be recovered to prevent a civil war."

Escalla whirred close to whisper frantically in the Justicar's ear. "Are you crazy? That dungeon was specifically designed as a hero-trap! It's a damned fortress!"

Ignoring the faerie, the baron sat back and folded up his arms in thought. "We will not entrust such a mission to a single ranger. We will need to send a team to represent all

interests in this matter. Geshtai and Bleredd shall each provide a priest as an observer. From my own garrison, I will
send a sorcerer, a paladin, and at least one archer to provide
you with proper fighting power." The baron laid his hands
flat upon the table, glaring at the assembled men. "Whelm
and Wave are all that matters. The other thefts this man has
done are of no consequence to me."

From across the table, Escalla's tall ears pricked like a
rabbit's. "*Other* thefts?"

"He has absconded with the library treasury of over
eighteen thousand nobles, as well as wands, jewels, relics,
magical scrolls, potions, and spellbooks."

With a noise like a crossbow bolt, Escalla shot through
the air, landed on her stomach in front of the baron and
batted her long lashes. Her artless smile had more teeth
than a shark.

"And these would be in your 'spoils of war, finders-keep-
ers category,' yes?"

"The state would requite a thirty-three percent tax upon
all such profits."

"Which as good servants of the state, we'll report to you
with unfailing accuracy!" Escalla raced back to Jus, hovered
above the hell hound's ears and polished the animal's black
nose with a rag. "Mister Baron, we are on the job one hundred percent at your command! My boys guarantee deliv-
ery!"

Geshtai's priest rolled his head to gaze at the girl and
said, "Why should we tolerate these filthy interlopers?"

The ranger stepped forward, his hand on the pommel of
his sword. This time the Justicar was clearly going to decap-
itate the priest. Winging brightly down to save the day,
Escalla blocked his path by happily shaking the baron's
hand.

"M'learned colleague here wishes to thank the county, city,
and municipality of Trigol for their kind offer of assistance

in his attempts to bring this dangerous thief to justice. My *goodness* but he'd like to thank you for your kind interest! Is a start tomorrow morning too early for you?"

The baron emptied another wine goblet and shoved the empty cup out for more. He glared at the priests in absolute contempt. "This man has a commission from the countess. This man has fought and killed along that border for the best part of a decade. The party would all be dead men without an experienced ranger. You are entering a region blanketed by Iuz's patrols and all sorts of lordless banditry. Do what he tells you. Once you cross the river into enemy territory, the party will be under his command."

Slurping wine, the baron pushed up from his chair. He ignored his visitors as priests, clerks, and scholars all stood to their feet.

"We will also offer you a guide, an experienced trail-blazer who is willing to guide the party into the Bandit Kingdoms." The baron snapped his fingers. "Summon him. Priests, bring your men. Plan your journey tonight. The recovery team leaves at dawn."

Men bowed as the baron, his wine jug, and his goblet all retired from the hall. Priests glared at one another then swept from the keep to summon their agents. Escalla brightly waved them all good-bye then helped herself to the largest remaining jug of wine.

"So, Jus, we dodge in, we flit out. We grab the treasure and run!" The faerie gave a great, expressive shrug. "What could be simpler?"

Sitting down at the abandoned table, the Justicar helped himself to wine, roast kid, and bread. "I don't like it. He knows we are coming. He *wants* us to come. For some reason, the librarian wants us in his lair."

Lair! Cinders grinned his big white grin. *Cinders sniff! Fire burn! Kill!*

Blissfully happy, Escalla raised her wine in a toast. "See? Cinders has it. Couldn't be simpler!" The faerie reclined on the table and helped herself to a large chunk of the Justicar's food. "Look, take it from me—adventuring is all just a matter of bringing the right talents to bear. We've got these Trigol City rubes for monster fodder, we've got you two guys for muscle, and *me* for brains! We've even got a guide!" The girl lay on her back and scissored her long legs in a twinkle of pure glee. "It's perfect! What could possibly go wrong?"

A soldier opened a door across the hall and admitted a new visitor. Striding happily into the room, the party's guide took one look at his new companions and brayed for joy.

"It's you, son! So there you are, finished skulking at last!"

The Justicar jackknifed forward, almost choking on his wine. Brimming with joy, Polk the teamster whacked the big man across his hell hound-covered shoulders. "We've got a job, son! You and me! There's a real adventure to be done. Real work, not this *investigation* stuff you waste your time on. A dungeon—now *that's* where a hero should be! You stick with me, son, and I'll make you a hero despite yourself!" Polk leaned to whisper loudly in Escalla's ear. "We gotta talk him up, give him confidence. Poor kid wouldn't know a portent from a portable hole."

Escalla looked up at Jus and gave the man a big smile. Polk reached for the wine and poured drinks for all, throwing arms about all three of his adopted friends.

"Here's to adventure! The stuff of legends and the spice of life!" Polk stuffed a beef bone between Cinders's jaws. "Drink, son, drink! We're off to make history!"

With a heavy sigh, the Justicar surrendered to his fate. By the time he finished the wine jug, the world had still steadfastly refused to improve.

In the gray hours before dawn, the baron's castle lay sleeping. Sentries leaned on the battlements while guard dogs snoozed. In the stables, a few yawning milkmaids and grooms stumbled about the first of the day's chores.

Cinders grinned happily, his teeth set and his eyes gleaming. Splayed on her belly in an old cot, Escalla made peaceful, ecstatic little noises as she clutched onto her bed. Jus had been tramping in and out of the room for almost half an hour, noisily getting ready for the journey. Escalla was aware that he was trying to wake her and perversely decided to remain exactly where she was.

An earth-shattering crash of metal, leather, and junk shuddered through the floorboards. Jus had deliberately dropped his armor and weapons belt right beside Escalla's bed. Escalla hugged the bed, finally lifting an eye up out of the blankets.

"Is there any particular reason why you can't just relax the way other people do?"

"We leave in three hours." Jus was noisily beginning his daily task of attending to the edge of his sword. After this would come exercises, armor maintenance, and breakfast. "We have to pack."

Escalla gave a mighty yawn. "Face it, man. There is nothing to pack. It all fits in one backpack."

Jus spread Cinders out across his bed and brushed the happy hell hound's fur. He shot a dire glance at Escalla, who still remained steadfastly in bed.

"Escalla, what are you doing?"

"I'm lying naked on an ermine fur blanket." The girl gave a happy wriggle. "What does it look like?"

Jus looked at her in confusion. "Why?"

"You know, you have *got* to loosen up more." The faerie sat up. "All right, I'm up! The world is saved! Show me a map of where we're going, and I'll try to find where breakfast is kept." The girl stretched again, showing a fine set of little white teeth. "Hey, Cinders, how's my favorite flaming pooch?"

Happy! Good smells. Pretty faerie!

"Cinders, you're a gem!"

Jus hefted his rawhide armor into place and jerked the fastenings tight. His suspicious eye glared at the little faerie as he said, "Where did you get an ermine skin?"

"Mrs. Baron lent it to me." Escalla sat up naked in bed and stretched luxuriously. "It's her best coat."

" 'Lent'?"

"In a sense. It was only for a night!" Escalla shook out her clothes and began getting dressed. "Faerie dust adds luster, man. Everyone knows that!"

The Justicar deliberately busied himself with his back turned to Escalla as the faerie wriggled into her skirt. Tying herself in, Escalla flitted through the air to hang above her friend's shoulder, looking down at the documents he had spread out across the tabletop.

"So partner, where's this map?"

"Here. It's a long march." Jus pointed to the painted lines scrawled all over his map. "River, canyon, here's the volcano—easy to spot, has a permanent steam cloud above it."

"Do we know what the labyrinth is like?"

"No maps of it." Jus folded the map and stuffed it carelessly into his backpack. "Maybe in Greyhawk, but we don't have the time."

"Hey, I'm game!" Escalla flew over to the door and struggled with the latch, laboring to swing the portal open.

"When in doubt, we send a priest down each corridor first. We'll find this trident and hammer, stop the civil war, kick the librarian's ass—simple!" The girl hovered happily, fluttering her wings.

"Come on," the Justicar growled, "let's eat."

Jus carried his backpack outside while Escalla followed her nose past the garrison kitchens and out into the officer's mess. Someone had thoughtfully laid out a breakfast of kippers, bacon, scrambled eggs, and strawberry tart for the baron. Escalla whistled happily as she cast a floating disk spell and absconded with the entire meal, plates and all, not forgetting the salt.

She found Jus sitting by a little flowerbed behind the stables. Escalla spread breakfast upon an old horse rug and settled herself down to a double helping of tart.

"A farewell breakfast, compliments of the baron. Dig in!"

Sniffing in puzzlement at the food, Jus sat down, oversalted his eggs, and began to eat. Escalla made herself comfortable on his knee and helped herself to anything and everything edible in sight. Cinders sucked on a kipper's tail, his red eyes gleaming above his eternal manic grin.

Thoughtfully breaking a piece of crisp bacon, Jus looked down at the faerie and said, "So you just found this?"

"Hey! No one said not to take it!"

The big man glowered. "I despair about you."

"Hey, we're partners." Escalla passed the man a large slice of tart. "Now eat up, and keep your eyes open."

Dawn stole across the castle yard. In the stables, Polk could be heard loudly advising a priest on how to say his morning prayers. A tall man armored in silver plate came out of the castle to stand beside an archer and a sorcerer, who were loitering around the stables. Watching the gathering of their new allies, both Jus and Escalla laid aside their meal and shared identical thoughts.

Jus settled his sword and said, "I'll watch your back."

"Same back at you." The girl flicked her wings and drifted off the ground. "Are we ready?"

"We're ready."

Ready!

The faerie heaved a sigh, headed out into the dawn, and said, "All right. Well, we're on the road to fame and glory."

❉   ❉   ❉   ❉   ❉

"You see, son, *determination*—that's the mark of a real hero. Grit! Stick-to-it-ness! The ability to look like you mean business!" Sitting happily atop his wagon, Polk left the driving to an assistant wagoner. Now that he was an official guide, he liked to leave himself free to talk and advise. *"Presence* is the first impact you make on an enemy. So one thing we have to work on is your image!"

Marching grimly beside the lead wagon, the Justicar gritted his teeth and tried to ignore Polk's constant monologue. Cinders failed to help matters. The hell hound kept his ears pricked up and his tail wagging, perfectly happy with the sights and smells of the road.

Sitting above his companions and behaving like a lord of creation, Polk took a drag from a stone jug full of whiskey. On the wagons behind him were arrayed two priests with their tents, baggage, portable altars, and relics; a lordly paladin encased in solid silver armor; and a close-mouthed pair of men from the baron's garrison. Three large wagons were rumbling along a ruined, broken roadway behind them, each carrying enough supplies to see an army through a thirty years' war.

Even this close to Trigol, the land still showed ghosts of battle. The skeletal shapes of farmhouses and villages jutted through the weeds, and wild grasses still followed the boundaries of long-forgotten fields. Only the bones were missing. The slaughtered had found no rest. Even now, their corpses toiled in the armies of Iuz, preparing for yet another war. Wind moaned through the wild oats beside a broken well.

Oblivious to the grim surroundings, Polk dragged in a breath of fresh morning air and gave a happy sigh. "Image, son! A hero has to have image." Polk corked his jug. "A clear-cut presence! A blazing eye! You ask the faerie, she'll back me!"

The faerie in question was lounging on the back of one of the great, hairy cart horses. No one could ever accuse Escalla of having a lack of personality. She reclined on her back eating wild strawberries taken from the fields, her toes wriggling happily inside her boots as she enjoyed the day. She rolled to watch Jus and gave the man a knowing smile.

"Hey, Jus! Bearing up?"

"The wagons are too slow." Jus seethed with annoyance at being made to cater to so much useless baggage. "Tomorrow we start to lose the roads."

"Yeah, well, enjoy it while we can." Escalla dipped strawberries in a little bowl of sugar crystals. "The muckity-mucks aren't going to give up their beds and bangles until they have to."

The two priests kept to their own wagons—watching one another, watching the road, and trying to prevent each other from speaking to the other party members. The baron's sorcerer carefully spied on the archer, and the archer kept a cold watch over the paladin. A whole day of march had passed without introductions, without chatter. Polk and Escalla filled the vacuum with a will. Casting an appraising gaze over her fellow travelers, Escalla sat up and hunted for the last few sugar crystals in her bowl.

"Well, this crew is just a laugh an hour!" Escalla tossed a strawberry up to Polk, who gave her a salute. "Polk's really hoopy, though! Where did you find him?"

Jus felt himself bristling like an angry hound. "I didn't. There's just no getting rid of him."

With his head up in the sun and his tail trailing in the breeze, Cinders gave a dry, sniggering little laugh. *Polk-man funny!*

Jus gave an irritated sigh then looked back along the caravan. Three full wagons—tons of supplies—and none of it could possibly be taken into the wilds. He felt a delicious surge of malice as he anticipated a future full of wails and cries.

Escalla flew up from her perch on the cart horse, whirring between the big animal's ears. She looped up and hovered, staring back along the line of wagons. Jus joined her, standing to watch the heavy vehicles rock and rumble slowly past them.

The Geshtai had sent a priestess on the expedition— a fat, powerful woman with cold eyes and a wealth of chins. Beneath her fish-patterned robes, bangles, and vestments of the river god, there came the gleam of metal armor, weapons, and charms. The big priestess sat in a nest of cushions and religious paraphernalia, spending her entire day keeping the Bleredd priest under surveillance.

Small, sharp-featured, and strangely weasel-like, the Bleredd priest wove subtle little spells to spy upon his rival—spells instantly countered by the Geshtai. The contest had kept them occupied in deadly earnest ever since the journey began at dawn.

Escalla gave a shiver, as though casting off the evil eye. "Lovely bunch we have here."

"Skilled killers." Jus shrugged his backpack into a better position. "The two priests are field agents. The Geshtai is a slaver, and the Bleredd priest is from Urnst—not a refugee from Tenh." The Justicar watched Escalla slyly appraising the other party members as they rolled by. "Our sorcerer is an ice mage. The paladin is called Olthwaite. The archer is Hanin. We were supposed to have an archer named Barkis, but he was stabbed in a tavern about an hour after he was assigned to us."

"Wow!" Escalla hovered in midair, her little fists planted on her hips a she surveyed the wagon train. "These guys haven't spoken to us all day. How did you pick all that up?"

"I talked to the baron's men." Jus gave a righteous sniff. "What did you think I was doing all last night?"

"I dunno. Ranger stuff?" Escalla shrugged, honestly confused. "Hey, man, I got my beauty sleep. *One* of us has to think about her complexion."

With the wagons finally passed, Jus walked into the pitted dirt roadway and crossed into the abandoned fields. He climbed up an overgrown apple tree, looked out across the wild hedges, and scanned for movement in the ruins of a farmhouse nearby. He let Cinders sniff the breeze, then tugged a trio of ripe apples from the bough. One he polished and tossed to Escalla, one he ate for himself, and the third he stuffed between Cinders's jaws. The hellhound grinned his mad grin, looking a little like a suckling pig as the apple gleamed between his teeth.

Jus looked at Escalla and gave a little shrug. "He likes them."

The ranger crunched his apple and slid to the ground. Escalla joined him, puzzling over how to eat the apple, which was far too large for her to sink her teeth into.

"So, Jus, you think the archer guy is a spy?"

"I think they're all spies." Jus glared at the departing wagons. "They're each on their own side, not ours."

"So should I do something?" Escalla passed Jus her apple. He scored the fruit with his nails and split it in two.

"I could fireball them all."

Burn! Burn paladin! Burn paladin! The hell hound's tail thumped against Jus's back.

The Justicar thought about the options, then heaved an irritated sigh and walked on in the wake of the wagons.

"No. The baron's been useful. We'd just be pushing Trigol closer to civil war. We'll leave them alone . . . for now."

Escalla cocked a sly eye at the Justicar. "Even Polk?"

"No. Him you have my personal permission to fireball."

*   *   *   *   *

Happily bathing in a copper cooking pot of scented water, Escalla whistled as she rubbed the soles of her pretty pink feet with a sandstone. Cinders's white fangs and baleful fires stood on watch above, covering Escalla's rear. The faerie gave a delicious sigh and relaxed back into the hot water, listening to the noises drifting on the nighttime breeze.

Polk followed the Justicar as he wandered about the camp, trying to bring the ranger to the path of proper thinking.

"Son, now I only say this because I really like you. Have you ever considered the advantages of dressing in white?"

"White?" This time Jus stopped in annoyance. "I'd stand out like dog's balls!"

"But that's the point—you don't hide, son! It's an invitation to attack! It's daring your enemies to try their blades against a champion of good."

Jus gave a snort. "How white will your robes be after a day on the march?"

"Now that's just mundanity. Son, my point is that a hero doesn't waste time with skulking." Polk gave a regal sniff. "Sir Olthwaite wears white."

"Yeah. His order bleaches cloth by soaking it for about a

year in urine." Jus seemed to be enjoying himself. "If you're talking to the paladin, I'd suggest you stay upwind."

Jus wandered off into the darkened scrub in an effort to get rid of the teamster, but Polk followed doggedly.

Escalla laughed. Jus was the heart and soul of diplomacy, just as ever. Rising from her tub, Escalla wrapped a towel about her middle, tucked it in tight, then wrung out her long golden hair and shook out her wet locks in the breeze.

"All right, pooch, blow!"

Blow!

The hell hound shot a stream of hot air from his muzzle, and Escalla hung her glorious hair in its path, spreading it out to dry.

As she worked her hairbrush, the faerie sang a song as she stood in the warm breeze. A slight tinge of sulphur was more than compensated for by sheer convenience. The girl threw back her hair, heaved a sigh . . . and then heard a twig break in the bushes at her back.

Escalla streaked sideways, a fireball already crackling in her hand. Dazed by her speed, the Bleredd priest squatted on the ground and raised his hands to shield himself from the blast. About to roast the man, Escalla bristled with fury, clinging tight to her damp towel.

"All right! What the hell do you want?"

With his head hunched forward at the neck just like a ferret, the priest moved his hands up and down, trying to placate the angry girl.

"To talk, to greet a comrade, to introduce." The man sank into a seated position, trying to make himself small and non-threatening. "I want nothing—merely a chance to say hello."

"Well, hello." Escalla let her hand drop slightly, the fireball still half-formed between her fingers. "I was getting dressed."

"Forgive me, dear forest princess, for this intrusion. I came out of worry—that is, out of *concern*." The priest folded his hands. "Concern for your companion the Justicar."

Her pointed ears lifted suspiciously, and Escalla raised one eyebrow. "Concern?"

"Your companion the Justicar . . ." The priest tilted his head like an animal coming at a problem. "For a man of his *devotion*, he seems strangely . . . impoverished."

Oh, this ought to be great! Escalla clapped her hands together and wore her most innocent face.

"Well, he's a special kind of guy. As long as he gets his head shaved once a month, he's happy."

"Yes . . . which I why I wished to ask for your advice."

The Bleredd priest no longer wore his armor, but a heavy warhammer still stuck its savage head through his belt. The man subtly moved to cover the brutal weapon with his sleeve.

"My temple is interested in furthering the cause of justice, perhaps even establishing a permanent corps of peace-keepers and investigators." The priest tilted his head. "Your friend would be the one man who could provide us with the proper guidance . . . for a suitable consulting fee, of course."

Escalla nodded sagely and looked duly serious. "Oh, of course!" The girl made a sorrowful noise. "But he really doesn't care so very much about money."

"Yes, therein lies our problem." The priest fixed a cool eye upon Escalla. "But *you* could perhaps persuade him to accept such a sum. He could then perhaps donate it to a worthy cause."

"Oh, *very* worthy!" Escalla fluttered her wings, the pure soul of innocence. "Or you could simply pay me, and *I* could handle all those details myself."

"And use your influence to guide him." The priest opened his hands. "You see? We are in agreement!"

Escalla kept herself well out of reach and nodded. "Oh, absolutely!"

"An alliance like this is all the stronger the sooner it begins." The priest made a pass with his hands, and an image of gold, jewels, and gems gleamed in the dark. "I'm sure you can now see that there are advantages to the two of you linking forces with Bleredd's temple . . . and with me." The man made illusory gemstones gleam. "When do you think we can begin our alliance?"

Escalla drew a big breath and put on a thoughtful face, hovering in midair.

"Hmm . . . yes . . . oooh . . ." The girl weighed time and schedules in her head. "Um, how's about when winged monkeys fly from my butt!" Escalla made a face and snapped her fingers at the priest. "Nice try, creepy boy, but I've got plans for a treasure all of my own!" The girl tucked her towel tight. "And I really, *really* suggest you don't try bothering J-man and me again."

The priest rose angrily and reached out to grab Escalla by the arm. She whirled, and suddenly a black sword flashed out from the night to hover beneath the priest's throat. The Justicar loomed in the darkness, his huge blade gleaming as it quivered just short of the priest's jugular.

"No one touches the faerie."

The ranger pushed the priest away with the tip of his sword, using the same distaste he would use to remove a piece of tainted meat. Stumbling, the priest backed away, gripped his hammer, then turned and marched off into the night.

Escalla coldly watched the priest leave, tucked in her towel, and flicked the spellfire from her fingertips.

"Thanks, man."

"No problem." The Justicar sheathed his sword with his usual fluid grace. "You weren't interested in a bribe?"

"Hey, I'm greedy, but I'm not dumb. As if they'd pay

anyone with anything other than a foot of steel between the shoulder blades!" The girl stooped to pick up her fallen hairbrush. "But, hey, as far as corruption of the innocent goes, these guys have really got an awful lot to learn."

13

After long days of travel, the party was leaving the last vestiges of safety behind. They had slept at one of the northern settlements and had been on the move before dawn. Now at long last they had entered enemy terrain, and the Justicar could forge ahead to the work at hand.

Enemy country was no laughing matter. Walking up the steep northern bank of the Artonsamay River, the Justicar slowly sank down amidst the weeds until he disappeared from view. Slithering forward in utter silence, he stared through the grasses into an alien land.

Years before, these plains had belonged to the Bandit Kingdoms. Petty warlords had lived here as brigands, raiding and reaving into the neighboring lands. Border patrols had fought bitter campaigns to keep the river lines clear, turning the region into a perpetual battlefield. With the coming of the Greyhawk Wars, however, all had changed. The Bandit Kingdoms had disintegrated under the onslaught of Iuz, and what few remained were no more than a sham, slave pits to Iuz and a refuge for the damned.

Wilderness had reclaimed the sparse few settlements. Where villages had stood, now only broken and burned skeletons of the once-proud halls lay stark against the sky. Where wagons had brought merchants and migrants, now there was only skittish wildlife and the occasional desperate bandit.

Near the river where the party waited, there was only the hollow buzz of flies and skeletal black bees.

This near the realm of Iuz, caution and skill divided the living from the dead. Taking no chances, the Justicar lay perfectly still, sensing the shift and stir of a hostile world. Before him, the undulating ground was covered knee deep in autumn grass, which looked gray and withered as if somehow drained of life. The gray stalks washed back and forth like an ocean in the breeze, sending ripples chasing far out toward the hills. Any trees on the land were restricted to scattered copses, but the nearest of these were over a mile away.

The sight would have been beautiful had it not been so dangerous. The motion of the grass could hide scouts and ambushers. The ranger stared toward the north where a distant volcano lifted plumes of thin white steam toward the clouds.

Cinders scanned the terrain with a nose sensitive to magic and eyes sensitive to heat. Tall canine ears lifted, and his tail slowly waved. After five long minutes, the hell hound finally seemed satisfied. His voice drifted ever-cheerful into Jus's mind.

Bones stood here. Gone now.

"How long ago?"

One sleep old.

The Justicar shifted position, moving almost without disturbing the grass. Soil had been disturbed on the crest of the riverbank beside him, and the footprints had been hazed over with a film of morning dew. Thin foot bones had left their shape across the grass, marking the tread of skeletal feet.

With a *pop*, Escalla appeared at his side. The little faerie lay flat and quiet in the grass, whispering cautiously into the breeze. "How's it going?"

"It looks clear." The Justicar could see nothing, yet it seemed unlikely that the border would be left unguarded for long. "Bring them across quickly. Tell them to shed anything they can't carry for eighty miles. We'll be travelling fast."

"Should we wait for dark?"

"We can't see in the dark. Most monsters can." The ranger turned awkwardly on his elbow to look back across the river. "And tell those priests we're keeping low. I'll kill any horse that so much as puts a foot across the shore."

The river made a dull, iron gray barrier between the living kingdoms and the dead. On the far side, blowing their cover with the twinkle of metal armor and silver swords, the rest of the party was trying to catch sight of the Justicar. Escalla looked at the fools as they tried to hide themselves, gave a sniff of professional disdain, then turned invisible and whirred away to deliver her messages.

Wagons had brought the party this far—wagons laden with food, tents, and all the luxuries required by paladins and priests. Encumbered by metal armor, shields, two-handed swords, bows, arrows, and spare bowstrings, the party made each day's travel into an enormous labor. They shot hurtful looks at the carefree faerie and the Justicar, who traipsed happily along in each other's company and made do with the simplest of gear.

But now that they were across the river, the party came under the Justicar's command. As the priests were instructed to abandon their equipment, a chorus of outraged voices drifted across the river. Two priests tried to cling to their horses, feeling that walking would be beneath their dignity. Unfortunately, out here on the plains a mounted man could be seen at twice the distance of a pedestrian. Escalla solved the problem by hosing the area with her favorite stinking cloud spell, instantly throwing horses, mules, servants, and wagons into a stampede away from the waterside.

Much to the Justicar's annoyance, Polk the teamster was still very much in evidence. Polk had skillfully assembled a raft from inflated skins to ferry the party members two by two. Both the Geshtai and the Bleredd priests insisted on being the first to cross, yet neither one deigned to help Polk with paddling the raft.

Rising from the weeds, Jus met the raft as it arrived and used his sword to hold it back from the shore.

"Robes off."

The priests—one male and one female—both swelled in indignation.

"These are the vestments of our station," said the Bleredd priest.

"We walk twenty miles each day. I won't slow my pace to suit your fashion needs."

Swathed in heavy brocaded robes and hung with collars, mitres, gold, and jewels, the two priests were poorly dressed for hiking. Polk hooted in glee as the two priests cursed and stripped away their vestments, each of them glaring at the Justicar in hate. Finally, they were left stripped down to just armor: suits of mail and plate.

"You pixie has chased away my pack mule," said the Geshtai priestess. "What am I to do for a tent?"

"Use a ground sheet," the Justicar answered tersely. "Your tents weigh too much."

The raft returned across the stream to pick up more travelers. As Polk poled away and sang a bawdy song, the Justicar sorted through a pile of equipment left on the shore and made a sour face.

"What's this?"

"Adventuring equipment." Bleredd's priest was short, weedy, and suspicious. He came complete with a suit of plate armor. "I am a professional."

The man had brought ropes, cords, parchment, a ten-foot pole, iron spikes, silver mirrors, lanterns, oil, holy water . . .

With a snort, the Justicar ignored the whole matter. It would all end up scattered behind the party after the first two miles. Jus's main worry was that it would leave a trail that an enemy could follow.

Popping into view and flying merrily across the river, Escalla invited herself over to inspect the equipment pile. She saw the huge mound of gear and instantly clasped her hands against her heart.

"Ooooh, *real* adventurers! Professionals at last!" Escalla rooted happily through the equipment pile. "Here's a question: just what exactly *is* the ten-foot pole for?"

"I would not expect a mere pixie to understand."

"Fine, fine! Just ring a little warning bell when you decide to use it, and I'll be there to watch." The faerie did a back flip through the air and hovered before the Justicar's eyes. "This is going to be more colorful than I thought."

The raft delivered two more men—the paladin resplendent in silver plate mail and a tall, cadaverous sorcerer rattling with wooden bandoliers of spell components—both from the baron's guard. The sorcerer labored up the shore. He looked across the landscape without the slightest bit of interest, seeming more concerned with taking an inventory of his magical charms.

Reaching the high ground, Sir Olthwaite the paladin struck a typical pose, leaning on his sword to survey the land.

Cinders's hackles rose, and the hell hound gave an evil mental growl. *Burn . . .*

"Not yet." The Justicar walked past the paladin. "Dump the armor. We're marching twenty miles a day."

Touching a scented handkerchief to his nose, Sir Olthwaite decided to ignore such uncouth suggestions.

"No need. I am used to hardship."

The Justicar never answered. His dark glance at the man's velvet cloak and silver armor spoke far more than words. Cinders gave another warning growl, and Jus reached up to pat the hell hound on the skull.

"Just do your job and stay away from my dog."

Cinders gave an unvocalized little growl. The hell hound's sinister appearance was enough to send most casual bystanders into retreat, but it appeared that the paladin was made of sterner stuff. He gave the hell hound a thoughtful look then simply walked away.

Rattling with quivers and sheathed in a swelteringly hot armor of plate and mail, the baron's archer looked suspiciously about the shoreline as he slicked back the black oily rat-tails of his hair. Avoiding the Justicar, the man made his own scan of the grasslands, keeping an arrow knocked to his heavy bow.

The Justicar looked away. His new allies had causes, none of which interested him. They wore equipment too heavy for the march, too noisy for stealth, and too clumsy for speed. Hating the encumbrance of his companions, Jus waved a hand to Escalla as she reappeared over the last raft load of goods. Much to Jus's annoyance, Polk the teamster stepped off the raft, unshipped the last supplies, and showed no inclination of returning to Trigol.

Polk's arrival was sealed by the man happily taking out an enormous stone jug of whiskey and slinging it like a back-pack across his shoulders. Seething, Jus felt his own foul temper rise to the boil.

As the teamster approached with a huge grin, the ranger simply looked at him and said, "Go away."

"Go and leave you? Cut you off without a guide?" Polk clipped a long hose to his belt. The ingenious arrangement apparently allowed him to sip from the whiskey jug as he walked. "Now see. That's what I'm talking about. Can't be done, not heroic. I'll have to educate by example."

With a strangled sound of frustration, Jus stomped off into the weeds. He checked his own light travel goods for comfort and was silencing the last tiny creaks and clanks as Escalla came whirring happily through the air.

"Hey, J-man, we moving out?"

"Time to go." The party tagging in their wake would slow them down. Jus was more than a tad annoyed by it all. "I'll lead these idiots as we march."

"Great! And I'll buzz around and check out the trail ahead. If you want, I can go invisible for half an hour and zoom up high to look for trouble."

"You can't stay invisible longer than that?"

"I told you, it itches and it gives me dandruff!" Standing on a hummock, the girl held out a long streamer of pure golden hair. "Look at this stuff, softer than a virgin's kiss." Escalla whirred her wings and rose into the air. "Hey, I'm two feet tall. Who'd set a trap for a wee flying girl?"

She began to whirr off into the weeds.

The Justicar gave a little frown and called out, "Be careful!"

"All right! All right!"

"Come back every fifteen minutes so I can see you're alive."

The girl looked back in annoyance. "No problem!"

"Right." Jus loosened his sword in its sheath. "And scream if you see anything!"

"I got it." Escalla hovered, her fists planted on her hips. "You know, I already *have* a mother."

"Does she know you dress like that?"

"Get bent!" The faerie dusted off her eye-opening little outfit. "Quit fussing about my safety. There's nothing I can't handle. Hey, remember"—the girl jabbed at herself confidently with one thumb—"no one touches the faerie!"

With that, Escalla fluttered off into the grass, leaving nothing behind her but a spicy scent of roses drifting in the breeze.

14

The long march proceeded hour after careful hour in an almost absolute silence. *Almost* absolute, for Polk the teamster had ideas of his own on how marches ought to be conducted. He strolled beside each party member for a while, burdening them with one of his monologues. Sir Olthwaite was affable. The two priests were cold. The sorcerer and archer were just suspicious enough to hedge their answers carefully. Polk fixed upon the Justicar as his firmest friend and his personal education project. Somehow, the teamster always managed to match Jus's pace, even though Polk had laden himself with enough adventuring equipment to last a thirty years' war.

Polk's services as a guide were thankfully unnecessary. On a grassy plain, the volcanic cone of White Plume Mountain was absurdly easy to spot. The continuous feathers of white smoke and steam shooting high into the clouds helped make the place even more conspicuous. The Justicar kept his party hugging the low ground while he alone crept across the low hummock lines and crests, hunting for the slightest sign that they had been discovered. Nothing larger than a plague fly stirred, and no tracks passed beneath his gaze.

Caution turned the Justicar's every sense into a perfect tool. Lying between the seed grasses atop a narrow rise of ground, he breathed the air and revelled in the simple fact of being alive. They were on the trail with work to be done.

Even here in the blighted lands, the wintry sun shone warm. He reached up to pat at Cinders's fur, hearing the thump-thump-thump of the hell hound's tail as they took the time to simply rest and listen to the breeze.

Down in the hollow behind them, the party had taken yet another rest. Unable to endure the sheer heat caused by walking in armor, the Bleredd priest had finally stripped off his arm and leg harness and loaded them upon his back. Unnecessary equipment had begun to disappear. After only half a day, the pace was beginning to beat them. Only the ever-resplendent paladin and the garrison archer, a silent professional, seemed able to keep up with the march.

Escalla had only checked in twice. However, it was now time for lunch, and even the thought of food had failed to make the faerie appear.

The little wretch still had a faerie cake hidden in Jus's backpack. Surely her sweet tooth would have called her back for a snack before now. Sitting up, the Justicar slowly turned to scan the grass, his face frozen in a frown.

"Where is she? What do you smell, old hound?"

Magic. Evil. The hell hound lifted up its ears. *No faerie girl.*

Jus sighed, sensing trouble in the wind, and took a swig of warm beer from his canteen. Checking his sword, he stood up and began to run swiftly ahead to sort out his partner's problems.

The clank of metal sounded from behind him and Cinders instantly gave a growl. The Justicar whirled, his hand on his sword and ready for a lightning-fast draw.

Frozen by the threat of the sword, Sir Olthwaite the paladin stood a few yards away.

Paladins were supposedly the ultimate embodiment of good, the white knights whose swords wielded justice. In the Justicar's experience, such men had far more interest in law than in actual justice. The Justicar had killed more than one lawman for just such cause, and he had few compunctions about adding another to his list. In Cinders's case, the hell hound simply resented having been made into a hearth rug.

With his hand still at his sword, the Justicar retained his fighting stance. Drifting through the wind around him came the ghostly sound of Cinders's growl.

"You move quietly."

"The breeze is blowing against you, but one can hardly play at being sneak thieves when dressed in steel." The paladin took a sniff at his perfumed kerchief as though offended by the scent of hell hound. "You have never asked my name. In some circles that might be considered rude. I am Sir Olthwaite, Knight Commander of the Dragon Star."

"I know. You're from Saint Cuthbert's temple."

Sir Olthwaite made a military bow. "Indeed! And you, sir, do you have a name?"

"I do."

If Olthwaite wanted anything more, the man could go get it from the faerie. Jus turned aside, indicating that the conversation was at an end, yet still the paladin persevered.

Sir Olthwaite took a breath of fresh air and said, "I met a man who saw you fighting in the market riots." The paladin smoothed his moustache as though pleased at sharing such knowledge. "You know a little priestly magic, it would seem."

"I get the job done." The Justicar took a last hard look into the sky, saw none of Iuz's scouts, and let his hand relax slightly on his sword. "My skills are my business. Stay here."

"Where are you going, sir? Surely this is a rest break."

"The faerie's missing. I'm going to find her."

Jus turned to go, taking a pace back out of sword reach before beginning to walk. Behind him, Sir Olthwaite moved forward in a clank of steel.

"You might need another sword. I shall accompany you."

Down in the hollow, the two priests had noticed the conversation above. Suspicious of conspiracies, they now climbed doggedly up the hillock to confront the two warriors.

"Where are you going?" The Geshtai priestess puffed hard from her climb. As priestess to a river god, she wore an armor of scales that seemed to get heavier and heavier with every step. "What have you both been hiding?"

Sir Olthwaite gave the priestess a droll glance and said, "We hide nothing, madam. We merely discuss the whereabouts of the faerie."

Bleredd's priest leaned on his warhammer and narrowed his eyes. He was clearly considering the likelihood that the faerie had flown to White Plume Mountain, stolen the lost weapons, and absconded with the goods. Simple common sense finally won over suspicion. A two-foot-tall faerie could hardly be expected to fly off with a magic hammer and a two-yard-long fishing spear.

"Why is she missing?" Bleredd's priest looked subtly left and right as though trying to divine whether the faerie was spying on his every move. "Why isn't she here?"

Ignoring paladins and priests, the Justicar simply turned to go. "She flew on ahead. I'm going to collect her."

"We will accompany you"—the Bleredd priest swung his hammer in his hands—"to make sure that you receive all the support you need."

Watching silently and coldly from a distance, the archer and sorcerer elected to join the group. Polk ambled after them, one of his interminable monologues echoing across the deserted wastes. Ignoring his volunteer help, the Justicar turned his back upon the party and set a hard pace as he jogged toward the mountain.

The landscape still held small signs of life. Dull blooms hung in the grass, and strange skeletal black bees visited the blossoms. The markings on the insects' backs looked disturbingly like human skulls. The drone of insect wings only made the land seem more desolate with their hollow counterpoint to the endless rustle of the grass.

There were few signs of Escalla's passing. Cinders sniffed the faintest of magic trails left by her whirring wings, but even this soon became lost as a chill, stinking breeze stirred through the grass. Finally slowing to a walk, Jus gazed across the emptiness and cursed the girl for risking her little pink hide.

The landscape seemed totally empty. It asked the question: Where would an idiotic busybody go to find trouble in the middle of an open plain?

The Justicar came to a halt, stared off into the grass, and said, "Polk, do you see anything interesting?"

"Interesting? Son, none of it's interesting." The little jog had winded the man—much to Jus's satisfaction. Polk glared at the ranger as though a treasured son had just stung him. "You're going about all this wrong, son. The hired help is dumping their armor, and there's no pack mule. How can you carry your loot away from a dungeon without a pack mule?" The teamster waved a chunk of bread in the air. "And you packed iron rations. How are we supposed to feast around the campfire on dry bread and jerky? The damned pixie ate the only pot of jam I had."

Jam . . . feeling an intuition filtering through his skull, the Justicar stared off across the seed grass. Here and there, one of the eerie bees drifted through the weeds as it took a last few loads of pollen home. Watching a bee slowly climb past his nose, Jus hunted for a hillock, found one, and raced to the crest so that he could stare across the plain.

Trees were scattered here and there, some alone and some in copses. He spied a clump of trees some way off their path and watched a bee go weaving off toward the thicket.

"Honey. The little git went looking for honey."

Sweet! Cinders pricked up his ears. *Honey good!*

Expecting that the girl had been stung to death or possibly eaten herself sick, Jus signaled the rest of the party.

Crouching low, he led the way over to a thicket of dry trees. As he neared the small copse he could hear a female voice amidst a swirl and hum of bees.

* * * * *

Under the trees, all was not well in Escalla's world. Trapped in a near-invisible sticky web, she swung beneath a pole borne by two shambling, rotting skeletons. More of the reeking monstrosities loped to either side, led by a tall, cadaverous figure with a face like jagged bone.

Determinedly cheerful, Escalla's voice bubbled brightly to fall upon seemingly deaf ears. "Did I say *three* wishes?" The faerie kept her voice at the high end of the bright and cheerful scale. "Hey, you guys set me free, and I'll grant you *four* wishes!"

With no immediate response, Escalla wriggled about to try to draw the attention of a walking corpse.

"All right, so you don't like wishes. Hey, I'm one-third leprechaun on my mother's side! Monsters like treasure, right? Would you believe I can lead you to a magic pot of gold?"

Writhing with maggots and worms, the monsters threw Escalla to the ground. She was inside some kind of camp-site. Cadaverous horses made of rotten flesh stood about a tent. Gagging as one of her captors leaned too close, Escalla tried to wiggle back from the creature's grasp.

It was time for a different approach.

"All right, you guys are undead. I can respect that! Beating the odds! Unconquered by death! Force of will, now *that's* what being undead says to me! And force of will means you've gotta have *self-respect.* That's what I like about you guys—you're straight, you're forceful, you're true blue."

Beating her points out one by one, the girl tried to keep the undead leader in range of her banter. "Now I know what you're all thinking. A guy with *real* self-respect would never go around picking on a helpless little faerie with a cute butt, and you'd be right!" The faerie affably slitted up her eyes. "Hey, we all have momentary lapses! I don't mind. So you just set me free, and we'll simply forget any of this happened. It's fine by me!"

The tent flaps swept aside and a tall, lethally thin figure appeared: a one-handed man with skin the texture of bubbling tar. The creature took a long, cold look at the captive faerie and bared its fangs with a hiss of evil joy. Escalla tried to meet the creature with a happy smile and gave a timid little wave.

"Boy, am I glad to see you!" A big bead of sweat traveled down Escalla's neck. "There's been a wee bit of a mix-up. Your gang here has mistaken me for someone else, but it's all cleared up now, so I was just about to go."

The black-skinned monster rubbed at the stump of its arm, then sidled silkily closer to the girl.

The faerie duly cleared her throat and said, "Ah, you're a cambion, right?" Escalla tried to shrink away. "That's fine! I can see where you're coming from. Now look, you're a demon, I'm a faerie. One's good, one's bad—but both are simply different sides of the same coin, right? I mean, you can't have good without evil! So if you kill me, you're just making life that much more difficult for yourself!"

The cambion slid a knife out of its belt and slowly began to advance toward the girl. Caught like a fly in a spider web, Escalla began to fight frenziedly against her bonds. She changed to a snake and was still stuck fast, then turned into a spiny urchin, a winged piranha, and a slimy slug. She found no way to escape but did manage to lose most of her clothes. The girl popped back into faerie form and gave a frightened squeal.

"*No!* Look, I'm really little! You don't wanna eat a faerie. You guys want to eat an elf! Just plant my feet in soil and water me for a few years and I'll grow . . . *honest!*" The girl tried to lift a hand and shape a deadly spell. "Look out! There's a psychopathic ranger standing behind you!" Her enemy refused to turn around. "Jus! Jus, time to cue the rescue party! *Juuuuuuuuus!*"

Instead of the Justicar, a heavyset man wielding a hammer gave a great shout from the brush nearby. He held up a holy symbol, screaming an invocation to Bleredd, and a blast of light thundered toward the skeletons. Shambling corpses were suddenly blasted apart, pieces of bone crashing down at Escalla's feet.

The white-faced cadaver withstood the storm, drew a sword, and ran toward the priest with an ululating cry. As it passed the man, the Justicar rose from the grass, pivoted, and sliced into the monster from behind. The creature stumbled forward with half of its torso severed from its trunk. Staggering, it tried to turn and attack with its sword, only to have the Justicar's black sword hack it in two.

✳   ✳   ✳   ✳   ✳

The Justicar felt power surge through him in a mad rush of battle rage as he rammed his blade into his foe. He whirled and saw the one-handed demon standing over Escalla. It was the same cambion he had fought beside the wagon trail a few days before.

The monster drew a dagger and stabbed straight for Escalla's heart. Jus bellowed a spell and the air wrenched with energies. Frozen in place, the demon's muscles bulged as it fought against the magic. The creature broke free and hurled itself backward an instant before the black sword could sever its head. The cambion dodged aside and cast a spell that struck and lifted the Justicar off his feet, throwing him a dozen feet through the air.

Huge with rage, the ranger surged back onto his feet. The ribs along his right side had broken. His enemy drew out a sword and ran to the attack, moving with the same blurring speed it had shown in the Razor Wood during their last battle. Jus whipped his blade downward and parried a lightning fast slash to his knee, ripped upward with his sword, and sliced into the teak-hard flesh of the demon's inner thigh. The monster staggered backward, took an arrow fired by the archer straight through its throat, yet still kept his feet to run screaming at the Justicar with weapon raised.

A lightning bolt whip-cracked across the grass from the sorcerer. With power grounding out through its flesh, the demon utterly ignored the spell and hacked down with its sword. The Justicar blurred his own weapon upward in a parry, deflected the demon's blade, then drove the creature back with a sharp stab.

"Allow me."

A silver blade smacked into the cambion and sent it spinning to the ground. The demon turned, looked up at the paladin, and its eyes widened with hate. An instant later, Sir Olthwaite rammed his sword two-handed down the creature's throat, twisting the weapon viciously to drill the monster to the sand.

Black blood spurted as the sword ripped free. With a flick of his blade, the paladin took a backward pace and let his target fall.

Breathing hard with exertion, Jus leaned on his sword and held a hand against his broken ribs.

"You know what that was?"

"Cambion, a type of lesser demon." The paladin sheathed his sword. "Rather nasty."

"And not used to being attacked from behind." Shaking his head to throw off his pain, Jus stooped over Escalla in her sticky web. "Did he mark you?"

The faerie swallowed, still seeing the cambion's dagger streaking for her heart. "No. What did you do—the magic, I mean?"

"Holding spell." Jus reeled, then forced himself to straighten. He drew in a deep, sharp breath, fought the pain, and then flicked a glance at Sir Olthwaite.

"Broken ribs. Can you heal it?"

Paladins had the healing touch, yet when Sir Olthwaite stretched his hands out to touch the wound, he frowned and slowly shook his head.

"Alas." Sir Olthwaite's voice rang with regret. "Such hellish magic radiates pure evil. I cannot heal you."

The Justicar held up his own hand, shaped a ball of light, and then stretched his ribs tight. As the magic hit them, his bones set with an audible *crack*.

It seemed . . . simple. The Justicar looked at Sir Olthwaite, then stooped to sweep Escalla up into his arms.

The web yielded to alcohol siphoned from Polk's whiskey jar. Reeking like a brewery, Escalla stood and unhappily allowed Jus to peel her carefully free. She still hovered halfway between gratitude, annoyance, and aftershock.

"All I wanted was some damned honey!"

"I wouldn't try it." Working doggedly, Jus untangled sticky web-strands from Escalla's hair. "These bees give you the mummy rot when they sting."

"Oh, great." Dazed, Escalla accepted it all. "Those damned corpses had a web strung between the trees for me."

"That cambion worked for our friend the librarian. I met him once before on the wagon trail." Jus tried to untangle gluey strands from Escalla's wings. "They know we're coming."

"Great." Somewhat chilled and sobered, Escalla sat herself upon a stump. "Hey, thanks. You know—for getting here on time."

"You're welcome." The Justicar pulled a last gummy strand free from the faerie's backside. "I liked that 'self-respect' line, by the way."

"Oh, really? It was pretty nice." The girl held out her hair and grimaced at the damage. "Too bad they were just zombies and let it ride over them. Damn, but I need a bath!"

Cinders instantly perked up. *Heat water? Make fire?*

"No!" Jus clapped a hand over the hell hound's nose. Escalla was still drenched in whiskey. "We'll stop by one of the streams running from the mountain. They're hot enough to make a decent bath."

From the bushes nearby, the Geshtai priestess quietly emerged. During the whole battle, she had been conspicuously absent. With a suspicious sideways glance, Escalla watched the woman go, feeling the hair prickle on the back of her neck.

"That woman gives me the creeps."

"Yes." The ranger watched her go. "Cinders says he smells bad magic in the party, but the priests won't let me close enough to try any scrying spells."

Escalla flew up to the hell hound and scratched him between the ears. "Cinders, you keep right on sniffing"

Polk wandered over, sniffed whiskey on the breeze, and reclaimed the last sad remnants of his whiskey store. The man glared at Jus, then wrinkled his moustache, and finally let his criticisms out into the open air.

"Son, you're just an uphill climb for me. I try, but I just can't reach you!" The man swirled his jug, decided to hoard his last few swigs, and slung the jug across his shoulders. *"Backstabbing?* It's just not heroic, son, a bad habit. A hero can't have bad habits."

Polk irritably pulled a strip of sticky spider web away from his heel and announced, "Now, come on. I have to get you into White Plume Mountain before you foul up again."

15

Over two more long days, the group moved from a land-scape of withered grass into a folded desolation of lava plains. Molten rock had rippled as it cooled, and little jets of steam made the rock slippery with algae-laden slime. The cancerous stone gleamed a dull gray-black while the algae shimmered a slick, foul green. The only brightness came from streaks of rust and sulphur salts that crusted the edges of thermal pools.

The only life in this foul place seemed to be skittering gray rats that licked the algae from the pools. Most of the party distastefully passed the animals by, but Jus quietly and reverently went searching through the rocks. The Justicar carefully examined the boiling waters of a geyser and found tiny transparent shrimp sidling through the shallows. He showed Escalla, gently reaching down to lift a crustacean into view. For once, Escalla knew enough to still her tongue and simply enjoy the moment.

High overhead, White Plume Mountain loomed. The volcano's cone seemed stark and bare. Vast geysers shot steam thousands of feet into the sky above the peak, thun-dering upward with a sound that echoed across the entire wilderness. When the wind changed, condensed spray came drifting down across the rocks, and Cinders sniffed happily at the stench of sulphur in the air.

The Justicar kept himself and Escalla directly in the midst of the group. Cold calculation insisted that the other party members could never be trusted. By keeping close, Jus reduced the chance of collecting a dagger in the back.

There now seemed to be small point in stealth. The owner of White Plume Mountain certainly knew that they were coming.

In the evenings, the group made a huddled camp about an oil stove. The party bedded down on hard, warm rock in the lee of sulphur-coated stones.

Keen to recruit secret converts to their cause, each of the two priests tried sounding out their companions one by one. Their hissed whispers carried hints of fantastic promises to nearby ears.

Ignoring the conspirators, Polk ostentatiously began to polish Sir Olthwaite's equipment. He sat deliberately close to the Justicar, holding up each piece of armor so that the ranger could see just what a proper adventurer carried into peril.

The Justicar had provided himself with an oilskin sheet that he spread over himself and the faerie. Escalla had made herself a bed inside the Justicar's backpack, and both slept safe and sound amidst the random spatter of condensation from on high. Cinders sat propped upon a pile of rocks, his eyes gleaming on unwinking watch. When anyone inside the camp made the slightest move toward the ranger or the faerie, a ghostly, half-heard canine growl would ripple through the air.

Of the entire party, only Escalla and the Justicar slept well.

On the final day of approach, the Justicar once again took the lead. A pathway of sorts existed—a rough-cut road flanked with moss-furred statues of Keraptis himself. The sorcerer's bifold mask was weathered into senile imbecility and pockmarked with fungi. Jus used the statues as stepping stones to climb up and avoid bends in the switch-back trail, guarding the party from ambushes as they trudged and struggled along the slippery stone road.

By evening, they had reached a flat plateau upon a shoulder of the mountain. The sun had begun to set, shining wine-red through the mists of sulphurous spray. With fat, stinking droplets raining down upon their necks, the party trudged upward through a darkening maze of rocks, dark pools, and shadow.

The road ended in a pile of moss-slimed ruins that might once have been a villa or a vast, impressive gate. A cave stood fifty yards away—a narrow cleft that hissed out a long blast of steam. Shuddering like a giant's breath, the steam suddenly halted. There was an indrawn sigh as air sucked slowly back into the cave—a minute's pause—and then the outrush of steam slowly began again.

Breathing slowly, with its mouth fanged by slime, the cavern lay in wait for its visitors. The whole mountain seemed plotting and aware, as though unseen shapes flickered through the distant rocks.

The mountain was waiting. . . .

Moving almost invisibly through the rocks, the Justicar approached the cave mouth from one side and carefully searched for enemies. He slithered to the ground only when the steam blasts proved themselves to be cool and the molds and slimes harmless. With Escalla at his side, he stooped and ran gloveless hands over the thin mud outside of the breathing cave, rubbing the muck thoughtfully between his fingertips.

"Mud. Boots have broken the soil crust and let the steam intermix. Probably yesterday." The man carefully wiped his hands clean upon his thighs. "This cave has had someone walk in but not walk out."

"How do you know they didn't walk out?" The faerie blinked. "The depth of the mud? Marks in the soil?"

"There's only one way down the mountain. We would have found them walking down the road."

"Yeah! Hey, you're pretty good at this."

The Justicar helped Escalla to her feet and said, "It's a ranger thing. It's what we do instead of parties." He turned and signalled the rest of the party, shouting to be heard above the hiss and roar of steam. "It's safe! This is our way in!"

The explorers gathered. Dripping fangs of algae framed the tunnel mouth. Wincing, Escalla stared at the entrance as it slowly breathed a dragon's breath of steam. She took one little pace away from the cave, nervously fluttering her wings.

"It doesn't look . . . *so* bad." She gave a fragile little smile, then made a ladylike curtsy to the paladin. "Hey, after you!"

Steam! Heat! Smell! Only Cinders seemed truly happy. *Good place!*

The faerie fluttered upward and swatted Cinders on the skull.

"Cinders, you suck in much more of this sulphur and you'll start to worry me!"

Tickles!

"Yeah, whatever." The girl took another look at the cave, watching the steam now slowly breathe back into the sinister mouth.

"Why does it keep doing that?" The girl backed away, then delved into the Justicar's backpack and pulled out a tiny little book. "Um, does anyone else feel like brushing up on a few spells?"

The Bleredd priest threw Escalla a sneer. "You're afraid of going in?"

"Hell, no! I just feel like cranking up a few spells." The girl preened herself, drawing proudly erect. *"Some* of us like to do these things properly!"

The Justicar remained standing beside the edge of the tunnel. He brushed at a strangely shiny patch of the rock. Sir Olthwaite strolled over beside him, his hands clasped regally behind his back. The man peered at the strange carvings uncovered by Jus's glove.

"What have you found, sir?"

"A welcome mat." Jus wiped clean an inscription burned into the stone. He sniffed in annoyance as he read the words aloud.

"Adventurers, come one, come all,
And enter the accursed halls.
Find the weapons, seek the prize.
The weak will rot—the strong survive.
The most worthy will attain the bliss
Of union with Keraptis."

Escalla slumped.

"Oh, great." The girl gave a dire look at the inscription. "Nothing I like more than being used as a test subject by a guy who thinks rhyming couplets are actually fashionable." The girl gave an irritated sigh. "I'm not sure I can deal with this sort of stuff without a good eight hours of beauty sleep."

The Justicar looked at the setting sun, gazed out across the plain, then turned his gaze to the damp, tired adventurers. After a long, silent stare at the other party members one by one, he jerked his chin toward the tangled stones down the road.

"She's right. Rest. Eat. Sleep." The man turned away from the tunnel. "We'll make a better job of it tomorrow."

Despite resenting his orders, the group walked a hundred yards back down the road. Amidst the pieces of a fallen statue of Keraptis, they made camp and shielded their miserable little stove from view.

Polk's sensibilities were offended by the overall mood of suspicion and gloom. The night before a great adventure was supposed to be a time for tales and splendor. The man ground jerky between two helmets and cooked up a surprisingly good stew, even managing to make a fresh, tasty flatbread upon a stone.

The Justicar ate, raised an eyebrow at the man, and slowly put his meal down. After a moment, he managed to make his sense of natural justice rise to the top.

"Polk, you did well." The Justicar fought a grumble back down where it belonged. "Thanks."

"You're welcome." Polk sniffed and fixed a dour gaze upon the Justicar. "So are you ready, son? Have you prayed to your patron gods to give strength to your avenging sword? Have you written a poem to a lady love? Have you readied parchment to make a map? "

"No."

Annoyed by Jus's total lack of proper sentiment, Polk went back to improving the morale of the adventurers. Smiling a nasty little smile, the Justicar rubbed his hands, pleased to be irritating one of the irritants at last.

A guard roster was set, and the party bedded down. Sleeping beneath Cinders's watchful gaze, Escalla and Jus wedged themselves into the rocks and tried to get some sleep.

After three solid hours of tossing and turning, Escalla grumpily sat up. With her hair hanging all over the place and her mouth tasting like an old bird's nest, she scratched herself in places where the sun seldom shone and looked blearily off into the dark.

The damned volcano geyser was drizzling mist all over the campsite yet again. Holding Jus's backpack above her as a roof, the faerie straightened a kink out of one wing and for the eleven thousandth time wished that she had a faerie cake for a little midnight snack.

Above her, Cinders's ears flicked high.

Movement.

"What?" Escalla jumped up, clutching a blanket to her skin. "Where?"

Path.

Hunched shapes skulked through the rocks, moving faster and faster as they slipped away from the campsite and headed toward the sighing cave. The clank and rattle of armor echoed above the sinister breath of steam.

Staring, Escalla hardly dared to move. Beside her, Jus levered himself up, scratching nails across the velvet stubble of his skull.

"Yep. There they go."

"What?" Escalla looked frantically about the camp, then saw that half the bedding piles lay empty. "That's some of the others?"

"Yup."

"Quick! We have to get in there after them!" The faerie dropped her blanket and hopped up and down on one foot drawing a legging up her thigh. "Jus! They're getting away!"

The Justicar gave an uncaring shrug.

"And?"

"And come *on!*" Escalla whined like a frantic little child. *"Ju-us,* they'll steal all our stuff!"

The Justicar sighed and rearranged his blankets.

"They always planned on ditching us. The Bleredd priest went an hour ago. The Geshtai only just found out." The big man gave a yawn filled with teeth. "Each priest wants to steal both the trident and the hammer."

Still half-clad, Escalla sped over to Jus and furiously grabbed him by his nipple hairs.

"Jus! Jus, are you listening to me? They are going to steal all the gold!"

"We have walked over four hundred miles—at least the last hundred of it through enemy territory to get here." The ranger regarded the tiny faerie through hooded eyes. "Just *who* were you planning on convincing to carry a hundredweight of gold coin all the way back home for you?"

Escalla folded her arms and hovered in midair.

"Look, we all have our little dreams. In your case, you want a world of justice for all." The faerie sulked and flicked long blonde hair into the wind. "In my case, I just want to roll buck naked on silk sheets big enough to drape a whale!"

Cinders eagerly began to flap his tail. *Faerie on silk! Faerie on silk!*

"Cinders, you're not helping!" The Justicar shifted his sword. "Escalla, we came here for the librarian. And wherever *he* is, then that's where your gold is going to be. I'll get some for you when we've killed the bastard."

The faerie's eyes sparkled. "Really true?"

"Really true, just for you. Now get some sleep, and we'll see who stayed here in the morning."

Considerably happier, Escalla jumped back into her bed. The sulphur mists smelled fresh and bracing, and the hiss of steam gave the mountainside a magnificent eldritch power. The faerie disappeared into her shelter, turned around and around like a dog treading a bed, and then wriggled down into the blankets. With a last careful glance about the camp, Jus patted Cinders, popped a coal into the hell hound's mouth, and lay back down.

The silence stretched for ten minutes, and then Escalla's muffled voice rose into the air.

"Hey, Jus?"

"Yes."

"How do we know they won't solve the maze, kill the librarian, and get the weapons, treasure and all?"

The Justicar lifted his head and replied, "This dungeon was designed to slaughter entire parties. How far do you think only a couple of people are going to get?"

"Oh, yeah. Yeah, that's right!"

Escalla settled herself back down. She lay still for almost a minute, and then her voice drifted out into the dark.

"Um, Jus?"

"Yes?"

"If it's going to wipe out the other guys because there's only one or two of them, why are you and I going to be all right?"

"Because you're a faerie." The human gave a huge, sleepy yawn. "No one touches the faerie."

"Jus, do I look too fat?"

"Nope." The ranger turned over in his bed. "Go to sleep."

16

Tying her long boots firmly in place, Escalla cast a glance about the empty camp. A dawn as weak as dishwater struggled through the clouds of volcanic steam, making light glitter from countless beads of dew. Steam hissed and shuddered out of the hideous mountain cave, blowing like a breath of evil into the morn.

Jus sat beside the remnants of a hot breakfast and carefully sharpened his sword, holding his whetstone at a precise angle as he worked the weapon's point.

The Tiger Nomads had a proverb that said, "Even a blind man can wreak havoc with a sharpened sword." The Justicar was a firm believer in giving a blade an edge that could cut like a razor, and he carefully tended his weapon every day. As Escalla watched, he finished his work, blew tiny fragments of metal dust from the ensorcelled steel, then carefully dusted the weapon with black carbon designed to stop light glinting from the blade.

Jus sensed Escalla seething as she tied on her gear. The faerie growled as she pulled bodice laces tight. "So what you're saying is that not one of the rotten bastards decided to stay? We have absolutely no help at all?"

"We've got *one.*" The Justicar carefully sheathed his sword. "What are you complaining about?"

Staggering around a corner, Polk carried a huge load of dungeoneering gear in his arms. He let the load collapse with a crash to the ground, pointedly dusting off his hands as he caught Escalla's eye.

"There! I brung the pick of the lot. Iron spikes, sixty feet of rope, six torches, and a flask of oil. There's a ground-sheet, a mirror, a flask of holy water, a holy symbol, mapping paper, a bullseye lantern, and six sticks of chalk. I've got parchment, pens, wax markers, ink, wolfsbane, garlic bud, and a ball of hairy string!" The man brandished a roll of twine. "Binding force of the universe, son! Can't go any-where without your hairy string!"

With her mouth stuffed full of pancake, Escalla raised an intolerant little brow and said, "Oh, gee. No ten-foot pole?"

"The priest took it. It's gone. We'll just hafta do with-out." Polk stood astride his mound of loot. "Now, who takes what?"

"I have all I need." The Justicar abandoned his backpack, hung his holy symbol about his neck, then clasped Cinders into place. "Escalla?"

"Faeries do not *carry.*" Escalla scorned the equipment pile with a glance. "Now let's get going."

Polk gaped at his companions in astonishment. "But what about sacks to carry the loot?"

"You want Jus to try sword fighting while carrying a pack?" Escalla whirred deftly up into the air. "If the loot was moved here, then it will have to be in boxes or bags. Even mad sorcerers have to obey the laws of common sense!"

The Justicar and Escalla hid their bedding beneath a rock then began a careful approach toward the hissing cave. Polk made a bad-tempered grab for the Justicar's abandoned back-pack, crammed it full of goods, then dumped the huge coil of rope about his own shoulders. He staggered after the two errant adventurers, rope coils slithering all about his neck.

"Son, you can't go dungeoneering without a rope!"

"You like rope, *you* carry it." The Justicar knelt beside the mud outside the cave mouth and looked down at the boot marks. "Here we go. We've got a party of two here going straight into the cave. The armored boot will be that Bleredd priest. The military boot will be the archer." The man outlined other footprints that came into the cave from the sides. "The next party took cover before going in. They thought the first ones were waiting in ambush."

"Oh, great!" Escalla hovered, fighting against the steamwind that thundered from the cave. "So now we have to worry about the other guys lying in wait somewhere inside?"

"Yup." Jus carefully looked left and right, scanning for danger. "Unless they've already taken each other out."

"Let's hope." The faerie pulled her leggings tight. "Polk? I'm serious, man. There's monsters down here. Go away!"

"Nope!" The teamster was more stubborn than a mule. "You won't get fifty feet without me!"

Jus walked to the center of the cave entrance and felt air being drawn into the tunnel. It whipped in past him for half a minute, paused, then came shuddering outward, mixed with steam. The vapor was unpleasant but not scalding. Reeking of the earth, it made clothes stick wetly to the skin and left an oily taste upon the tongue.

Whistling merrily, Escalla rummaged through a little bag hanging from the rear of the backpack. She pulled out bandages, lint, a lucky rabbit's foot, and a few assorted pieces of Polk's trash until finally she unearthed three pebbles wrapped in dirty cloth. Standing at the opening to a dungeon packed with monsters, traps, and hideous engines of death, her three companions watched with growing impatience.

The girl polished the three little rocks, happily preoccupied until she noticed the others glowering at her in silent expectation.

"What?"

Jus simply looked at her. "What are you doing?"

"Permanent light spells!" The faerie proudly held up three glowing rocks made into pendants through an imaginative use of string. "See? Bright light, no heat, and no hands. Perfect for your dungeoneering needs."

When unwrapped, the magic pendants flooded the whole area with light. Suitably impressed, Jus inspected the girl's creations.

"You made these?"

"Last night, while all those other guys were off whispering with each other." Escalla seemed inordinately pleased with her handiwork as she slipped pendants over the necks of Jus and Polk. "One each! That's all I had time for." The girl hovered in midair and looked back at the other two as though they had been dawdling and wasting time. "Well, come on! Are we going in?"

The unpleasant gush of steam came again, and Escalla huddled behind Cinders to shelter from the blast. Walking carefully, his sword searching the shadows, the Justicar moved forward. His ears deafened by the gush and roar of the steam, he cautiously led the way into the dark.

The cave pierced only a few dozen feet into the mountainside and then dead-ended. A jagged horizontal crevice near the roof sucked air in a mighty rush, paused, then shuddered as vast clouds of steam shot into the cave. The sulphurous breath gushed out of the tunnel and into the open air, almost blinding the adventurers, who fought to keep their feet amidst the blast.

Slime, dirt, and steam had formed a fine mud all across the floors, but at the center of the floor, the muck had been disturbed. Using a dagger blade, someone had dug down almost two handspan's deep. Inside the hole, there lay a square trapdoor with an iron ring mounted on one side.

The door would open upward, swinging back toward the cave mouth. The Justicar circled the door with the greatest of care, then held back Escalla when she made to touch the iron ring.

"Careful."

Cinders growled, confirming Jus's fears. Hunching down beside the trapdoor, the ranger sheathed his sword carefully.

"Polk, give me the rope."

Behind him, the teamster instantly cheered up. "You need it. I told you that you would."

"Yeah. Now, shut up."

Escalla raised one brow in sly approval as Jus gently slipped an end of the rope through the iron ring, moving carefully so as to never move or jiggle the handle. He passed the rope through until he reached the midsection of the line, then paid the rope out as he backed slowly away down the passageway. After ten paces, he signalled his companions to lie down and used his own broad back for cover.

Steam thundered all about him, rushing out into the open air. As the breath came to its pause, the Justicar held Cinders up in front of him as a fire shield and hauled backward on the rope.

An explosion suddenly blasted through the trapdoor, ripping it from its hinges and slamming the iron plate into the ceiling. A rockfall thundered downward from the roof. Dust and debris were sucked away from the party as the cave's breath was drawn sharply in.

The silence after the explosion seemed deafening. A last few rocks slammed down from the ceiling as the adventurers slowly rose to their feet.

Below the ruined trapdoor, a circular stair plunged down into the dark. Blinking, Escalla looked down into the rubble-cluttered hole.

"Oooh, not good!"

"A rune trap. Our *allies* don't want us following them." Jus tried to brush free the dust that clung to Cinders's wet, bedraggled fur. "Cinders? Sorry about the dust."

'S all right.

The ranger risked one quick look down into the dark space below then jumped down onto the spiral stair. He tossed his magic light down and followed after it in a rush, his black sword out and ready to stab into the shadows. The sheer speed and aggression of the man made Escalla feel like a professional. She dived down after him, hovering behind his shoulder with a spell hanging half-readied in one hand.

The stair descended in a dizzy spiral, around and around. The Justicar slowed his initial rush, stood silently to listen to the sounds of the caverns below, then retrieved his magic light.

"Polk?"

"I'm here! 'Course I'm here!"

"Stand still."

Jus closed his eyes, sheathed the magic light, and let the stairwell plunge into impenetrable darkness. The stairwell seemed to thrum and shudder with the pulsebeat of the volcano's steam. The air hung thick with a swampy stench that scratched mercilessly at the sinuses.

Cinders stirred slightly as he tested the subterranean air. *Smell slime. Hear water. Much magic.* The hell hound gave a snort and then a sneeze. *Evil walked here, little while ago.*

Escalla slowly unshielded her light and said, "He scents evil, huh?"

"Evil passed here." Jus settled the hell hound's snout firmly into place. "Meaning it walked *in* here from *outside.*"

"Oh, lovely." Escalla looked a little miffed. "Our ex-comrades are sounding better and better."

A slow, careful descent began. They marched down the stairs for interminable minutes, until finally the stairway opened out onto a square-hewn room. The pure, clean light from three necklaces flooded out to fill in the details of the room. Rough-surfaced walls gleamed slick as mucus with mottled patches of algae. Oily water—filthy, blood-warm, and smelling like an abyssal swamp—reflected rainbows from the floor. A rotten stench hung in the thick air. A slow lap of water echoed in the distance, and the atmosphere clung warm and sticky to their skin.

A prod of the water with Jus's sword revealed that the floor was about one foot below the surface. It would be unpleasantly easy to hide traps and tripwires underneath the muck. Enclosed by untold thousands of tons of volcanic rock, Escalla had turned slightly pale.

"So, um, this is a dungeon, then?"

"Yep." The Justicar carefully prodded his sword into the mire. "Claustrophobic?"

"Me?" The faerie shook her head, keeping careful watch as if the walls and ceilings were about to mash her as flat as a bug. "Never! Nope! Not me! No way am *I* longing for the wide open spaces!"

"Good."

Cinders could see and smell nothing lying in wait under the water. Even so, it could hide a monster lying in ambush. With no choice except to move forward, the Justicar secured his sword to one wrist with a leather thong and stepped cautiously down into the scum.

The filthy stuff was warm as phlegm and crept insidiously inward through his bootlace holes. With a curse, the Justicar waded forward, his motion making far too much noise. The way things were going, the whole dungeon would be able to hear him coming.

A short corridor extended away into the dark. Jus looked back to see Polk holding a scroll upon a clipboard and scribbling notes as fast as he could write. Though he half-wished the man would be swallowed up by a carrion crawler, Jus seemed to be cursed with a streak of responsibility.

"Polk! Stop that, and stay close."

"I'm chronicling, son!" The teamster held up a page covered with awful, childish letters written with a waterproof wax marker. "Don't pay me no mind. I'm just an observer. Hey, how do you spell 'thews'?"

Jus muttered, exchanged a look of annoyance with Escalla, then jerked his chin toward the tunnel ahead. The faerie gave her partner a confident nod, then popped instantly out of view. On invisible wings, she whirred sightly ahead of the Justicar as he felt his way forward through the water.

They moved slowly onward, senses testing at the darkness beyond. Moments later, Escalla came back to hover at Jus's side.

"What is a thew anyway?" she asked.

"Who knows."

The tunnel took a sudden ninety-degree turn. Jus flattened himself against a corner, knelt down in the muck on all fours, and peeked around the bend with his head down low.

"Let's go."

The faerie whirred invisibly ahead, and Jus followed. With a clang and a rattle, Polk brought up the rear, diligently watching for the slightest slip in his companions' professional codes.

Cinders gave a warning growl. *Cat smell.*

"Cat?"

Wet cat. The hell hound didn't seem particularly worried. *Big wet cat, sitting in water.*

Far down the tunnel, a lamp cast a little yellow pool of light. The Justicar moved carefully forward, and a figure slowly materialized out of the gloom.

The passage up ahead forked three ways. Just in front of the junction, a large female sphinx sat unhappily in the mire. Bigger than a cart horse, with her fur matted and her hair hanging limp, she looked rather like a huge, bedraggled lion. The creature sat up as she noticed her visitors and tried to make herself look haughty and prim.

She wore a natty headdress made out of gold and gems. Straight brown hair had been cut into a rather attractive little bob, but the effect was spoiled by the horrible humidity of the tunnels. Brown eyes and a smattering of freckles made the sphinx's face look rather more like the girl next door rather than a carnivorous monster.

A shimmering, transparent wall of force screened the sphinx and her intersection from the adventurers' end of the corridor. Smoothing back her hair, the creature drew herself up and tried to make herself presentable as Jus, Polk, and the faerie drew near.

With one paw laid importantly upon her breast, the sphinx cleared her throat, then spoke a rhyme.

> "Round she is, yet flat as a board
> Altar of the Lupine Lords
> Jewel on black velvet, pearl in the sea
> Unchanged but e'erchanging eternally."

The sphinx intoned her riddle in a beautifully cultured voice. Before anyone else could move, Escalla popped into view and waved to the two men to keep away from the action.

"Guys, back off." The faerie cracked her knuckles. "It's time for auntie to do her stuff."

The faerie fluttered joyously toward the force wall and waved quite happily at the sphinx. "Hey, that's a really great riddle! No one seems to make them with that sort of quality anymore."

The sphinx recoiled a little in surprise, then shrugged her furry shoulders and nodded. "Thank you. Answer the riddle, and I shall let you pass."

"Again, *classic* technique used to best possible effect!" Escalla shook her head in admiration. "Riddle-solve, magic door. I mean, you just take tradition, and *you* make it work!"

"Oh." Combing at her muddy hair, the sphinx sat up a little straighter. "Well . . . well, thank you."

"Oh, you're welcome! I'm Escalla, by the way." The faerie hovered happily in midair. "Boys, come up and meet . . . ?" Escalla tilted her head at the sphinx. "Sorry, I didn't quite catch your name?"

The sphinx gave a shy little smile and said, "It's Enid."

"*Enid!* Really?" Escalla raised one brow and introduced her companions. "Well, here's Polk, the world's most pedantic wagon driver, and this is Ev—" The Justicar's warning growl cut the faerie off. "Um, ev-everyone's friend, Jus the Justicar." The girl leaned a little closer to the sphinx. "Overdeveloped sense of justice but has pecs to *die* for!"

"Really?"

"Oooh, yeah!" Escalla decided to sit upon Jus's shoulders to talk with the sphinx. "So anyway! You're magically held here in place, or are you working freelance?"

"Hmmm? Oh, magically held." Enid the sphinx minced about in a circle, trying to find a place out of the slime. "That little two-toned reprobate put an enchantment on me. I'm stuck here for a whole month!"

"A month!" Escalla clapped her face to her hands. "Sitting here in the mud? You could get swamp itch! You could get fur fungus! Isn't there even a dry place to sit?"

"No. Not at all." The woman-headed cat shook out her ruined fur. "They give me eight hours to sleep over in a pokey little room—no brush, no comb, and raw meat for supper. There's not a book to read, not a thing to do but make spell symbols and cook up new riddles!"

The faerie joined the sphinx in a shared bond of feminine indignation.

"Oooh, I *hate* that! Some damned sorceress up north had me doing almost the exact same thing—had me delivering portents! Had to fly to some 'chosen child's' village and be his mentor for a whole year." Escalla had never had to do anything of the kind, but she instantly threw herself into her role. "Damned little brat tried to pull my wings off!"

"No consideration. None at all." The sphinx grumbled. She tried to sit down and fold her paws, but the filthy water deterred her.

"But still, you get time to make up good riddles." Escalla looked about the floor. "Hey, did some other guys come through here just before?"

"Sods snuck past me!" The sphinx grumbled, flexing her claws. "Both sets of them guessed my riddle in seconds!"

"That quickly?"

"Straight off the cuff. Said 'moon' in less time than it takes to draw a breath!"

"Really?" Escalla looked suitably distraught, even while filing the information away. "Well it's going to keep me guessing for a while, I can tell you!"

The sphinx would hear none of it.

"Oh, I can't imagine that! A girl like you? You'll have it in a trice!" Enid scratched her ear with one hind leg. "Go on, give it a try—do!"

"Well, since you insist." Escalla thoughtfully cupped her chin. "So, let's see . . . I mean, it's a *classic*. You've got really good, pure simplicity working for you here." The faerie bit her lip, flew in a circle, and then came to a stop. "I'm gonna go right out on a limb here. I'm thinking . . . *moon?*"

Enid opened her front paws in joy and shouted. "See, you got it! I knew you could!"

"Well, it took a lot of doing. But hey—*moon*—something everyone sees, right in front of your face, so you never think about it! *Classic* misdirection, Enid! You really have the touch."

Enid reached up to remove a slip of papyrus from the ceiling above the portal. She simpered as the force wall came down.

"Well, thanks. You know, one tries one's best."

"Well, your best is pretty good." Escalla crossed the line of the force wall and ushered the two men through. "So Enid, the big J here is thinking something along the lines of finding the guy who summoned you and maybe chopping him into at least eleven pieces. Do you want to come?"

"Aaaaah." Enid gave a disappointed sigh. "I have to stay here. Magic spell, you know."

"Oh, sure, I can see that. But hey, we'll try to kill the guy and set you free."

"Oh, thank you!" The sphinx seemed utterly relieved. "Look, just for you, here's a little help." The sphinx gave the faerie the slip of papyrus from above the force wall. "It's a stun symbol. Anyone passing through a door you place this on—instant knock out! I made it as a little extra for anyone trying to break down the force wall."

Holding the little gift with unfeigned delight, Escalla held the papyrus out in the light where it could be admired.

"You made this?"

"Certainly!" The sphinx looked a little shy. "It's a sphinx thing."

"Well, thank you! That's really generous." Escalla noticed Jus and Polk waiting for her impatiently in the right-hand passageway. "Wish us luck, and we'll do our best for you!"

"Be careful!" Enid the sphinx waved the party on their way. "It's one treasure per tunnel."

Escalla tucked the papyrus down her cleavage then whirred up the passageway to meet Polk and the Justicar. The two men stared at her, and Escalla opened her hands in innocence.

"What? Just because we're adventuring, we can't be nice?"

The Justicar shook his head and motioned down the corridor. "Come on. We have a wizard to kill."

They moved down the eastern tunnel—Escalla flying invisibly to the fore, followed by the Justicar with Cinders grinning from his helm. Polk came behind, taking a pull from his whiskey flask to clear his sinuses from the smell of mold. The teamster flicked a glance up the corridor then back to Jus and clucked his tongue in disappointment.

"It's a shame, son, a shame to see you letting a woman take the lead."

"The woman happens to be invisible." The Justicar let his voice drop to a mutter. "And she can fry you like an egg, you old coot."

With his front leg hovering mid-step in the water, Jus suddenly heard Cinders bark an alarm.

Stop.

The Justicar froze in position. Above his head, Cinders's red eyes shone. *New smell. Danger in water.*

"Escalla?"

A bow floated on the water nearby. The faerie's wings disturbed the water surface as she hovered low, her magic light peeping out to illuminate the murk.

"Yeah, yeah, I see it. Some sort of . . . ewwwww!"

A corpse lay half submerged in the shallow water. A screaming skull thrust up toward the surface, with crooked finger bones already dissolving even as they reached upward for escape. The skeleton's flesh had turned into a vile, putrescent ooze, floating in green streamers all about the dissolving bones.

Escalla contributed to affairs by being violently ill. Coming as it did from an invisible source, this was no sight for gentle eyes. As vomit struck the green slime, it instantly began to discolor. Moments later, the slime had grown, absorbing the new matter with terrifying speed.

Escalla popped back into view, looking haggard as she stared down at the skeleton.

"What the . . . ?"

"Green slime." Jus inspected his boots, which still seemed free of the infection. "It's on the floor under the water. Gods only know how far it goes. Escalla, take a look."

The faerie looked ill. A swig from a water bottle set her to rights. With a nod at Jus, the girl began hovering above the water and trying to peer below. Watching this display of inordinate, cowardly caution, Polk licked his wax marker and flipped open his chronicle scroll with a *snap*.

"Son, I fail to see why a hero should be concerned about a little slime."

"That slime can eat through anything you care to touch it with. We'd be dead in minutes." The ranger held his sword carefully away from the water as he inspected the skeleton. "He was running toward us when he fell."

The floating bow seemed to identify the fallen man as the baron's archer. How many other men had been in his party was anybody's guess, but only one had lived to flee this far back down the corridor.

This did not bode well. Jus scratched the stubble of his chin as he stared at the dead, dissolving bones.

"He's pointing toward us. He must have already safely crossed this slime patch on the way down the corridor."

Hovering, the faerie cocked an eye. "So?"

"So something at the other end scared him so much that he forgot about the slime."

"Oh . . ." Escalla looked a little dazed as she looked down the dark, foreboding corridor. "Maybe he was just a little shy?"

"Maybe."

The ranger drew in a big sigh then held out a hand to Polk.

"Polk, no comments. We need the iron spikes. Twelve for you, twelve for me."

The iron climbing pitons had loops and serrations designed for mountain climbing. Leaning against one wall, the two men lashed the spikes to the edges of their boots, pointing down. Elevated a few inches above the floor, they took a nervous breath and strode carefully past the dissolving green skeleton. The spike points grated on the floor underneath the water; Polk almost slipped, wailed, and was caught by one of the Justicar's huge hands. The ranger hauled Polk to safety in one great surge of strength, propelling the teamster far down the corridor where he landed with a splash. Jus waded powerfully after him for a dozen feet more, then frantically began to tear away the spikes about his boots.

The spikes had dissolved almost halfway. Acid from the slime still clung to the metal and was eating it away. Polk and Jus cleared their boots and hurled the spikes away, watching them fall into the oily muck near the slime.

Polk wriggled his moustache in thought.

"Improvisation, boy. You're learning. That's the mark of a great hero." The man gave another tug at his moustache. "But the spikes are gone. How will we get back?"

"Deal with it later."

Escalla hovered above the green slime, keeping carefully away from the water.

"So this stuff eats through flesh, leather, metal . . . But it hasn't gone through the stone floor. So it leaves stone alone?"

The Justicar shrugged. "Pretty much. Otherwise it would burn through to the Abyss."

"Polk, give me one of your oil flasks."

"Aha!" The teamster swelled with triumph. "You've thought of a way to burn off the slime?"

"Nope. I thought of a thousand and one uses for one of the local tricks and traps."

Escalla seized hold of the clay oil bottle, uncorked it, and poured the oil out into the water. She then carefully collected green slime with the dissolving tip of the dead archer's bow and dropped it into the oil bottle. She dropped a piece of waybread into the jug to keep the slime fed and happy, then carefully cleaned the spout and popped the cork back home.

"Aaand there we are." The job done, Escalla carefully washed the bottle in the water well away from the slime.

"We'll have to keep it upright so it doesn't eat its way through the cork. I'd hate to see what happens if we accidentally smash the jug."

There was a moment's pause and then the faerie passed the deadly cargo to Polk.

"Here, *you* carry it!"

The teamster instantly recoiled. "It's a monster! I'll be soiled!"

"Do I look soiled?" Escalla posed above the water, flipping out long sheets of soft blonde hair. "Hey, I'm a lovable icon of forest fun. You can trust my integrity!"

"But you're a faerie." Polk sniffed. "An underhanded breed."

"Hey!" The faerie proudly waved her little parchment with the stun rune. "When you're my size, it's gotta be brains over brawn. Now just carry the damned slime!"

Polk gingerly accepted his deadly load. He wrapped a piece of rope about the bottleneck and carried it before him as though it might explode at any instant. With a shake of her head, Escalla turned invisible and rose to scout her way along the unknown corridor.

They came to a junction in the passage with a tunnel turning away from the mother route. Escalla peered both ways, shrugged, and continued along the main passageway. She gave a piercing whistle to summon her companions and flew erratically onward down a corridor that was still knee-deep in mire.

"Hey, guys, this way feels good, don't you think? I mean, none of it looks lived in, but maybe that's the idea."

"Escalla!" Jus waded forward, holding his sword on guard. *"Shhh!"*

"But maybe we should be more scientific? Maybe the wizard is with the weapons? We could have tried to use magic to find the trident and stuff." The girl's voice echoed eerily in the gloom. "Should I have memorised a locate object spell? I mean, I learned fireball, stinking cloud, and lightning bolt. I did web and a couple of magic missiles. . . . Does that make me sound too combat-heavy to you?"

She approached a door that sealed the corridor. After carefully inspecting for signs of insects, tentacles, explosive runes, and poisoned needles, Escalla pressed one tall pointy ear against the wood.

"Eww! Mildew!" The girl jerked back and scrubbed at her besmirched little face. "Anyway, it's empty, not a soul stirring, all that kind of stuff. Face it: We've been smart enough to let someone else pioneer the route. Anything dangerous, the archer and his pals will already have solved!" The girl motioned to the door. "J-man, do the boot thing."

The Justicar could have tried to kick the old door down. Instead, he turned the door handle and shoved.

"The door's ajar, dimwit."

Escalla sniffed, the very image of offended dignity.

Jus poised his sword, then with a rush he threw open the door and stood ready to fight. Miffed at having made a little blunder, the faerie took one look into the deserted room and flew right on in.

"Come on, Polk! Time's wasting!"

Behind her, the teamster began fussing about in his backpack, finally finding a few iron spikes at the bottom. The man knelt down in the water and began splashing away with a hammer, trying to jam a spike home underneath the door.

Escalla flew to perch atop the door.

"Um, Polk? Guy, we may be working to a slight time limit here. We don't want the others to sneak past us with all the treasure and stuff." Polk ignored her, and Escalla leaned closer. "Just how many spikes did you bring with you anyhow?"

"This is the last one!"

"Really?" The faerie cleared her throat politely. "Um, Polk? What the hell are you doing?"

"I'm *spiking*, girl! That's what you have to do in a dungeon: spike the doors! Keeps 'em open."

The faerie gave a malicious little smile and hovered close to Polk's ear. "Hey Polk, why do we want the doors pegged open?"

"So they're not in the way if we have to . . ." Suddenly catching onto the appalling implications, Polk stood up and quickly abandoned the whole idea. "Right! No more spikes for you two! Not now, not ever!"

Escalla ushered Polk into the room with a sigh. In a universe of idiots, she was the only pure and shining star. The faerie tugged her bodice straight, flicked back her hair, and then flew stylishly into her very first dungeon room.

The door instantly slammed shut behind her, locking itself with magical bolts of force.

"Damn!"

They were trapped in a room without exits. The faerie looked at the door, then at Polk. Not deigning to say a word, she went across the room to find the Justicar.

17

Unamused, Jus glared at the locked door. Magical force shimmered across the portal, sealing it shut. Only a golden keyhole remained uncovered, twinkling and glittering in invitation.

"Great."

There were no other possible exits from the room. The chamber was broad and square and strangely decorated. Nine evenly spaced globes hung from the ceiling by wires. Huge and silvery, they dangled just above the ranger's head.

Jus grumbled, looking as though he wanted to cleave something with his sword.

"Cinders, can you smell anything?"

Muck and water. The hell hound sniffed. *Magic. Boring. Go now?*

"We're working on it." Jus tried an experimental shove against the door and found his hand repelled from the portal. "Any of you find any secret doors?"

"No." Escalla gave a shrug. "What's a secret door look like, anyhow?"

"If I knew that, it wouldn't be secret." Jus hammered on the walls with the hilt of his sword, tapping carefully, high and low. He moved with an absolute thoroughness until he noticed that Polk and Escalla were merely content to watch.

Annoyed, the ranger slitted up his eyes and said, "You *could* help."

Shrugging, Escalla fluttered over to one of the silver globes. "Sure!" She rapped the sphere with her fingertips. "Hey these things are glass! Want me to break one?"

"Don't touch it!"

The Justicar held up his hand to halt the girl. He waved everyone away from the globes.

"They're obvious, so we don't mess with them. Remember this whole place is set up as a test." The Justicar went back to his careful search of the walls and floor. "Look for other solutions first—ones the designer didn't think of. Escalla, take a careful look at the lock and see what you think."

"I'm on it!"

The girl whirred busily away. Interested scholarly noises followed as she took a thorough appraisal of the lock, and then the faerie came back to the Justicar's side. He had his gauntlets off and was kneeling in the muck probing the floor.

Jus looked up at Escalla, raised his brows, and said, "So did you look at it?"

"Yep!"

"Can you open it?"

"Nope!" Shrugging, the girl seemed to wonder why Jus looked so hurt. "Hey, I'm a sorceress not a cat burglar! What did you expect?"

The only other option seemed to be the globes. Polk walked underneath one and inspected it, his face reflected into silly shapes in the silver glass.

"Son, these here are a cryptic puzzle. That's a classic element of dungeon design."

"They're a trap." Jus shook his head and approached one sphere. "Any bets? One should have the exit key, and the others will probably explode or contain a shower of rot grubs."

"You miss the point, son!" The teamster slapped Jus on his armored shoulder, trying to cheer him up. "Come on. A dungeon is a foe, a challenge!"

With a dire glance at Polk, the Justicar carefully touched a globe. It weighed about as much as bowl of gruel and didn't rattle when shaken. A light held behind the globe did not shine through. Each of the globes seemed to be exactly the same. There was no way to tell what was inside without shattering one.

Escalla met her friend's eye and gave a helpless little shrug.

"What the hell? Pick one and bust the thing!" The girl pointed out one sphere hanging in a corner. "Try this one!"

"Why that one?"

"It feels lucky!" Making a little pirouette, Escalla fluttered through the air. "Trust me. I'm a faerie."

Blowing out a heavy breath, Jus shook his head and approached the chosen globe. He took his sword and gave it a couple of experimental swipes to loosen up his wrists, then slid the weapon back into its sheath.

"Polk, spread a groundsheet under it to catch the contents as they fall. Escalla, go invisible." The man waited until all was ready. He motioned for Polk to go to the farthest corner of the room. "Stay there."

The manic sounds of a happy hell hound drifted into their minds. *Burn! Monster come, Cinders flame!*

Jus shook his head. "You've only got three shots. Don't breathe flame unless I ask for it."

Cinders sulked, his tall ears flattening and a dissatisfied mumble echoing in everyone's mind.

With everything ready, the Justicar moved to stand beside the chosen globe. His feet moved into a measured combat stance, and he took two deep, slow breaths.

An instant later, his sword was out of its sheath, had smashed through the globe, and was already moving in a second cut. The sphere had just begun to fly apart, black shapes still frozen inside, as the Justicar's sword whipped through the glass a second time.

Shattered glass flew through the air, and flat black shapes suddenly screamed as they exploded from their prison. Unfolding like lethal sheets of paper, they scythed through the air toward the Justicar.

"Shadows!" Jus's sword blurred toward one of the black shapes, but the monster simply dodged aside. "Escalla, stay away!"

Three monsters had been in the sphere. One slid to the water's surface, already cut to ribbons. Jus ducked as another turned itself sideways, invisibly thin, and sliced at his throat.

The shadows attacked, numblingly swift, their voices screaming like children lost down a distant well. His teeth set, the Justicar swatted at black shapes with his blade, and they rippled like silk sheets as they tumbled, dipped, and streaked across the room. Like flying razors, they hissed and sliced at living flesh, swirling sideways as the black sword came whipping out to slash them.

As the Justicar hammered one shadow aside, a frightened faerie voice twittered from above.

"Jus!"

"Stay back!" His blade ringing as the shadows swirled and spun into the attack, Jus parried each razor cut that sliced toward his flesh. "They can kill you, but they can only hurt me!"

"Jus, get clear! I can shoot!"

"Stay invisible and stay there!"

A shadow ripped a line across the Justicar, but instead of slicing into his flesh, it seemed to incise a wound into his soul. Chill spread into his body. He cursed and whipped his blade in a blinding maze of cuts, and the two shadows flapped backward, tatters flying from their edges as they were sliced and punctured by the Justicar's blade.

One shadow caught sight of Polk and flew at him with a keening scream. Jus caught the motion from the corner of his eye and whirled, his blade flashing to split the monster in two. Like a sliced bedsheet it coiled and fluttered as it fell, its voice fading as its hellish life-force leaked into the mire.

The final shadow gave a piercing, bloodcurdling scream. Turning sideways into an invisibly thin line, it streaked straight toward the Justicar, ready to shear his soul. One instant, Jus stood in the path of the charge. Escalla screamed in fright, and then suddenly Jus had pivoted aside, his blade whipping down. The lethally sharp sword slit the entire shadow in half. The monster flew past him, swerved to avoid the wall, and then suddenly fell apart. With an echoing wail of horror, the entity peeled into two pieces, its form fading as it disappeared like scraps of mist inside a wind.

With a curse, Jus sheathed his sword. Escalla popped into view, fluttering and anxious as she came down to swirl about her friend.

"Hot damn, man! You are *awesome* with that sword!" The girl blew out a breath of relief and made a face of disapproval. "You should have let me take one. I could have helped."

"Shadows." Jus touched at the chill spot where the monster had cut at him. "They suck out strength. I've got lots, but you've got little. Safer to keep you out of their way."

"You were protecting me like that?" The girl blinked at him, a little smile on her face. "That's sweet!"

"Yeah." Jus rubbed at the wound. "Normally it takes about an hour to heal, but here's a trick they never teach at priest school." The ranger took a long drink from his canteen of beer. He heaved a sigh, flexed his arm, and simply shrugged away the injury.

Polk nudged at the waters where a shadow had once lain. "You shouldn't drink on the job, son. It's bad form."

"*You* drink."

"I'm the chronicler. It helps my creative flow." Polk folded up his arms. "So, have you figured out the cryptic clues? Have you solved the trap? Come on, time's a-wasting!"

Among the shards of shattered glass, Escalla found a little key. She took it to the door and touched it to the keyhole. It passed into the lock, turned, and achieved absolutely nothing. The faerie took out the key and looked through the keyhole in indignation, seeing the empty corridor outside the room mocking at her.

"Damn it! It's the wrong key!" She kicked at the door in spite, but magical force made her foot rebound from the wood. "What are we supposed to do now?"

They all looked up at the eight remaining globes. Clearly, they were supposed to break the globes one at a time, fighting monster after monster until they wore themselves out. With no humor for the wizard's little games, Jus growled in ill-temper, then flashed a glance from Escalla to the door and back again, then pulled Cinders tight.

He nodded once as he stared at the door lock, then said, "Escalla, can you turn into something really, really thin"—he glanced over at the portal—"something thin enough to go through the keyhole?"

Pursing her lips, Escalla eyed the door with the air of a consummate shapechanging professional.

"Sure! But why? It still leaves you guys locked in here."

"Humor me."

Jus put out his hands, and Escalla did a backflip as she turned into an absurdly long, thin earthworm. She could change her shape but never her mass. Threading herself into the keyhole and slipping swiftly through, she left her clothes lying in Jus's grasp.

On the far side of the door, the girl had no light. Changing back into her usual form, she cowered nude and nervous in the dark.

"I'm out! What now?"

Jus nodded thoughtfully to himself and said, "Go away from the door, then turn around and try to open it."

The girl's voice could be heard muttering in the dark outside. Polk and Cinders both exchanged idle glances as though comparing notes on Jus's sanity. The big man caught the roll of Polk's eye and gave a scowl.

"Bear with me." Jus stood back from the door. "Escalla?"

"I'm coming! I'm coming!" The girl's voice was muffled as she came back from her little trip. "What now?"

"Turn the door handle and push!"

The door swept open. Apparently, the trap was set to let new visitors in. Jus tossed Polk into the corridor, leaping along with him in a rush as they raced out of the room. The door slammed shut behind them with a rush, the leaden *boom* of it echoing out along the pitch-black corridors.

Polk and Jus heaved a sigh of relief then looked along the empty passage.

Something was missing. Jus flicked a glance left and right and frowned. "Where's Escalla?"

The faerie was nowhere to be seen. Jus made a weary noise, turned back to the door and opened it to find a nude, wet Escalla glaring at him from inside. The girl's cheeks blazed pink with embarrassment.

"Don't say it!"

Without another word, the girl flew back out of the room and snatched her clothes out of the ranger's grasp. She dressed herself while hovering in midair and casting a suspicious glance behind her to see if anyone had dared to watch.

Red eyes gleamed, and Escalla gave a sniff. "Whatta you looking at, mutt?"

Faerie butt! The hell hound's tail wagged. *Neat!*

"Hmph! Well at least you've got good taste." The girl pulled on her long gloves. "All right crew, show's over, trap's solved. Let's get moving and find this damned wizard!"

They returned to the side passage that had led them astray. Escalla flipped herself invisible, peeked about the corner, and then led the way into the dark. Jus surged through the water just behind her, his sword out and his eyes searching everywhere. Above his helm, Cinders grinned like a mad piranha. The dog's big white teeth were the only things clean in the entire dungeon.

The teamster gradually fell behind. Carefully drawing on his scrolls, the man looked up only when hailed from a great distance ahead. A small ball of light floated in the darkness behind Jus and the faerie.

Staring in irritation back at Polk, the Justicar growled and said, "What in the name of Zagyg are you doing?"

"Maps!" Polk refused to be disturbed at his task. "A chronicle has to have a map."

"Right." The ranger walked on down the passage. "Come on. If you fall back too far, we won't hear it if you get eaten by a monster."

Polk blinked, looked behind himself, then sped hastily after Jus's departing back, his feet splashing madly in the water. He made sure to tread in the big man's footsteps and stayed as close behind him as he dared.

* * * * *

The corridor ended in a plain wooden door. Escalla became visible as she neglected to concentrate on her magic and instead played at being a dungeoneer. With her wings whirring away, she made a careful inspection of the portal.

"Is this one teak?" The faerie made a face of mock distaste. "The last door was oak. These people ought to decorate according to some kind of theme." She carefully kept away from the moldy, slimy wood. "No traps, no runes, no ear borers, no guillotines." Escalla motioned to the door.

"Wood rot is really bad for my complexion. Anyone want to listen at the thing?"

Jus made an irritated noise and simply kicked the door down. Rotten wood flew apart and fell bouncing all over the floor. With his sword ready, the Justicar advanced through the doorway and glared into the room beyond.

Magic light flooded harsh and bright into a large stone chamber. A single door stood opposite the entryway, and four huge, terrifying shapes stood hunched in the gloom. Huge creatures made of malformed flesh, eight feet tall and rippling with misshapen muscle, each seemed to have been badly stitched together out of spare parts from a mad doctor's refuse bin.

The Justicar looked at the creatures and hefted his sword, ready to parry or run one through.

"Flesh golems."

They stood in niches—four monsters with an empty niche beside them. Each monster had a number burned into its chest: five, seven, eleven, and thirteen.

One of the monsters stirred. Its breath bubbled wetly as it turned foul, cold eyes upon the three interlopers and said, "One of us does not belong with the others. If you can pick it out, it will serve you. If you pick the wrong one, we will kill you. You have sixty seconds."

Frightened into visibility and hovering ahead of her two companions, Escalla looked at the numbers and blinked.

"Um, look, did some other guys come through here just before?"

"Fifty-five seconds."

"Yeah, look, do you always ask the same question when people come in, or do you change it?" The faerie nervously fluttered her wings. "Because if the other guys came through here and answered right, then the odd monster out went with them."

"Forty seconds."

Escalla flitted in front of the door with anxiety. "Look! If there was a fifth monster and he went along with the other guys, then *he's* the one who didn't belong! So that's your answer, yeah? It's the missing guy!"

"Thirty seconds."

The faerie fluttered madly back and forth, her voice pitched into a whine.

"But it's not *fair!* You're doin' it all wrong!" Escalla began to go into a tantrum. "I can't answer it if you don't listen to me! Hello? Hey, fleshfreaks, pay attention to the faerie!"

The monsters turned toward Escalla and flexed fingertips hard enough to carve though stone.

"Ten seconds!"

"All right! All right! I can solve this!" The girl tried to hold Jus back. "There's a solution, trust me. Brains over brawn."

The Justicar turned, shoved Polk back down the corridor, then grabbed Escalla underneath one arm. The faerie's eyes bugged, and she angrily kicked her little feet.

"Hey! No one touches the faerie!"

"Shut up and shoot!"

Escalla looked back into the room behind her to see all four monsters lumbering toward the door. She laughed and opened her hands, a swirling surge of energy whirling inside her grasp.

"Ha! *Fireball!*"

Jus tried to stop her. "For gods' sake *no!*"

Too late. Escalla screeched with glee and punched the spell down the passageway. With a foul curse, the Justicar managed to tackle Polk and shove both the teamster and the faerie down into the mire. The ranger thudded on top of them, Cinders's fur cloaking his back as a wild explosion blasted through the air.

The fireball was a spell far too large for such a tiny room. The room shook with explosive force, and then a roaring lance of flame came shooting down the corridor. It ripped above the Justicar, the heat of it licking steam from Cinders's fireproof fur. Greasy sludge atop the water caught fire with horrid little flames, lighting the scene as Polk and Escalla fought up from the filth and coughed the muck out of their mouths.

They were suddenly alone. The air was filled with smoke and the stench of scorched muck. Dazed and almost drowned, Escalla peeled back her hair from her face. Polk half raised himself from the mire and looked around as though expecting a new blast of fire.

The Justicar's magic light had disappeared.

Thrashing sounds came from the room as the massive creatures beat in a frenzy at the walls. Burned and furious, all four of the flesh golems came staggering through the doorway, caught sight of Polk and Escalla, and screamed in bloodcurdling hate. Escalla shrieked and instantly disappeared. Suddenly alone, Polk sat on his backside and began to skid rapidly backward through the mire.

All four monsters blundered toward him, when suddenly a dripping shape heaved upward from the water. Dripping mud, his hell hound skin outlined by fire, the Justicar rose and hacked his black sword straight into the trailing creature's skull. The bone clove with a hideous *crack*, and the black blade ripped free in a trail of blood.

The monster spun and staggered blindly against a wall, thrashing in the mud with an appalling unwillingness to die. A second monster whirled and flailed with its fist, catching Jus across the shoulder and smashing him against the wall, but the ranger rebounded and hacked through the creature's arms. The golem shrieked in agony and rage, but the ranger wasted no time. Following through with his sword, he plunged over half the blade through his foe's chest. The creature staggered and fell.

Burn! Burn!

Cinders sent a bolt of flame thundering into the corridor. One flesh-monster roared and screamed. Another simply put its hands over its eyes. The Justicar dodged a clumsy strike by one of the monsters, split one creature's shoulder half from its body, then with a second chop almost ripped the creature in two.

The last remaining abomination made a charge, blundering through the water. Jus hefted his sword and let loose a roar that shook the entire tunnel. Hurling himself into his enemy, the ranger met its punch with a swift slice of his blade. The monster's arm fell, injured and bleeding. It flailed the limb at him like a club, battering the Justicar's shoulder so that the bone snapped with an audible crack.

Snarling as he shook away the pain, Jus staggered backward. The flesh monster clenched its fist and rose to smash him to the floor. The ranger kicked the creature in its crotch, and his boot making a sickening sound. The monster pitched forward, and the Justicar hacked his sword down one-handed with stunning force. The flesh monster's head fell, almost severed from its neck. Still fighting, it lurched around and punched a wall, shattering the stone. With blood spraying from its neck, the golem came around to make another devastating charge.

The water made footwork nightmarishly awkward. It was a place for blade work and not for dodging. Jus reversed his sword into a backhanded grip, holding it like a huge ice pick as the flesh golem charged. The ranger whipped the sword upward as the golem ripped at him with its remaining arm. The sword sliced, deflecting the monster's blow and ripping its target from elbow to armpit.

It all happened in a single fluid blur. Jus pivoted and swung, throwing his entire weight behind the sword. The blade ripped into the golem's spine as it passed through, and the monster arched, its eyes going wide. Already dead, its momentum carried it forward. The black sword whirled back and hissed into the monster's neck on the uninjured side. Thick as a tree-trunk, the neck was finally sliced through. The golem struck the dungeon wall, and the impact shook the severed head free from its shoulders. Decapitated, the titanic torso struck the passageway, shattering stone blocks and spraying blood until it finally slid into the mire.

His sword dripping blood and his shoulder broken, the Justicar whirled on his companions in an apocalyptic rage.

"Who the hell told you to use a damned fireball?"

Escalla popped into view, hiding behind Polk.

"Sorry!" The girl took cover. "Girlish enthusiasm! The blast was smaller last time I used it. I swear!"

"You almost killed us all!"

"Hey, don't sweat it!" Escalla came happily out of hiding. "I set them up for you. Four in, four down! They mess with *us*, and they get what's coming!"

His head swimming, his shoulder broken, and one side of his body a livid bruise, the Justicar shot the girl a seething glance. Polk was looking at him and chewing his moustache.

The Justicar reacted with a growl. "Well?"

Retrieving the fallen slime bottle intact from the mud, the teamster shook his head in disappointment. "You should have fought them in the doorway one at a time, son, man to monster flashing blades!" The teamster gave a sigh. "Backstabbing . . ."

". . . is just not done. Right." The Justicar slumped against the wall and fought to stand. "How many of those damned healing potions do we have?"

Escalla's eyes opened wide, and an instant later she was at the ranger's side. She ran a hand across his face and asked, "Are you really hurt?"

"Maybe." The man slid down the wall and ended up sitting in the water. "Get me the healing potion, the big one."

The baron's only sliver of aid had been to provide each of his adventurers with a powerful magic medicine. Escalla pulled a potion from Polk's load of equipment and grimaced as she heard the Justicar snap his own broken bones into place. She held the potion to his lips and tipped it up to make him drink, her wings fanning his brow delicately.

Pale, Escalla watched as the Justicar breathed hard and let the magic potion do its work.

"Hey, Jus?"

"Yeah?"

"Sorry, man. It seemed a good idea, you know?"

"I know." The warrior gave a weary sigh. "Just be careful."

"Sure." The girl tossed away the empty potion bottle and sat on Jus's knee. She looked up at him for long, quiet moments, watching him in concern.

"I didn't know you *could* be hurt, man." Escalla ruefully wiped at the man's face. "You're like a juggernaut, big and indestructible and always there."

"Take the pain and keep hitting." Slowly, Jus began breathing more easily. "First combat lesson worth learning."

"Hey, that was some pretty sword stuff you were doing, though." The faerie shook her head. "Great moves, J-man."

"Thanks. I try." The ranger opened his eyes and sat up, testing his newly healed shoulder. "Potion's working."

"Hoopy."

The girl patted Cinders's wet, soggy fur. "Hey, pooch. You all right?"

All right.

It took few minutes of rest to get the Justicar back on his feet. He explored his shoulder slowly, shook his head, and used one of his few precious spells to heal the lingering damage.

The spell did the trick. Jus almost instantly felt as good as new. Swinging his arms in satisfaction, the big man trod on monster backs and marched into the fire-blackened room.

"Whoever came through here last, this wasn't what they fled from. There's still something nasty up ahead."

The Justicar wrenched the exit door open. It showed signs of being scuffed and opened. Jus took a swift look up the newfound passageway and waved the others onward.

"Come on."

Happily drawing his maps, Polk followed after the warrior.

＊　＊　＊　＊　＊

Hovering anxiously back in the flesh-monsters' room, Escalla fluttered here and there, poking about for treasure. Finding nothing, she gave a frustrated little noise and hastened off after her colleagues.

The corridor wended onward into the darkness, but the dark now had a half-heard pulse and flow of steam. Stairs led a few steps upward out of the muck, and the rough stone walls became beaded with warm, sticky droplets of water. From far down the tunnel, a sudden blast and shudder shook the air. A prolonged hiss of steam echoed down the hall, followed by a ripple of heat washing through the air.

Above the stairs, a broken pile of metal junk half-filled the corridor. The Justicar shook his head and simply bent iron bars aside then picked his way forward along the hall. A growing stink of sulphur and the roar of steam made the going slower as they crept cautiously into the gloom.

A broken door opened upon a rough stone ledge. Beyond the ledge, great swirls of steam eddied inside a huge natural cave. Water dripped and spattered from a ceiling hundreds of feet above, while the floor seemed to be a seething sea of bubbling mud.

The reeking steam made the air almost unbreathable. Cinders wagged his bedraggled tail quite happily, but the remainder of the group shied back and shielded their faces from the heat as they crept forward onto the ledge to stare into the cave.

The walls glowed with sickly phosphorescent light, showing a hellish space of boiling water and bubbling mud. Far across the cave there lay another ledge, beyond which a new tunnel gaped in sinister black welcome.

The gulf between the ledges was at least a hundred feet wide. Between the two ledges, there hung long and slimy chains, the end of each one hanging a dozen feet above the boiling mud. Rotten fragments of wood showed that the chains might have once supported strips of wood— perhaps a bridge or walkway of some sort, but there was no longer any way to tell.

Escalla looked about herself in wonder then lay down on her stomach to peer at the pools thirty feet below. She smiled, her eyes opening wide in sheer joy of discovery.

"Hey, guys, you should see this! It's incredible. There's a couple of geysers down here!"

A sudden shudder of force filled the air. The Justicar snatched Escalla back from the brink, whipping her backward by the heels as a huge jet of boiling water shot up past her perch and smacked into the ceiling above. Steam thundered up into the sky, smacking into the rock ceiling to make a boiling rain. The raw power of the blast made the entire dungeon shudder and filled the cavern with a swirling sulphurous fog.

Escalla sat in the Justicar's arms, blinking at the geyser. Jus held Escalla in the crook of one arm and brushed her hair back from her face.

"All right?"

"This had better be *some* damned treasure we find!" The faerie blew out a breath, shook her head, and took back to the air. "This dungeon is really getting on my hit list."

The cave shook as multiple geyser blasts thundered lethal columns of boiling water into the air. Escalla hovered safely back, timing the geyser blasts and watching the mud pools with a frown. Fists planted on her hips, she set her willpower to work and came up with the only sensible plan.

"All right, you guys can't climb the chains. One slip and you'll be broiled." She gazed competently across the cave, measuring the distance with her eyes. "I tell you what. I'll fly over to the other ledge and take a look down the new tunnel. If it looks like you guys will have to cross, we'll try to figure something out. If not, there's no point risking it."

It seemed the only thing to do, but Jus didn't like it. He tucked the girl's healing potion into her belt and helped her tie back her bedraggled hair.

"All right, but just *look*." The Justicar ducked as yet another titanic column of boiling water shot to the roof of the cave. "Get in, look, and get out. Don't risk the geysers, and don't touch anything!"

"You got it!" Escalla's wings fluttered happily as she hovered. She waited for a second geyser blast and then darted forward. "Back in five minutes!"

Great scalding drops of water rained down from the roof as Escalla wove between the hanging chains. She looked upon the bubbling mud pools below and banked hard sideways as a big gush of hot water spurted upward from a geyser mouth. Weaving nimbly back and forth, she sailed past a geyser at the far edge of the cave just as a jet of steam shot up into the sky. The steam ripped across her rear, and Escalla squawked and flung herself madly down out of the way. She hit the ledge and ducked into a doorway just as a geyser exploded into life in the cave.

Unprotected by her leather clothes, the faerie's left thigh stung like wildfire.

Across the cave, the Justicar dodged steam and bellowed in alarm. "Are you all right?"

"Ouch! Damn! I've burned my butt!" The girl pulled at her backside and glared at a livid scald mark. "This dungeon has no respect for quality!"

Fanning at her rump, Escalla rose painfully to her feet. She sighed, anointed her bottom with a few drops of healing potion, then looked into the dark tunnel mouth beyond the door.

A body lay stretched out in the doorway, lying on its back. Plate armor lay bent and buckled, and the open visor showed a pale, staring face.

Escalla kept her distance, nudging at the fallen figure as it lay lifeless on the floor.

"Um, guys? I just found the Bleredd priest!"

The man's armor had been battered. He lay frozen in terror, his face bleached white as paper, his lips and fingernails pale blue, and blood showing at a tear upon his throat. Out of respect for the dead, Escalla refrained from searching him for gold teeth, contenting herself with going through his purse for loose coins.

"Guys? He's really dead!" Escalla looked down the narrow corridor just beyond and saw a door waiting invitingly ajar. "But there's a room here. I'll go take a look and see if the passage goes on!"

She flew into the passageway, peering this way and that. From behind her, Jus's voice shook the walls. *"Escalla? Escalla!"* The ranger's voice boomed out over the roar and hiss of geysers and boiling mud. "Escalla, don't touch anything!"

"Hey, it's just one little door! Just a peek!" The faerie turned the latch. "How much danger can there be?"

The door had been deliberately perforated by dozens of little holes. Mist seemed to swirl out past Escalla and into the corridor. The girl threw all her tiny strength into shoving at the door, her wings beating and her legs straining as she tried to swing it open. She managed to open the portal by a shoulder's width. The mist slithered and coiled past her, leaving Escalla blinking into the dark.

The space beyond the door was utterly dark. The faerie's magical light seemed to fail at the threshold as though running into an invisible black wall. Escalla poked a finger at the darkness and found it to be made of empty air. She bit her lip as a foul, crawling sensation rippled down her spine.

Something seemed terribly, terribly wrong. Despite the geysers and volcanic mud a few yards behind, the air had taken on a distinct deathly chill.

A cold sweat ran down the faerie's spine. Conceding that she might have been just a *little* rash, Escalla eased away from the door and turned around.

Looming above her, a black figure was coalescing from the mists. A dark cloak swirled, and claws seemed to trail off into icy wisps of fog. Tall, cadaverous, and pale, the creature gave a predatory smile, his incisors gleaming, as he filled the air above the frozen faerie.

With a leer upon his face, the vampire loomed and spread his claws. Escalla made a little move backward, her antennae falling limp and flat.

"Oooh, *joy* . . ."

Escalla's day had definitely taken a turn for the worse.

18

Grinning a big placatory grin, Escalla backed slowly away. Quite suddenly she gave the vampire a friendly little wave.

"Um, hello! Look, I'm just having a look. Didn't touch a thing, I swear! So I'll just be on my way now. Sorry to have bothered you."

The vampire came toward her, and Escalla's antennae drooped.

"Aaaw, come on! I'm just a snack for you! You keep eating like this between priests and you'll get all fat and bloated!"

Lean as a strand of wire, the vampire bared his fangs. Claws shot from the ends of his fingertips as the last of his body coalesced from the swirling mists.

With a *pop*, Escalla instantly changed form.

"Look, I'm a skunk, a talking skunk!" Now a pink and lavender female skunk, Escalla waved her tail. "One more step and I do the musk thing! Yeah! *Pow!*" The skunk retreated as the vampire continued his slow, deliberate advance. "You guys *do* have a sense of smell, don't you? Come on, man, I'm serious! One step closer and you're gonna reek like the dead! Just like the dead . . ." The skunk suddenly looked a little anxious. "Then again, you already *are* dead. Oh, *damn!*"

Radiating a lifeless cold, the vampire spread his claws wide and gave a feral hiss. Quavering, Escalla changed herself into a spiny sea urchin and enthusiastically waved her prongs.

"Look, I'm all spiky! You'll pierce your lips if you try to bite! Definitely a stupid meal!" Seeing the vampire still coming toward her, Escalla changed herself into a floating rock. "Whups! Silicon life form! Look! No blood, I swear!"

A vampire claw ripped past her. The rock that was Escalla screamed and dodged aside. She turned back into faerie form, back-flipped, and then ricocheted from the ceiling as the vampire slashed at her with blinding speed. After an evasive somersault, Escalla hung hovering in the air, gleefully readying her last remaining battle spell.

"Oh yeah? You think you're pretty tough?" The whole dungeon lit up as brilliant sparks arced between the faerie's hands. "Well suck on *this* you undead yo-yo!"

Escalla screamed with laughter as sorcerous power blasted into life between her palms!

"Lightning bolt, *attack!*"

A blast of electricity stabbed out from the faerie's palms, sheeting the entire tunnel with light. The lightning bolt blasted into the vampire, arcing out to snake coils of power all across the floor and walls. Escalla fluttered her wings in triumph as she saw her enemy ripped apart by the spell.

"Escalla! Escalla!" The Justicar's booming voice drifted from across the carvern. "What's going on?"

The hole blown through the vampire simply closed itself. Scarcely even ruffled, the creature resolidified from mist.

"Oops!" Escalla's face fell, and she hovered in midair. "Look, about that 'undead yo-yo' thing . . ."

Furious, the vampire flexed his talons. Clearing her throat, Escalla steepled her fingers and became the soul of calm.

"Look, let's be reasonable about this. I'm sure we can both come to a mutually advantageous—"

With a scream of wild hunger, the vampire attacked. He ripped the air with his talons, missing Escalla by the barest fraction of an inch. Fluttering madly back and forth, the girl screeched in panic as the creature howled for her soul.

"Jus! Jus, there's a vampire here!"

The answer came echoing back past the sound of geyser steam.

"Don't let it touch you!"

"Don't let it touch me!" Escalla roared as she dodged vampire's claws. "What kind of damned fool advice is that?" The faerie tried to lunge between the vampire's feet, only to have a claw smash into the stone and block her path. "Six foot four, shaven headed, and the brains of a dead ant!"

Escalla tried to dodge past the vampire and into the corridor that led to her friends. The fanged monstrosity blocked her every move, snatching at her with claws that seemed to rip the heat from the air.

"Jus, I could use some help here!"

"Hold on! I'm coming!"

The vampire whipped his head about and gave an ululating cry. From the little crevices and shadows hidden in the corridors, a chittering, squealing horde of bats came whirling through the air. They descended about the Justicar in an enraged black cloud, blinding him with their wings. The ranger cursed, shielded his eyes, and retreated as he swatted at the bat clouds with his hands.

Hissing as he summoned his winged minions to harass the Justicar, the vampire's instant of distraction gave Escalla an opening. The girl hurled herself backward into the pitch black room from whence the vampire must have come. Hitting the magical zone of blackness, Escalla's magic light instantly flared and failed, breaking both spells but plunging the room into utter darkness.

"Oh, great!"

The darkness seemed less complete—merely a "bowels of the earth" darkness as opposed to the "magical spell" kind. Escalla shot up to the door lintel, licked, slapped her hand on the stone, then hovered a few feet behind the frame of the door.

"*Yoooo-hooooo!* Hey, fang boy! Nice coffin! Wanna bet I can break it?"

The vampire whirled.

Escalla twiddled her fingers at the creature and waved in mock friendliness. "What, you're so lame you can't even take down a faerie?"

With a snarl, the vampire lunged for Escalla's throat. He passed beneath the portal, and a massive *crash* of force pounded downward from the sphinx's parchment stuck above the doorframe. The vampire spun and dropped like a stone, lying stunned and twitching weakly on the floor.

Leaping in utter glee, Escalla gave a screech of victory.

"*Yes!* I did it! He's out like a light!"

With the bats dispersing, Jus answered the faerie's cry. "*What? You stunned it?*"

"With the sphinx's papyrus-thingie! *Wham!* One in, one down!" Escalla weaved back and forth, boxing at shadows. "*Pow!* You better watch yourself if you try takin' on *this* faerie!"

"It won't hold for long!" Jus bellowed across the geyser cave. "You'll have to kill the vampire while he's down!"

Having changed shape into a large firefly to light the room, Escalla blinked and looked down at the vampire.

"Kill it! How? I just used my last major spell!"

"What spells do you still have?"

"Ummm, lessee . . ." The firefly ticked its list of spells off on its feet. "Um, two magic missiles, a sleep spell, web spell, a stinking cloud, and Tensor's floating disk!"

"Floating *what?*"

"*Disk!* It levitates stuff! I wanna use it to haul all my treasure out of the dungeon!" Escalla hovered over a long wooden box in the middle of the square room. "Hey, he has a coffin in here!"

✿ ✿ ✿ ✿ ✿

In the geyser cave, Jus retreated as a lethal blast of steam shot up through the mud. There was no way to cross the chasm in the few scant minutes Escalla had left.

"Escalla, listen to me! Use a magic missile! Hurry! Blast his coffin and use a sliver of the wood as a stake!"

The man cocked his head, Cinders helpfully lending his own keen hearing as the girl's voice drifted back through the steam.

"Wood slivers? What, you want me to kindle a fire?"

"No!" Jus leaned over the ledge to give his voice an extra ounce of force. "Hammer the stake through his heart!"

"No way!"

"Just do it! Hurry!"

"But I'm a girl!" Escalla wailed. *"I'm a faerie! Blood'll splurt over my dress!"*

"Just do it!" Jus felt a thrill of fright as though the vampire was already reaching for the girl. "Hurry, before it wakes up!"

A flash came from the distant tunnel. Seconds later, there was a revolting sound of hammering, and Escalla's wail managed to carry across the intervening yards.

"Eeeeew! Eeeeeew—ick! I can't believe you're making me do this!"

Jus helplessly clenched his sword.

"Is it done?"

"Yes, damn it! I staked him, and there's black guck all over me! Are you happy now?"

Jus breathed out a deep sigh of relief, swapped a brief look with Polk, and felt Cinders happily wagging his tail.

"She did it."

Whack in heart! Splat splat splat! Cinders dwelt on the cool sound effects and jiggled in glee. *Stick bad monster again!*

"Yeah, time to finish it." The Justicar turned back to bellow out across the open cave. "Escalla?"

"Yeah?"

"The vampire's out, but he's not dead. To kill it, you have to do something more."

"What *now*?"

Jus stood at the edge of the mud and folded up his arms. Smiling, he shouted, "Now turn into a big rat or something and gnaw off his head!"

There was a long moment's pause.

Spattered with goo and utterly unamused, Escalla appeared at the ledge opposite the Justicar's perch.

"You have *got* to be kidding."

"Just do it!"

"No way, no where, no how!" Escalla met Jus eye to eye and planted her fists upon her skinny hips. "You want someone's head gnawed off, you come over here and do it!"

The Justicar sighed.

"All right, take my sword and do it."

"Yeah, right!" The faerie gave a toss of her gooey hair. "Like I can really carry that chunk of ironmongery all the way over the mud!"

"Well, find another way!" The Justicar clenching his fists in frustration. "Your magic missile spell fires darts! Saw his head off with a stream of those!"

The faerie glared at her friend.

"You are a sick, *sick* man, you know that?" The girl turned back down the tunnel. "I am doing this under *serious* protest—and only because this vampire really pissed me off!"

Holding a torch made from a chunk of vampire coffin, the girl tramped off into the gloom. A staccato series of little blasts revealed that the grisly job was being done.

Spattered, bedraggled, and extremely annoyed, Escalla appeared back at the ledge.

"Hey Jus, what about the dead priest? Isn't he gonna turn into a vampire too?"

"No!" The geyser gave its customary warning cough, and Jus ducked down low. "You don't turn into a vampire unless you're buried in the earth! That's why you leave the bodies out for the scavengers."

"Oh, great!" Escalla stood on the chest of the dead Bleredd priest to give her voice more height so it would carry. "Great, I can see it all now. You get fanged to death by a vampire, and just to add insult to injury, your friends just leave you on a roadside to get eaten up by crows!" Pausing, Escalla considered the point. "Hey, but what if you were *half* eaten by crows, but then someone came back and buried you? Would you turn into a sort of half-skeleton, half-vampire?

She disappeared back into the gloom. Flinching back from hot steam, Jus edged closer to his own rim of the ledge.

"Escalla? Escalla, get back here!"

Jus heard a warning rumble from the boiling mud down in the cavern and dodged back as a geyser spurted its lethal column up into the cave. When the steam and raining water had finally cleared, Polk, Cinders, and the Justicar blinked to see Escalla leaping and waving excitedly from the opposite ledge.

The faerie made a little dance of triumph in the air and shouted, "I found it! I found it!"

The Justicar's heart gave a surge of joy. "One of the magic weapons?"

"No!" Escalla came dancing out onto the ledge holding a little coin. "I found gold! The vampire had a big bag of treasure!"

Shaking his head to clear a rain of hot sulphur-water from Cinders's snout, Jus gave a sigh.

"Does the dungeon go on?"

"Naah, dead end." Escalla shoved her gold coin down her cleavage for safekeeping. "But there's treasure here, bags and bags of it! Oh, and there's a big hammer hidden underneath the coffin!"

Polk applauded, jerking his head in approval. The faerie took a bow as the teamster showered her with praise.

"That's it! That's got to be the magic hammer. She did good! She did damned good!"

"Damned good." Jus felt himself relaxing piece by piece. His fingers had almost stamped their outline into the handle of his sword. The man blew out his breath and fixed the faerie with his eye.

"You be careful!"

"Why Jus, are you concerned for little me?" Escalla posed and fluttered her lashes. "Now wait there! I'll go get the treasure!"

The girl disappeared, and Jus tried to see where she had gone.

"Escalla? Escalla! Don't touch the hammer with your bare hands! You'll get a power shock unless you're aligned with the damned thing's god!"

A flash came from down the dark corridor, joined with a screech of pain. Jus closed his eyes and rubbed at his forehead with his fingertips.

"You touched it, didn't you?"

"Shut up!" The girl's distant voice went into a sulk. "I'm going to drink my healing potion now."

Long minutes passed, and then Escalla came fluttering into view. Behind her came a big floating force-disk, upon which rode a dozen huge bags of coin, a hammer wrapped in scraps of the vampire's cloak, and the undead creature's raggedly severed head, riding on the prow like a figurehead.

✳   ✳   ✳   ✳   ✳

Grinning, Escalla timed the geysers, picked a gap and flew happily over the mud. The floating disk behind her went out into the open air then plunged down to ride three feet above the boiling morass.

Her wings whirring, Escalla flew past the swinging, dripping chains and came hovering up to land in the Justicar's arms.

"I'm here! I'm a vampire slayer!" The girl helped herself to the ranger's canteen, pleased to find that the scoundrel was carrying beer rather than water. The girl wiped foam from her mouth. "Right! That's *my* blow struck for truth and light! Let's go!"

The disk, however, remained stubbornly stuck three feet above the mud. Annoyed, Escalla peered over the ledge at the disk in alarm and knitted her alabaster brows.

"Damn it! Stupid floating disk spell!" The girl signed for Polk's rope. "Right! Gimme the rope! We'll bring the gold up the old fashioned way. I'll go tie the sacks to the line."

Jus looked at the steam-drenched cavern in glowering disbelief.

"You'll be be cooked like a dumpling!"

"No way! Three minutes between the geyser over there going off, and five minutes between blasts for this one! That gives me a window of . . . of two minutes!" The faerie dived down toward the mud, trailing a noose in her grasp. "Now come on! We'll get your magic hammer first!"

The magic hammer Whelm was hauled up from below, with the severed vampire head dangling below it on the rope. Jus removed the grisly head and tossed it over to Polk.

"Here. Catch!"

Polk held the head and almost screamed in fright.

"What am I supposed to do with this?"

"Stuff the mouth with holy wafers."

"Wafers?" The teamster stared. "Where in damnation am I supposed to get wafers from?"

"You forgot the wafers?" Jus shook his head in disappointment as he hauled up the first heavy bag of gold. "I don't know what adventure parties are coming to. Well, just stick it in your pack."

Escalla helped push the first heavy bag of gold onto the ledge and began to frenziedly untie the rope. She ignored the warning rumble from the geyser down below and triumphantly pulled the rope free.

"Right! Next bag!"

"Escalla?" Jus crouched as the ground began to shudder. "Escalla, get back!"

"What? No way!" The faerie blinked. She began edging back toward the ledge. "I have time! Just a few more bags!"

A sudden roar came from the mud pits as the geyser exploded into life. Already running for cover, Jus tackled the girl and dived with her back into the passageway. An instant later, a vast roaring column of boiling water shot into the air. Amidst the steam, gold and silver coins could be seen showering through the cavern.

"No! My treasure!"

Flapping and fighting, Escalla desperately tried to reach the gold. Jus grimly held her fast, and the girl slumped as she watched the coins go dancing down into the boiling mud. Finally, the girl simply ceased struggling. When the geyser finally halted, she clung miserably in the Justicar's arms with a tear welling in her eye.

"My gold! My beautiful gold!"

The ranger's face brimmed with sympathy.

"Hey, cheer up. I'll get you more treasure."

"But it was *my* gold!" Escalla made a miserable little noise, looking wanly off into the boiling mud. "I won it on my very own."

Shooting a glance toward Polk, who was no damned help at all, Jus patted Escalla on the back.

"You did well. You took out a vampire all on your own. We'll make a Justicar out of you yet."

"You'd have to eradicate my fashion sense first." The girl gave a sigh for lost glories then seemed to cheer up. "Easy come, easy go, I guess."

"Hey, you've still got one bag and the hammer. And the piece down your front can be your lucky piece, hey?" Jus tried his to cheer her up. "Come on, let's get back to the sphinx."

The man sat Escalla up on his shoulder where she could talk to Cinders, and the hell hound did his best to wag his tail and nuzzle at her hand. Jus picked up the little sack of gold and stuffed the money into Polk's backpack.

"Polk, give Escalla your magic light."

"But I need it for my chronicle!" The teamster bridled in alarm. "How can I see to write?"

"I don't care. She needs it more than you do." The Justicar rapped his knuckles against the man's bulging pack-load of gear. "Use a lantern."

Polk muttered, tucked his parchment under his arm and fussed with flint and tinder. Creeping out of her sulk, Escalla leaned over and plucked one of the parchments from Polk's grasp.

"So what are you writing there, anyway?"

"It is a chronicle of our adventure." Polk shot a meaningful glance at Jus. "Assuming the two of you both end up doing things worth chronicling."

Escalla read a few lines of Polk's horrible scrawl and blinked in surprise.

"Hey! This is all about me and the vampire!"

"Of course." Scorching his fingers, the teamster adjusted the lens of his bullseye lantern. "A heroic act! One slip of a girl fighting a triumphant battle against a creature of darkness."

"Hoopy!" Always happy to have her ego stroked, Escalla puffed herself up with pride, lost treasures instantly forgotten. "Hey Jus! This is actually pretty good! Check it out!"

The girl read a line from the top of the scroll. "Ooh! 'Escalla, siren of the sylvan forest, slayer of the shadow-fiend!' I like that!"

"Thank you." Polk bowed.

"Yeah!" The girl read more. "And what's this? 'Sensuous, sinful silky-thighed seductress of the . . .'" Suddenly unamused, Escalla began flipping back through pages of the scrolls.

"What's this? 'Love hungry,' 'perfect peach,' 'pinched, lissome bounty of her tightly curved . . . '" The girl put the scrolls aside and flicked a hard sidewise glance to Polk.

"You don't get out much, do you?"

"This is the recognized heroic literary style." Polk swelled himself up with an enormous, fragile dignity.

"Really?" Escalla tossed the man his scroll. "Well if I catch you staring at my silken thighs again, I'm gonna turn into a giant bedbug and visit you in the dark!"

It was time to retrace their tracks. Wearily trying to keep the peace, Jus lead the march into the dark. "Polk, stop writing purple prose about Escalla's thighs. Escalla, stop hassling the sidekick. Now come on, there's still two more weapons and a wizard to find."

Ducking a cobweb, Escalla frowned.

"Isn't there only one weapon left?"

"The city wants Wave and Whelm, and the erinyes must still be after Blackrazor. It's a good guess that our old allies are hoping to collect all three." Jus led the way down steps and back into the waterlogged corridors of the main dungeon. "Let's get back to that first junction and see your friend the sphinx."

＊　＊　＊　＊　＊

Back at the intersection, Enid the sphinx rose from her soggy vigil and waved one big paw as the party approached.

Tramping squishily through the muck, Jus, Cinders, Escalla, and Polk all waved in return.

The green slime in the corridor had been bypassed in the brusquest possible style. Thick overshoes of rope for Polk and Jus had used up the bulk of Polk's climbing gear. Polk muttered and grumbled, unhappy at the slow attrition of his dungeoneering equipment. He wrote his chronicles while glaring at the Justicar's back, the harsh sweeps of his wax marker showing the color of his mood.

Sitting upon Cinders and Jus, Escalla gave the sphinx a merry little salute and said, "Hey, Enid!"

"Hello." Enid looked up from teasing knots out of her tail. "Did you beat the vampire?"

"Yeah." Escalla made a twiddling little motion of her hand, unsure quite how to broach an uncomfortable topic. "Hey, about that . . . so you *did* know he was down there?"

"Oh, yes." Enid nodded as bright as can be. "I heard the magicians talking about him."

"Um, for future reference, a vampire is a pretty *major* encounter." The faerie gave a sigh. "Is there anything *else* you might want to fill us in on before we go down any more of these tunnels?"

It seemed to be a brand new thought to poor Enid. The sphinx turned to look down the northern tunnel and gave a little frown.

"Well, no one tells me much, but seafood or something is down *this* tunnel. When the breeze blows from that direction, my allergies break out." The cat woman gave a puzzled shrug. "They deliver about a ton of fish heads down there every day or two."

"Fish heads." Escalla nodded, storing the information duly away. "Uh-huh. And the other way?"

Enid shrugged.

"Umm, every day at about nightfall, someone delivers livestock down the western tunnel. Goats, cows, sheep, a few peasants on occasion. It gets pretty noisy down there for about five minutes or so." The sphinx frowned. "Then it all just stops."

"Oh, good." Overjoyed at the thought of all the toothy monsters just waiting for faerie snacks, Escalla sighed. "Gentlemen, thoughts please?"

Jus looked from one tunnel to another.

"Big hungry things in the west tunnel, maybe lots of tiny hungry things in the north where the fish heads go." The Justicar approached Enid the sphinx. "Thank you for the stun symbol."

"You liked it? Oh, good!" Immensely pleased, Enid preened her muddy hair. "So few people appreciate quality spells."

"It helped." Jus stood with one hand on his sword, looking dark and powerful. Above his head, Cinders grinned and let his eyes gleam bright red. "You said you sometimes see the wizards?"

"Every day!" The sphinx settled proudly in her place. "The librarian and his two acolytes, the keepers of Keraptis."

"*Keepers* of Keraptis?" Escalla raised her eyebrows and skimmed a meaningful glance at Jus. "Oh, really?"

"Those're the chaps! They're making a new Keraptis." Enid scratched at her slightly flea-bitten hide. "Dedicated to their job, they've worked ever so hard to restore this place just the way it was! My older sister was the sphinx in this dungeon ten years ago."

The Justicar scowled and carefully weighed this little gem of knowledge in his mind. Settling his sword, he reached up to pat the sphinx's flank and thoughtfully passed the creature by.

"Thank you, Enid. We'll see you again soon."

"All right." Enid settled into the mud. "Have a nice time!"

❧   ❧   ❧   ❧   ❧

It was time to pick a new route. Jus swiveled Cinders so that the hound could take a good sniff at the dungeon airs.

"Cinders, what do you think, old friend?"

Cinders smelled the western tunnel. *That way is beasts— cats, bugs.*

"Yup." The Justicar opened his badger-skin purse and took out a piece of snack-coal for the hell hound. "And the other way?"

Fish this way. The hell hound sniffed at the north tunnel. *Evil this way. Fresh blood, dead things, slimy water.*

"Evil again?" The Justicar narrowed his eyes. "Interesting . . ."

Escalla rose up from the ranger's shoulders and hovered in the air.

"Hey! I vote north! I vote for the fish heads! One vampire is enough. This time, I say we face something *small.*" The faerie whirred northward and turned invisible. "Now, come on! Let's go find some cash and get those weapons back!"

With the invisible faerie in the lead, a slow, careful advance began. Like the other tunnels, this passage seemed to have been burned and gouged out of the mountain's heart. Algae caked the walls and spread horrid color across the surface of the mire. The knee-deep waters were unpleasantly warm and made the tunnel echo with the splash of walking feet. Ripples in the surface sent refracted light dancing madly back and forth across the walls.

Cinders tracked Escalla with his sharp eyes. The girl flew up to a dark alcove leading off the passageway, inspected the darkness within, and even unveiled her borrowed magic light to take a closer look. She seemed satisfied. The light waved her companions down the main route, and the little faerie light swiftly disappeared.

The Justicar moved forward slowly. As he drew near the alcove, Cinders began to growl, the fur rising up all along his shoulders. Jus cleared his sword out of its scabbard in a single flawless blur, his weapon suddenly hovering in midair.

"Out."

Cinders's flames seethed, and a sinister little tongue of flame lit the alcove. A shadow against one wall stirred and moved as the Justicar's sword point whipped toward its throat and stopped a hair's breadth away.

Sir Olthwaite the paladin—pale, filth-spattered and much the worse for wear—edged into the light.

"Greetings, fellows! Well met, well met." The man raised a hand in wary greeting. "If you will forgive me, I thought you might be some of *them.*"

Polk made a sound of joy and stamped his foot, splashing his inside leg with dungeon soup.

"Sir Olthwaite! It's Sir Olthwaite!" The teamster slapped Jus hard on the back. "Now we'll go places! We've got a *real* hero for this dungeon!"

"Polk, sir! My dear chap what a pleasure to see you well!" The paladin made to advance and embrace, only to be halted by the Justicar's sword at his throat. "Yes, quite well . . ."

His face shadowed by the hell hound's twisting flames, the Justicar did not sheathe his sword. He held the point directly under the paladin's jaw and asked, "Where is the rest of your party, Sir Paladin?"

Clearing his throat, Sir Olthwaite gave a little shrug.

"There were only three of us: myself, the magician, and the priestess of Geshtai." The man gave a genteel nod of his chin back toward the sphinx. "That way. The western tunnel. We met wights, two of them. They took a fair amount of defeating."

The Justicar's sword remained poised for an instant kill, his stance low and spread.

"Yet *you* managed to survive."

"Not unscathed, I fear." The paladin managed to look a little pale. "They seem to have left me a tad drained of life. I'm not my old self quite yet." The knight swallowed and tried to move the ranger's sword point aside with his fingertips. "Look, well met on the trail and all that! Forgive and forget—what?"

Cinders's growl became almost audible, his fur rising like porcupine bristles as his barred teeth ran with flames. Escalla popped into visibility between Cinders and the paladin, resting one hand upon the dog's wet nose.

"Cinders, down boy! Enough!"

Burn!

"Not now!" The faerie coiled close to the hell hound and whispered in his ear. "Let him take hits from a few dozen monsters first, then toast him from behind!"

Unhappy, Cinders drooped and muttered canine curses in the air. Escalla fluttered brightly over to the paladin, inspecting the man by the glow of her magic light. Her tilted eyes shone with innocent surprise.

"So here you are! We were sooo worried!" The girl used one finger to lower Jus's sword.

"Jus, ease it back a bit just for now . . ." The faerie kept herself carefully out of reach of their newfound friend. "So you went down the west tunnel, huh? What was there?"

"Wights, my dear, as I said." Sir Olthwaite took his chance and moved closer to Polk, patting the pleased teamster on the shoulder. "My friend Polk here can tell you that underground exploration has its dangers."

"Really?" Having just polished off a vampire single-handedly, Escalla clasped her hands in mock concern. "Do tell: What else was down there?"

"A pit trap and a corridor that heated metal as you entered it." The paladin scornfully adjusted the coil of rope that dangled from his belt. "It's of no consequence! Come.

I can lead you back there. We can pass the traps and find the missing weapons!"

Posing like a confused little girl, the faerie put her finger against her chin. "Oh, but since we're already partway down this tunnel, why don't we keep going?"

"There are no weapons down *this* tunnel!" The paladin's voice snapped like a whip. "We have a job to do!"

"Yeah?" Escalla pivoted slowly in midair. "But my good friend Enid tells me that each of these three tunnels has a weapon at the end of it!"

Bristling in indignation, Polk tottered forward beneath his huge backpack full of gear.

"You listen to Sir Olthwaite! Veteran adventurers get a nose for treasure!"

"But I'm a girl, and girls are just *sooo* curious!" Ever suspicious, Escalla's sly eyes gleamed as she flew circles about the party. "I wanna go up *this* tunnel!"

Sir Olthwaite flexed his fingers.

"There is more profit to the west. We used a spell to tell us so."

"Oh?" Escalla flew down to pluck at the burnt end of the paladin's rope. "But your gear seems to have gotten all scorched and scratched! North seems so much safer."

The Justicar had heard enough. With his sword still out, he jerked his head toward the end of the northern tunnel.

"Move out. We're going north." The ranger shifted his grip on his sword. "And the great adventurer can show us how it's done. Polk, give him a torch."

"A torch?" The paladin bridled. "Why must *I* carry a torch?"

"Because you're leading." His sword held deceptively light in his hand, Jus nodded down the corridor. "Be my guest."

Sir Olthwaite took a light from Polk's lantern, spared an unfathomable glance for the Justicar, and then moved down the passageway. Escalla flicked Jus a glance, smiled, and popped swiftly out of view.

Polk was left glaring at Jus in bitter disappointment. The teamster shook his head slowly from side to side like a judge passing sentence.

Jus ignored the man and walked on.

"Keep that hammer safe."

"It's safe." Polk sniffed in disdain. "Son, I'm disappointed. Disappointed! A knight of the Silver Dragon walks among us, and do you pay him the slightest mind?" The little man swelled up like a puffer fish in indignation. "I suppose you don't care to hear what I think?"

"No."

Sir Olthwaite had reached the end of the corridor, where his torchlight showed an open room. The paladin lifted high his light, and Escalla came whirring beneath his arm, her passage shown by the scent of magic in her wake. Coming steadily forward, Jus paused in the doorway and looked out over a great waterlogged room.

A wide expanse of water glittered in the light. Polk's lantern beam searched out the limits of a large, echoing chamber. At the far side of the room, a stairway led upward into a new corridor. The whole place echoed to the lap and swirl of water, and algae-stink made the air as thick as rotting blood.

Jus lifted his own light to carefully inspect the ceiling, then took a careful, responsive grip upon his blade. Cinders's voice suddenly flickered in his mind.

Deep water. The hell hound went suddenly stiff. *Motion!*

Jus whipped his sword up to cover the dark water, and the paladin followed suit. Algae all across the water's surface rippled into life. Escalla a squeaked as she flew hastily aside.

The center of the room was far deeper than the verge. Water-weeds surged up out of the depths and boiled with life. Moving fast as thought, the dank strands wrapped themselves into a weird parody of human limbs.

The weeds shimmered with magic, the weedy textures disappeared, and quite suddenly two bodies swam happily in the water. Two stunningly beautiful maidens waved eagerly to the men. The girl on the left had long dark pigtails, and the costume of a minstrel girl clung wet and transparent against her curves. To the right, a voluptuous, bright-eyed elfmaid swam stark naked except for a little necklace of flowers.

"You've come!" The minstrel girl yearned upward with big dark puppy eyes. "We've been so lonely!"

"Yes!" The elf girl reached up dripping arms. "Lonely! Stuck here pining away for companionship!"

The minstrel girl swam imploring little circles. As she pleaded, the elf girl echoed her every phrase.

"Come to us!"

"Yes! Come to us!"

"Pleasure us!"

"Yes, in every possible way!"

Pleading hands reached up toward the human men. "Please rescue us! Come into the water and we'll give you *anything* you like!"

Flying high above, Escalla wearily rolled her eyes.

"Oh, *brother!* Who are you two kidding?"

"But it's true!" The minstrel girl pouted, stung to tears by the nasty-old faerie. She looked imploringly up at the Justicar. "I'm an innocent girl trapped here by a spell! I've been so lonely! I'm human, and I'm *aching* to be yours!"

The elf fought her way to the fore.

"I'm aching too! I bet *I* ache more!"

"You do not!" The brunette whirled and began arguing with her companion. "I was aching this morning!"

"Well I was aching yesterday!"

The minstrel maid went into a sulk. "That's just like you! You never want to share!" She turned and flicked a hand toward the human males. "Oh, just come in the water and take me!"

Jus felt an ensorcellment rippling across his soul, only to flare out and die against the well-tried power of his magic ring. Sir Olthwaite also seemed magically immune. Bereft of such protection, Polk gave a howl of joy and ran straight toward the women.

The Justicar spun, punched Polk unconscious with a single massive left to the jaw, and caught the man by the scruff of the neck as he fell. He sat the man up against the wall, then glared down at the two girls in the water.

"Kelpies. Gods, but Kelpies annoy me."

The two water-women made an "Awww!" of disappointment and looked imploringly up out of the water.

"We can do drow." The elfmaid's form shifted, her silky white skin deepening to coal black and her hair shimmering into a silvery white. "Is this better?"

"Knock it off!" Hovering high above the water, Escalla frowned. "Jus? What are they?"

"Kelpies—intelligent weeds." The Justicar dragged Polk upright with one heave of his arm. "They charm males, let them drown, then chew them up for plant food."

The faerie bridled in alarm.

"But that's horrid!"

"We're sorry." The two women hung their heads, then cast a little glance up at the Justicar. "You should probably spank us."

"Shut up, or I'll come back with a bucket of weed poison." The ranger managed to drag Polk, backpack and all, around the rim of the room. He tested the way ahead with the tip of his sword. "The edges are shallow, the middle's deep. Head for the stairs.

The two kelpies were left behind as Sir Olthwaite, the Justicar, and Escalla scaled the stairs. Pouting unhappily, the kelpies sniffed as Jus tramped past. "Mammals have no sense of fun!"

Jus ignored them. Stamping his boots to try to free them of some of their burden of dungeon water, the big man reached the top of the stairs, dropped Polk against the wall, then felt in the teamster's pockets for the inevitable flask of liquor. He trickled a little of the alcohol into the man's open mouth, took a pull on the flask himself, and passed it up to the faerie.

Escalla drank, coughed as though she had just swallowed acid, and tossed the drink back down to the Justicar.

"*Ooooh*, amphisbanae piss! You don't get much of that nowadays." The girl sounded hoarse. "How is he?"

Jus shrugged, hardly caring. At his feet, Polk swallowed, stirred, and opened an accusing eye. Mightily offended, the man cradled his jaw and said, "What did you do that for?"

"They were evil animated water weeds, and they wanted to grind you up for fertilizer."

"The fiends!" Polk bridled and shot a regretful glance back down the stairs. "Even the minstrel girl?"

"*Definitely* the minstrel girl." Jus hauled the little man up to his feet. "You're all right. Take another drink, and let's get going."

Blinking in amazement, Polk suddenly gazed up at the Justicar and sputtered, "You saved me! You saved my life!"

"Yup."

"You're a hero!"

"If you say so."

Suddenly Polk felt the weight of his backpack and raised a suspicious brow.

"You just didn't want to have to dive into the water to retrieve the magic hammer."

"Yup." The Justicar smiled.

The little teamster muttered, took a drink from his flask, and cast an eye about the room. Sir Olthwaite stood guard against the upper passage while light still reflected from the kelpie pool below. Feeling victimized, Polk tenderly probed his own jaw.

"Kelpies, eh? How did you throw off the evil spell?"

The Justicar held up a hand and removed his gauntlet. A bone ring shone on his finger.

"Useful trinket. Protection against fear and charm spells." The man cast a glance up at Escalla. "And Escalla's safe. It's not like the kelpies have anything to offer *her*."

Biting her knuckle and casting an eye back down the stairs, Escalla gave a start.

"What? Oh, yeah! Didn't do a thing for me! Not even the elfmaid!"

All eyes now turned toward the paladin. Sir Olthwaite drew himself up proudly, his chiselled face radiating a superior air, and he said, "Vows of chastity armor a man against such feminine wiles."

Escalla and Jus both raised a brow. Sneering from atop the ranger's helm, Cinders snarled at the paladin.

Burn . . .

"Later." The Justicar looked at the plain wooden door at the side of the steps and then at the huge double-flanged metal portal that sealed off the corridor. He jerked his chin toward the metal doors. "That way."

Escalla fluttered curiously in front of the metal doors and frowned.

"Must be something really important on the other side."

"Something that eats fish heads." Polk sniffed. "Can't be much."

"Yeah, you're right!" The girl let the humans push open the way. "Well, we've had vampires, giant flesh monsters, green slime, and talking kelp. There can't be much left." Her wings whirring, the girl made a toast with Polk's own flask and then flew into the dark. "Here's to something small!"

19

"Ha! A fish head!" Forgetting to remain invisible, Escalla darted back and forth over the floor finding clues. "And another one! We're on the right track!"

It took a nose less sensitive than Cinders's to sense the trail ahead. The first huge metallic doors had swung open upon a short passageway that led to a duplicate portal of the first. Fish heads had been dropped here and there, and the tracks of some kind of handcart trailed mud across the floors.

Escalla fluttered about impatiently as Sir Olthwaite and Jus put their shoulders to the next doors and swung them slowly outward, revealing yet another chamber blocked by metal doors. The fish reek came more strongly as the doors opened wide. An old fish head had clearly fallen free as it was carried over stone flanges in the floor, and the stench was enough to bring water to the eyes.

Escalla fluttered about the last pair of doors. Halting to the rear, Jus knelt and examined the previous portal, inspecting the perfect fit of the doors against heavy stone flanges built into the corridor. The doors were absurdly easy to open from the south but seemed to be built to stop an assault of some kind from the north.

"These doors seal perfectly against the stone. The seal is even lined with leather." The Justicar touched the well-oiled hinges with his fingers. "Of all doors in the dungeon, these are the only ones anybody cares for."

"Yeah, whatever." Escalla had finished her inspection of the latest set of metal doors. "No runes, no tripwires, no traps. Pooch says there's no smell of spells. You will observe, the faerie now listens with one graceful ear." The girl pressed her head against the door and listened carefully. "Clear! See, I'm getting this adventure thing down after all!" Posing in midair, Escalla stretched indulgently as the humans opened the way.

Swinging slowly outward, the heavy metal doors flooded a baleful red light into the corridor. The air swirled stifling hot with steam, and the fish smell hovered thicker than flies. Escalla snorted in disgust and drifted onward down the passageway, looking at walls that now dripped with condensation.

She emerged into a great, transparent tube. The floor was stone, yet the clear, curved walls and ceiling roiled violently with bubbles. Escalla looked nervously about and shrank away from the dripping surface of the tube. The impression of savage heat looming in on every side made the little faerie quail.

The passage apparently went beneath the waters of a boiling lake. From somewhere far below, the light of the volcano ebbed and pulsed, lighting the lake with all the colors of clotting blood. The faerie stared at it all, then hesitantly approached the ceiling to reach upward with one delicate little finger.

From behind her, the Justicar called out a warning. The faerie waved him down and softly prodded the hot, transparent surface of the passageway. It stretched slightly away from her touch.

The walls felt red hot, rubbery, and dangerously thin. Hot as they were, the waters beyond boiled with all the force of a superheated kettle, sending vast bubbles wobbling upward through the baleful glare. Escalla carefully touched a water droplet on the walls, then tasted it with her tongue and made a face.

"*Ewwww!* Sulphur! Must be an underground lake that touches the lava." The girl prodded her finger against the ceiling. "Dunno what this stuff is. It feels kinda flimsy. Let's see if we can poke a hole right through!"

"Let's *not*." Jus grabbed the girl by an ankle and hauled her down. "Leave it alone."

"Hey!" Escalla snatched her foot back. "No one touches the faerie!"

Ignoring her protests, Jus made a careful inspection of the walls, making sure Sir Olthwaite was well in front of him. "Those doors behind us are waterproof—all three sets of them. They're there to stop boiling water from flooding the dungeon if this tunnel gives out. The outrush of water would automatically slam the doors closed."

Everyone stopped and stared at the boiling lake. Even Polk's pen-scratching halted.

Escalla took a sudden retreat to the rear.

"So it's a trap? They slam the doors on us then boil us like crayfish to kill us all?"

"No, I don't think that's what this place is for." Jus looked carefully down the tunnel. "Everything has been a careful test of one kind or another, like an obstacle course. If they simply wanted to kill us, they'd just have filled all the tunnels with poison gas."

Escalla blinked. "Really?"

"Yup. Don't worry. We won't get to that stage until we beat all the tests and try to leave."

With a patronizing smile, Escalla patted the Justicar upon his head. "Well, that's *very* reassuring, Jus! I feel *sooo* much better now."

"Good." The ranger jerked his chin toward the far end of the tunnel. "Keep going."

A fish head here and a fish head there marked the pathway down the boiling tunnel. The passageway stretched into the center of the volcanic lake, slowly opening outward until it formed a vast hemisphere. The chamber echoed to the sound of boiling bubbles in the lake beyond. Even with a ceiling arching ten feet overhead, the transparent cavern had a horrid, claustrophobic feel. One stab into the walls could rip it open like a curtain, bringing the whole lake thundering inward through the hole.

Garbage all across the chamber reeked in the heat. A wide pile of stinking refuse lay upon the floor. There were festering fish heads, mounds of weed, and broken human bones. The stench of it all made Escalla gag, and even Cinders set up a mournful whine.

Escalla landed near the garbage, trying to cover her nose and mouth as she pointed at a huge chest just beyond.

"Dead end, but there's a treasure chest!" The girl shied away from rotting chunks of dead fish. "So what's supposed to be down here: hordes of rats, killer cockroaches? The fish patrol?"

A sudden flash of movement flickered through the room. Cinders whipped his face to the right, and the Justicar instantly ducked. A vast crab claw blasted out of the pile of decaying trash, almost shearing Jus's head off his shoulders. The Justicar's sword shot upward to deflect the blow, but he had to duck aside as another claw erupted into the gloom.

With a ponderous rumble, the entire trash pile lumbered upward. Shedding a rain of fish heads and bones, a gargantuan crab rose from the refuse and lurched toward the intruders with frightening speed. Two huge pincers snapped and clashed. The adventurers stared for one brief instant at the monster that had lain hidden underneath the trash, then they scattered wildly back as the thing lashed at them with its claws.

The crab towered overhead, arcing its claws wide. The beast had a shell at least thirty feet wide, with claws large enough to shear through a horse. Festooned with garbage and sheathed in its own natural armor, the giant crab gave a bubbling roar then surged forward straight toward Escalla.

The faerie's smile simply froze on her face.

"Mother!"

A crab claw scythed toward her. Escalla turned invisible, tumbled sideways, and fired a spell. A thick green cloud of vapor wrapped itself about the crab. Unperturbed, the creature surged out of the gas and waded straight toward Sir Olthwaite and the Justicar as the two men backed away with drawn swords. Beating a hasty retreat, Escalla backpedaled through the air.

"Oooh, that is the second largest crustacean I ever clapped my eyes on!"

Staring in terror at the crab, Polk cleared his throat.

"Wh-what was the largest?"

"Do you know Farewell Island?"

"I've heard of it."

"The bad news is, it's not an island." Jerking well away from the clashing claws, Escalla bellowed toward the Justicar. "Jus, you're a ranger! Don't you have some kind of affinity for wildlife?"

Both men charged forward, the paladin leaping fully armored over a blow from the crab's gigantic claw, while Jus simply smashed a pincer aside with a massive blow of his sword. The ranger stepped in to hack at the crab's arm, his blade moving almost too fast to see. His weapon rebounded off the crab's hard shell, ringing as though it had just been smashed into an anvil. A claw bashed backward into him, lifting Jus from his feet. He clung to the vast pincers and hammered his blade down at the creature's limb, unable to crack a fracture through its thick shell. Cinders leaked sulphur through his barred teeth and let flames spill out into the air.

Cinders burn crab!

"It's covered in wet weeds!" Jus felt his blade rebound off the crab's armor. "Wait till we find a soft spot!"

Beside him, Sir Olthwaite fought in utter silence, tumbling aside like an acrobat as a claw almost cut him in two.

The paladin came up against the walls, made the transparent substance stretch, and sped away as a little spurt of boiling water fountained into the air.

Fluttering in panic, the invisible faerie hung at the Justicar's side.

"Jus, what do we do?"

"Fight!" The Justicar battered aside a crab claw then chopped down into the creature's shell. He finally felt the black sword bite, but it was a mere scratch that the titanic creature ignored. "Throw a spell at the damned thing! And don't bust the walls!"

Escalla's spell repertoire had come down to a single spell—her web spell—and the crab was certainly too powerful to be slowed by that for more than an instant. The faerie panted, backed through the air, and tried to come up with a plan.

"Jus, have you got any spells left?"

"A silence spell!" The man smashed a sweeping claw aside. "I'm saving it!"

"Why?"

"Because I have to!"

Slipping on a fish head, Jus went down on one knee. A pincer nearly ripped off his arm but caught instead on the black sword. Cursing the rotten slimy floor, Jus ripped his sword free and stabbed it into the crab, the point punching through the creature's chitin and driving back the claw.

Escalla suddenly went stiff with excitement and whirled backward through the air. "Jus, hold the fort! Hold it off!"

"What?" The Justicar ducked another blow. "How?"

"Just fight defensively!"

Narrowly missing having his head sheared off, Jus gave a snarl.

"Defensively! What in the name of Nerull's backside do you think we're doing?"

As the faerie flew away, Jus cursed and returned to the job of killing the crustacean. The crab had switched its attention to Sir Olthwaite, and the paladin ducked and dodged with an inhuman turn of speed. Claws clashed beneath his feet, but the paladin nimbly danced aside.

Suddenly the crab saw Jus and pivoted its huge body in a lightning-fast turn. Jus swerved into the beast, spun, and threw his whole weight into a vicious blow at the creature's elbow joint. The blade sheared through the monster's flesh and sent a claw bouncing on the ground. The crab whirled and smashed the Justicar aside with its stump, hurling the man to the ground and then stabbing down at him with its other claw. Jus abandoned his blade as both halves of the claw clamped about his waist. He seized hold of the chitin, his muscles bulging as he fought to keep the beast from slicing him in two.

"Paladin! Hit the joints! Cut the claw!"

✳   ✳   ✳   ✳   ✳

In the corridor leading back to the dungeon, Escalla shot swiftly through the air. She found Polk cowering behind the last set of metal doors, his knees knocking like dice shaking in a cup. The faerie landed on his backpack and began frantically tearing at buckles, straps, and ties.

"Quick! Where's my oil flask?"

"What?" Polk had eyes only for the giant crab. "Flaming oil won't hurt *that*, woman! Have you any idea of that thing's size!"

"No, the *other* oil flask!" Burrowing through the pack, Escalla showered the dungeon floor with useless gear. For some reason, Polk was carrying at least three sets of clean underwear. "Where did you put my gods damned slime?"

His eyes going wide, Polk flapped his lower lip like a landed fish.

"What? You can't use it! It's not done!"

"I'll use it on you in a moment!" The faerie burrowed down amidst a cornucopia of wax candles, tallow candles, hourglasses, bells, and beads. "Where in the name of Orcus's sagging gut did you put it?"

Wrapped inside a blanket and sealed inside a cooking pot lay the oil flask. Escalla grabbed the thing with two hands and hauled it up into the air, flinging wrappings aside as she whirred back into the battle.

"Jus, hold on! I'm coming!"

The ranger lay trapped by the crab's claw, his armor cut and buckling as he slowly lost headway against the giant beast. As Escalla whirred past him, Sir Olthwaite jerked into action and smacked at the crab with his sword.

Jus gathered himself, took a hard grip on the crab's claws, and roared like a maddened bear as he slowly forced the pincer blades apart. He flung his head sideways as the crab loomed above him with its open maw.

"Cinders!"

The hell hound blasted flame into the crab's gaping mouth and the giant crustacean gave a piercing scream. The Justicar heaved, wrenching the crab's claw open and tossing the limb aside. The crab backed away, shielding itself in panic from Cinders's flames.

Hovering above the monster, Escalla gave a shriek of triumph and cast the oil pot down. The ceramic jug instantly rebounded from the creature's algae-padded shell and landed safe and sound amongst the fish heads on the floor.

Holding his side, the Justicar lurched backward as the crab came at him again.

"Escalla, whatever you're doing, do it fast!"

The girl picked up the oil flask, sensed a sudden wind, and looked across her shoulder to see the giant crab's claws blurring straight toward her throat. She changed herself into a fish head and fell bouncing to the floor, the oil flask thudding into the trash.

The crab flailed its claw down like a club, flattening trash and smashing at the refuse. The oil jar broke with a crash, and green slime spattered up onto the monster's arm.

A fish head rolled one big yellow eye, screamed like a frightened child, and suddenly sprouted spider's legs. Yelping in fright, the faerie grabbed her fallen clothes and ran between the crab's feet, leaping onto the Justicar as the monster slowly turned around.

The beast saw all its prey together in once place and lumbered down the corridor. Jus, Sir Olthwaite, and Escalla scrabbled frantically back as green slime spread like wildfire up the crustacean's arm.

The slime attack finally registered somewhere in the crab's dull brain. The creature screamed and battered its claw against the ground, slime spattering all across the stone. Jus peeled the spider-legged fish head from his back and held the faerie dangling in the air.

"Escalla! The chest! Hurry!"

Naked, the faerie popped back into her usual form, took a look at the rampaging crab, then sped like an arrow straight past the creature's thrashing limbs. The crab had smeared slime on its face, covering its eyes with the predatory sludge. It swiped blindly at the faerie as she passed then turned to lumber after her to protect its treasure horde.

The faerie flung herself down beside the heavy treasure chest and wrenched open the lid. Inside lay a long silver trident, a beautiful magic wand inlaid with ice-worm's shell, and a dazzling carpet of pearls.

"Pearls!" The girl jammed her fingers in among the heaps of gems, then stared in hunger at the magic wand. "Wand!"

"*The trident!*" Jus bellowed as the crab bore down upon the girl. "*Hurry!*"

"Pearls!" The faerie held three priceless black pearls in her hand.

The trident lay gleaming at her feet—as much as a faerie could possibly hope to haul. Escalla rammed the big black pearls into her mouth and swallowed the things whole. She jammed the wand between her teeth, used a wad of algae to shield her hands, and took a grip upon the trident's head. She dragged the thing out of the chest, gave a great heave of relief, then threw herself wildly aside as a crab claw smashed the chest to flinders.

Entirely covered in pustulous green slime, the crab gave a bubbling cry of fury and pain. It smacked its claw down to try and crush the faerie. Escalla ducked as green slime spattered through the room. Sizzling gobbets missing her skull to land among the fish heads and the algae.

Lurching in a blind frenzy, the crab began slashing at the empty air with its claw. Her teeth clamped on her magic wand, Escalla ran. The trident bounced and clattered as she dragged it across the stone floors. Hearing the noise, the crab turned and whipped its dissolving claw to smash the little creature to the ground.

The claw rose high in the air, ripping a hole in the transparent membrane of the roof, and a column of boiling water thundered down onto the crab. Escalla risked one brief look across her shoulder, saw the entire ceiling rip apart behind her, and then fled before a foaming tidal wave of boiling water and steam.

Jus hung in the metal doorway, blocking it as Sir Olthwaite made to slam the huge doors shut. Escalla ran as she had never run before, her wings blurring to push her into greater speed as she clung grimly to the trident. The boiling water wall foamed and roared behind her, consuming crab, algae, fish heads, and green slime. The girl flung herself the last few yards toward the doors. She felt Jus catch her by the neck and physically fling her on into the corridor. The big man turned and shielded her from the first blast of boiling water as he lunged inward through the doors. A sizzling wall of water crashed into him from behind, splashing deadly foam across Cinders's fur. The force of the water smashed the metal doors shut behind him with a thunderous clang. Water surged about the floor, steaming evilly as Jus thrashed forward into the next chamber and hauled shut the second set of doors.

The Justicar was badly burned about the legs yet never stopped moving until his companions were safe. The boiling water slammed into the outer doors, but their strong metal frames held. The ranger stared at the doors for one moment, then his knees gave way and he fell to the floor. He skin was red and already beginning to blister in several places.

Landing upon Polk's backpack, Escalla dug out the last healing potion and raced it over to her friend.

"This is the last one! Do you have a healing spell?"

"I'm out!" Jus hissed, the pain of the burns making him squeeze shut his eyes. "Give me the potion!"

She fed it to him herself, then stripped away his trousers to inspect the damage. The backs of his legs were blistered and red. Wincing, Escalla poured cool water from a canteen across the burns. The potion slowly eased the damage, making it fade before the faerie's eyes.

With all damage gone, the girl heaved out a long-held sigh, then patted the man upon one hairy thigh.

"Well, *that* one must have hurt like hell." The girl took a great deal of reassurance from the touch. "Hey Cinders, you all right?"

Fine.

"Well, at least you got a bath."

Escalla looked down, discovered she was naked, and retrieved her clothes from a silent Polk. She picked up her new magic wand, read the runes along its side, and looked up in hostility as the paladin came near.

Sir Olthwaite cleared his throat. "Do you know how to work the wand?"

Escalla turned away, holding her new treasure against her chest. The wand was covered with ice runes. "I might."

A thunderous boom echoed from the boiling lake beyond as the last of the air-filled chamber collapsed under the water. "What the hell were you doing while Jus was fighting the crab?"

"I fought the crab!" The armored man drew himself proudly erect. "I have already told you, the wights have diminished my fighting powers!"

"Really?"

The paladin gave a distasteful sniff.

"I hardly think this is the place for a mere faerie to comment upon the fighting prowess of a knight of the realm."

For once, Escalla did not deign to answer. Instead, she looked down the barrel of her wand, patted it twice, and then cradled it in her arms. Backing away in midair, she swirled over toward the gear left lying in the water on the floor.

"Well, here's Wave. That's two magic weapons down and one to go." Escalla kicked at the trident with her booted foot. "Polk, you carry it. Use rags to protect your hands." The girl lifted her chin. "Touching these things can cause you power burns, you know."

Sir Olthwaite looked from the trident to the girl in puzzlement.

"Why did you take the trident? You could have had the gems!"

"Jus wants the trident."

"But you didn't get any treasure! You're still poor!"

The faerie shrugged and smiled wickedly. "That too shall pass." The girl rested a hand upon the Justicar's shoulders. "Hey J-man, you all right?"

"I'm fine." The man rose slowly, testing his legs for burns. Battered and wet with the hell hound pelt upon his head, he looked like a wolverine that had been brushed the wrong way. "Let's go."

They moved down the corridor, heading for the kelpie pool. Hanging back to walk at the Justicar's side, Sir Olthwaite tapped thoughtfully at his own chin.

"So you have the city's two weapons? Will you be leaving now?"

Jus kept his head down, thinking as he walked.

"No."

"No?"

"Blackrazor." The Justicar settled his grip upon his black sword. "We'll fetch it."

Escalla looked back at her friend and gave an enigmatic smile. Sir Olthwaite drew in a proud breath and nodded.

"Yes. Why settle for two weapons? We shall overawe the baron by retrieving all three."

"I'm not working for the baron." The Justicar breathed easier as the healing potion finished its work. "I like to make sure nothing ends up in the wrong hands."

"Wrong hands?"

"Ones I have judged and found *wanting*—"

The paladin heard the words, frowned, and looked at the ranger.

"I regret that I have already used up my own healing gift upon my slain companions." The man tugged at his chin. "You still seem injured. What is this spell you are reserving? Surely it cannot be more important than your health?"

"A silence spell." The Justicar pushed his way into the kelpie's room and watched the two weed-women dive away in fright. "And it *is* more important than my health."

20

"Hey, Enid."

"Oh, hello!" Enid the Sphinx sat primly upright in her place at the dungeon's main junction. "Still at it?"

"Still going." Escalla gave a sigh. "Anyway, Enid, Sir Olthwaite. Sir Olthwaite, Enid."

Enid obviously remembered the paladin. She grumpily flexed her claws and said, "We've met. He guessed my riddle."

"Ah, he's a student of the classics. It happens—no point grumbling. We move on, we learn." Escalla put a comradely arm about Enid's shoulders then tapped Polk upon the skull. "Polk, oil flask! I'm going to go get more slime!"

The Justicar raised one thoughtful eyebrow.

"Really?"

"Yeah, it's great stuff!" The faerie whizzed down the eastern corridor. "Back in a flash. Meanwhile, did anyone bring lunch?"

Lunch! Cinders wagged his damp tail. *Burnt bones and coal!*

"And I even brought you naphtha for afterward." Jus removed the hell hound skin and affectionately began to tidy its fur. "Here we go. Eat hearty."

Escalla returned to find her compatriots wrestling with strips of hardened jerky. Enid delicately nibbled on a piece of bread, showering crumbs across the watery floor. The faerie descended and gave a full slime-jug to Polk, who unhappily stored the thing away. Snatching Polk's lunch while the man's back was turned, Escalla settled upon Enid's furry back.

"Lunch looks . . . challenging."

Jus gnawed his jerky and shrugged. Sir Olthwaite distastefully put his food away. Having grown used to the ranger's camp cooking, Escalla happily stuffed her face and enjoyed her meal, though it didn't last long.

Sitting in the midst of a shower of crumbs, she announced, "So, we ready to go?"

"Yup." Jus passed the faerie his canteen. "Let's move."

The group waded off down the western tunnel. Behind them, Enid waved a cheerful paw.

"Have a nice time!"

"You too!" Escalla flew backward to wave goodbye. "We'll play riddles tonight, but no eating people anymore, all right?"

"I'm relatively over that little phase now!" Enid gave a final wave. "See you!"

❖　❖　❖　❖　❖

The western tunnel's trap provided a few minute's pause. Walking ahead of the Justicar, Sir Olthwaite halted and flexed his fingers in frustrated indecision. After a moment, he pointed to the water-covered ground ahead.

"The floor drops away here. It is only a ten-foot of gap, but that's quite enough to drown in."

The Justicar lifted his magic light and squinted at the water. Escalla popped into visibility and tried to see whether anything lurked down below.

"How did you cross last time?" she asked.

"We swam. I removed my armor and drew it across the hole with a rope."

It seemed a simple enough plan. Jus took one pace backward, sheathed his sword, and said, "Good. You go first."

With a sharp glance of distaste at the ranger, Sir Olthwaite unbuckled his pauldrons and let his arm pieces slide off. Chunk by chunk he divested himself of his armor, letting the metal plates collect at his feet. Dressed in a soiled blue undersuit, the man bundled up his equipment and wrapped it with a few turns of his thin rope. He tied off the scorched rope end and without a backward glance, slipped into the water and began to swim across the gap.

Jus watched carefully then jerked his chin at the water trap.

"Polk, you're next."

Polk swallowed, eyeing the oily, filthy pool.

"Now, son, this seems a grand place to hide a monster! You have to realize that evil lurks—it *lurks*—meanin' it likes to hide."

Jus kept careful eyes and ears on the passageway.

"We already dangled some bait. Nothing's there." The Justicar helped Polk from his backpack. "Can you swim?"

"Well, son, now that's another point of contention in yer plan."

Jus leaned the trident against one wall. He helpfully stuffed Polk's chronicles inside one of his waterproof scroll tubes and handed the man one end of his own rope.

"You don't swim?"

"Nope, not a stroke. That's what I'm saying!"

"Time to learn."

Jus threw the other end of the rope to a dripping, fuming Sir Olthwaite and unceremoniously pushed Polk into the pool. The teamster squawked and thrashed like a drowning rat until the paladin hauled the rope and landed him on the far side of the pit.

Escalla hovered behind and above Sir Olthwaite, her new wand tucked under one arm and pointing at the paladin. Jus gave a nod to the faerie, then patted Cinders on the head. Sword, boots, armor, and all, he jumped into the water, swam across, and emerged dripping at the far side. The big man shook himself dry like a wolf, sending water flying out to spatter the paladin.

Sir Olthwaite grimaced angrily then turned to point down the corridor.

"We were attacked just around the corner." Hanging his sword from his belt, the man shouldered his armor bundle. "There's no point re-armoring. I shall show you why."

The group trudged down the corridor, their skin filthy with muck from the water. Marginally cleaner than the other adventurers, Escalla whistled a little tune between her teeth. The ranger threw a clod of algae at her invisible rear end in an effort to silence her. The faerie went into a huff, zipped around a corner, and then suddenly unveiled her magic light.

"Hey! There's dead guys here!"

The party rounded the corner. Escalla hovered in midair above a human body that lay floating face-up in the water. Dressed in a slashed robe and hat, the corpse was clearly that of the baron's sorcerer.

Two other corpses floated nearby. They were *wights*, gray skinned and leathery, and had obviously been slashed with swords. The Justicar strode forward and checked the monsters for signs of life in the simplest possible way: he hacked their heads off one by one. With that job done, he prodded at the dead sorcerer from a distance with his sword.

"Life drain. See the burns?"

Escalla hovered at her friend's side and asked, "What does that?"

"Negative energy creatures, wights, vampires." The Justicar knelt and relieved the body of a healing potion jammed into its belt. "But that isn't what killed him. This man was stabbed from behind."

Sir Olthwaite managed to appear sanctimonious as he spoke. "A creature slain by a wight becomes a wight. I therefore performed the final office of a friend."

The Justicar said nothing.

Escalla flew a few paces farther out of reach and said, "All right! Let's just remain *acquaintances* then, shall we?"

Jus uncorked the healing potion, sniffed at it in suspicion, and seemed satisfied enough to clip it to his own belt.

"The potion seems all right." Jus checked the smooth slide of his sword inside its sheath. "Paladin, you left a perfectly good potion behind? Why?"

Sir Olthwaite seared the Justicar with a disdainful glance and replied, "*Some* of us have a distaste for robbing the dead."

"The worms don't need it. We do." Jus rose and took a close look at the corridor ahead. "Tell us about this passageway."

"The tunnel up ahead is lined with copper slabs," the paladin explained. "A hum of power seems to ripple through the metal, making the dank air shimmer with force." Sir Olthwaite touched the bare copper with his hand. "It's a trap designed to strip away your weapons and armor. Metal heats as you walk down the tunnel."

"Getting hotter over distance or hotter over time?" asked the Justicar.

"Time." The paladin seemed evasive. "So it seemed."

The Justicar watched Sir Olthwaite for a moment then said, "Where's the Geshtai priestess?"

"I sent her through the tunnel. She did not return."

Sent her? That was interesting. The Justicar nodded slowly, then looked down the corridor.

Hovering up near the ceiling, Escalla stuck a hand into the passage and twiddled her fingertips.

"Feels all right. I can go take a look." The girl frowned. "Cinders, what do you smell?"

Undead. Evil!

"Now that's not good." Lifting her magic light, Escalla gave a swirl. "Shall I go?"

"Do it." The Justicar kept his eyes on the corridor. "Paladin, guard the rear."

Once Sir Olthwaite's attention was partially divided, Escalla stealthily slipped off her anti-charm ring and dropped it in Jus's palm. The Justicar traded it for his own bone ring, shielding the faerie from view until the ring slipped it in place upon her finger. With a happy salute, Escalla flipped her wings wide and turned invisible, the magic light bobbing softly as she flew into the corridor.

She flew a mere ten feet and then screeched in pain. An instant later, a hot gold piece came flying at the Justicar.

"My lucky gold piece!" Visible again, the girl rubbed angrily at her cleavage. "Damned thing almost branded me!"

"You'll get it back." Jus caught the rapidly cooling coin and tucked it into his scabbard. "Tell me you didn't swallow any coins."

The girl raised one brow, put her fingers against her stomach, and looked a little blank. "Are pearls metallic?"

"Not that I've heard."

"Oh, good." The girl turned invisible again. "Well, undead, here I come!"

She flew off into the unknown, her light glittering from the great copper slabs lining the passage walls. Far down the tunnel, the light seemed to flare as it caught the walls of a larger room. Escalla's cheery little voice could be heard echoing out into the halls.

"*Helloooo!*" The light swirled and bobbed. "Yoo-hoooo! Undead? The vampire crusher is here!"

There was a sudden sound of a door crashing open, followed by a chorus of bestial snarls. Escalla's war cry could be heard as frost and mist came billowing down the metal corridor. Whooping, the unseen girl blasted at her enemies.

"Oh, you want some of this? Yeah? You want some more?"

Frosty vapors drifted into the copper passageway, and Jus lunged forward to the tunnel mouth.

"Escalla!"

"Hey, I'm fine!" The faerie could be seen framed against the light as she waved her new magic wand above her head. "Oh, man, this thing is wild!"

"What happened?"

"Dunno. Some kind of ghouls or something. I froze them into corpsicles!" The faerie turned a cartwheel in the air. "Come on down! The water's fine!"

It was easier said than done. The Justicar carefully held a coin out into the corridor, dropping it when it suddenly became hot enough to scorch him through his leather glove. The coin hissed steam as it hit the water and disappeared from view.

Simply tying the arms and armor into a bundle and towing it through the corridor would be useless. The metal would heat itself enough to burn through the ropes. Jus removed his helmet, scratched at his head stubble and then settled his ideas. After long moments, inspiration came, and he settled into the details of a proper plan.

"Escalla, come back! Olthwaite, watch the rear."

The faerie drifted into view, waving her wand over her head.

"Ta-daaaaah!" Hey, killing undead is a real breeze. I may start renting myself out."

"Don't get too fond of it. None of them have hit you yet." The man lifted his arm to provide Escalla with a perch. "What's down the corridor?"

"Icicles and ghouls! There's a dead priestess in the room, all eaten up." Escalla waved a potion over her head. "She was carrying this, though. Pretty useful, huh?"

"Good." Jus took the potion and tossed it to Polk. "Did you figure out the wand?"

"Oh, it's a frost thingie! It shoots out a cone of cold." The faerie pointed at three different runes upon the side. "Red means kill, this one makes a great big ice wall, but I dunno what the last one means. The blue line fades as its charges wear out." The wand looked to be about two-thirds empty. "Pretty hoopy, huh?"

"You need it. It gives you a sting." The Justicar looked down at the paladin's pile of armor. "We can use it, too."

The room at the far end of the tunnel seemed no more dangerous than half a dozen traps already passed and gone. Jus faced the passageway and folded his arms in thought.

"Paladin, why didn't you go farther?" The man narrowed his eyes as he glared into the dark. "The wights were dead, the priestess had traversed the copper tunnel . . ."

"I had no allies." Sir Olthwaite tugged at his wet, filthy undersuit. "Dungeons are dangerous. I felt it best to find some companions before proceeding farther. I searched— and I found you."

"Go down the tunnel, then. It's safe." Jus held out his hand for the man's sword. "Leave your sword and we'll tow it through."

"How? A rope will burn through within sixty feet!"

"The wand." Jus took a blanket from Polk's backpack and soaked it in the water. "We wrap the weapons and freeze them inside a block of ice. We wrap the block with groundsheets and tow it through the water, moving at a run."

"Ah!" The paladin stroked his moustache. "Then I shall help you. By all means bundle the weapons and metal."

"Scout the passage." Dark and forbidding, the Justicar refused to look at the man. "Make sure there're no obstacles in the water. Polk and I will do the carrying. It's going to be dirty work."

Sir Olthwaite took a torch and began to walk down the tunnel. Happily playing with her wand, Escalla encased armor, weapons, and sundry bits of treasure inside a block of ice. Polk seemed to approve of the whole idea and began wrapping the mass in cloaks and blankets.

Jus wore leather armor, but his belt had a metal buckle. After removing the belt, he tied his trousers up with string. As he did so, he moved quietly closer to the faerie.

"Follow Sir Olthwaite."

"You got it!" The faerie worked the slide on her wand with a harsh *clack-clack*, setting it to kill. "See you in a few minutes."

The faerie sped away. Jus and Polk lifted the big block of ice between them on a cradle of blankets. They looked at one another, drew a deep breath, and then ran like hell through the corridor.

Water foamed about their shins as they blundered through the mire. Steam rose from the ungainly ice block as the metal inside began to overheat. Halfway down the passageway, the ice gave a *crack*. With the block dripping and already beginning to sag, Polk and Jus careened into the open room and hurled the ice block over at a set of stairs. The ice split, and heated metal tumbled in the steam. Jus dove to retrieve Escalla's golden ring. He cooled it with a chunk of ice and jammed it onto his finger before reaching down to rescue his helmet and sword.

Carefully inspecting his much-cherished sword, the Justicar slowly relaxed. The blade seemed unharmed. Rubbing the pommel with ice until it cooled, Jus slid the weapon back into the leather scabbard at his belt. The silky *click* of the sword sinking home sounded loud and comforting.

The chamber at the end of the copper passage was square. Issuing from a still-open secret panel were a group of fanged, skeletal humanoids all frozen in ice. Frost starred the walls and had frozen the floors into a sheet of ice. Escalla hovered self-importantly above the frozen ghouls, hoping that someone would choose to comment upon her handiwork.

The one man who saw fit to make a fuss was Polk. Over-joyed, the teamster licked the end of his wax marker as he circled the ghouls.

"Eight! She got eight! Now this girl has the right stuff!" Polk began scribbling notes into his chronicles. "Beauty and brains, son! Take heed!" The man shot a glance up at Escalla. "Can I write 'mistress of mayhem'?"

"As long as you don't mention my leather duds in the same paragraph, sure!" The faerie polished her knuckles on one breast. "Did I mention the fact that I took 'em all in one shot?"

"I'll put it in big letters." Polk suddenly seemed far hap-pier with his day. "Now see? There's no reason not to fight fair. No slimes needed. You're a combat kitten now!"

With her head swollen, the faerie drifted down to watch her companions rescuing their gear. The paladin had not yet bothered to climb back into his armor. Escalla kept her eye casually upon Sir Olthwaite's back as she came closer to the ground. "So, Jus, nothing broken?"

"Doesn't look like it." The Justicar tossed Sir Olthwaite his silver sword. "Here."

The paladin caught the weapon with a deft left-handed catch, then used the implement to point at a set of steps leading up out of the muck. The top of the steps had been sealed off with a door made out of something akin to solid ivory. Runes had been inscribed about a central indenta-tion, and the whole portal had been fixed deep into the living stone. The door seemed massive, solid, and unbreak-able.

Looking over at the new discovery, Cinders gave a sniff and then a sudden sneeze. *Bah! Magic! Strong magic!*

There seemed to be no explosive runes. Jus walked up to the white door and wiped it with a fingertip. The surface was free of algae, and the edges of the runes still showed stone dust that had drifted from above.

"This is new construction. The rest of the dungeon is old, but this has only been here a few days."

Escalla flew over and pushed at the door, then twisted at a ring-latch set below the runes and said, "I can't turn it."

"It'll be a mystic clue." Polk looked immensely self-important. "One of us should talk to it and see what it wants!"

No one seemed keen to speak to the dungeon fittings just yet. Watched intently by Sir Olthwaite, the Justicar held up his light and carefully traced the patterns cut into the door.

Someone had already unsuccessfully tried to break the door down. Mud marks showed where a foot had kicked at the ivory. Jus touched the still-wet mud then returned to the runes.

"Glyphs." The man traced two symbols on either side of the indentation in the door. "Sir Olthwaite?"

"Glyphs are for rangers and priests." Intensely interested, the paladin edged closer. "Can you read them?"

"Yup." The ranger stood. "The one on the left means 'good.' The one on the right is 'blood.'" Jus carefully removed his gauntlet. "It's a magic lock."

The man nicked his thumb and pressed a droplet into the hollow of the door. A heavy click sounded as the door unlocked itself and suddenly sprang open. Jus snorted, licked his cut, and looked into the corridor beyond.

A shocking whip crack echoed through the hall. Sir Olthwaite lashed out his rope and snapped it about the ranger's neck. With a scream of triumph, the paladin seemed to swell, a new creature bursting up out of the abandoned skin. White wings unfolded as a naked female figure discarded her disguise to the floor.

Wrapped in a scorched magic rope, Jus snarled and rolled aside. Naked, savage, and powerful, the erinyes laughed in triumph and flung out a clawed hand toward the faerie girl.

Magic twisted through the air to slam into Escalla. "Obey me! Kill the others with your wand!"

The faerie rocked beneath the magic blast, then held up her hand with the Justicar's magic ring and gave a nasty smile.

"Think again, bitch!"

Escalla turned the wand upon the erinyes. Screaming in anger and frustration, the devil-woman instantly fled. With Jus still in her line of fire, the faerie could only curse and fire her web spell down the hall to block the erinyes's escape. The devil-creature gave a peal of laughter and evaded the web with ease, disappearing quickly into the dark.

Swearing, Escalla stared into the dark and hunted targets for her wand.

"Damn it!" Furious, Escalla half-made to fly after the erinyes. "Jus! Do I ice the bitch?"

"Stay together!" The big man managed to wrench himself free from the erinyes's abandoned rope. "She can't beat us if we stay together!"

Escalla swore and slammed her little fist against the wall.

"She's after Blackrazor!" The girl shouted curses. "Damn it! I thought the paladin was just an agent for one of the temples!"

Polk blinked. Still covered by wet scraps of Sir Olthwaite's old skin, the man sat on the floor in a daze.

"You-you knew he wasn't a paladin?"

Annoyed with himself, Jus gave a growl.

"A baatezu. No wonder the creature couldn't use a healing potion." The Justicar cursed himself as he carefully coiled the erinyes's magic rope. "But Cinders hated him so much I thought he must have really been a paladin!"

"Well, good boy, Cinders." Escalla patted the hound upon the head. "You tried to tell us."

Cinders good dog! Evil smell gone!

The faerie cocked an eye at Jus and asked, "Hey, erinyes come from somewhere really awful, don't they? Are they immune to hell hound fire?"

"Yup." Jus scratched at Cinders's snout. "So I'm told."

"Ah well, he can gnaw off the bits of her when we're done! Pooch, sniff deep and start tracking!" Escalla assumed combat stance in midair, her wand covering the way ahead. "Jus, let's go make some iced devil-bitch!"

21

"You have *got* to be kidding!"

Fluttering in midair, Escalla looked down at the floor of the dungeon's latest room. Two trenches blocked access across the floor, and the bottom of each trench was filled with jagged, rusted blades. The floor between the two ditches gleamed as slick as polished silver.

Escalla thoughtfully hovered above the floor and touched it with a fingertip. The floor was so smooth that it would be impossible to keep a grip. It was literally slipperier than grease and made a deadly trap between the two pits. Were Polk or Jus to venture out onto the floor, they would fall, slide down, and come to a grisly end.

"Lovely." Becoming more annoyed by the obstacle course, Escalla breathed out an angry puff of breath and shook her head. "I gotta get you two guys some wings!" The girl twisted her wand in frustration. "Jus, if you're going to get an idea, get it quick! That bitch is getting away!"

Standing in the doorway and measuring the room with his eyes, Jus drummed fingers on the pommel of his sword. Above his helmet, Cinders sniffed at the air, keeping watch for the elusive erinyes.

Polk peered out from behind the Justicar, uncorking his scroll case to once again begin his chronicles. He shook his head sadly as he flicked a glance at the Justicar.

"Son, the place has got you this time! Stymied! Flummoxed! This is the end of the road." The teamster licked his wax marker and began to write. "You just weren't up to the challenge of evil, I guess."

"Polk, shut up." The Justicar nodded over at Escalla. "That wand of yours . . . Can you mold an ice wall into different shapes?"

"What? You mean ice sculpt?" The girl looked at her wand. "Dunno. You want me to do you a nice little elf or a dragon?"

Jus gave the girl an impatient glare. "Lay an ice wall on the floor like a sheet. Bridge the pits. Polk and I will slide over on the ice."

"Hey, now *that's* thinking!" Escalla unstrapped her weapon. "This thing doesn't have that many charges left, though. I've probably only got a dozen shots before I have to get it recharged."

Despite the drawbacks, the Justicar's plan was the best possible solution. Happy to be useful, Escalla thumbed her wand and flew backward, the ice wand hosing frost down onto the ground. A broad layer of ice made a flat road along the frictionless floor and above its two chasms. Escalla gave the ice an extra layer of thickness beneath the bridges, then switched off the wand and fanned away the frost vapors with her wings.

A gleaming causeway now stretched across the room. Six inches thick, the ice glittered as it stretched above the trenches and their rusty blades. More than satisfied, Escalla fluttered down to rap a bridge with her knuckles. The echo rattled through the hall.

"Solid as a frost giant's privy!" The faerie rubbed her hands together and looked expectantly at the two humans. "All right, guys, it's over to you!"

Jus grabbed Polk's backpack full of gear and threw it skating across the room, following it with the magic trident and hammer. The ranger then grabbed Polk by the belt and the scruff of his neck and held him facedown above the ground.

Struggling like a captured bug, Polk thrashed and stammered in fright.

"No, son! Stop! I can't go!" The teamster wailed as he felt himself being swung to and fro. "Son, someone has to outlive you to write the chronicles! Son, *just think this through!*"

With a mighty heave, Jus sent Polk shooting like a toboggan over the ice. The man gibbered as he whizzed above the razor-sharp spikes. When he hit the far wall, he clung like a monkey to the stone.

From the far side of the hall, Jus frowned and asked, "Are you all right?"

"Yes, dagnabbit!"

"Damn."

The Justicar shook his head then sank carefully down on all fours. He arranged Cinders carefully across his back and slid slowly upon his belly out on the ice. He used rags bound about his gloves to give him some grip as he stolidly wormed his way above the lethal traps.

Escalla hovered overhead, being rather less than helpful and beating time with her hands. "Come on! *Hurry-hurry-hurry-hurry-hurry!* We have to beat the erinyes to the sword!"

Ice creaked and groaned in the gloomy hall. As Jus reached the mid-point of the first bridge, the ice suddenly fractured beneath his weight. Long cracks whipped out across the bridge and a flake of ice fell tinkling from the bridge's underside. The man froze, his eyes wide as he felt the entire bridge threatening to give way.

Flitting between the ranger and the exit, Escalla irritably drummed her wand with her fingertips. "Hey, Jus, did I mention the need for a little speed here?"

The man sent her a furious look and slithered carefully on his way. The second bridge seemed even thinner and more brittle than the first. Jus blew out a breath, tested the ice with his hand, then slid carefully across the ice.

As he began to cross the second bridge, Escalla came closer and whispered, "Do you need a push or something?"

With a snarl of annoyance, the ranger rose up onto his hands and shouted, "Shut up! It's slippery, and the stuff's too damned thin!"

A cracking sound came from the bridge, and Jus's eyes went wide. With a sudden *snap*, the whole mass broke free. Escalla screamed in fright as the bridge slammed down onto the steel blades below. The faerie flung her hands to her face and flew through a cloud of frost to flap madly in the air.

"*Jus!*" In a panic, Escalla bit her hands. "Jus, did you die?"

Five feet below the rim, Jus lay sprawled on an intact six-inch-thick slab of ice. The blades had penetrated halfway through the ice, but they managed to make the bridge more stable than before. Muttering to himself, Jus picked his way from ice chunk to ice chunk and crept across the lip of the trench onto proper stony ground.

Safe at last, Jus kicked at a random piece of ice. He wiped off the frosted front of his armor and peeled Polk away from the wall.

"Let's get moving."

Escalla let Jus kick open the exit door, took a swift peek about the corner, then zipped forward to scout the way ahead. Jus dragged Polk along in his wake, the teamster struggling vainly to come to terms with his handful of scrolls, the magic trident, and a lantern.

"Hold up!" the teamster protested.

"Come on, *move!*" Jus took a swift look into the corridor then hauled Polk behind him. "Keep close and keep quiet!"

The corridor came to a branch. Escalla risked a swift glance both ways, saw nothing, and ducked back into cover. With his sword at the ready, Jus planted his back against a wall and edged up to the intersection.

"Cinders?"

The hell hound sniffed at traces of monster stench and said, *Left.*

Jus jerked his chin at the faerie. The girl turned down the left-hand passage and flew on her way.

It was yet another corridor, this time dry floored and well traveled. The long walkway led down to yet another door. This time the door hung open, and a horrific stable-like stink wafted through the air from beyond. In haste to catch her foe, Escalla flew into the room, saw that it sank deeper into the ground in a series of huge steps, then caught a flash of white wings at the lowest level of the room.

The little faerie yelled, *"There she is!"*

Wand at the ready, Escalla shot down at the erinyes. She gave a whoop of victory that suddenly turned into a scream as a cloud of silver came hissing through the air. A line of spikes stitched a line in the wall behind her, three darts smacking into her midriff and hurtling her aside.

The Justicar threw himself in front of the faerie as three more darts came flashing up at her. The black blade whipped in a figure eight, battering aside the missiles. He backed away from the room, going to ground and gathering Escalla up by the roots of her wings.

The ranger snatched a glimpse of a flat arena below as the erinyes raced through a door. Behind the erinyes, three man-headed lions screamed in hate. The three manticores whipped their spike-studded tails through the air. Jus ducked an instant before a fresh cloud of iron darts hammered into the wall behind him. With Escalla cradled bleeding in his arms, he backed back in the dungeon corridor so that he could study the room from relative safety.

The room had been constructed like an inverted ziggurat. A huge space sank downward step by step, each layer forming a platform in which monsters roamed. Three manticores occupied the lowest level, screeching as they shot darts up toward the passageway. Jus kept flat on the floor out of the manticores' firing line and wrenched the darts out of Escalla's side.

He worked with grim efficiency, holding the girl with an uncommon gentleness as he staunched her wounds.

Doubled up in agony, the faerie tried to push Jus away and said through clenched teeth, "Get her! Get after her!"

"To hell with that!" Jus crammed his hand against the girl's wounds, then wrapped her in a length of bandage. He poured their last healing potion down her throat, cupping her in his arms until she swallowed every drop.

"Lie still! Let the potion work!"

Potions made for humans would take their own sweet time to work upon a faerie. Stirring weakly, the girl tried to rise up and help. Jus put a hand on Escalla to reinforce his order to stay down. Slithering flat on his stomach, he took a swift glance over the edge of the floor, ducked a shower of manticore spikes, and then looked again. Below him, the manticores screamed for blood.

Polk slithered forward in a clatter of trident, hammer, and backpack. "Son, ain't this dangerous? Don't manticores fly?"

"They're trapped down there. And the erinyes has held them off herself with some kind of spell." The Justicar risked a final glimpse of the room from a different angle. "Stay down!"

The huge chamber dropped down at least forty feet toward a central arena. Three square, concentric levels separated the adventurers from the lowest level—and the lowest level held the only other door that exited from the room.

The descending levels each formed a pen, and in each pen, monsters roamed. The first and third were filled with water and giant lobsters. The middle level had been dusted with sand, and here six giant scorpions roamed. The creatures lifted their claws and spread them wide, sensing prey above. From the central arena down below, the manticores roared and struck sparks from stone with their spiked iron tails.

Sitting down to think, the Justicar pondered distances and options. His concentration was spoiled by Polk's voice and the scratching of the teamster's wax marker against one of his parchments.

"Held back by fear, hesitatin' right at the very brink o' greatness . . ." Polk frowned. "Is 'lassitude' a real word?"

"Shut up!" Jus wriggled back from the edge, the motion provoking fresh howls from below. Somewhere beyond the door, light flashed and a distant battle raged. "Sounds like the erinyes is fighting a guardian."

"And she'll win!" Polk sat up too straight and ducked as a blast of manticore spikes showered overhead. "She'll get Blackrazor and get away! So then where will our legend be?"

"Nowhere."

"How do we get down?"

Jus collected up the faerie and cradled her against his chest. Her injuries were healing, but the shock of them had left her quaking and pale. She put her arms weakly about the Justicar's neck as he carried her farther back out into the corridor.

Polk scuttled nervously backward, hurrying after the Justicar.

"Son? Hey son! How are you planning to get down?"

"I'm not."

Unamused, Polk folded up his arms.

"So you're just giving up. You're sayin' you have no idea how to get down there?"

"Of course there are ways." Jus tenderly lifted Escalla up, and the faerie clung against him, still leaking blood into her bandages. "We can wait until Escalla gets better, have her make a sloping ice wall and just toboggan our way down."

Polk's eyes went wide as he immediately fancied the idea and asked eagerly, "So that's what you're going to do?"

"Nope." Jus passed the lolling faerie into Polk's care and pushed the man farther along down the corridor. "Take her out of the mountain."

"Son? Son, you have a devil to catch!"

The Justicar turned to plant himself in the center of the passageway. Facing the manticore room, he slowly unsheathed his sword and tested the deadly edge of the blade.

"One way in, one way out." Square, dark, and powerful, the big man rested with his sword cradled in his arms. "If she wants to get out of the dungeon, then she has to get past me."

"*Very good, Justicar.*"

Cruel as a sugared knife, a female voice carried down the hall. The erinyes stood in the door to the monster chamber, her body framed by her pure white wings.

In her hand she held a black-scabbarded sword. Naked, the creature's skin shone pale as bone. Around her waist was clasped a string of rubies that still dripped with dark green blood. Exquisitely, lethally sensual, the erinyes walked slowly down the corridor.

"You are quite right, of course. I was expected. Whoever built this dungeon has shielded the corridors. I cannot teleport." She halted just short of the Justicar and delicately folded her wings. "It seems I shall have to pass by you the old-fashioned way."

Dark and savage, the Justicar lowered his sword into position.

"Polk, leave!"

The teamster hid with only his head poking about the corner of the passageway, reluctant to entirely abscond.

"Final conflict, son! I can't just leave you!"

The erinyes spoke mocking admiration. "Aww, isn't that sweet? But Escalla looks so hurt, poor thing. And your doggie's flames are useless. So it seems you are alone, *Justicar.*"

She sidled closer—just out of sword reach—and speared a sly sidewise glance at the ranger.

"*Justicar.* You never were a man for talk. Can you guess what was guarding Blackrazor? No?" The erinyes shrugged then fingered the bloodstained rubies at her waist. "No matter. It was a relatively minor entity. I fed it to the manticores." The erinyes held up the black sword, a spark of pure venom glittering in her eyes. "And so now I have regained possession of my toy."

She sank slightly down into a combat stance, the dungeon light glittering from her naked skin.

"I can't charm you, fear spells don't work on you, and your little doggie sees straight through illusions, so I suppose I shall have to kill you." The devil-woman walked forward, framing herself with her wings. "You have annoyed me once too often."

Jus stared flatly at the erinyes as though measuring her for a coffin. Framing his helm, Cinders grinned in feral glee, slowly waving his tail. The Justicar gently flexed his grip upon his sword, the blade responding to his touch like a living stream of steel.

"You can't wield the sword, can you?" he said mirthlessly. "That's why you were using thieves as minions."

"The sword has an *ego,* dear. It has a mind." The woman slowly drew the demonic sword from its sheath. "However, it now knows that through me it will gain the souls it craves. So you see, for once, I can use Blackrazor quite easily."

Blackrazor shimmered evilly as it slid free. Dancing with the light of countless stars, the weapon gibbered madly in its need to feed.

The evil sword blasted a storm of energy up into its mistress. Her naked body jerked, and the erinyes spread her wings and arched in ecstasy. Her slitted pupils dilated. Breathing deep and ragged, the creature turned toward her enemy and slowly gaped her fangs.

"Oh, this is *sweet!*" The erinyes moved with a syrupy slowness, like a creature soaring through its own ultimate dream. "I'm not just going to kill you, *Justicar*. I'm going to obliterate your soul!"

The sword stabbed energy into the devil-woman, and she suddenly blurred with speed. With a haste spell burning through her blood, she streaked into the attack, her blade slicing the air with stars.

The Justicar's sword snapped up to parry, sparks spattering as the enchanted steel wailed in agony. The screaming erinyes whirled like a dervish, whipping the soul-blade in an almost invisible blur. The Justicar stood like a rock, his own sword blocking Blackrazor time and time again. The soulsword howled in hunger as it lunged and slashed, but the Justicar smashed it aside even as it screeched for his blood. Sparks showered and skittered all across the dungeon floor. Still lying helpless, Escalla made a little sound of fright as she saw Jus standing at the center of a dizzy blur of steel.

Never once going over to the attack, Jus stood his ground and gave a display of pure, savage skill. He reserved his strength, letting the erinyes come at him in a wild storm of hate. Magical speed accelerating her to fantastic speeds, the erinyes screeched and swirled like a whirlwind. The sword blows rained down faster and faster, high and low, coming at unbelievable speed. A tuft of hair sprang free from Cinders, and then a slash ripped through the hell hound's hide. A line of blood appeared on the Justicar's thigh as if by magic, and leather scales went flying from his cuirass. Still the ranger stood in place, his blade flashing short, staccato arcs as he fought against Blackrazor's speed.

The erinyes cut high, cut low, then made three lightning fast thrusts at the Justicar's flesh. The blade flashed left and right as Jus slightly swayed aside—then suddenly the man whirled and trapped the erinyes's arm against himself. He locked her wrist and hammered viciously against her elbow, breaking her arm with a horrific snap. Moving inhumanly fast, the devil-woman ripped free, transferring Blackrazor to her other hand.

The erinyes danced back out of range, her sword arm hanging broken at her side. The Justicar breathed hard, gave a cold growl, and then surged forward like an attacking bear. His enemy let her venomous hiss trail up into a scream of manic hate and spun into the attack behind a whirlwind of sorcerous steel.

She snarled in from above—cut high, cut low, and cut again. Blackrazor's passage was marked by screams as it smacked time and time again against the Justicar's black sword. The Justicar shifted his weight back and forth, his face cold with concentration as he moved with the short, efficient motions of a master swordsman.

Watching the big man fight, Polk simply gaped in awe. Escalla managed to raise herself up, watching in amazement as she saw Jus fight the ensorcelled monster to an utter standstill. Framed by a maze of sparks, the Justicar scarcely seemed to move, his huge bearlike figure moving slowly forward through a storm of screaming steel.

Damage slipped through piece by piece. More fur flew from Cinders, with blood welling up from the Justicar's shoulder to soak into the fur. The ranger's magic light suddenly went flying from his chest as Blackrazor slashed a line of blood across his chest. Cinders immediately trickled flames from his mouth, filling the corridor with blood-red light. The combatants cast huge shadows as they battled back and forth along the hall.

And then suddenly the erinyes's power was gone. Blackrazor had squandered its energy. The erinyes faltered, and the Justicar instantly sliced his black sword down. In response, the devil-woman threw Blackrazor up to block the blow, the immense power of the attack slamming her off her feet. Knocked backward, she slid along the corridor, dodging wildly as the Justicar's blade came smashing down. One wing was sheared through as she tried to roll aside, and the she-devil screamed in utter agony. The Justicar's sword slashed in a blur of steel. She dodged left, right, then left again. Despite her best efforts, she lost the other wing in a sudden horrific swipe of the Justicar's sword.

Blood sprayed across the corridor. One handed and without her magic speed, the erinyes was no match for the raw violence of the Justicar. The man roared in anger, and the entire dungeon seemed to shudder to his rage. The erinyes blocked a cut that would have sheared her in two, panic suddenly sparking in her eyes. She retreated in fright, only just meeting each attack as the warrior's raw force smashed her blade aside. Blackrazor came back into the attack, only to be flicked away as the Justicar ripped his sword across the erinyes's waist. Rubies fell skittering on the ground, and the devil-woman staggered backward with black blood springing beneath her hands.

Clutching Blackrazor, the erinyes backed into the monster room. Satiated manticores still tore at their meal, while giant scorpions scuttled angrily toward the sound of prey. In the water levels, the surface foamed as predators fought to come closer to the battle up above.

Sheathed in blood, the two combatants poised themselves a dozen feet apart, then charged toward each other in a titanic clash of force. The two black swords met in a blast of force, the erinyes whirling in a circle to hack at the Justicar's heels. The big man jumped the blade and kicked his enemy in her broken arm, hammering his boot into the wound. Broken bones grated, and the erinyes gave a screech of agony.

Reeling free, the devil-woman staggered to the edge of the first ring of pens, and a huge crayfish claw lunged upward at her from the water. She whirled and hacked away the claw—then gave a feral hiss of excitement and jammed her soul-blade down into the crayfish as it rose toward her. Blackrazor plunged into the crayfish's tiny brain, the star-spattered steel cackling as it ripped the life-force out of its prey.

A black surge of stolen energy thundered into the erinyes. Blood flow from her wounds instantly stopped, and her injuries closed and healed. With the storm of stolen life-force rippling across her skin, she whirled and came racing at the Justicar.

He smashed her blade high and then chopped a lethal blow across her breast. Black energy sucked into the injury, healing it the instant it was made. The devil-woman laughed in victory, hacked out with Blackrazor and stabbed the blade through the skin of the Justicar's waist. He snarled and smashed his elbow hard across her jaw, making monster and her soul-blade stagger free.

Running with blood, Jus shook his head and parried a lethal lunge aimed straight at his eye. He blocked the blow one-handed, ramming the heel of his fist up into the erinyes's chin. His enemy rocked, and the Justicar's black sword whipped to tear great slashes across her hide.

The erinyes's wounds closed instantly, each one diminishing the haze of stolen energy. As she stabbed at him, Jus roared and made a killing thrust, ramming his sword into the devil's heart. He viciously twisted the blade like a corkscrew, and the erinyes screeched in torment on his hook. She ripped free, the black life-force from the sword hissing into the wound. The energy flickered out and died. Only half-healed, the erinyes's breast ran with blood.

Panting, the erinyes bared her fangs. She clutched her wound and slowly backed away. With a malicious hiss, she flicked up her hand. A brilliant flash of magic flooded from a ring upon the creature's hand.

Nine identical erinyes suddenly made a circle about the Justicar, all of them running sideways in a hellish carousel.

Nine mouths laughed, and nine Blackrazors whirled. She sped around and around the Justicar, Blackrazor glittering in a stream of deadly stars.

Surrounded by screaming death, the Justicar stood his ground and tried to pick his enemy amongst the ring of illusions.

"Cinders, which one is she?"

Can't tell! The hell hound twitched, trying to focus on the swirling images. *Moves too fast!*

The erinyes laughed like a woman winning trophies at a fair.

"Time to die, Justicar!" A peal of mirth rose into the air. "I'll get you! And your little dog too!"

From the corridor, Escalla tried to drag herself forward.

"Jus! Jus, hold her off! I'm coming!" The little faerie tried to drag herself forward, her bandages wet with blood. "Jus, I'm coming!"

The ring of devils raced faster and faster, coming closer to the Justicar. The erinyes gave a cry of joy—then halted as she saw the Justicar bow his head and close his eyes.

Freezing in place, the erinyes stared in amazement. The ranger stood with his blade on guard, his stance spread, and his breathing deliberately slow and calm. With his eyes closed, he left himself open to attack. The devil-woman faltered in surprise, then gave a wild, triumphant cry. She swirled like a mad dancer, and then the entire ring of images lunged inward for the kill, nine soul-swords raised to smash the human to the ground.

Cinders's ears twitched. Moving with vicious speed, Jus whipped his blade up behind his back and caught the real Blackrazor as it came scything at his spine. The man spun, his sword blurring forward in a lunge. With a horrific sound, it rammed into the monster's flesh and nine erinyes images screamed in horror as they were run through the heart.

Eight images flashed and disappeared, leaving the Justicar's enemy impaled on his blade. The Justicar twisted his sword, ripped it free, then brought the weapon down in one enormous blow. He hacked the screaming devil in two, his blade scything down to clang against the stone floor. With blood exploding from her flesh, the erinyes fell in two twitching halves, her last scream echoing as Blackrazor fell impotent against the ground.

Breathing hard, Jus slowly lowered his sword. Blood ran from his back, waist, arms, and thighs. He knelt and wiped his blade clean in his dead foe's hair, then grimly slammed the blade back in its sheath.

Back in the corridor, Escalla panted with pain. Her eyes fell on the glittering rubbish left behind in the erinyes's retreat. Amidst the rubies that had fallen from the erinyes's waist, there lay a potion flask. Escalla uncorked the thing, sniffed at it, then drank. She threw the empty bottle away, then felt Polk scuttling forward to lift her to her feet. The teamster carried her into the monster room, where both he and the faerie stared at the Justicar standing amidst the horrific remains of his foe.

Polk gaped at the ranger, thoroughly amazed.

"You did it." Surveying the damage, the teamster set his cap back on his head. "Son, you can swordfight! I never saw nothing like it in my life!"

Jus felt at the blood running from his wounds and gave an irritated scowl.

"I told you: If they can hit back, you're doing something wrong."

He reached for the faerie. Escalla clenched a bloody hand against her bandages and reached out to climb into the Justicar's arms. She shook her head in disbelief as she gazed about the room.

"Then that's it. We did it! That's all three weapons found." The faerie blinked in a daze. "We beat White Plume Mountain."

With a roar of laughter, a voice flooded into the room from above.

"All three weapons! Well done, little insects. Well done indeed!"

A crash of magic flooded the room, and an unseen fist clamped about Escalla and the Justicar. Polk screeched and tried to jab the trident at something, only to stagger and fall as a spell put him to sleep.

A huge image hovered above the monster pen—a human face painted in complex patterns of black and white. The librarian of Trigol laughed and squeezed his victims inside a gigantic magic fist, lifting them slowly into the air.

"Two survivors. Or is it three?" The librarian shouted out a spell. A glowing circular portal opened, and two of his assistants stepped through to lift Polk up from the floor. "Come along, then! It's high time we showed you exactly why you are here!"

The fallen magical weapons were collected and brought into the magic gate. An instant later, Jus and Escalla were drawn through into the glowing hole and the entire universe seemed to explode with light.

22

In a vast chasm lit by blood-red light, the molten heart of White Plume Mountain roared. High above, the chasm soared into a ceiling vaulted by the world's own bones. Hundreds of feet down below, a huge lake of magma roiled. From this molten blood of the earth, five giant columns of transparent crystal soared upward, thrusting aloft a platform high in the air. Fields of force shielded the platform from the raw heat of the lava, the planes shimmering as energy ebbed and flowed into the air.

Power crackled from the crystal columns, arcing like lightning bolts against the chasm walls. The heads of the columns emerged through the platform floor, each one forming one point of a gigantic pentagram painted in congealed human blood. Power arced from the columns and into pathways gouged into the floor. The chasm shuddered and echoed to the forces gathering deep inside the mountain's bowels.

All the power, all the force, fed into a single, brilliant point. The center of the giant pentagram held a long, open trough of clear glass. Inside the trough, a human skeleton lay wreathed with power. Tendrils of flesh were creeping ever so slowly to wrap the bones. At each point of the pentagram, a heavy stone table equipped with manacles gleamed evilly in the light. Branches of power crept from the pentagram to lick over the dangling chains before pulsing and flowing back to the trough with its obscene skeleton.

The transparent platform of force hung above the lava lake. Suspended above the magma, the floor shimmered in the lightning light. Trapped inside a small hemisphere with invisible walls, the Justicar stirred slowly and painfully awake, his head still thudding from the agony of a stun spell.

The prison's ceiling was too low. Jus had to hunch over to fit his head beneath the surface of the invisible dome. The big man discovered Escalla and Polk lying at his feet. He gently picked up the faerie—small, frail, and swathed in bloody bandages—and cradled her in his arms as he took stock of the scene outside his cage.

A tangled pile of equipment lay carelessly beside the pentagram. Two black swords, one shimmering slightly from the pinpoint lights of a myriad of stars, joined a trident and a hammer. Thrown about, almost as an afterthought, were their backpacks and the erinyes's magic rope. Cinders lay draped upside down over it all like a throw rug, the light in his eyes gleaming slyly. Jus met the hell hound's gaze, nodded, and felt the cunning hound hiss slightly in reply.

Far below the transparent floor, lava bubbled. A brilliant coil of power lanced up from the crystal columns and out into the pentagram. The hideous skeleton in the trough took on glistening new flesh, sucking obscenely on the energy that crawled across the floor.

The volcano shuddered as magma welled into the fire lake far below. Here and there, a few flecks of fallen rock passed through the screen that shielded the open platform from the heat. The rock chips spattered to the floor like a brittle rain.

The noise of bubbling lava made the platform shiver. Escalla stirred and sat up, rubbing at the side of her skull. She worked a bad taste out of her mouth and looked around at the volcanic chamber.

The faerie sighed and rested a hand against her wounds. "I guess we passed the librarian's test, huh?"

"Looks like it."

"Jus? If you had a great plan for this moment, this is a good time to clue me in."

"I have one." The big man remained calculating and calm. "But I need to get free and get close to the librarian."

"Oh, great." Escalla craned her neck to see the skeleton trough and its surrounding array of torture tables. "Oh, I *really* like the look of that. Gotta admire a host who really knows how to entertain."

Jus pointed to the skeleton trough with his chin. "Keraptis?"

"Cloned from his own hair strands." Escalla looked carefully at the pentagram arrangement, the crystal columns, and the ring of tables with their manacles. Blood-red magma light made the very air seem to boil. "This stuff is all really major magical construct. This must be Keraptis's old haunts beneath the mountain." The girl tilted her slanted eyes, her intelligence sharp as a razor. "Those torture tables are new, though. See—it's all new-sawn wood."

The Justicar carefully put Escalla down on the transparent floor. She sat there with lava bubbling two hundred feet below her bottom while the Justicar stood and pressed his hands against the ceiling of his prison. He rapped the dome with his knuckles, raising his eyebrows as it gave off a metallic *clang*.

Escalla winced as she touched her bandages.

"So what—are they going to do human sacrifices to get the power to raise this mage?"

"It might be worse than that." The Justicar carefully traced the join of the prison's walls to the floor. The dome felt cold and hard. The floor seemed to be a living, pulsing slab of pure force. "They set this labyrinth up deliberately to kill the weak but let a few heroes through."

The faerie cocked an eye. "You're saying we're heroes?"

"No, I'm saying the maze is actually a filter." The Justicar seemed satisfied with his examination of the prison. "Polk, wake up."

The teamster came suddenly awake and sat up, eyes wide open and his head spinning. "I'm up, son! I'm up!"

"Good. We're leaving."

The Justicar took a quick look over the open platform above the lava. The place still seemed utterly devoid of life. "We're in Keraptis's laboratories now. They won't expect us to get free. We'll get into the mountain and hunt the librarian down on our own terms."

Escalla gave an elegant gesture to indicate the little dome that held them prisoner. "And this jail-thingie we're in? What? Did you find a key?"

Jus sniffed. "It's not part of the original room. It's not a force field. It's magical steel. It rings when you rap it with your knuckles." The big man planted his shoulders against the ceiling. "They even put in some air holes! I think it's just resting on the floor."

Both the teamster and the faerie looked around as if they could somehow test the truth of the Justicar's words.

Jus braced himself. "I'll lift it. You two get out, get my sword, and use it to prop up the dome so I can escape."

"Gotcha!" The faerie instantly ran over to the edge of the prison, then turned and looked at Jus with a dubious eye. "You're really going to be able to lift this thing?"

Jus never answered. He planted his body beneath the invisible prison dome and took the weight upon his shoulders. He shot the faerie a rare smile—full of shared pleasure—and slowly began to stand.

With a noise like the lid being raised upon a cooking pot, the dome slowly began to lift. Escalla probed at the edge of the invisible prison, felt a gap beginning to open, and slid beneath the edge and into the open air. She stood, brushing roughly at her bandages, and grinned with feral delight at her friend the Justicar.

"Oh, man! You can be my hero anytime!"

She spread her wings and turned toward the equipment pile. "Polk? Come on, man. I need you to lift the sword!"

Polk stared at the Justicar in absolute approval and total joy. Slapping his hands together in satisfaction, he backed away and wriggled beneath the invisible dome. Escalla caught the teamster by the hand, and they both ran side by side toward the welcoming grin of Cinders.

A sudden huge blow lifted Escalla up into the air, crushing her inside a giant fist. Polk fell skidding on the floor, knocked almost senseless by the massive ghostly hand that snatched itself about Escalla's body.

A second fist lifted up the invisible prison dome, cast it aside, then snatched up the Justicar as well. The huge fists trailed tendrils of force, magical links running back toward the cavern mouth that led into the mountain.

Walking coolly through the portal came the librarian. His two acolytes followed at his back. The man lifted his hands and squeezed. The ghostly fists copied the motion, making Escalla croak with pain as she and the Justicar were held dangling like toys.

"A superior man proves his superiority by leaving nothing to chance." The librarian cast a brief glance toward the faint shimmer of the overturned prison dome.

"You were right. It was glass steel. You made an impressive show of deduction, a good display of physical force." The librarian turned his fists as he finally walked onto the vast, invisible platform. He examined the Justicar like an imprisoned insect in his grasp. "It will be interesting to discover what you do and how you do it. The erinyes was a poor match. She lacked your cunning." The librarian thoughtfully turned the Justicar this way and that. "A very *useful* cunning . . ."

The librarian nodded to his acolytes, and both men immediately walked over to the tables at the edges of the pentagram. Manacles were unclasped and chains attached. One table was conspicuously adjusted to hold a victim of faerie-size.

Polk sat up, blinking. He sat beside the pile of abandoned equipment, looked dazedly at Cinders where the hell hound lay draped across his backpack, then the teamster finally seemed to see the librarian and his acolytes.

The sorcerers went about their business as a plume of lava hissed upward from the pool far below. Staring at the librarian, Polk changed colors, from pale white to bright red with fury.

"Good triumphs over evil!" The teamster puffed up like a frog, utterly incensed. "You may think you've got us, but you've lost!"

"Ah, the insect speaks." The librarian was carefully inspecting the skeleton inside the trough. Muscle fibres coiled wetly about the bones while power surged up through the mighty pillars that held the force platform up out of the mountain's molten heart. "I was never in a contest, little man. Therefore I cannot lose." Still holding his two prisoners in his ghostly fists, the librarian carefully observed his acolytes making adjustments to their equipment. "I have no time for selecting worthy donors, so we let the labyrinth perform our selection process for us. The trap was baited, set, and sprung. The rewards"—the librarian looked closer at the half-formed body deep inside its tank—"the rewards are about to be achieved."

Jus looked at Escalla. He needed time. He needed to find a way to break free. The girl read his intention. She blew out a big breath, engaged her enthusiasm, and suddenly made a mocking, raucous laugh.

The noise turned the heads of librarian, the assistants—and even Polk as the girl made a flippant little sneer. "Trap?

Trap? Ha! You blew it!" The faerie wriggled inside the giant fist of force. "We got hold of all the weapons!"

"The weapons were always where I wanted them to be." The librarian sniffed. "Simple enough to seize them again at need. Until then, they form an admirable part of the sifting process."

"But we killed all your little pet monsters!"

"Then we will use a spell to summon some more." The librarian seemed finished with his work at the tank and turned to look at the Justicar and Escalla. "The two of you make a promising start. There will be others—hopefully *better*. We shall examine ways of snaring tougher prey."

Polk sat, frozen. The librarian's two assistants both cast glances up at their master's victims and then stood carefully over to one side. Behind them, the giant pentagram glowed with force, magical pathways rippling as energy flowed up into the transparent coffin. Strand by strand the body in the trough rebuilt itself, the muscle strands shining sticky-wet beneath the flickering light.

Hanging in midair, Escalla cast a glance into the magic trough and insolently blew a strand of hair back from her eyes. "So *this* is the triumph you're wasting your time on? All you did was clone some old wizard from his hair strands?"

"This is *Keraptis!*" With his assistants still busy at their chores, the librarian suddenly had time to educate lesser entities. He turned his back to the abyss and walked beneath his two victims. "A most unusual being. Did you know his structure was physically different from other men? He visited the plane of limbo and reshaped himself, allowing himself to store more magical energy that is normally possible for a mortal frame!"

Escalla gave a mocking shrug. "Whoopie! So now you're gonna collect a reward from the guy when he comes awake." The faerie let her antenna make a sarcastic little droop. *"This is a new plan."*

Lava shuddered far below, and a tongue of flame shot skyward past the force platform. Curtains of energy at the platform's sides kept away the heat, yet allowed a few pieces of pumice ash to land streaming and hissing beside the pentagram.

Breathing deeply at the stench of sulphur, the librarian slowly turned and continued, "We are not copying Keraptis. We are *replacing*—or rather, *I* am replacing him. His physical form was perfectly designed, but his mind shall be my own."

Escalla made a rude noise and rolled her eyes in mock agony. "Oh, *please!* Oh for the gods' sakes, *please* tell me you're not going to hold us captive while you reveal your evil plan!"

The librarian came to stand beneath the faerie and stare up at her in disdain. "Of all the potential donors, you are the only one whose survival irks me. You are a *nasty* little thing, arrogant, vain, and overconfident."

"Oh, really!" The faerie let her eyebrows raise in a droll little arc of surprise. "It's called *class*, egghead. Try it sometime—maybe you'll like it!"

"Yes. Quite nasty." The librarian gave a sniff of distaste. "The winnowing process may yet be imperfect."

The librarian made to turn away, and Escalla swore and struggled, frantically trying to snare back his attention. *"Hey!* Hey, you bucket of phlegm! Yeah, I'm talking to you!" The girl kicked her legs in a frenzy of hate. "You think you're a match for me? You wouldn't know a decent faerie spell if it bit you on the ass!"

Quite suddenly, the librarian gave an arrogant smile. "But I shall, my dear! I am going to *absorb* you, your skills, your experience, your strengths—and the Justicar's as well." The man hefted up his fists and squeezed. Escalla cried out, her bandages suddenly soaking with more blood. "We shall find new trinkets to make bait for new mazes. We shall skim all of the Flanaess for the greatest powers and talents this world has to offer. All shall contribute themselves to the structure of the Overman."

The man slowly opened out his hands to encompass his mighty works. Behind him, vast energies roared upward from the core of the world.

"*Here* is the experiment Keraptis feared to do! His body structure was a potential even he never understood! But we are grateful. He has laid the foundations for the world's first true Overman!" The man drew in a breath of sulphurous air, revelling in his vision.

Trapped inside a huge transparent fist high above, the Justicar looked down at his prey through cold eyes. "I have heard enough. You are an enemy of the people. You have chosen to prey upon the weak." The Justicar's voice came low and powerful, cutting through the noise of magma steam. "*You have been judged.*"

The librarian's painted mask of a face froze. A moment later, the man snarled in fury, his magic fist crushing tight about the Justicar.

"An overman has no moral constraints! An overman shapes the world to the needs of his own intellect!" The librarian's voice shook in a roar. "Good and evil are labels! Small minds paint the universe shades of black and white to allow themselves to comprehend! An overman *is* the black and white!" The librarian lifted up his painted face. "I am both blurred into one!"

Squeezed breathless by the invisible fist, Escalla struggled to make herself heard. "Th-then that makes dirty gray!" The girl arched in agony. "And that's r-real hard to color c-coordinate!"

With a snarl, the librarian clenched his hand, and the giant fist mirrored his fury. Escalla croaked, squealed, and then suddenly fell limp. With the faerie unconscious, the librarian dropped her to the floor. She landed with her wings crushed and broken and blood spilling from her mouth onto the ground.

Jus roared in anger and fright, his muscles bulging as he fought to break free. *"Escalla!"*

Laughing, the librarian held Jus dangling helplessly in the air. "She was weak, weak and unworthy!" The librarian flicked a sneer over at the broken little figure on the floor. "No matter. We shall use her."

He walked back toward the pentagram, towing the Justicar behind him through the air. Stopping beside the mound of discarded trident, sword, and hell hound skin, the man nodded to his acolytes. "We will drain him."

"Wait!" The Justicar's cold voice boomed out above the sounds of lava and steam. Sour and triumphant, the librarian turned to look up at him.

"A plea, Justicar?"

"A message." The Justicar's dark eyes gleamed. He gazed down at his enemy, then jerked his chin off to one side. "Someone wants you."

The librarian frowned, turned, and looked at the empty space behind him. There was nothing except a backpack, a bundle of weapons, and a barbaric, mangy wolf skin. The pelt's red eyes suddenly sparked with feral glee.

Hi!

Fire blasted out to smash into the librarian's face. The sheer force of it threw the man backward, his hair and robes going instantly up in flames. Still hanging up above, Jus watched the librarian stagger burning and blinded past his feet.

"Polk! Sword!"

The teamster kicked one of his captors in the crotch. Dodging free, Polk snatched up a black sword from the loose equipment and hacked clumsily at the strand that anchored the magician's translucent magic fist to his hands. The black blade clove, and suddenly the Justicar fell free. He crashed to the ground, stretched up a hand, and Polk threw him the sword. The Justicar held the blade and jerked with pain, almost dropping the weapon. He shook his head then surged onto his feet, bellowing in fury.

One of the librarian's two assistants cast a spell, the energies shearing past the Justicar to knock Polk off his feet. The teamster picked himself up, surged forward, and kicked his man again. The teamster then gave the man a shove in the chest that sent the apprentice stumbling back through the energy veil. He shrieked as he fell hundreds of feet down into the magma.

The second assistant threw himself between his injured master and the Justicar. The apprentice screamed symbols and sent a rain of darts scything through the air. The Justicar growled and waded forward through the storm, ignored the pounding, and finally punched the apprentice across the face. The apprentice fell, sprawling on the ground. Jus turned and found the librarian standing, grinning in triumph through a mutilated, blistered skull.

The librarian hissed, his breath bubbling. In one hand he held a black-bladed sword. With his back to the abyss, the man lifted his hand and readied a spell, ready to blast the Justicar to atoms.

Suddenly a clear voice pealed in from a dozen yards away. *"Hey! Brain boy!"*

The librarian jerked his head to stare at the center of the pentagram. Escalla, her wounds gone and her body utterly undamaged, gave the man a wave. She tapped at the unmarked skin of her midriff and gave a smile. "Polymorph! I do a good fake death scene, huh?"

The girl stood astride the half-formed body of Keraptis in its glass trough. She had her flask of green slime lying directly above Keraptis's chest. Sloping over her shoulder, she held the hammer Polk used for his iron spikes and pitons. "Say bye-bye to your super clone!"

The librarian screamed as Escalla whipped the hammer down onto the slime jar. The flask shattered, spurting green slime all over Keraptis's naked flesh. The savage infection instantly took hold, bubbling as the skeleton melted into a formless morass of bubbling flesh.

Jus was already moving. He cast his last spell—long-horded and long-planned for—straight at the librarian's feet. A surge of force ripped through the air, spreading outward in a sphere about the librarian. The sorcerer saw his enemy charging at him and whipped up his hand to smash Jus apart with a spell. He opened his mouth to scream the spell's syllables—and no sound came from his throat.

Horror lit the librarian's eyes. The Justicar's battle scream cut off the instant he crossed the edge of his own silence spell. Unable to cast magic, the librarian shrank back against the edge of the abyss, his own acolyte held before him as a shield.

He had no magic, but he *did* have Blackrazor! Suddenly inspired, the librarian whirled and rammed the black sword through his assistant's heart. The victim bucked and died, clawing at the blade jutting from his chest. Grinning, the librarian awaited the surge of energy that would rush up Blackrazor's blade, knowing he could use the power to smash the ranger to the ground.

No energy surge came. The librarian looked at the sword in astonishment, staring at the wolf-skull pommel in dawning shock.

An instant later, the Justicar fell on him in fury. A savage chop of Blackrazor hacked the librarian's hand free from its wrist. The librarian's black, skull-pommelled sword fell to the floor as Jus stepped forward with Blackrazor flicking down into a thrust. He rammed the soul-sword through the librarian's guts and instantly released the blade.

The librarian gripped Blackrazor in shock, staggering slightly back until he stood at the brink of the abyss. Retrieving his own much-beloved sword, the Justicar simply smacked off the librarian's head. With a contemptuous push, he then shoved sorcerer, severed head, and soul-sword over the edge into the abyss.

With a look of annoyance on his face, the big man walked out of the sphere of silence, wiping off his blade. He gathered Escalla in one arm as both of them watched the librarian splash down into the magma far below.

Jus sniffed, watching the flare of light in grim satisfaction. *"No one touches the faerie."*

"Right on, J-man!" Escalla retrieved her frost wand from the loot pile and thrust it through her belt. Satisfied with a job well done, Escalla reached out to thump Polk on the skull. "Hey! Well done, big nose!"

A blast of light suddenly burst up from the lava. Blackrazor's destruction unleashed a storm of energy that blew sideways, shearing huge cracks into the columns of crystal. The force platform began to tilt, sliding Keraptis's slime-covered body inexorably toward the edges of the ledge. Another explosion sounded deep down in the magma lake as Blackrazor blew apart with a massive blast of force. The power of countless thousands of drained souls shuddered through the earth to bring White Plume Mountain startlingly awake.

A shower of stones from above began to smash down onto the platform, rebounding and tumbling off into the empty air. The platform tilted sharply sideways as two crystal columns cracked apart. Escalla saw Cinders start sliding off toward the abyss and flew over in a rush to catch him by the tail. The hell hound hung half over the edges of the platform, staring into the surging magma. Burned by heat, the faerie wrestled him back from the edge and dragged the creature back up toward the Justicar.

Thank you.

"You're welcome!" The faerie watched her bag of gold pieces falling down into the lava. "Aww, man! That was my treasure!"

Jus and Polk seized the magic weapons, clinging onto Whelm and Wave as the whole platform lurched sideways. The only exit seemed to be through a single jagged cave. As the platform sizzled with energy, Jus caught hold of Polk, gave him Wave and Whelm, and then physically threw the teamster toward safety. Polk clawed over the lip of the rock shelf, hunching as hot rocks crashed and fell about him.

The force platform hung sloping straight down toward the lava. Jus clung onto a projecting knob of crystal pillar a dozen feet short of the ledge.

Still attached to Polk's backpack, the erinyes's magic rope came slithering by. Jus frantically kicked and caught the rope loop around his boot. He snatched the rope, dragged it free, then whipped it up toward Polk's reaching hands.

The magic rope cracked through the air. Braced in the cave mouth, Polk took the strain as Jus climbed hand over hand into the cavern.

Yards behind him, Escalla flew clumsily through the air, dragging Cinders by the tail. The whole force platform went spinning down toward the magma lake, the magic flaring and disappearing as the crystal columns broke. Raw heat came fountaining upward, catching the faerie and wrapping her in Cinders's pelt. Shielded from the furnace, she was hurled straight into Jus's hands, blistering winds jetting into the tunnel mouth and almost bowling the adventurers from their feet.

A long corridor ran past rooms filled with laboratory equipment, books, and scrolls. Jus snatched Cinders and pushed the others ahead, hanging the hell hound skin about his neck to shield the party from the heat. Behind them, the lava bubbled like a stew, the whole mountain beginning to throb with building force.

The group pelted down a jagged corridor. As they passed a table, Jus ducked beneath a tongue of fire and snatched up a bag of gems. Escalla blinked at it in shock as Jus shielded her from a fire blast.

"Yours!" The Justicar sheltered Escalla as chunks of rock rained from the ceiling. *"I promised I'd get you treasure!"*

The entire mountain shook as the adventurers sped onward down the hall. Escalla snatched a ruby from a shelf as she passed. Stuffing the treasure down her meagre cleavage, she sped down the passageway, shooting up an overhead tunnel as the corridor took a turn straight into the air.

Jus shoved Polk up the steel ladder rungs then began to climb hastily behind the teamster. Keeping just ahead of Polk and his rather careless trident, Escalla discovered a hatchway and threw her tiny strength into trying to turn the wheel that opened the door. Below the tunnel entrance, flame sheeted through the air, heat blasting up the tunnel to lick in hunger at their feet.

"Polk! Press the catch!" Shielding himself unsuccessfully from the heat, Jus clung onto the ladder rungs. "Get the damned thing open!"

Encumbered by his trident, Polk fought past and rammed his hand against the hatch. The trapdoor flung backward, and a cascade of filthy water began to tumble inward through the open hole.

The adventurers fought their way past the flow to find themselves in familiar algae-spattered corridors. They were in the north passage of the dungeon, and Enid the sphinx's backside faced them only a few yards away. The Justicar tried to slam shut the trapdoor, but steam shot out to fill the corridor with a choking fog.

"Out! Kelpies! Enid! Move! Get out of the mountain!"

Enid looked about, saw the adventurers pelting pell-mell down the passageway toward her, then saw a lick of flames come shooting from the hole just behind. Hard on the Justicar's heels came two shrieking women made of bundled kelp, their weed-strands steaming as fire licked into the passageway. Escalla shot past Enid and grabbed the big cat-woman by the ear.

"Enid, the spell's broken! *Run like hell!*"

They all ran down the corridor and reached the spiral stair. Jus thrust the two kelpies ahead of him, shoving them up the stairs and bringing up the rear. Behind him, ceilings shattered and rock cracked in two, superheated steam blasting through the cracks to jet into the halls.

The fugitives blundered up the steps and out into a cave. Daylight streamed inward, making humans and non-humans alike begin to blink and stagger. Escalla led the way ahead of Enid, breaking out onto the open mountainside. Steam and smoke jetted from fissures in the rocks, the whole mountain heaving underfoot as it shuddered in fury.

A steep series of cliffs switchbacked below them. Even as Escalla watched, a rumble deep inside the mountain made the land before them split open in a crevasse. With a mighty roar, the roadway fell away for two hundred feet, turning into a maze of jagged rubble far below.

High above the cave, the lip of the volcano blasted lava through the air. Red-hot stones spattered all across the ground, and a great wave of lava tumbled slowly down toward the adventurers. Escalla stared at the lava—then at the jagged slope below, and ripped the frost wand quickly from her belt.

"You damned flightless twits will be the death of me!" The girl used her wings to fight the recoil as she hosed ice across the jagged slope and made it into a toboggan run. "All right, people! *Slide-slide-slide!*"

The faerie dove away, plastering ice in front of her as she plunged toward the road below. The two kelpies and the sphinx hesitated in fear until Polk blundered into them from behind. All four went shooting off downslope, wailing in fright as they slid away at lightning speed.

Jus stood at the brink of the toboggan slope. He looked back at the erupting volcano behind him, gazing at the lava flow and the spurting steam. Despite a volcanic eruption behind him, the man remained unhurried and calm. The erinyes's magic rope was coiled carefully at his belt. He tied Cinders tight about his neck, settled sword and hammer in his hand, then looked down at the rest of the party spilling out onto the road below.

"Cinders, we did good."

Did good! Cinders eternal grin lit up. *Cinders has some holes.*

"I'll get you mended back in town." The Justicar watched the two kelpies sheltering in a nearby stream. "Ready to go?"

Go now. Eat coals later. Then chase girls.

"Right." Jus jumped down onto the toboggan slope and sped down the slide. Behind him, an entire underground fortress went up in flames, shooting great white plumes of smoke high up into an evening sky.